A TIME OF MADNESS

Lance Koster is a ruthless young thug whose sordid, petty hold-up misfires into a vicious knifing and death. To escape arrest he hurriedly leaves South Africa to join the Rhodesian Army, little realising that he has traded one savage existence for another—the remorseless fight against terrorism.

Richard Kelly, the hardened detective inspector in Salisbury's Special Branch, is investigating the burning down of a remote mission station and the disappearance of its inhabitants when an act of horrific barbarism pierces his cynicism and impels him into a crusade of vengeance. Detailed police work and Kelly's obsessive drive lead him first into the pursuit of the killer gang and then into the heart of the Communist organisation directing the terrorist incursions. Kelly's disregard of established police procedure and his acute perception of human nature help him through one crisis after another.

The parallel stories of Kelly and Koster, caught up in tragic conflict, are grippingly told as the chain of events races to an unbearably tense climax.

A TIME OF MADNESS

Robert Early

ALLAN WINGATE · London
A Howard & Wyndham Company
1978

This edition 1978

Originally published in Rhodesia by
The Graham Publishing Company (Pvt) Ltd, 1977

Printed and bound in Great Britain by
Redwood Burn Limited, Trowbridge & Esher
for the Publishers
Allan Wingate Ltd, 44 Hill Street, London W1X 8LB

ISBN 85523 400 8

For Rosemary Jean

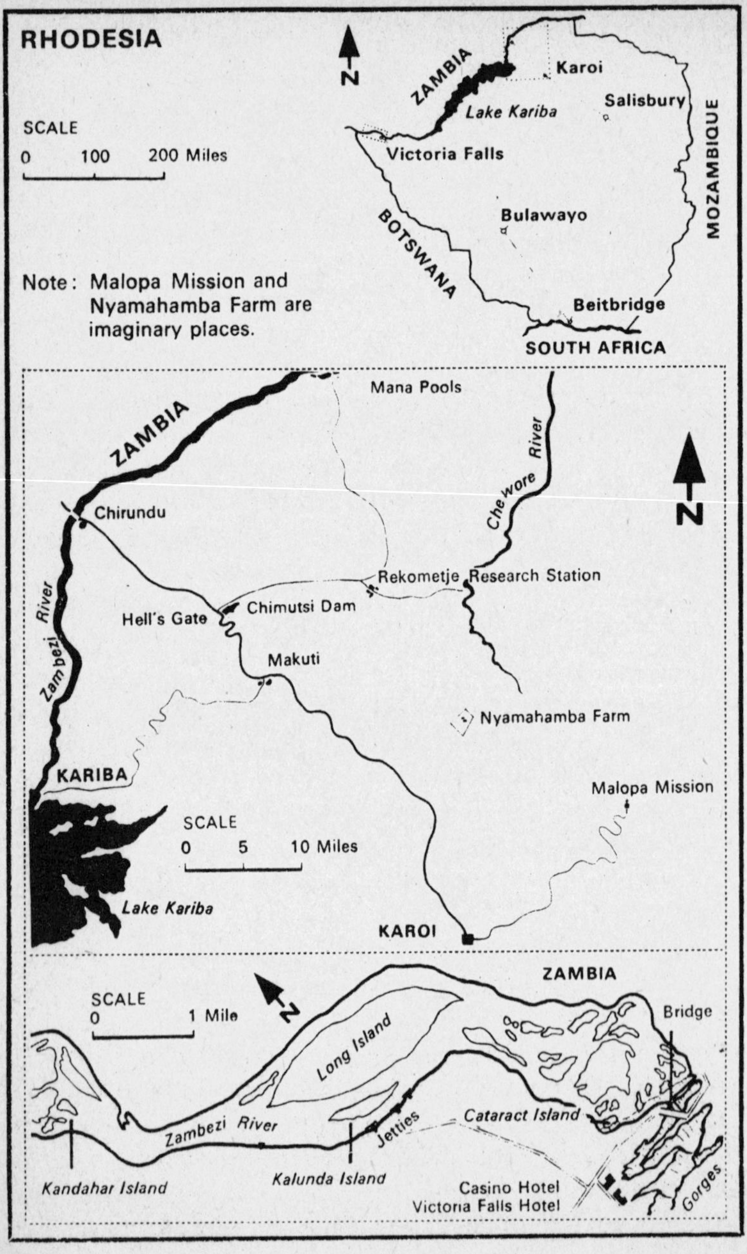

RHODESIA
N
ZAMBIA
Karoi
Lake Kariba
Salisbury
SCALE
0 100 200 Miles
Victoria Falls
MOZAMBIQUE
BOTSWANA
Bulawayo
Note: Malopa Mission and Nyamahamba Farm are imaginary places.
Beitbridge
SOUTH AFRICA
Mana Pools
ZAMBIA
Chewore River
N
Chirundu
Rekometje Research Station
Zambezi River
Chimutsi Dam
Hell's Gate
Makuti
Nyamahamba Farm
KARIBA
Malopa Mission
SCALE
0 5 10 Miles
Lake Kariba
KAROI
ZAMBIA
SCALE
0 1 Mile
N
Bridge
Long Island
Cataract Island
Zambezi River
Jetties
Kandahar Island
Kalunda Island
Casino Hotel
Victoria Falls Hotel
Gorges

Prologue

FROM the dark mouth of a service lane Lance Koster watched the diminishing stream of late night traffic moving along Twist Street and mumbled a curse. He was cold, wet and slightly drunk. He shouldn't have had that last vodka but, Jesus, he needed it, and anyway it didn't affect his judgement. Just helped to keep the cold out, that's all.

The rain hit the street and fought its sluggish way along the garbage-choked gutters with stinking, muted protest. The overhead lights turned the black tar surface into a long, shimmering mirror reflecting distorted images of flashing fluorescent signs.

Lance was young and wiry but tough and he wore an old denim jacket, black shirt and black trousers. They contrasted with his pallid complexion. Long brown hair matched his eyes and framed cocky, pugnacious features. He also wore a gold Omega wrist watch with someone else's initials engraved on the back. The Omega told him the time was twelve minutes past one.

Through the slightly misted windows of the Clarendon Café he watched the last of the late night customers approach the cash desk. About bloody time. Standing around in the sodding rain had done nothing to improve either his appearance or his disposition, and the warming effect of the alcohol was beginning to wear off.

He shivered, feeling water run down the back of his neck. His feet squelched in his shoes as he shifted his position to get a better view of the interior of the café.

The man was helping the woman into a light raincoat and smiling at her. She was a good-looking doll and Lance felt a twinge of envy which lasted just until he remembered that Carol was waiting for him.

The slow heat of desire crept through his loins. Carol, with her over-developed breasts and frantic hips. Carol, on the big eiderdown, sated with pleasure and moaning softly. She was waiting for him right now and he knew he would be late. Hurry up, you bastards. He glared at the couple through the glass, willing them to leave.

Finally they came out onto the street, passing within ten feet of Lance. They didn't see him. The man was fondling the woman's breast under her coat. Randy bugger.

Lance shrank back into the shadows, glancing at the bus stop near the café entrance. A well-dressed figure lay sprawled across the bench in drunken sleep. Not an unusual sight early on a Sunday morning in Johannesburg's Hillbrow. He approved of the performance the man was giving. When old Nick the Greek left the café with the takings of a particularly busy night in his battered old briefcase, he was in for one hell of a shock.

The African waiters finished stacking chairs in the café and left in a group. One of them pointed at the figure on the bench and they laughed derisively. They did not notice Lance.

Suddenly the lights went out in the café and old Nick was on the pavement, a bunch of keys in his hand. He locked the door while clutching the briefcase under his left arm. He glanced up and down the street, took in the figure on the bench and dismissed it. He had seen thousands like it during his eighteen years of life in Hillbrow. He had watched the kids on the block graduate from shoplifting juvenile delinquents to swaggering young punks, to whores, pimps, pushers, muggers and con artists second to none. And through the years his genuine concern for them had slowly been ground down to mild regret and, very occasionally, to pleased surprise when one or two of the kids had climbed the slime-ridden rungs of the stinking sewer that was Hillbrow and broken away from their criminal upbringing to become solid, respected members of society. Honesty was another word for starvation and very few even tried.

The traffic flow had eased considerably and Nick was pleased to be able to close up fairly early. That last couple had looked as if they would stay until the sun came up, and he wanted a good night's sleep, especially as he had to face his three grandchildren in the morning. He loved them totally, spoilt them completely and shared with them the affinity of the old for the young.

But that son of mine has not turned out so well, he thought to himself. Mr Bigshot Lawyer, always making out that his father was not high class, just because he owned a café in Hillbrow. He forgot maybe where the money for the university came from. So now Spiro was a lawyer with a fancy society practice and an eighty-thousand rand house in Sandton and considered his father a peasant because he lived in a two-roomed flat in Kotze Street. If it were not for the children, he wouldn't bother to travel the twelve miles out to Sandton in the morning. And that wife of Spiro's. Now there was a snooty bitch. Always on about tennis and golf and the servant problem, looking down on him and talking through her nose. He wondered what Spiro saw in her. All bones and adenoids. No meat on her at all. He made a mental note to give her a big kiss when he arrived at the house. He knew it would infuriate her.

Grinning slightly to himself he headed up the street towards his flat. He would make a cup of hot Milo, take a bath and be asleep inside an hour. He had just over two thousand rand in the briefcase. He would drop the money into the night deposit safe at the Standard Bank near his flat. It would go to join the seventy thousand he had in his account. Nick thought he would retire at the end of the year and build a house on his stand in Umhlanga Rocks. He would enjoy teaching the grandchildren to fish. He had been a good fisherman before he emigrated to South Africa.

The hairs on the back of Nick's neck started to prickle. Something was wrong. The figure on the bench had risen and was running towards him. There was no trace of drunkenness now. With a sense of horror Nick saw that the man had a nylon stocking pulled over his head. Nick wasn't a coward, but he was sixty-seven years old. He turned and ran.

From the service lane Lance had seen Roy begin his move. As Roy stood up, Lance pulled a bone-handled flick knife from the pocket of his denim jacket. Despite the rain-chilled wind the knife was slippery with sweat, his mouth was desert dry and he could feel his heart beginning to pound. He thumbed the release catch and the five-inch blade gleamed dully in the dim light. Crêpe soles making no noise, he ran up behind the old café owner.

At that moment Nick turned to run from Roy. He saw Lance closing in on him and swung wildly with the briefcase. Lance ducked and slipped on the wet pavement. Nick tried desperately to check himself but he was moving too fast. He tripped over Lance's outstretched legs and fell across him. Five inches of cheap German steel slid easily into his stomach just below the navel.

Nick screamed.

Lance felt something warm gush across his hand and for a moment didn't understand what it was. He pushed the old man away and as he stood up he shook the knife, wiping his hand across the front of his jacket. Christ! It was blood. Funny how brown it looked under the street lights. He stared down at the old man who lay on his side clutching his stomach and groaning.

'You stupid old bastard!' Lance yelled. 'I didn't mean to cut you. You fell on my knife.'

Roy grabbed the briefcase and tried to run. It jerked out of his hand. 'Jesus wept! The goddam thing's chained to his wrist.' He pulled at the briefcase with sobbing frustration. 'Lance, for God's sake cut it free. Use your knife.'

Lance didn't move. He stood there staring down at the old man. A car full of late night revellers pulled up at the curb. A drunken voice shouted, 'Lookit that guy. He's more pissed than I am.' The car pulled away and disappeared erratically down the street.

'For Christ's sake, Lance,' Roy screamed, 'cut this bloody thing free!' His voice had more than a touch of panic.

The street had seemed empty before. From nowhere half-a-dozen people had appeared and were moving closer. Lance shook his head like a swimmer coming up for air and suddenly reached across the old man and hacked savagely with the knife at the leather handle of the briefcase. Down the street a woman started screaming. Roy turned and ran. The briefcase came free. Lance tucked it under his arm like a rugby ball. As he turned to follow Roy into the service lane he saw a policeman come round the corner. He had a gun in his hand and a dog on a leash. A bloody great Alsatian.

Lance ran for his life.

The escape route had been planned three days ago. One hundred yards down the lane there was an entrance to a private garage which served a block of flats. The goddam cop was at the entrance of the lane yelling something. Christ, I didn't mean to cut the old bastard, Lance thought. He paid no attention to the shouting behind him. He swerved past a row of dustbins. The dog caught him in the hip and ripped half his jacket away. He felt a searing pain, then he was rolling away from the snapping jaws, terror rising in him like an engulfing tide. As he spun to face the eighty pounds of snarling fury, he scooped up a dustbin lid, dropping the briefcase onto a heap of sodden garbage. The dog attacked again, fast and high, going for the throat. Lance flicked the lid up and the dog's teeth closed with a clash on the galvanized rim. He brought the knife up very fast and stabbed the dog twice in the chest. It howled loudly and the dustbin lid was suddenly free in his hand.

The cop was shouting, only twenty feet away and moving in fast. Lance saw the flash of orange suddenly blossom from the cop's hand and felt the bullet tug at his sleeve, the whiplash crash of the detonation reverberating loudly in the confined space. He threw the lid at the cop's face and followed it. The man put up his arm to fend off the flying lid and Lance kicked him, very hard and very expertly, in the groin. The cop doubled over in agony; the gun slid across the wet tar and came to rest in a puddle of dirty water. He must be a new boy to Hillbrow, Lance thought, he doesn't even wear a box. He retrieved the dustbin lid and hit the cop hard on the right collarbone with the rim. The bone snapped with a wet popping sound. He threw the lid at the still whimpering Alsatian, picked up the briefcase and ran into the garage.

A large crowd of spectators had gathered at the entrance to the service lane, all shouting and gesticulating, but not one of them moved off the flimsy security of the lighted street to help the groaning police officer. If the cop kicked it, it would be tough tit and three cheers.

This was Hillbrow, not Saint Mary's convent for refined young ladies, and good Samaritans were as common as bikinis in winter.

Lance ran through the garage and up the service stairs to the first floor of the building. He swung over a low guard-wall separating the building from the roof of an old house next to it and crossed the slippery corrugated iron sheeting carefully. There was a gap of six feet between the old house and the fire escape of the highrise apartment block flanking it.

He closed the flick knife and put it away. Very carefully he threw the briefcase across the six-foot gap. It landed with a wet slap on the fire escape platform. He jumped for the iron railing surrounding the platform. His hands slipped on the rain-slick surface of the railing and his injured side smashed heavily into the rigid iron. A wave of agony swept through him and he hung over the rail, heaving for air while bright white lights flashed and little red circles spun in crazy kaleidoscope behind his eyes. The spasm passed in a few seconds and dragging himself painfully onto the platform he picked up the briefcase.

The fire escape led to the main first floor corridor, which he limped along slowly and in pain. The bite in his side was really beginning to hurt. He went down a flight of steps, through the darkened foyer and came out on the street behind the café. Apart from an old African night watchman huddled in an army surplus coat and fast asleep in the doorway of a shop, the street was deserted.

Ten feet from where Lance emerged a Vincent Black Prince rested on its stand next to the curb. Casually, despite the pain, he sauntered over to the motorcycle, wedged the briefcase between his thigh and the saddle and eased the big machine forward off the stand. The Vincent was one of the few things he had acquired honestly and he was exceptionally proud of it. It looked as if it had just left the showroom and was superbly tuned; it could do a hundred and fifteen easily and the girls flipped over it, clinging tightly to him. It was worth every cent he had spent on it.

It was only after he had travelled a couple of hundred yards that he began to think about Roy. Where was the yellow bastard? All big talk and bullshit. As soon as the crap hits the blades he pulls a fade. I took the money; I got bitten by that bloody police dog; I dropped the cop and if Roy thinks he's getting a split of the bread he's out of his lousy skull.

The thought of keeping the stolen money to himself cheered him up considerably. His shock at the time of the accidental stabbing was wearing off, and although he felt vaguely sorry for the old Greek and hoped the wound wasn't fatal, he was not particularly concerned either way. Silly old bugger should have known better than to walk around unprotected with all that cash. Teach him a bloody good lesson, if he lived. Lance shrugged mentally and carefully turned a corner.

In the distance he could hear the sirens approaching from the direction of Hospital Hill Police Station. Their banshee shriek rent the night. He rode with excessive care, not wanting to attract attention, and the street was thankfully deserted. His breathing was almost normal but he could still feel the blood pounding through his body. Christ, it had been close. Much too close.

He moved his body slightly to reassure himself that the briefcase was still there. The movement sent fiery fingers of pain twisting through his side. Involuntarily cringing from the pain, he jerked the handbrake on the Vincent. The front wheel locked and the motorcycle went into a wild side skid, the tyres finding no grip on the wet road surface. Lance corrected the skid and brought the bike to a halt in the middle of the road. The briefcase slipped and almost fell from position. Cursing with pain and fear, he forced it under his backside, flipped the Vincent into first gear and twisted the throttle. The big machine surged forward as the rear tyre suddenly gripped . . . and he did not see the Volvo.

He heard the squeal of brakes and felt the jarring impact as the Vincent hit the right wing of the car, then he was accelerating away to the sound of broken glass tinkling on the road.

Panic swept through him as he passed three cars on the wrong side, screamed through two red traffic lights and almost came off as he skidded round a corner with the offside footrest gouging a rut in the tar. It was not until he had narrowly missed a collision with a taxi that he began to regain control of himself. The booming roar of the Vincent's exhaust dropped to a low growl as he gently closed the throttle and eased to a stop in a dark section of the street.

Trembling with reaction, he took a packet of twenty Texan and a box of matches from his shirt pocket. The shirt was soaked with rain and sweat and the matches were damp. He tore the heads off four of them before he managed to light a cigarette. He had difficulty controlling his shaking hands. Of all the bastard luck!

With his panic slowly subsiding and coherent thought beginning to return, he tried to assess his position. Perhaps it wasn't so bad after all. No one had been close enough to identify him when he had stabbed the old man and taken the briefcase. No one had followed him during the getaway. Of that he was certain. The driver of the Volvo wouldn't be able to recognise him: the accident had happened too fast. So although it had given him a hell of a shock, he had left nothing behind to link him with the robbery.

The relief he felt was tremendous as he flicked the half-smoked butt away in a shower of sparks and kicked the Vincent into life. He noted with surprise that he was in Empire Road, at least six miles from the scene of the crash with absolutely no idea of how he had got there.

Feeling very confident and cocky, he rode slowly past the Fort, Johannesburg's main prison. The pigs will never get me inside there, he thought. It's only a matter of planning. Plan right and you can get away with anything.

He rode past the Quirinal Hotel into Pretoria Street. Ahead of him a policeman was directing the remnants of the late night traffic. Beyond him Lance could see three Flying Squad cars pulled up outside the Clarendon Café.

'What's going on?' he asked as he pulled up beside the police officer. 'Somebody shoot the president?' The fact that his childish show of bravado was not only incredibly stupid but also highly dangerous didn't occur to him.

'Move along,' the policeman snarled, 'before I knock you off for taking old Nick.'

'You mean someone finally nailed the silly old bugger?'

'I told you to move, so move. Now!' He was not in a good

mood. He had returned to the single quarters after four frustrating hours of trying to convince his fiancée that sex before marriage was an experiment all engaged couples took part in and a whole lot of fun as well. He had been at his persuasive best but she wouldn't believe him and he knew he would have to marry her to get her into bed. Trouble was he didn't want to get married, and anyway he couldn't afford a wife on a constable's salary. The engagement had only been to make the bed bit easier. Now it looked like he was stuck with her and it didn't appeal to him at all. He wondered how the hell he was going to get out of it. He didn't notice Lance's ripped jacket or the broken tail light on the Vincent. He had his own troubles.

Apart from the fast, controlled activity around the Clarendon Café, the streets were completely deserted now. Even old Molly, who had been hustling the area for more years than anyone could remember and retailed it desperately for fifty cents with anyone drunk enough not to care how old she was, had been forced off the streets by the wet, biting wind. Lance, with his confidence fully restored, made his way to an ugly, grey block of flats. He passed no traffic and no one saw him.

In the street-level garage under the concrete building he parked the Vincent in its usual place. He grinned as he pulled it back onto the stand. He was home and dry; even the pain in his side was beginning to ease off. From behind the lagging of a hot water pipe, which ran along the back wall, he took a folded OK Bazaars carrier bag. He shook it open and tipped the contents of the battered old briefcase into it, and walked through a doorway into the passage.

It was an old building with peeling paint, a manual lift and a coal-fired boiler. He went into the boiler-room and opened the fire grate with an empty coal sack he found on the floor. The flames were not high, but the heat was intense. He tossed the briefcase onto the glowing bed of coals and watched the hungry flames lick greedily at the old leather, twisting and distorting it beyond recognition. He picked up a spade and shovelled a heap of coal on top of the blackened remnants. Satisfied, he closed the grate and used the fire escape to reach the first floor.

He stopped outside flat number 112 and reached into his pocket for the keys. Sudden fear constricted his throat and his heart began its wild pounding again.

There was no pocket. It had been ripped away by that bloody police dog.

Frantically he searched the other pockets of his clothing. It was no use. The keys had been in the left-hand pocket of the jacket and almost the entire side had been ripped away, and he hadn't realised it. Thank Christ that cop hadn't noticed it either. If he had it would have been the end. Trembling, he tried frantically to remember if anything else had been in that pocket. He forced himself to calm down and think. If he lost control now he would be finished. Slowly his trembling subsided. No, there had been nothing else. Only the keys, and there must be thousands like them in Johannesburg. They were ordinary Yale keys and would be impossible to trace. The building had been up for over forty years, so the locks were at least as old, and no one keeps records that long.

He lifted the loose tile on the window-sill and found the spare key he left for Carol. Quietly he let himself into the flat. He was relieved to find Carol asleep on the double bed under the eiderdown, her long blonde hair framing her face on the pillow. He wasn't in the mood to handle a sulky woman, and sulk she would if he woke her up. He was over two hours late.

He stripped off his sodden clothing, wincing with pain as congealed blood stuck to the material and jerked at the wound. He slipped into the bath and, as gently as he could, sponged the blood away from his hip. The wound looked much worse than it felt. There were two pairs of jagged tears a couple of inches long just above his hipbone. He thought briefly about rabies, but it was for sure that the cops would use only healthy dogs. The bastards!

He climbed out of the bath and carefully dried himself, using Elastoplast strips to cover the bite which had started bleeding again. He kicked his clothes into a heap in the corner of the bathroom, reminding himself to get rid of them in the morning.

In the bedroom he brushed Carol's hair gently off the pillow and slid in next to her. He stuffed the carrier bag between the headboard and the mattress, too tired to count the contents. Carol stirred restlessly beside him, her breasts brushing his right arm and he felt a mild wakening of passion. But she turned away from him and the moment died. He thought he would buy himself a present on Monday. After all, it was November 3rd, 1970, and his birthday. He had just turned nineteen.

* * *

Lance woke up with the sun streaming through the open window into his face. He climbed out of bed and limped over to the window to close the curtains. His hip was stiff but no longer painful. The clouds of the previous night had retreated in the face of the sun and the sky was a bright, brassy blue. It was going to be a hot day. Carol wasn't in bed. He heard her moving around in the kitchen and glanced at his watch. It was nine forty-five.

Moving over to the wardrobe he laid out a pair of trousers and a shirt, and after dressing quickly, lifted the carrier bag from between the mattress and the headboard, and tipped the contents onto the bed. The silver coins formed a small, gleaming pool round which the brown, purple and green notes settled like foliage. He counted the money carefully, sorting the paper notes into piles of one-, five- and ten-rand denominations. He built little towers of coins on the bedside table. Together they totalled two thousand one hundred and fifty-seven rand, sixty-seven cents. The Clarendon Café was a bloody gold mine! Excitedly he called over his shoulder, 'Carol! Come and look at this. We've got enough here to get ourselves married.'

'But I don't want to marry you, man,' a male voice said quietly.

Lance spun away from the bed, shock twisting his features into an animal snarl. Roy stood in the doorway nonchalantly tapping a rolled up newspaper against his leg.

'You bastard! What's the idea of sneaking up on me like that? Where the hell's Carol?'

Roy smiled without warmth. His eyes were black and unblinking, like a lizard's. 'Sonny boy, first let me set you straight. I am not a bastard and if you ever say that again I'll break your cruddy neck.'

He shook the paper chidingly. 'Secondly, I'm here to finalise the conclusion of our successful business venture of last night. I've come for the bread. Do I make myself clear, or would you like me to repeat it?' He was relaxed and completely confident.

'Go to hell, you chicken bastard. You ran out on me last night and you got no claim to the money now. You want any, try taking it. Just try.' He lunged angrily toward the older man.

The gun in Roy's hand stopped him cold.

Lance worked as a counter salesman for the Buffalo Arms Company in Eloff Street and he knew guns. The one pointed at him now was an Astra .38 Special with a 1½-inch barrel. Not the best revolver in the world, but a long way from the worst.

'I used to like you, sonny boy, but right now you're not top of the hit parade.' Roy grinned wolfishly at him. 'I was going to give you a couple of hundred bucks for your trouble, but now you're going to get your teeth stuffed down your throat. You've upset me, little man, but believe me you're going to be a bloody sight more upset pretty soon. Now pick up that bag and put the money into it. But do it very carefully because, as I said, I don't like you very much any more and it wouldn't trouble me to kill you right now.'

Lance measured the distance between them. It was too far; Roy wasn't stupid. He knew he couldn't hope to reach him before Roy pulled the trigger, and he was afraid. With a show of bravado he was far from feeling he sneered, shrugged his shoulders and began stuffing money into the carrier bag. With his back to Roy he said, 'I asked you where Carol is.'

'Now *there's* a smart piece of tail. I told her to take a long walk as I had some very private business to talk over with you and she took off as quietly as a little mouse. A switched-on goose, that one. I may even shack up with her myself.'

'She wouldn't give an ugly tit like you one of her old bras.'

'Lance baby, I may not be a Greek god, but by the time I've finished with you I'll look like a combination of Cary Grant and Rock Hudson compared to you. Now pick up the bread and move out in front of me. Don't get any fancy ideas because shooting the guy who cut old Nick would only make me a hero. Move.'

Lance walked down the stairs out into the street and stopped next to Roy's battered 1950 Plymouth.

Roy tossed the keys onto the front seat. 'You drive, little man. Remember I'll be sitting right behind you and I'll blow your bloody brains out if you try anything cute. Now head out towards Wemmerpan, and watch your driving. We wouldn't want to have an accident, would we?'

Lance was thinking furiously as he nursed the twenty-year-old heap through the Sunday morning traffic. He wasn't sure if Roy would shoot but he wasn't prepared to find out. He didn't want to die. So far Roy had been very careful and given him no chance. He would just have to wait and hope for the opening which must come. Jesus wept, Roy had to boob sometime. He had to.

Lance eased the car off the road and came to a halt in the shadow of a mine dump which bordered the waters of Wemmerpan Dam. Surrounded by tall pine and blue-gum trees, it was completely screened from the road. A notice-board warned of the constant danger of cave-ins on the dump and instructed people to keep off it. A number of children had lost their lives playing on the treacherous golden sand.

'Out, sonny boy. This is where your education starts,' growled Roy.

He climbed out of the car and with the gun viciously prodded Lance along a gully leading into the dump. The gullies, cut by wind and rain and undermined by water, were what made the dumps so dangerous, and no sane person would choose the area for a stroll. Which suited Roy perfectly.

Lance could feel the sweat trickling down between his shoulder blades. Roy was a coward but with the odds in his favour he was a savage bastard and could put him in hospital for months, or possibly cripple him permanently . . . if he didn't kill him! He took delight in maiming helpless victims and there was more than one human wreck hobbling around the city as terrifying testimony to his sadism.

The blow smashed into Lance just above his kidneys and hurled him into the gully wall. The pain rocketed to his brain and, for an instant, he thought he had been shot. He dug his hands into the soft wall, trying desperately to stay on his feet. He knew that once he was down he was finished. The sand crumbled under his clawing fingers and he slid down the wall, followed by a small cascade of golden dust.

'What's the matter, big deal?' Roy's voice reached him through a haze of pain-filled red mist. 'Did Uncle Roy hurt you a little bit?'

Lance pushed himself into a sitting position and Roy kicked him in the ribs. Not very hard, but with enough force to snap him back into the sand.

'You're not so tough after all, are you? Two little taps and you flop around on your back like a virgin after a gang bang. But you won't be doing any banging any more, sonny boy. I'm going to make bloody sure of that.'

Roy put the revolver away and the sun glinted on the brass knuckles now covering his right fist.

With the terrified look of a cowering animal Lance pleaded, 'Roy, I'm sorry for what I said to you. I didn't mean it. You gave me a fright. I didn't mean anything I said. Honestly, Roy. You take all the money and Carol. I don't want anything. Only please, for Jesus' sake, don't hit me again.'

The unmistakable whine in Lance's voice heightened Roy's perverted anticipation. He flexed his right hand and slowly tightened his grip on the brass knuckles.

'You got a few lessons to learn, little man, and I'm just the right person to teach you,' he said. 'But there's no rush. I've got all day.'

Lance sank back dejectedly onto the sand. But he was neither dejected nor terrified. He knew he had a chance and he had to force the elation from his tone. If Roy had kept the gun in his hand there would have been no chance at all, but with it tucked safely away in Roy's pocket, he felt the first glimmerings of hope.

When the sand had collapsed with Lance, a section of rusted, long-forgotten barbed wire fencing had been exposed. The wire was about four-foot long with six inches of broken fencing standard attached to one end. His right hand, partly buried under the sand, gripped the broken standard and he could feel the barbs sticking into his back where the wire lay curled under him.

'Get up, you little tit,' Roy snarled. 'I said I've got all day, but that doesn't mean I'm going to waste it.'

Lance shook his head groggily, but made no move to stand.

'Okay, sonny boy, I'll just kick the hell out of you while you lie there and think about how good looking you used to be.'

The kick, full of savage fury, would have broken Lance's jaw if it had connected. But it didn't. He felt a stinging burn as the heavy-soled shoe grazed his cheek. Then he was rolling away, the wire held in his hand like a whip. He lurched to his feet and almost lost his balance as pain from his injured side swept through his body.

The momentum of his missed kick had sent Roy sprawling onto his back and before he could move the wire whistled through the air and an ugly, bloody gash opened up across the side of his face. As he scrambled to his feet the wire struck again, tearing away part of his left ear. He turned to run, but the gully ended a few yards behind him and the walls were of soft, unclimbable sand, fifteen feet high.

Again and again the darting wire frustrated every move Roy made and he began to scream. A high, continuous scream of blind terror. He tried to grab the wire but it was torn out of his hands, ripping his palms to shreds. His face was transformed into a bloody mess, strips of skin and red flesh hanging down from his cheeks like some hideous carnival mask.

Pain and terror destroyed his judgement and ignoring the wire he ran for the exit of the gully, frantically trying to pull the revolver from his pocket. The brass knuckles jammed in his pocket and he couldn't free his hand. The wire struck again and the standard was almost wrenched from Lance's hand as Roy tripped. His scream faded to a gentle gurgle and finally stopped.

'Okay, you bastard son-of-a-bitch!' Lance panted triumphantly. 'Now tell me what you're going to do to me.'

But Roy couldn't hear him. Roy would never be able to hear anything again. The wire had wrapped round his throat and as he fell, the rusty barbs had sunk deep into his flesh and severed his jugular vein. His life had pumped out onto the golden sand, staining it bright red. He was quite dead.

Lance stood looking down at what he had done. The features

were unrecognisable. Blood and sand covered the face like a thick obscene carpet, and already a few flies had discovered the jagged hole in the neck.

Lance dropped the wire and was sick—as sick as he had ever been in his life. He staggered out of the gully and collapsed on the back seat of Roy's car, shuddering with delayed reaction.

Gradually the shuddering subsided and he began to think coherently. He found a toolkit in the boot of the car and removed the numberplates. Taking them with him he returned to the gully and, without looking at the corpse, began to tunnel into the rear wall, using one of the numberplates as a spade.

It was hard, hot work, the sand continually collapsing into the excavation, and it took him over an hour to tunnel a space big enough to hold the body. The first few flies which had gathered at the gaping wound had now swollen to a dense, black cloud and they buzzed angrily round him as he forced the corpse into the tunnel. Throwing the gore-covered wire in with the body, he hacked at the soft sand above the tunnel until it collapsed and effectively buried the body. It wasn't a foolproof job. With luck the entire wall would crumble and bury the grave under tons of sand. It was possible that the rain would wash the sand away, leaving the corpse exposed. He had to take that chance; it was the best he could do.

Back at the car, he jacked it up and removed the wheels. With the wheelbrace he smashed the windows and headlights and then destroyed the licence discs. He spent fifteen minutes carefully going over the car with a cloth to wipe away any traces of fingerprints. With a knife he found in the toolkit he punctured the tyres, cutting large squares out of the side walls. He rolled them into the dam, holding them under water until the air bubbled out of the holes and they sank swiftly. He cursed himself bitterly for not searching the body and destroying any identification, but he couldn't face the prospect of exhuming it now. The tools and the numberplates followed the wheels into the water and he stepped back and examined the car critically.

Finally he was satisfied that from a distance at least, it gave the appearance of just another old abandoned wreck. He toyed with the idea of setting fire to it, but decided it would draw too much attention. He hoped whoever discovered it would strip it of everything saleable and not report the finding to the police. In any event the police would have a hell of a job tracing it through the engine number. He picked up the red and white carrier bag and walked away through the trees.

* * *

Two hours later Lance walked into his flat. He had mingled with the Sunday crowd at the motoring museum near Wemmerpan and then caught a bus back to Hillbrow. No one had paid the slightest attention to him and the journey had been uneventful. He was under no illusions. The situation could become critical at any time and he had to be prepared to face and withstand a police investigation. He wasn't prepared to find Carol in the bedroom, packing.

'What the hell are you doing, kid?' He walked up to her and put his arm around her waist.

She spun away from him, her expression harsh and tear-stained. 'Packing. What does it look like to you?' she cried as she flung the last of her clothes into the suitcase and slammed it shut.

'Why? Christ, Carol, you can't just walk out on me like this for no reason. Hell, I want to marry you!'

'Marry me? That's good, that is. I wouldn't marry you if you were the last man on earth.'

'Why the hell not? What have I done to upset you? Or did Roy have something to do with it?'

'Roy, you, me, the whole lousy, stinking world. You stay out all night whenever you feel like it. You treat me like your private whore—only a whore gets paid for it. But when your peculiar friends start ordering me around, that's the end. I've had enough of them and you. That Roy is nothing but bad news, so are you. Exit Carol Winters.'

She grabbed the suitcase off the bed and moved towards the door. Lance put up his arm to bar her way and she raked her nails across his face.

'Get out of my bloody way,' she spat at him. 'I never want to see you again.'

After a long moment Lance dropped his arm and passively watched her leave. There was no way he could tell her that Roy couldn't bother her, would never bother anyone ever again. The front door slammed with a deafening crash.

He wiped the blood off his cheek with his handkerchief and wandered into the lounge. He thought that this was possibly not his day. Grudgingly he admitted to himself that Carol was at least partway right. He was turning into a no-good bum. In the short space of ten hours he had stabbed and possibly killed an inoffensive old man, had very definitely killed his ex-partner and had lost a girl he was just beginning to love. Roy's death had been necessary for survival and he wouldn't be missed, but Carol would be. God damn the entire stinking mess to hell and back.

Listlessly he flicked the switch on the radio and took a canned beer from the refrigerator in the kitchen. He flopped into a chair in the lounge and began paging disinterestedly through the Sunday newspaper Roy had dropped on the floor. He wondered what he was going to do about his life. The money had lost a little of its lure. It would last a couple of months and then he would be back to square one. Christ, he thought, what the hell am I doing to myself?

The morse code dots and dashes pinging from the radio and the newscaster's voice saying, '*The World At One PM*', followed by the usual blurb extolling the virtues of Peter Stuyvesant cigarettes broke his chain of thought. He reached out and turned the volume up. He paid no attention to the reports of sabre rattling by the OAU foaming about white minorities in Southern Africa. The cultured tones of the announcer continued:

'In the early hours of this morning a restaurant owner, Mr Nikolaos Eleftheriadis, was attacked and stabbed outside his place of business in Hillbrow. His assailants, described only as two European men, escaped with over two thousand rand in cash. During the escape a police dog was stabbed to death and a police officer, Sergeant Reitz, was injured. It is believed one of the assailants was bitten by the

police dog. Doctors and hospitals in the Witwatersrand area have been requested to report any person requiring medical attention for a dog bite to the police. Mr Eleftheriadis and Sergeant Reitz are in hospital in a satisfactory condition. The police are in possession of a number of clues and early arrests are anticipated. The Hillbrow Murder and Robbery Squad are conducting the investigation.'

Lance started sweating. The seriousness of his actions had suddenly hit him. It had started out as a simple snatch, and at the very worst, if he had been caught, the sentence wouldn't have exceeded two years, at the most. If they caught him now they would throw the book at him, and probably the judge's bench as well. He imagined how the indictment would read: Robbery with violence; attempted murder; destruction of government property—one police dog; assault with intent to do grievous bodily harm—on police (they'd nail him on that one—the law look after their own); resisting arrest; murder.

He would be lucky to get off with fifteen years. Hell, they'd probably drop him in a hole and forget him. And no one who assaults a cop could expect decent treatment in prison. He'd be lucky if he lived long enough to complete his sentence.

He suddenly realised he was thinking in terms of being caught. A few dimly-remembered phrases rolled through his mind: 'Brilliant police work!' 'Determined investigation!'—the sort of comments made by judges to police officers in court and reported in the Press.

He was painfully aware that his knowledge of the police was confined to the young constable on the beat and the fat, disinterested desk sergeant at Hospital Hill Police Station who clung tenaciously to his minimum-effort position while he counted the hours towards his retirement. But now the full attention of the Murder and Robbery Squad would be focused on this crime. Especially as a colleague had been injured. And the Murder and Robbery Squad did not consist of raw young constables or fat desk sergeants. They were experienced men—hard, dedicated, sometimes brilliant and, without exception, relentlessly thorough. They wouldn't give up. Lance knew they would get onto him sooner or later. There were too many leads. They had his keys and the section of his torn jacket. They would find Roy's car and possibly the body. In Hillbrow he was known to be a friend of Roy's. A little money spread around in the right circles and the police would know it too. He had to get out, to run, to hide. But where? He'd been an idiot to imagine he could brazen it out. He had to move, and fast.

The bold black type of an advertisement in the Sunday paper, lying spread out on the floor, drew his attention.

ARE YOU MAN ENOUGH TO DO A MAN'S JOB?
JOIN THE RHODESIAN LIGHT INFANTRY—
Rhodesia's elite commando unit.

If you are young (18 to 24), physically fit and want a career which offers excitement, good pay, excellent sporting facilities and the chance of rapid promotion, apply now to the Recruiting Officer, Rhodesian Light Infantry, Post Bag 7720, Causeway, Salisbury.

DO A MAN'S JOB IN A MAN'S WORLD.

A full colour photograph showed a troop of camouflaged soldiers throwing hand grenades and firing machine-guns into the bush. They were all grinning and gave the impression of having a ball. It didn't look like fun to Lance, it looked bloody dangerous. But why not? Why the hell not?

Rhodesia had been hot news for some years. She had seized independence from Britain, Lance vaguely recalled from his school history lessons, because the British Government had refused to grant legal independence to the Colony. Britain had retaliated by imposing economic sanctions to force her into submission. So far this had failed, and a few British back-benchers were still advocating the use of their armed forces to whip the rebels into line but, according to the newspapers, they appeared to be largely ignored. Christ, he thought, Rhodesians, black and white, had fought side by side with British troops in three major wars and a lot of small ones, and most of the whites in Rhodesia were of British stock anyway. Englishman against Englishman? No ways!

To Lance, the possibility of serious trouble developing was as remote as Mars, even though he'd heard there had been sporadic terrorist incidents. This suited him perfectly. He had no intention of getting his head blown off. He didn't know, or much care, which country was right or wrong. Justice was seldom part of his calculations. All that concerned him was the fact that he could vanish into those camouflaged ranks, and after a few years, when the scene had cooled in Hillbrow, he could return. He had no intention of burying himself in the Rhodesian sticks for any longer than was absolutely necessary.

He pulled out the file which contained all his personal papers and checked through it. Passport valid until January, 1973; health certificate valid for another six months. All okay there. Thank God he had taken that trip to Mozambique last year. He packed his clothes and personal belongings into the two panniers which had been designed to hang over the pillion of the Vincent. The panniers bulged but he managed to close them.

The flat was fully furnished, down to the sheets and towels. So these presented no disposal problem. If they had he would simply have abandoned them. He sat down at the table and wrote two letters, the first to the Buffalo Arms Company informing them he had been offered a job with an arms manufacturing company in Australia which gave him the opportunity to qualify as an armourer. He apologised for the lack of notice but hoped they would understand.

The second letter was addressed to the rental agency responsible for the block of flats. He informed them of his intention to vacate the premises immediately. As the rent was paid up to the end of the month he envisaged no comeback from that direction.

The money!

The goddam money. It was stacked in the middle of the table as sweet and innocent as a fully-primed time bomb. He had killed for it and he wanted it, but discarded the idea of taking it with him. If the customs check at the border uncovered it, he would be finished. He considered the possibility of hiding it, pending his return, but time was short and he couldn't think of a suitable place to stash it. For a long time he sat at the table trying to figure out some way of keeping both the money and his freedom. He opened another beer and paced the lounge, wrestling with the problem.

In the end he did what he had known he would have to do from the beginning. He separated three hundred rand in ten-rand notes from the pile and wrapped the remainder in a sheet of plain brown paper. He addressed the parcel to Mr N Eleftheriadis, c/o Johannesburg General Hospital, Klein Street. He used his left hand. It bore no resemblance to his normal writing.

He retrieved the torn and bloody clothing from the bathroom floor and it followed the briefcase into the boiler-room furnace. He scrubbed the bathroom floor until it gleamed, using the flick knife to scrape the last vestiges of dried blood from between the tiles, then he scrubbed the floor again.

Slipping into a leather jacket he left the flat with the panniers slung over his shoulder.

The two letters were posted in a box in the city centre; the money he forced into another box in Pretoria, thirty-five miles to the north. After carefully wiping the flick knife with his handkerchief, he threw it into a deep section of the Apies River, which runs through the city.

As he swung the big Vincent into Paul Kruger Street, which led north to Beit Bridge and the Rhodesian border over three hundred miles away, he was amazed how simple it was to disappear. With two letters he had severed all ties with his life in Johannesburg. For all practical purposes, he had ceased to exist. He rode for the border confident that in a few years at the most he could return and pick up the threads of his life.

Four days later he stood before a board of officers and attested as a trooper in the Rhodesian Light Infantry. The next day he began his recruit training at First Battalion Depot, Queensway, Salisbury.

Christ, I made it, he thought. No one will ever be able to trace me here. But he was wrong. He had not made it. For Lance Koster nothing would ever be the same again.

1

IT was hot at Malopa Mission. Heat waves shimmered elusively across the dry, dusty land, changing and distorting the shape and character of the distant purple hills. Above the escarpment of the Zambezi valley the clouds hung heavy and dark, pregnant with the promise of impending rain. Dust devils danced and weaved along the ploughed furrows, sucking up little plumes of parched, unresisting soil.

Gara Paratema crumbled a clod of the dark, rich soil between his fingers and hoped it would rain soon. Everything was ready. The lands had been ploughed and fertilised just as the Conex officer had instructed. This year they were trying out a new hybrid maize seed which, the Conex officer had said, had given a yield of eighty bags to the acre on the Government Research Farm near Salisbury. Gara knew that he could not hope to match that yield, which had been achieved under strict control conditions, but with good rains he hoped to reap at least forty bags to the acre.

After last season's disastrous drought, the mission's financial position was desperate. Work had come to a halt on the half-completed school dormitory wing and a good crop would provide the capital necessary to finish the much-needed building. At the moment over thirty children were sleeping on the floor in the school classrooms — which was a big improvement, Gara grinned to himself.

When he had first arrived at the mission as an orphan, sixteen years ago, there had been no classrooms. Lessons had been learnt in the shade of a massive old baobab tree. When it rained the whole school had simply moved into the mud-walled church, which had been the only building on the mission apart from Father Antonio's primitive shack.

The passing years had brought many changes and improvements to the mission. A brick church now stood on the site of the old pole-and-dagga building. The hospital had forty beds and a small fee was charged for treatment, if patients could afford it. Many could not, but Matthew Makeba, who was a state registered nurse, turned no one away. Father Antonio had fought for and obtained a government grant to assist with the purchasing of drugs, but there never seemed to be enough money.

The massive old baobab tree still stood outside the school building, its function recreational rather than academic now. Gone were the nights when Father Antonio would creep off into the bush with his hunting lamp and old .22 rifle, returning hours later with an impala or duiker to supplement their meagre diet of sadza and beans. The game laws were very strict and the fact that he was never caught poaching was due, according to Father Antonio, to divine intervention. Gara was more inclined to believe in the benevolence of the Game Department rangers.

Pupils had come and gone, but somehow Gara had stayed, gradually assuming full control of all the mission's farming activities, learning all he could from farming journals and haunting the Conex office in Karoi for advice and inspiration. The small dairy herd, presented to the mission by a philanthropic society in Salisbury, had become his pride and joy. The sight of the black and white Frieslands never failed to thrill him, and under his management the milk yield had risen considerably.

The strident clanging of the school bell interrupted his thoughts and he made his way slowly back to the building, checking the list of supplies he needed from the Farmers' Co-op in Karoi. The Land-Rover, which at long last had replaced the old bicycle, previously the only transport on the mission, was a joy to drive and he looked forward to the monthly shopping trips with Father Antonio. Now that Gara had his driving licence, Father Antonio would not do any driving but would spend most of the four-hour trip dozing in the passenger seat.

'Right. Are you ready then, Gara?' Father Antonio came slowly down the steps.

The years of rugged, unceasing labour in this northern corner of Rhodesia had not been kind to Father Antonio. The spring had gone from his step, his once magnificent mane of thick black hair was thinning rapidly, bleached by the sun to a washed-out brown, and his eyesight was steadily declining. But with the stubbornness common to the very young and the very old, he refused to wear the glasses he needed. He waved absently to a group of dusty children playing happily in the scant shade of the leafless baobab tree and climbed with difficulty into the high passenger seat of the Land-Rover.

Gara slid contentedly behind the steering-wheel. He drove carefully out of the mission yard onto the dirt road which led to Karoi, a great cloud of red dust suspended in the air behind them marking the passage of the vehicle.

For about two hours Father Antonio stared vacantly out of the window, perspiration gathering in the creases and folds of the wrinkled skin around his mouth and nose, to drip unnoticed from his chin. From time to time he glanced at Gara and a troubled, cloudy expression flitted across the priest's careworn features.

Gara was pleased his passenger was not in a talkative mood. He didn't enjoy conversation as he drove. It interfered with his concentration and detracted from the pleasure somehow.

The road wound through a large tract of mopani forest and a hundred yards ahead of the vehicle a herd of graceful impala leapt across the road, their tawny bodies gleaming in the sun, white tails flicking derisively as they made their way deeper into the trees. The sight seemed to rouse Father Antonio from his reverie.

'Pull over and stop for a moment, Gara,' he said.

Gara's frown of concentration deepened as he slowly brought the Land-Rover to a standstill, taking great care not to scratch the paintwork on the tangle of mopani scrub which lined the road. The impala watched suspiciously from the dubious safety of the trees.

'Father, you cannot shoot here,' he said with a flashing display of teeth. 'We are very close to the main road and it would be asking for trouble to take the carcass into Karoi.'

'It is not my intention to shoot anything, Gara. I'm tired of the bumping and would like to rest for a few minutes. Check the water in the radiator and be careful not to burn yourself.'

Gara climbed out of the Land-Rover and took the water bag from its place in the middle of the spare wheel on the bonnet. He topped up the radiator, careful to release the steam first, and closed the bonnet.

Father Antonio climbed out and leaned against the front mudguard, wiping his face with his handkerchief. The perspiration had conspired with the dust to turn his cleric's collar into a limp, vaguely pink strip of material.

'Gara, you have been on the mission station for about sixteen years now, haven't you?'

'Yes, Father. It will be sixteen years on the twenty-second of December.'

'So you know more about the affairs of the mission than anyone, apart from myself.' It was a flat statement.

'It is possible, Father.' Gara's answer was guarded. He wondered what Father Antonio was leading up to. He knew the old man well enough to realise that this was not just a casual conversation.

'So perhaps you can tell me what it is that is troubling the young men on the mission and in the Tribal Trust Lands?' He was casual and offhand, as if the answer did not really matter, but he watched Gara's reaction with deep and bitter disappointment.

The blank, uncomprehending, slightly idiotic look which has baffled, intrigued and infuriated white men in Africa for hundreds of years, clamped across Gara's features like a shutter, giving the impression that a light had gone out behind his eyes.

'I know of no trouble, Father,' he said with studied deliberation, then added brusquely, 'It is getting late and we should go now.' He got back into the Land-Rover and revved the engine with unnecessary violence, staring fixedly through the windscreen.

Father Antonio climbed wearily into the vehicle. All his experience of working with Africans, helping them in their times of need, curing their sicknesses and teaching them to live better lives had, if anything, taught him that over a thousand years of savage, pagan existence could not be wiped out at one stroke. It would take many generations of dedicated men to eliminate the fears and superstitions which were fundamental to the tribal African's make-up.

And this change was possibly not in the best interests of the African himself. To deprive him of the spirits he knew and feared, spirits which were sometimes kind and sometimes astonishingly cruel, but always understood, and to replace them with an all-powerful, all-seeing, mystical spirit called God, which he had never seen and never would, led to a confused and troubled state of mind which did him no good at all.

Father Antonio knew that a place on the mission station staff was a desired and much envied position among the young men in the Tribal Trust Lands, but he sometimes wondered if this was due to the privileges of good food, decent clothing, education and nothing whatever to do with Christianity. He thought that perhaps he was growing cynical with the passing years.

He had brought civilization and the doctrine of Christ to thousands of ignorant peasants over the years, so that the peasants were no longer ignorant; they could read and write; would defend their long trousers, sunglasses and transistor radios to the death; and would cast off the veneer of Christian principles like a worn-out cloak as soon and as often as it suited them.

Sometimes, in the dark and lonely reaches of the night he would lie awake and listen to the howling of the wind or the harsh and uncompromising snarl of thunder, while vivid lightning flashes chased the blackness round the room, casting obscene and terrifying pictures onto the walls of his crudely-built shack, and he would question the ways of a God who could permit His servant to labour as he had done, to cut himself off from civilized contact as he had done, to live in passionless piety and poverty as he had done, and in the end to be rewarded with nothing more than expedient lip service from those he had attempted to lead into the paths of righteousness, and he would come to the bitter conclusion that as soon as the members of his flock were convinced that the advantages of Christianity had been exploited to the limit, they would slink back to the old ways and to their witchdoctors with no more regret than a snake shedding its skin. In those dark and lonely hours he would curse his God and all the burdens He placed upon those who loved Him, and he would consign all His teachings to the deepest pits of hell.

Father Antonio would rise with the sun and watch the miracle of the birth of a new day, watch the mist dissipate in the valley and the dawn bring new life to the vast land and he would feel ashamed. Ashamed that the terrors of the night and his own failures had combined to render his faith a useless thing, he would pray to his God to forgive him his sins and he would redouble his efforts in the name of Christ the King.

Although he did not doubt the existence of his God, nor the correctness of His ways, he prayed for a sign that would convince his flock of the power and might of God and turn them into true Christians and believers. But this sign never came and he had to be content with what he considered were his own lack of ability and shortcomings.

He had believed that Gara was his one personal success. Of all the Africans on the mission he would have staked his life that Gara was the one true Christian. Now he sat in the passenger seat of the Land-Rover and cursed himself. He had been in Africa far too long not to recognise the undercurrents which ran like an insidious thread through all aspects of tribal life. And now he recognised the signs in Gara's attitude. For Father Antonio was no fool. In days gone by he could stalk an impala herd across a dry bed of mopani leaves or a buffalo through the dense reeds which grew in profusion along the banks of the Zambezi River. And he had not lost this skill.

The previous night the pressures under which he worked had become so unbearable that he had not been able to sleep. These pressures had driven him from his bed and he had attempted to find solace by walking around the mission in the bright moonlight. God or the devil had directed his steps towards the pole-and-dagga huts which he had permitted to be erected on the mission by the subsistence farmers who had been wiped out by the drought of the preceding year.

These unfortunate people had arrived at the mission with little more than the clothes on their backs and Father Antonio had allocated them land on which to build their huts, had satisfied their hunger, which was prodigious, tended their sick, of which there were many, and for the past six months they had enjoyed his hospitality and appeared quite content to continue to do so for the foreseeable future. To Father Antonio it was only one of the many problems he had to deal with through the year. The mission could not feed all and sundry and as soon as it rained he would tactfully suggest that they return to their ancestral homes. Being tactful in this case could amount to him chasing them off the mission with a sjambok, if need be: once he had been fed through the lean winter months the average tribal African saw no reason why that inimitable state should not continue for the rest of his life.

But the need for that sort of action did not enter Father Antonio's head this night. All he saw was the bright eye of the fire in the middle of the compound. Around the fire was a group of figures who appeared deep in conversation. From fifty yards away he could not identify any of them and he knew then that he would have to consult the optician on one of his monthly trips to Karoi.

Normally he would have approached the gathering in an open and straightforward manner, but there was something furtive and unwholesome in the way they were huddled together and some forgotten instinct warned him that he would not be welcome at this fire. Using tracking and stalking skills which he thought had been buried in his past, he dropped to his stomach and inched his way through the dry branches and burnt-out grass until he was within ten yards of the fire.

The first figure he recognised was Gara. Gara, the only one on the mission whom he believed had been completely converted to the ways of Christianity. Gara who now held above his head an AK 47 rifle.

Father Antonio recognised at once the sinister outline of the weapon's short barrel and curved magazine. Bastion of communist power, the AK 47 had readily been handed out to the peasants in a score of countries wherever there was a possibility of trouble. Invented in Russia and copied by the Chinese it required little maintenance and was a superb weapon in the hands of semi-trained terrorists sponsored by the expansionist dreams of Marx, Lenin and Mao for the overthrow of established order, be it in Korea, Vietnam, the Middle East or Southern Africa.

It took a little while for the implications to penetrate the old priest's confused mind. He wouldn't believe it. But when Gara began speaking, he had no choice.

'The Chinese have done it.' Gara did not raise his voice but the low, growling tones carried clearly to where Father Antonio lay, just beyond the perimeter of the huts. 'They have given to us in Zimbabwe the key to our salvation and freedom.' He paused for breath and the perspiration running down his face was visible even to Father Antonio. 'These weapons have been given to us to use in the struggle against the oppressors of our country, and that struggle is now in our hands. Are we children to be told that the only work is in the white man's homes, on the white man's farms or in the white man's mines? I tell you my brothers that one day the white men will serve our food, clean our shoes and work on our farms while their bleating she-goats will scrub our floors. The time to use these weapons is now—to kill the white pigs or drive them into the country of the Boers below the Limpopo River.'

He raised the AK above his head and shouted, 'I tell you the time is now!'

He sat down among the Africans in front of the squatters' huts and a thirteen-year-old youth, who happened to be a favourite of Father Antonio's, leapt into the firelight to proclaim his hatred for the white man and his undying love for Chairman Mao and all that he advocated.

Father Antonio stared in disbelief. The scene was beyond his comprehension. As a man of God he had lived his life according to His lights, and these lights had on occasion played him false, but never to the extent of his renouncing his God.

A battered and confused old man, he worked his way fearfully from the fire, every rustle and crack of the dry bush seeming to scream his presence to the intent figures crouched in the flickering light. At last he rose to his feet and staggered blindly in the direction of his hut, shock overcoming all instincts of self-preservation and he neither wondered nor cared if he had been heard.

Father Antonio was not a physical coward. He had faced more than his share of wounded buffalo, charging lions and berserk Africans, without flinching. But now he needed much more than physical courage. He needed the moral courage to admit that he had wasted his entire life. And he did not have it. He could not concede that every drop of sweat, every tear shed in loneliness and desperation and hope had been wasted. His God would not, could not, burden His faithful servant with this final crushing defeat.

He knew he should use the Land-Rover and leave the mission immediately. The Tsetse Fly Control camp was at Matsikiti, only fifteen miles away. He could use the radio there to call the police at Karoi, and he knew that before dawn the mission would be surrounded and the agitators either dead or captured. But he could not destroy all that he had created, for in doing so he would make a mockery of his life. Although he was a servant of God, he was also a man, with man's vulnerability to the sin of pride. He sincerely believed he had built a lasting testament to God at the mission, and in the space of a few moments that belief had been shattered. He could not assist in its dismemberment.

It was a long, restless and despairing night that Father Antonio spent. In the morning, praying that what he had seen around the fire was nothing but a dream, he waited until all the mission staff had gone about their duties. Then slowly and casually, with racing heart, he worked his way over to the squatters' huts. In the friendly light of day he surveyed the scene and almost convinced himself that nothing sinister could possibly have taken place at so innocent a venue. It must have been a dream brought on by overwork and old age. But in turning to leave he disturbed a pile of ash and something glinted in the sun. It was a medium-calibre 7,62 mm bullet, and Father Antonio could no longer hide behind the possibility of a dream.

This was conclusive proof and he could not deny it. But equally he could not bring himself to report his findings to the authorities. The fact that he was endangering innocent lives by his silence simply did not occur to him. Communism, as far as he was concerned, was a state of non-existence, the antithesis of the teachings of Christ. He convinced himself that he would talk to Gara about what he had seen and he knew that his arguments would compel Gara to tell the communist-inspired agitators to leave Malopa Mission.

He had endured the bone-shaking trip in the Land-Rover in silence, hoping that Gara would confide in him. But as time progressed this became a forlorn hope.

As they approached the main tarred road, in desperation he reached into his pocket and dropped the 7,62 mm bullet onto the seat between them.

Gara's reaction was startling. He twisted the wheel savagely and brought the Land-Rover to a skidding halt in the middle of the road, and the pursuing dustcloud enveloped them like a shroud of doom. Gone was the blank, uncomprehending expression. Gara's eyes blazed with naked fury.

'Where did you get that?' he snarled, thick lips peeling back over his teeth.

'Gara, my son,' Father Antonio implored, 'I saw you last night with a rifle in your hands. What do you need a rifle for? Together we can make the mission a place of peace and refuge for all our people. A place to be proud of. We do not need Godless communistic ideals to teach us wrong from right.' All the appeal of his considerable personality went into his last sentence. 'Gara, for the love of our Father in heaven, please help me. I need you.'

The Tokarev appeared in Gara's hand and the whiplash crack of the pistol rolled away over the empty land. Father Antonio's blood left bright splashes of crimson on the grey seat as the force of the bullet spun him round.

Gara climbed out of the Land-Rover and walking round the front of the vehicle opened the passenger door to let the body of the dead priest spill to the ground. Father Antonio's last action had been to clutch the cross hanging from his belt.

Gara looked down at the body. 'Let your God give you freedom, old man. I will take my freedom with a gun.'

He sprang into the Land-Rover and, scattering stones and dust, spun the vehicle round and headed back toward the mission. In turning, the back wheel crushed Father Antonio's skull and before Gara was out of sight, the ants had found the feast of dark blood and grey pulp which leaked slowly onto the road to mingle with the rich, red soil of Africa.

2

DAMN the phone!

I pulled the blankets over my head but the insistent and impersonal tones still penetrated loudly enough to grab hold of my frayed nerve ends and tie them together. Finally I threw back the covers and stepped out of bed, planting my heel firmly onto the half-full champagne glass, shattering it. I forced an eyelid open and the luminous dial of my wrist watch told me it was 0430 hours. I stumbled over to the phone and wrenched the receiver off the cradle.

'Kelly,' I barked, or tried to. Even to my ears my voice sounded like the squeak of a dirty disc brake.

'Good morning, sir.' The voice was cool, crisp and efficient. 'DPO Rawson here. Sorry to wake you up so early, but something has come up that I thought you should know about.'

He was sorry? 'Give.' I managed to get more authority into it this time.

'A report has just come in from Karoi, sir.' He sounded a little contrite. 'Malopa Mission has been burnt down and most of the people living there have joined the attackers and left the area.'

'How do you know they've joined the attackers?' I was being petty and I knew it. My brain needed a chance to catch up to the report. 'They may have been abducted or they could be lying scattered around in the bush with their guts shot out.'

'Yes, sir.' Very distant now. He didn't appreciate my tone at all, which was just too bad. I was the inspector, not him.

'Malopa Mission is about . . . '

'I know where the goddam place is,' I growled. 'Send a car for me.' I slammed the receiver down.

I could imagine Rawson turning to the others in the Special Branch duty office and telling them what a son-of-a-bitch I was. I didn't blame him. I had once been a detective patrol officer myself. But at last I was fully awake with my brain shifting into top.

I walked back into the bedroom, switched on the light and gave Cathy a healthy clout on the backside.

'Ouch!' She sat up and glared at me. I knew she had been awake all the time.

'You shouldn't listen to other peoples' conversations.' I threw her a mock glare. 'Didn't your mother ever teach you any manners?'

'Of course, she did,' Cathy answered, lowering her eyes coyly as she stepped out of the bed. She walked over to me with that slow, feline grace which is so typically Cathy, her lovely body and expression still giving off that warm, lazy glow which follows a night of love.

She was blonde, twenty-seven years old, about five-foot six tall and built like the playmate of the year. I had known her for six months and was in no hurry to file her away as a memory.

She kissed me gently on the cheek, her breasts brushing slowly across my chest. I felt the slow fire of desire building up and she was aware of the effect she was having on me. I fought down the urge to jump back into bed with her and pushed her away, regretfully.

She followed me to the shower, mischievous lights dancing in her deep blue eyes.

'My mother taught me a lot,' she said. 'She taught me never to sleep with strange policemen who blunder about in the middle of the night, bellowing down telephones, smashing things and assaulting innocent maidens in the bedroom.'

I threw a towel at her. 'Coffee, woman,' I commanded pompously. 'In return for outstanding bravery, the elite of the British South Africa Police have a right to expect unstinting service . . . especially from maidens who never were innocent.'

She threw the towel back.

'Coffee, woman,' I repeated.

'At once, oh master of a thousand desires.'

She started toward me, when I said quietly, 'Sorry kid. This is serious.'

She reacted immediately to the change in mood. 'What is it, Rich?' concern replacing the banter.

'You know better than to ask questions like that,' I said, smiling to take the sting out of the words. We had been over this before.

I am a member of Special Branch and on call twenty-four hours a day, but I don't take my cases to bed. Most of my life is spent with every kind of human scum that contaminates society and I was determined none of it would rub off on to Cathy.

'Okay,' Cathy nodded, 'I'll read about it in the *Sunday Mail*.' She turned and walked into the kitchen. 'Coffee in two minutes,' she called.

Thank God for mature women. The scene had changed and she could accept it, instantly.

I dried off, ran the electric razor round my jaw and checked with the mirror that I hadn't left any stubble. The face that looked back at me was average, the brown hair and blue eyes a legacy of combined Irish/Spanish ancestry dating back to the time Drake had played havoc with the armada off the coast of Ireland. The nose was slightly crooked, the result of a few scrimmages with paid-up members of the fractious mob. The strong jaw-line gave the face a rugged appearance. I had lived behind it for thirty-four uncompromising years and I carried enough muscle on my five-foot eleven frame to ensure that no one pushed it around just for laughs.

I was pulling on a shirt when Cathy walked into the bedroom with a cup of coffee in one hand and a packet of Elastoplast in the other.

'What's the plaster for?'

'I always knew you were an unfeeling brute. There's blood all over the floor in the passage.'

I looked down at my foot and found a deep gash about an inch long in my heel. Damn, the glass. I hadn't even felt it. In fact I still couldn't feel it.

I took a strip of plaster out of the packet. 'My mother told me never to drink champagne in bed. I should have listened to her.'

The doorbell chimes sounded through the flat.

Cathy shrugged into a floral housecoat, slowly and provocatively doing up the buttons, starting at the top. Giving me a look that was more teasing than seductive she began to sway her hips in an exaggerated, sensuous movement.

'Stop messing around, Cathy,' I chuckled, 'and open the door. I don't have any pants on.'

She finished buttoning the housecoat, laughed at me and walked out of the bedroom. I thought that marriage with Cathy could just work. She might kill me in a year, but it would be worth finding out.

I finished dressing, adjusted the Smith & Wesson .38 comfortably in its shoulder holster, and went through to the lounge.

Cathy had given the young uniformed Information Room driver a cup of coffee. In return he was staring at her like a mesmerised rabbit. I couldn't blame him. The way her breasts were standing out behind the thin cotton material was enough to convince a bishop to sell the altar and take off for the nearest strip joint.

'Good morning, sir.' He stood up respectfully without taking his eyes off her. 'I was just telling your wife that I'm sorry to have to disturb you so early in the morning.'

He didn't look sorry to me.

'She's not my wife,' I growled. 'She's my mother. Let's go.'

His eyes widened and he looked at me and then back at Cathy. She rewarded him by opening a top button on her coat. He saw more than he could handle and walked out of the flat in a daze.

I grabbed her and kissed her hard. 'Bitch,' I murmured softly.

'Goodbye, son. Have a good day at school,' she said, pressing her body against me. She was warm, hard and soft all at the same time. She nibbled my ear and suddenly bit, hard. 'Come back soon,' she whispered.

I knew what she meant, and suddenly I fell in love. Just like that. At thirty-four I had finally fallen in love. Don't ask me why. I don't know. I dug my fingers into her shoulders and held her away from me.

She felt the moment, too. The lights in her eyes came up like the sun after a long, dark night.

'Cathy,' I whispered, 'I . . . '

She put a cool, slim finger across my lips.

'Not now, Rich. Come back and tell me when we have time to listen to each other. I don't want to hear that you love me when you're standing in the doorway with a gun under your arm.' She brushed a long strand of blonde hair off her forehead. 'I want you to tell me when we are in bed and I can feel you beside me.'

I knew she was right. I kissed her softly and walked out.

What she didn't realise was that I would always have a gun under my arm. It was the way I lived and would probably be the way I died.

I climbed into the blue and white B-car. The driver was looking a little glassy-eyed, no doubt still bemused by that flash of breast. Hell, he would probably remember it for the rest of his life.

'Okay, son,' I interrupted his dream, 'let's see if this old heap can move.'

'Blue light and siren, sir?' He shot me a hopeful look.

'Yeah.'

These Information Room characters can drive. The tests they go through would turn a good civilian driver green, and not with envy.

He slammed the souped-up Peugeot into first and took off.

We made the nine miles in six minutes. The roads were empty and he drove as if he was at Le Mans. I knew he would be just as good in heavy traffic. I was glad the taxpayers were footing the tyre bill.

I walked into Salisbury's Central Police Station through the Information Room. The stink of early morning crime and tears hit me like a physical blow. After ten years on the force it was something I should have become accustomed to, but I never would.

The suckers at the Charge Office counter were complaining about the whores who had robbed them; distraught parents with tears in their eyes and confused expressions on their faces were looking for children who would have stayed at home if their parents had given them the love they needed; and a woman was loudly insisting that the pile of underclothes she had brought with her should be tested for seminal stains because her daughter was only fourteen years old.

I walked past the line of handcuffed garbage waiting their turn to be documented by the Cells Detail: the proud, defiant ones, the scared and trembling ones, and the ones who had been arrested so often that nothing was new anymore. At least half of them would be released by the magistrate in a couple of hours' time or fined piddling amounts that could be paid out of a child's pocket money. And they would be back. Next time the cautioning would be a little more severe, the fine would be a little higher, but the result would be the same. And when it had happened often enough the magistrate would reluctantly impose a jail sentence.

Even in prison, sentences would be reduced for good behaviour. Good behaviour! Hell, of course they would behave themselves. They had very little option.

Once they were released the whole deal would begin again, and it was the police who had to do all the work and take the blame for the rising crime rate. I sometimes wondered why we didn't just put them up in Meikles Hotel instead of sending them to prison. It would surely save us a lot of work and probably be a damn sight cheaper as well.

I hated their guts and they knew it.

Not one of them would meet my eyes as I walked slowly past.

The bored uniformed cops behind the counter had seen and heard it all a thousand times before and were wishing the hours away so that they could go off duty and pretend the world was a good place to live in. They would go home, take a shower and try to scrub away the filth that had surrounded them for the last eight hours. But they never could. It was under the skin where no soap can reach. You could read it in their faces. Bright, young, shining, twenty-year-old faces with forty-year-old eyes. Hard, cynical, disbelieving eyes that would set them apart from other men for the rest of their lives. It's true. You can pick out a cop in a room full of people. Just look at the eyes.

Nurses and policemen make such felicitous marriage partners

because both have seen the end of the world too often to have any delusions left about life.

I waved to Beth at her desk behind the Control radio. The three gold bars on her shoulders shone in the harsh glare of the fluorescent tubes and she managed to look as though she had just stepped out of the glossy pages of *Fair Lady*, even in the unattractive uniform of the BSA Police and after a long, hard shift.

At one time we had had something going between us, but she outranked most of the youngsters in the Information Room and she had tried to outrank me in a very personal way. She couldn't, and when she finally realised that she never would, she married an inspector in Traffic Section. He couldn't hold her and the marriage had come apart. It had really upset her and on a few nights she had cried herself to sleep in my arms, blaming herself for the break-up, and maybe she had been right. There weren't many men around capable of handling her. Her ex-husband had been transferred to Bulawayo and she had settled down to work, passing her promotion exams at the top of her squad.

So now she was a woman section officer in charge of an Information Room crew, doing a man's job and doing it better than most. She was also a clean and welcoming oasis in that stinking atmosphere.

A small spark passed between us as I sat down at her desk. She rubbed her leg against mine and I rubbed back. She had nice legs.

'Hi, Rich.' Her voice was low, controlled and very sexy. The pressure of her leg increased. 'What are you doing up so early? Her husband come home unexpectedly?' Her lips twitched in an impudent little smile.

'Don't you ever have any thoughts that are pure?' I grinned back. I liked this girl.

'Quite often, but I do my best to ignore them.'

'Get your mind up where it belongs and find DPO Rawson for me. He's somewhere in the building.' The pressure of her leg eased as she lifted the receiver.

I sat back and compared her to Cathy. Physically they were equally attractive. If they were both featured in the same issue of *Playboy* it would be a sellout. With Beth, though, something intangible was missing. I had no idea what it was, but for me it just wasn't there. I knew then that my love for Cathy was no passing emotion. It was a good feeling. I hoped I wouldn't louse it up like Beth had done. This was something I wanted to last.

'He's in the SB duty room, Rich.' Beth put the receiver down and looked at me with intimate familiarity.

'You will address me as "sir",' I chided her.

'Yes, *sir*! Now get the hell out of here before I shock all these youngsters.' Her expression was one of longing. 'Call me when you're free.'

'Sorry, girl, I'm not free anymore.'

'My God! The great Detective Inspector Kelly has fallen at last.' She looked really happy. 'What's she like, Rich?'

'Like a woman.'

I left her reaching to answer the strident clanging of the 99 emergency phone. Her 'Bugger off . . . sir!' followed me along the passage.

I wiped the smile off my face as I turned into the SB duty room. Rawson was sitting at a desk hammering out his report on an old Imperial typewriter.

'Morning, sir,' he said, glancing up briefly. 'Almost finished.'

He typed a couple of lines, pulled the report out of the machine and handed it to me. The script was out of line and some of the letters were difficult to read, which was not surprising as it was the same machine I had used when I had been transferred to Special Branch eight years ago. It had been old then. The Government expects us to work with antiquated equipment on a severely restricted budget, and somehow we manage. And manage very well. The British South Africa Police are rated second only to the Los Angeles Police Department in respect of crimes reported and crimes solved. And we do it without computers. The only modern piece of equipment in my office was a new and very expensive Xerox photocopier.

I read quickly through the report. Rawson's English was concise, meticulous and to the point.

An African had staggered into Matsikiti Tsetse Camp at 2330 hours with a bullet in his shoulder and another in his stomach. He told the tsetse officer that Malopa Mission had been attacked and all the buildings burnt down. The tsetse officer, John Conraad, whom I remembered as a slim, intent character who took his job very seriously, had contacted the police at Karoi by radio and the patrol sent to investigate had hit a TMH landmine just before reaching the mission. The Land-Rover was a write-off but none of the occupants had been injured. They had continued to the mission on foot, finding the buildings gutted by fire and the place deserted. They were waiting for daylight to carry out a recce of the area. End of report.

I turned to Rawson. He had written a good report, but I wasn't about to let it show.

'What have you done about this, besides giving vent to your literary talents and waking me up?'

'Nothing, sir.' His compressed lips were white with anger, which was exactly the reaction I wanted to see.

All the detectives working under me hated my guts and I worked at maintaining their feelings. I wasn't running a boy scout club. I needed angry men. No contented cop has ever solved a case yet, unless it was by accident. I have no use for the contented ones. My detectives worked their backsides off to prove they weren't as stupid as they thought I thought they were. It got a little complicated, but it was a damn good system. We solved a hell of a lot of cases.

'Get hold of Mr Hamilton and let him know the score,' I said. 'You're good at waking people up.'

His lips were even whiter as he reached for the phone. He would have loved to take a swing at me, but I was a little too big and my rank was out of his reach. Discipline is a wonderful thing. One day he would have my job and he'd be good at it—he was getting the right training.

James Hamilton was a detective chief superintendent and my boss. He had that rare combination of compassion and iron will—as well as the ability and sharpness to cut straight through to the heart of a case without ruffling anyone's feathers. Everyone on the station would have gone to hell and back for him, including me.

He had remained a gentleman in a profession which invariably destroyed gentlemen. We had argued long and hard. He disliked my methods and had no hesitation in telling me so. But we had one thing in common: we both hated the jackals of the night, the hyenas who preyed on the defenceless and unsuspecting. We also shared a deep-seated respect for each other.

I picked up the receiver on the second phone and dialled.

'Rhodesian Light Infantry. Good morning, may I help you?'

RLI officers trained their soldiers very well.

'Put me through to the duty officer, please.' He wasn't one of my staff and I didn't have to be rude.

'One moment, please, sir.'

The receiver spluttered and crackled against my ear. Eventually a strong, crisp voice answered, 'Captain Powers.'

I was in luck. I had known Mike Powers for years.

'Mike, Rich Kelly here. If you guys aren't too busy saluting flags and whitewashing stones I've got something here which may just interest you.'

'Get stuffed.' The grin came right through the receiver. 'We have better things to do than help you incompetents issue traffic tickets.'

I filled him in with a couple of quick sentences and told him what I needed: 'A couple of choppers filled with RLI troopies and a lift to Malopa Mission.'

'I'll have to get clearance from the brigadier at Two Brigade HQ.' No messing around, just cool competence and acceptance of the facts. 'How soon can you be ready to leave?'

'Can you do it in an hour?' I asked, expecting protests.

'Make it thirty minutes,' he shot back and the phone went dead.

'The Old Man wants a car to pick him up right away,' Rawson told me, looking at a spot on the wall above my head.

'There are no old men around here,' I glowered at him. 'Only men and young cubs who think they are men.'

The spot on the wall climbed higher. Possibly I was overdoing the Humphrey Bogart bit, but there was no time to worry about it.

'Tell Info Room to send a car for Mr Hamilton and another one to APTS to pick up Sergeant Moses.'

Sergeant Moses and I had joined the police at more or less the same time and I had first met him when I had been posted to Chirundu on the Zambezi River. I had been a young, innocent and ignorant patrol officer and he had been a constable.

The crime rate in Chirundu was very low, averaging about twelve CR's a month and most of those were traffic violations. The majority of our duties consisted of foot patrols along the banks of the Zambezi River. We walked many miles, spent days poaching in Mana Pools Game Reserve and had taken great delight in outwitting the game rangers who tried to catch us.

Although hunting without a licence was, and still is, a criminal offence, we took exception to the fact that game rangers could virtually shoot where and what they pleased, while we were forced to buy our meat at exorbitant prices from the butchery on the Chirundu Sugar Estates. The rangers sanctimoniously justified their actions by claiming they shot only for boys' rations, which was not true. Anyway, it was for sure that we weren't girls, and we felt justified in claiming our share.

Once, after a long, hot and very hard patrol, we had been sitting under a tree on the bank of the Zambezi near the mouth of Kariba Gorge, when a herd of impala stepped daintily out of the bush to drink. I had an old Lee-Enfield .303 and ten rounds. Constable Moses had a Greener shotgun and two AAA twelve-bore cartridges.

My Lee-Enfield was stamped 1897 and the bolt would lock solid after four rounds of rapid. The cartridges Moses had were issued to patrol after patrol, and as African constables had instructions to carry both of them in their pocket and not to load the shotgun unless the situation demanded it, the cartridges were so swollen and distorted by heat and sweat that they could not be forced into the breech of the Greener.

We were one hell of a fighting force. We could have held off a determined attack by half-a-dozen unarmed four-year-olds for about twenty seconds.

The impala never sensed us. I looked at Moses, he looked at the Lee-Enfield and I shot the ram just behind the ear.

A tall, lanky game ranger stepped out from the cover of a mopani tree about thirty yards away.

'Afternoon, gentlemen,' he smirked. 'I've been following you for the last five miles in the hopes that you'd do something stupid.'

He was right. We had been stupid. We hadn't even suspected his presence. He was one hell of a game ranger, though. In his position I'd have made sure no one shot anything in my area. Not him. The dead impala didn't bother him in the least. He followed us until I did shoot something, then he started to crow.

There was nothing I could do about it. He had me nailed to the barn door.

As previously arranged, the pick-up Land-Rover from Chirundu arrived.

Ginger Walker jumped out and walked towards us. 'Move it, you guys.' Sweat was pouring down his face. 'I have a date at the club tonight and women, like the Dunkeld bus, wait for no man . . . '

He looked at the dead impala on the ground. 'Jesus! I knew it was hot in this damn valley, but when the animals start dropping dead with heatstroke, it's time for a transfer.' His grey police shirt was almost black with perspiration.

'It didn't die of heatstroke.' The lanky ranger was very smug. 'It's been shot.'

'You're a very observant person. Or did somebody tell you?' Ginger looked at him suspiciously.

'Can it, Ginger,' I said. 'I'm in the crap. Let's leave the zoo-keeper here to gloat and push off to Chirundu.'

We climbed into the Land-Rover and Constable Moses hopped over the tailboard into the back.

The ranger came running over. 'My truck's five miles away. How am I going to get the evidence to Chirundu?'

'You've got a problem.' Ginger was unsympathetic.

I had had enough of buggering around.

'Throw the carcass in the back,' I said, 'and we'll take it in for you.'

Constable Moses helped him load the impala and we took off.

'You're a stupid sod,' Ginger muttered. He didn't look at me. He couldn't. The road was in terrible condition and demanded all his attention.

'Shut up and drive,' I told him. I didn't need any sermons.

We arrived at the police station in Chirundu at about 1630 hours. I walked into the member-in-charge's office and gave him the story. He was a hard-nosed bastard and I expected the roof to fall in on me. He looked at me mildly and walked out to the Land-Rover. He got a couple of off-duty constables to butcher the carcass; the skin, horns and hooves went into the Zambezi River; the meat went into the paraffin deepfreeze.

When the game ranger finally arrived he was met with blank looks and uncomprehending expressions. He wasn't so stupid. He left the police station swearing and fuming. No evidence, no case. I pulled eight straight weeks night duty and a transfer to Salisbury. The report the ranger turned in disappeared quietly somewhere, and I suspect the member-in-charge had something to do with that as well.

His name was James Hamilton.

* * *

I finished briefing Mr Hamilton as the B-car pulled up next to the landing zone at New Sarum. DPO Rawson and Sergeant Moses were in the back. We had changed into camouflage kit bummed from the army and had drawn Sterlings from the Salisbury Central Armoury.

Four helicopters on the concrete LZ churned the early morning mists. Mike Powers ran up to the car and saluted.

'Morning, Mr Hamilton,' he yelled and glanced at me. 'I've kept the choppers on the ground long enough. You guys are late, so let's move it.'

I looked at my watch. He was dead right, we were late. It had been exactly thirty-six minutes since my phone call.

We climbed out of the Peugeot and ducking low under the rotors, ran towards the helicopters. I tossed my pack in and squeezed in next to a corporal. He shifted over to give me room. Rawson and Sergeant Moses found room for themselves in another chopper.

The four helicopters took off simultaneously.

The lights of Salisbury vanished and then there was nothing to do but watch the shadows grow on the ground as the sun came up behind us. Conversation was impossible. There were no doors on Seven Squadron helicopters and every time the pilot banked I thought I would fall out. Somehow I didn't and two hours later we landed at Malopa Mission.

As the helicopters settled, the soldiers hit the ground with their rifles on full cock, and spread out in defensive positions. I am a cop, not a soldier, but I hit the dirt with the best of them.

The choppers took off and the dust cloud they left behind made it difficult to see anything until the wind moved in.

Four figures walked towards us and when we recognised the police uniforms and the antiquated .303 rifles, we stood up, dusted ourselves off and looked round.

The stark, blackened remnant of the church building seemed to tower over everything. Next to it was the roofless shell of a solid brick building. I knew this had been the mission hospital. It was still smouldering, the thin white plumes vivid against the blue sky.

Malopa Mission was, strictly speaking, in the Karoi area, but the Chirundu patrol border was only a few miles to the north and in the old days Father Antonio had always been good for a bed and a meal. I knew this place well.

I didn't recognise any of the four-man police detail. The section officer walked over to Powers and saluted.

'Morning, sir.' He looked tired and drawn. They all did. It couldn't have been a whole lot of fun to hit a landmine in the dark and then, armed with relics of the Boer War and knowing that the enemy were armed with modern automatic weapons, to carry on with the patrol. I noticed all four of them casting longing looks at the SLRs carried by the troopies.

The detail wore the regulation grey shirts and blue riot trousers issued to police for bush work. I swore under my breath. It may have been great camouflage in Kentucky, but there sure as hell is no blue grass in Rhodesia. Good God, even their belt brasses had been polished. It was pointless kicking against the regulations. Some senior assistant commissioner who should have been retired long ago, insisted that the police were not army and should be recognised as police wherever they happened to be.

ZAPU and ZANU must have loved him. Policemen were easier to see and shoot in the bush than a one-legged stripper in purple panties. I couldn't change the regulations but that didn't mean I had to obey them. The camouflage kit that Rawson, Sergeant Moses and I had appropriated from the army may just help to keep us alive, and anything which helped to do that came out way in front of all the outmoded regulations in the book.

Powers didn't return the section officer's salute. He stuck out his hand instead.

'I'm Mike Powers.' He looked grim. The destruction all around us was having an effect. 'Officer commanding 3 Commando. Who are you?'

'John Mitcher.' He shook Powers' hand. 'And very glad to see you, Mike.' He gestured towards the old baobab tree. 'My radio and maps are over there. Let's go into the shade and I'll give you a full sit. rep. As far as I know it, that is.'

'I don't want to know your troubles, mate,' Powers answered. He jerked his thumb in my direction. 'Open your heart to the DI over there. First thing I've got to do is carry out a clearance patrol.' He pumped his arm up and down in some mysterious army signal to the troopies.

The troopies understood his signal and as he ran around the corner of the burnt-out church, they scattered through the ruined mission and into the bush beyond.

Mitcher introduced himself to me and the others did likewise. After I had shaken hands all round, we squatted on our heels in the shade of the big baobab. Mitcher spread his map on the ground, keeping it pinned down with his boot heel on one corner and his rifle across the top.

'We hit the mine about here.' He jabbed his finger at the map. He had a deep gash across the back of his hand. It didn't seem to bother him. He looked hard and tough and I didn't think much would bother Section Officer Mitcher.

'We were a bit dazed by the explosion and it took a while for us to get going again.' No bragging, no modesty. Just facts. 'The truck was a write-off, but fortunately no one was hurt, and we were only about two miles from the mission, thank God.' He looked over the map at a young patrol officer. 'Hill, get a fire going and brew up some tea.' He crumpled an empty Gold Flake box and threw it away. 'And find me a cigarette before I have a bloody nicotine fit.'

My brand. I opened my carton and gave him a pack of thirty.

'Thanks, sir.'

I'm not Mike Powers. Christian names have no future around me.

Mitcher lit a cigarette and stuck the packet into his pocket. I had given him thirty and he took them. No buggering around trying to give the rest back.

'We circled the mission and approached from the east side,' he continued. 'The sun was coming up and made things easier. As it turned out, it didn't matter. There was no one here. Only a few bodies in the hospital.' He pointed towards the burnt-out building. 'From the number of tracks leading northwest it seems that the ters have abducted everyone left alive. We were just about to follow them when we heard the choppers arrive.'

Abduction was a frequent terrorist tactic. They used everyone, old men, women and children as porters, cooks or labourers on their flight back to sanctuary. Those who couldn't take the pace were shot as an example to the others. The survivors were held virtually as slaves in terrorist camps in Zambia or Mozambique. Occasionally if there were too many in the abducted group or the terrorists too hotly pursued, they were simply abandoned to make their own way to safety or die in the bush. It didn't seem to worry the ters either way.

Mitcher rocked back on his heels and waited for my comments, his eyes telling me that if I wanted him to obey my orders, now was the time to prove that I knew what I was doing, and the fact that I outranked him didn't matter a damn.

I studied the map. Ignoring the contours, the mission was about eighty-five miles from the Zambezi River. Eighty-five dead straight miles with a farm on the line. If the terrorists stuck to a north-westerly path, they had to cross that farm. In all probability they would head in that direction. It was the easiest route to the Zambian border, and Zambia was the only safety they would find this side of hell. The direct northerly route was rugged, impossible terrain and, although slightly shorter, would take them at least twice the time to cover.

I switched on the TR 28 set, waited for it to warm up, then pushed the tit. '221, 221, 221, Sierra Bravo.'

Karoi's call-sign was 221, and they were maintaining a listening watch. I was Sierra Bravo.

They answered immediately. 'Sierra Bravo, 221.' The voice was distorted by distance, heat and the limitations of the set. 'Reading you threes, over.'

Threes was good enough.

All messages were supposed to be sent in Shackle code. Zambia may have been monitoring our transmissions, but I didn't think it was likely. Anyway time was short and I decided to chance it. I sent in clear:

'221, Sierra Bravo. Instruct the South African Police at Mana Pools to set up a stop-line between Hell's Gate on the Chirundu Road and Rekometje Research Station. Unknown number of CTs heading in that direction. Instruct Lomagundi HQ that I want a base camp set up at Makuti.'

I didn't have the weight to swing that one, but I knew Mr Hamilton could do it and he would back me up, I hoped. Makuti is a tiny settlement right on the edge of the Zambezi escarpment and one of my favourite places. It consists of a police camp, roads department camp, a tsetse control camp, a post office relay tower and a motel. On a clear day, from the motel verandah, you can see the waters of Kariba Dam, fifty miles away. If the terrorists stuck to a northerly route they would have to pass within fifteen miles of Makuti, and with luck, that's where we would nail them.

'Also contact Nyamahamba Farm. It is on the direct line of escape. Immediate protection is to be afforded to this farm and the occupants to be moved out, if they agree.'

If the people on the farm elected to stay, there was nothing we could do about it. We could try, but I know farmers. They would stay. They would take precautions as far as they were able, but they would stay. The remote, wild and lonely lands had soaked up too many tears, too much sweat and sometimes blood, to be abandoned for even a short period. They would defy the devil himself, but they would stay. And in consequence make our job doubly difficult. We had more than enough to do without having to worry about women and children running around and fouling things up.

'We are commencing follow-up. Confirm message understood. Over.'

The reply was sharp and clear.

'Sierra Bravo, 221. Message understood. Oscar Charlie instructs you are to remain at the mission to await his arrival. You are not, repeat not, to accompany Romeo Lima India. Confirm. Over.'

I held the mike as far away from my mouth as possible and dropped my voice to a whisper. '221, Sierra Bravo. You are unreadable. Receiving you strength one. Please repeat last transmission. Over.'

They came back at fours. 'Sierra Bravo, 221. You are to remain at the mission to await arrival of Oscar Charlie. You are not to accompany Romeo Lima India. Confirm understood. Over.'

If anyone thought I was going to sit around the mission twiddling my thumbs, they were out of their tiny minds. The RLI held the police in enough contempt as it was. It was time to show them we did more than issue traffic tickets.

'221, Sierra Bravo,' I continued in the whisper. 'Receiving you ones. You are unreadable. Nothing heard. Out.'

I unscrewed the mike lead and stuffed it into the pocket on the set pack. I sized-up the men grouped round me. Rawson looked resigned, Sergeant Moses was smiling broadly and Mitcher looked strangely content. Maybe I had passed the test. The other three looked astounded.

Hill handed me a steaming mug of tea. I used the silver paper from my cigarette packet to line the rim of the aluminium mug. I had burnt my mouth too often in the past to be caught again.

I was wilfully disobeying a direct order, but I didn't expect anyone else to drop into the manure with me.

'Gentlemen,' I was being very polite, 'you all heard the order. I am going with the army. DPO Rawson is coming with me because he has no choice. Sergeant Moses is coming because he wants to.' I paused to let the words sink in. 'What you guys do is entirely up to you.'

'I always knew those TR 28 sets were a load of crap,' Mitcher said seriously. 'I never heard a thing.'

'Have we got time to finish our tea, sir?' Hill looked as happy as a boy scout going on a picnic. I grinned at him. He was risking a severe disciplinary rebuke at best, and a bullet in the guts if we were unlucky. And he knew it.

The other two went into a private huddle. Finally the one called Henderson said to me, 'Sir, we all heard the order.' He glanced at the other policeman and got a back-up nod. 'Patrol Officer Pell and I feel we should obey it. We are going to wait for the OC's arrival.' He sat back, looking grim.

I was disappointed, but didn't show it. They were probably the only sensible ones among us.

'Yellow bastards!' Rawson muttered. He surprised me, I didn't know he had it in him.

'You can't talk to me that way.' Henderson stood up, ready for trouble. He looked as if he could handle himself and I was sorry he wasn't coming with us.

As Rawson scrambled to his feet, I stepped between them. 'Knock it off. There's enough going on round here without you two girls trying to pull each other's hair out.'

Rawson gave a disgusted grunt and turned away. He knew me. Henderson didn't. He glared at me. I smiled back.

Mitcher growled, 'Shut up, Henderson.'

Henderson obviously knew Mitcher. He sat down next to Pell and shut up.

I looked at the two dissenters. 'As you're not coming with us, please be good enough to hand over all foodstuffs you may have in your packs to Sergeant Moses.' It was time I did a little glaring of my own. 'We're liable to need it more than you are.' I turned to Mitcher. 'Let's have a look round.'

'There's not much to look at, sir.' He uncoiled himself. 'Only the bodies in the hospital.'

'So, let's take a look anyway.'

The hospital was a burnt-out shell. As we walked between rows of what had once been beds, I felt the anger and hatred rise up in my throat. The twisted metal conspired with the sunlight to throw grotesque shadows against the walls. How the hell could they do it? These were their own people. I had been able to speak Shona before I could speak English, and I still didn't understand them.

There were three bodies in the ruins of the hospital. Two had died in their beds. The third had tried for life. It was impossible to tell whether it had been a man or a woman. The distorted, burnt shape told a story of its own. It had collapsed underneath a window, a burning rafter across its back. The rafter had held it from freedom. Neither hand had any nails left. The blood trails down the wall bore mute testimony to the last, futile struggle.

A shudder ran up my spine, and I hoped to God that I would never find myself in that position.

We left the hospital and did a quick tour of the mission. There was, as Mitcher had said, not much to see. Even the squatters' huts had been burnt down. Strangely, Father Antonio's shack had not been touched. The bed was unmade, but everything else was in order.

'Looks like he took off with the rest of them.' Henderson's voice came up from behind us.

I had known Father Antonio for a long time. The idea of him charging through the bush waving an AK, his cassock flapping behind him, would have made me laugh, if there had been anything to laugh about. His only weapon was his faith. And one thing was for certain, he would never have allowed the terrorists to take him as a hostage. If I knew him at all, he would either be chasing after the ters trying to convert them, or he would be dead. And I didn't think he was chasing them.

'Don't talk crap,' I snapped at Henderson.

'But why didn't they burn down his hut as well?' Pell's voice had a built-in whine that irritated me.

‘Probably ran out of matches,’ Hill said, looking at no one in particular.

‘The army is coming back, sir,’ interrupted Mitcher.

I turned and walked to meet Powers.

‘They’ve taken off northwest and they’re really moving,’ Powers said, pausing to wipe the sweat off his face. ‘Or they were. If they keep up the pace they’ll kill the old people and the children.’ He dug out a cigarette and lit it. ‘We found tyre tracks moving ahead of the main body, so it looks like the big shots are travelling in style, for the moment anyway. They’ll run into jesse bush about fifteen miles from here and will have to abandon the vehicle. They’ll never be able to drive through that mess. The only way through is on foot and even then it’s bloody hard going.’

He nodded his thanks as Hill passed him a mug of tea.

‘I’ve sent a patrol under Corporal Koster after them,’ Powers continued, ‘with orders not to engage, but to report any sightings. We’re doing a follow-up in extended line. I’d hate to lose the big cheese in this trap.’

He finished the tea and handed the mug back to Hill. Then turning to the men he said, ‘If you gentlemen are ready, we’ll move out now.’

We moved, and left Henderson and Pell a couple of lonely figures under the big baobab tree.

I glanced at my watch. It was 0800 hours and already as hot as hell. Powers was the captain and this was his show. We were policemen, not soldiers. He asked us to stay close to the MAG gunner and that’s where we stayed.

In a couple of hours the sling of my Sterling sub-machine-gun had started chafing my shoulder. The troopie with the MAG seemed oblivious of the weight he was carrying. The heavy machine-gun was at least ten times the weight of my Sterling and it didn’t bother him at all. He was garlanded with five-hundred rounds of belt ammo and that didn’t seem to worry him either.

* * *

It was 1200 hours when we found the first body.

It was an old woman who had been shot through the back of the head. Koster's patrol had found her first and blazed the trees round the body. Her shrivelled black face looked at peace, and I hoped she was. We moved on.

From then on we found bodies. But time was against us and we didn't stop, except once. That was when we found an elderly African man pegged down across an anthill. A stake had been driven into his stomach and his genitals had been hacked off. He was still alive. Sergeant Moses gently lifted his head and tried to pour a trickle of water down his throat. He couldn't take it and he gagged, blood seeping from the corner of his mouth. The RLI medic finally got the stake out of the old man's stomach after pumping him full of morphine. The blood gushed out in a rich, red stream and the medic turned away. There was nothing more he could do.

Despite the morphine, the old man screamed. I flipped the Sterling onto single shot and put a bullet through his head.

They all stared at me. There was disgust in their eyes, but there was respect as well. No one said a word. I felt like hell.

* * *

At 1830 hours, just as the sun was beginning to sink below the horizon, we found the Land-Rover and ran into an ambush. The terrorists were lying in the jesse about thirty yards to the left of the Land-Rover. They must have watched Koster's patrol move through and then taken up their position, knowing that a follow-up was bound to come.

The MAG gunner had treated me with contempt until the incident at the anthill. I couldn't blame him. In Salisbury the army and the police mixed like paint and petrol. Neither understood the other nor wanted to. Until I had shot the old man I had been just another cop. Now I was a person he could understand. He had been trying to talk to me ever since, but I couldn't respond. I didn't like myself very much right then. Someone had had to do it, but that didn't make it any easier.

He stepped out of the cover of the mopani trees and pointed at the Land-Rover, fifty yards away. 'Look, sir. We've nailed the bastards now,' he said and swung the MAG toward the jesse.

'Get down, you bloody fool!'

Powers' shout was too late. Far too late. A burst of automatic fire split the air and a line of red dots stitched themselves across the trooper's green army shirt, hurling him back into the trees. He was dead before he hit the ground.

I emptied the Sterling into the jesse, not feeling the recoil. At fifty yards I might as well have been throwing pebbles. I dived toward the MAG. Rawson was suddenly beside me, ripping ammunition belts off the dead trooper, and together we got that beautiful weapon working.

I slammed the butt into my shoulder and raked the jesse. There was no target to aim at, but that didn't stop me. It didn't stop anyone else either. The whole commando were on their stomachs sending a withering hail of death screaming into the dense bush. It lasted for about a minute and then stopped abruptly. The silence almost deafened me. After the initial RPD burst, no return fire had come our way, and I was sure the ambushing bastards were dead. Nothing could have lived through that murderous fire.

Powers leapt to his feet and ran straight toward the ambush, an indescribable high-pitched whine coming from his mouth—the same sound an angry bull terrier makes when going in for the kill. Mitcher was right behind him. He didn't make a sound, but his eyes were alight with unholy joy, and he looked the more dangerous of the two.

When the rest of us caught up with them, we found Mitcher grinding his boot into the face of a struggling terrorist. The terrorist had caught a burst right through his thighs. I could see the bone poking its way out between the layers of flesh, starkly white against the black skin. An AK lay half hidden in the dry grass about four feet away, where he had thrown it when the bullets hit him.

I had no sympathy for him but I needed him alive. I grabbed Mitcher's shoulder and spun him away. But I was too late. The bullets had cut the terrorist's femoral artery and he bled to death as I knelt down next to him. You can't get information out of a corpse. I stood up. The killing lust died slowly in Mitcher's eyes and he shrugged apologetically.

We found one other body. The MAG had cut it in half. It was a youngster, not more than fifteen years old. He had fallen over the RPD and the hot barrel had scorched his shirt. You don't have to be mature to pull a trigger.

The dead trooper was loaded aboard the Land-Rover with the two terrorists and a soldier was detailed to drive the bodies back to the mission. He looked unhappy, but he didn't argue.

From the tracks that we found, there had been at least eight terrorists lying in the ambush. A corporal found another AK and a faint blood trail leading northwest. How six terrorists had walked away through that murderous curtain of lead I will never know.

Sergeant Moses unshipped the radio and I called Karoi, in code this time. I reported the finding of twenty-eight corpses murdered by the fleeing terrorist gang, and the contact.

When I had decoded the reply I called Mike Powers over. 'We're about forty miles from the South African Police stop-line, which has been extended from Hell's Gate along the bottom of the escarpment to the Chewore River.'

Powers studied the map a moment. 'They've either got a hell of a lot of men, or they're bloody thin on the ground.' He looked up in surprise. 'That's a thirty-five-mile long stop-line. Stupid buggers won't be able to see each other, never mind the ters.'

'Special Air Services are parachuting into the area about fifteen miles in front of the SAP,' I told him. 'They'll work the flanks and we'll squeeze the ters to death between us, we hope.'

'A brilliant plan. Bloody brilliant. I wonder which idiot at Sunray Major with more rank than brains thought that one up?' He folded the map disgustedly. 'By tomorrow we'll probably walk into the SAS and then the fun will start. How do I tell my troopers to be careful before they fire. They're keyed up to hell and the first thing that moves in front of us is going to get shot.'

The growing roar of the three Dakotas shut him up. They passed almost directly overhead, the Rhodesian Air Force insignia showing faintly in the fading light.

'Jesus, it's too late to stop it now. I hope the fat, desk-bound pensucker who ordered that sleeps well tonight.' He watched the fast-disappearing aircraft, anger tightening the tendons of his neck. 'Screw them.' He looked at his watch. 'The moon should rise about 2100 hours. We'll bivvie here and move out then.' He shouted over his shoulder, 'Sergeant Jamieson!'

'Sir.'

'Tell the men to take a break and get something to eat. We're moving out at 2100.'

'Yes, sir.' The unseen Sergeant Jamieson sounded grateful. It had been a long, hard day.

I broke out my tiny Gaz cooker. Wonderful people the French. They've invented a lot of useful things. I had finished my mug of instant soup and was just setting fire to a Gold Flake, when Henderson staggered up to us and flopped down.

'Bloody hell!' Rawson regarded him with amazement. 'What happened? Pell get tired of holding your hand and chase you away?'

Henderson ignored him. He turned to me. 'Sorry, sir,' he said sheepishly, 'I stayed at the mission until I heard the OC's chopper coming in to land and suddenly I knew you'd been right. I grabbed my rifle and came after you. I hope you don't mind if I join you.'

I didn't mind. In fact I was pleased to see him.

For some reason his presence seemed to upset Rawson. 'Of course we don't mind, my dear.' His tone was cold and sarcastic. 'We can do with a young lady to cook our food, stitch on our buttons, and maybe dry our tears when we hurt ourselves.' Then he flared, 'Why don't you run back to your mummy? We have grown-up work to do.'

Henderson got slowly to his feet. He was about four inches taller than Rawson and thirty pounds heavier. None of it fat. 'You run off at the mouth like a blocked sewer and I've had enough of your crap. Put up or shut up, little man,' he growled, and Rawson hit him in the mouth. Accurately and very hard.

Henderson staggered back a few feet, recovered quickly, and kicked Rawson in the stomach. The air spewing out of Rawson's throat made a whistling sound. Henderson closed in and Rawson's knee hit him in the groin. Neither of them could breathe properly and they waltzed a few crazy paces hanging on to each other.

I would have made a great spectator in ancient Rome. Normally I wouldn't have interfered. They were both adults, or thought they were, and if they wanted to pound the hell out of each other, they were welcome to carry on. But times were not normal and we needed them both.

Mitcher and I separated them. For a few moments they sat glaring at each other, and then by mutual consent they decided that neither existed, which was fine with me.

It had been a long, weary day. I leant back against a tree, pulled my camouflage cap over my face and went to sleep.

3

THE moon climbed slowly and majestically into the black night sky. It hung full and heavy behind us and gave off enough light to read by.

We moved out. Very carefully and very quietly, every piece of equipment that could shine or rattle was wrapped or stuffed away in packs or tied down.

The dry jesse bush was harsh and uninviting and looked like a weird, nightmare lunar landscape. There were no colours left in the world. Everything stood out in brilliant black and white relief.

Our progress was slow. The RLI tracker lost the spoor often. Tracking conditions were almost impossible. No matter how good a tracker you are, nothing looks the same in moonlight. You can't tell the difference between old, dry, naturally-dead grass flattened by the wind and growing grass unnaturally flattened by recent passings.

Henderson moved over to me quietly during one of the lulls while we waited for the tracker to find the spoor again.

'I've done a bit of tracking, sir.' He smelt of sweat and dust. 'Do you think it would be in order if I helped the tracker out?'

The troopies didn't like it, but Powers okay'd it. Henderson moved up with the tracker.

They were bloody good, once they had overcome a little initial animosity and the tracker had realised that Henderson was there to help him, not to take over the show. Gradually they began to work as a team and we really started to move through the jesse.

But the terrorists had been running, and unless they staged another ambush, we had no hope of catching up with them that night.

Three things happened simultaneously. We burst out of the jesse into comparatively open mopani forest, the moon sank down below the horizon and the rains came. Suddenly it was pitch black and very, very wet. We stopped where we were. It was not only pointless to go on, it was impossible. For three-and-a-half wet, miserable, stinking hours we sat there. Tourist brochures tell us that the temperature in Rhodesia in November ranges from hot to hotter. My teeth hadn't read the brochure. They wouldn't stop chattering and I damn near froze. If I ever meet a brass monkey we can form a club.

Towards dawn the rain eased to a gentle drizzle. The sky turned into a solid grey blanket. Henderson came back to us. No one mentioned tracks. I tried to light a cigarette but the goddam thing fell apart in a soggy mess. My fingers were blue and fumbling, which didn't help a great deal. I tossed it disgustedly into the bush.

Hill had my Gaz cooker and was playing tea boy again. He handed me a steaming mug. I fished out the tea bag and squeezed half a tube of condensed milk into the liquid. That hot, sweet tea hit my stomach like a revolution and it was one of the most refreshing drinks I'd ever tasted.

Mike Powers walked over to me. He had a contraceptive stretched over the muzzle of his SLR to keep the water out. So there was another use for them, and the French got another good mark.

'I've been onto Sunray Major,' he said. 'They seem a little subdued this morning. I don't think they appreciated my comments on their brilliant SAS strategy.' His lips twisted into a sardonic grin. 'Let's have a look at the map.'

The ground was too wet to spread the map out, so we stood in the drizzle holding it up between us.

The ters must have had a good compass. They were following a dead straight, northwest line of escape. And on that line was Nyamahamba Farm, only seven miles ahead of us.

'For Christ's sake,' I said, 'unless the sods swung round Nyamahamba Farm, they'll have gone right through it by now. I hope those people had some protection.'

'Only one way to find out,' Powers answered, then shouted, 'Sergeant Jamieson!'

'Yes, sir?'

'Get the lead out. We're moving.'

'Yes, sir.'

One of these days I supposed I would get a look at the mysterious Sergeant Jamieson.

And move we did. And the rain came down again in barrels. And my heel began to hurt. Really hurt.

We reached the farm just after 0630 hours. Seven miles in an hour. I limped in five hundred yards behind everyone else. My foot was on fire. I forgot the pain as I walked through the compound.

The terrorists had tried to burn the huts but the rain had kept the fire from spreading. It hadn't stopped the killing. There were seven bodies in the compound. Four had been shot. The other three had been hacked to death.

The farm store was a wreck. What they couldn't carry away the terrorists had scattered in the mud. Smashed transitor radios shared soggy puddles with bolts of brightly-coloured cloth. Sunglasses and smashed Surf packets added to the destruction.

An African woman lay huddled over a paraffin lamp. She had been stripped naked and the bayonet wounds had stopped bleeding. The rain had washed the blood away and it was easy to see the holes in her back. A paraffin lamp is a hell of a thing to die for. I walked on.

In the lounge of the farmhouse we found Ronson. An empty Browning self-loading shotgun lay on the carpet beside him. Dozens of expended AK cartridge cases littered the floor and there was scarcely a square foot of wall space unmarked by bullet holes. Ronson had not died quietly.

It was impossible to determine how many times he had been shot. The terrorists had vented their animal insanity on the corpse, leaving Ronson an almost unrecognizable, bloody carcass. They must have used their serrated Russian bayonets to rip through his body again and again—there were even pieces of flesh clinging to the ceiling.

There was also one dead terrorist. I couldn't tell how old he had been. He had taken a full blast of SG shot in the face, and there wasn't much left of his features. He was crumpled up against the side of the slate-finished fireplace.

'Medic!' The frantic scream outside the house jerked my attention from the senseless savagery in the lounge. I ran out to investigate, and finally met Sergeant Jamieson.

He came out of a tobacco barn with Mrs Ronson in his arms. She was naked and her left breast had been cut off. Thin trickles of blood ran down her thighs from the black triangle between her legs. I couldn't even begin to imagine her agony as those bastards had mounted her, one after the other, and then viciously mutilated her. She must have been tough, because she was, incredulously, still alive. But only just.

She mumbled something, but it was difficult to understand her. She had chewed through her lips.

I put my ear close to her mouth.

'My . . . my . . . children,' she finally managed to breathe. A tremor ran through her body, and then she was still.

There was nothing I could do for her. She had lived just long enough to ask after her children.

I turned and raced back to the house.

I ran through the lounge and up the passage to the bedroom at the end. I kicked the door open, and was almost sick.

It was a slaughterhouse. Great splashes of blood left vivid streaks through the chaos of splintered cupboard doors, torn, scattered clothing, smashed furniture and broken glass.

There were two little bodies on the floor. One was about five years old and the other about three. Their arms had been hacked off at the elbows and their legs at the knees.

The thick trails of blood across the floor showed that they had lived for a short time. A mercifully short time. There were boot-prints in the blood.

The bastards had stood and watched them die. Two little children flopping around on the floor, not understanding their hideous agony, nor able to escape it. They had died screaming and terrified.

It was then that I really learnt to hate.

The terrorists had stood and watched them die. The inhuman, sadistic, fucking animals.

I lifted the small, pitiful bodies onto the bed. Even in death their faces were twisted and distorted with terror. Their eyes were open and accusing, following my movements with flat, dead questions. Why had I allowed this to happen to them? It was my job to protect them, wasn't it? I hadn't done my job, had I? Why had I allowed them to die like this? Why? Why? Why? I had no answer to offer.

I covered them gently with a sheet and walked out of the room, blood pounding behind my eyes. The accusing memory of those two little faces will damn me until the day I die.

Sergeant Jamieson came into the bedroom carrying Mrs Ronson's body and laid it down gently next to her children. At least they were together in death.

I grabbed Sergeant Moses, unloaded the radio and encoded a message as quickly as I could. We were now closer to Chirundu than Karoi, and two-zero-five was Chirundu's call sign.

'205, 205, 205, Sierra Bravo.'

All I received was silence. I tried calling them for a couple of minutes without making contact, and finally called Karoi. They came back at strength one. This time I really couldn't read them.

Someone fired a shot in the compound and we all hit the dirt. Jamieson appeared round the corner of one of the huts. He had something in his hand. He walked over to Powers and extended it. His face was grey and the sheen on his forehead wasn't all rain. He held it out . . . a tiny ripped, white arm. The fingers and nails looked like a doll's.

'A dog was chewing this. I shot the sodding thing.'

Powers stood stupefied, not moving. I took the arm from Jamieson.

No dog could have got into that room, not through a closed door. The godless bastards had fed the severed limbs to the compound scavengers.

I returned to the bedroom and, pulling back the sheet on the bed, placed the mangled arm next to the children.

'Christ!'

I hadn't heard Powers come in but he was standing just behind me. He stared at the tiny bodies for a moment. His face was ashen. He spun round and walked out of the room.

'Sergeant Jamieson,' he shouted hoarsely from the verandah of the house. I wondered irrelevently if he knew the names of any of the rest of his troop.

'Sir?' The reply was subdued but clear.

'Fall the commando in and send them in here one at a time.'

To each in turn he showed them the bodies. He didn't say a word, just pointed. A few came close to fainting, a couple vomited in the passage, and no one who walked into that room would ever be the same again.

We covered the bodies and went outside. There were no youngsters left. Some were only eighteen or nineteen years old, but there were no youngsters. Their faces were drawn and hard.

Powers stopped in front of them. 'Now we know what we're chasing.' He paused, then added roughly, 'Let's get the bastards. Move out. Arrowhead formation.' We moved out.

The men were strangely silent and withdrawn, each avoiding the eyes of the others; each lost in his private hell of cold hate and revenge . . . each a self-appointed executioner. Vengeance is an ugly and cancerous emotion. Mine was all-consuming and I knew I would never be purged of it until I had put those accusing little eyes finally to rest. I had to exact bloody retribution from the murderous swine, not only for the Ronson children but to quiet the churning hatred in my soul. I wanted revenge, and by God I would have it.

We had gone about a mile when Powers moved over to me. 'I meant to tell you,' he said, 'I was in touch with Koster just before we left the farm. His patrol never came anywhere near the Ronsons. The ters abandoned the old people and the kids last night and in the dark Koster followed the wrong tracks. By the time he had caught up with them and realised his mistake the rains had started and had wiped out the tracks. It was impossible for Koster to double back and pick up the terrorists' trail. He says some of the old people are in pretty bad shape, so I've instructed him to escort the whole group to the Karoi Road to await transport.

'I also contacted the SAS, and their CO was just as cheesed-off as I was about Sunray Major's suicidal tactics—he didn't fancy us running into each other any more than I did. So we've changed the plans slightly. They are still forming the east and west flanks, but they won't advance. So they'll be almost out of our direct line of sweep. If Sunray Major doesn't like it, it's just too bloody bad.

'It looks as if the ters are heading straight into the SAP stop-line somewhere near Chimutsi Dam at the base of the escarpment.'

I knew the area well. It was my old backyard and we had the terrorists boxed in. The SAP were in front of them, the SAS flanked them and we were moving up behind them. They had no way out.

The low-slung clouds were dark and threatening, but the rain held off as we worked our slow and tortuous way down the rugged and mountainous Zambezi escarpment. My foot had given me hell for a while before going completely numb. I knew it was there, but I couldn't feel it.

It had been virtually impossible to maintain an extended line coming down the escarpment. We hadn't bunched, but the line had been ragged and there had been gaps. Even so I was fairly certain we hadn't left any terrorists in the deep gorges or on the high peaks behind us. The line reformed properly on the flat terrain of the valley floor and we swept forward toward Chimutsi Dam and the South African Police.

The heavy clouds seemed to trap the heat in the valley and it was like walking through warm, thick pea soup after the cool, fresh winds of the escarpment.

First the mopani bees found us, then the tsetse flies came. I still don't know which are worse. A tsetse can saw its proboscis through the thickest clothing. It actually has tiny hacksaw-type teeth on the proboscis and it doesn't need to look for exposed spots like the mosquito does. It simply hacks its way through to the blood it needs to breed, leaving fiercely irritating lumps at the site. Strangely, the more you are exposed to the tsetses, the less effect their bites have, but enough of them can drive you nuts.

Mopani bees, on the other hand, are harmless. They don't sting or bite. They simply exist. In thousands. They look like slightly-fattened black mosquitoes and they get into everything. Eyes, nostrils, mouth, ears and hair. They stick in the perspiration running down your face and if you crush one, the scent seems to attract a thousand more. After a while you learn to leave them alone, except for spitting the dead ones out of your mouth. And you learn to live with both them and the tsetses. Only because you have no choice.

The bush was very quiet. Normally the country would have been swarming with game and birds, but there had been no rain for many months and all the waterholes had either dried up or were minute, muddy puddles in the centre of circles of hard, dry, cracked earth. The rain that had fallen during the night had disappeared into the thirsty earth and left little sign of its coming.

Once we found a spot in the dry river bed where elephants had dug for, and found, water. There were long trails of wet mud across the sand where the elephants had blown the residue out of the hole they had dug. But there was no trace of the hole itself. Elephants are jealous of their water and they had filled the hole in as soon as the herd had finished drinking.

We approached Chimutsi Dam very carefully, but not carefully enough.

The bullets screamed through the leafless bush, chopping branches and ripping chunks of bark from the trees. I dived into a shallow depression and stayed there.

It was no RPD firing at us. An RPD sounds like thick paper being torn very fast. This was different. It was a heavy-calibre boom like a continuous roll of loud and vicious thunder. Powers recognised it too.

'Hold your fire!'

His voice was loud in the sudden silence as the machine-gun coincidentally stopped firing. The RLI troopies had earned my respect. Not one of them had returned the fire. They lay tense and ready behind their cover, but they didn't fire. All of them had recognised the sound of the MAG. We had either run into the SAP or the SAS. I had a mental bet that it would be the SAP. The SAS would not have opened fire, nor missed if they had.

'This is Captain Powers, RLI.' He didn't show himself. He

wasn't running in the stupidity stakes. It was not impossible that the ters had managed to get hold of a MAG. 'Identify yourselves.' No one replied.

The silence stretched out for five long minutes. The only sounds were the breeze gently caressing the naked branches and the soft, low call of a dove near the dam. Apart from that there was no sound at all and it could have been the most peaceful place on earth if it hadn't been for the perforated barrel of the Sterling pressing into my cheek hard enough to leave a pattern.

Eventually Powers lost patience.

'Identify yourselves or we will over-run your position.' There was unmistakable anger in his voice. The troopies around me tensed themselves for the rush and a burly figure stood up in the grass at the foot of the earthen dam wall. He wore South African camouflage which is a different colour and pattern to ours. Another bloody ridiculous anomaly, and I won my private bet.

'Okay, man.' The slightly guttural tones of an Afrikaner speaking English carried clearly across the seventy yards of waving grass that separated us. 'We is B Company, South African Police.'

We relaxed slowly, and gratefully.

'Tell your men to stand in the open where we can see them.' Powers wasn't about to take any chances with a bunch of trigger-happy greenhorns.

They came out slowly and reluctantly, but they came, the RLI men swopping glares with them and each resenting the other's presence.

The South African Police were just that—policemen, but out of their element. They were pulled off the beat in Durban or out of a squad car in Johannesburg, given a couple of weeks' training and dumped straight into the middle of a war. And not really their war, either.

They were not good soldiers. Under the circumstances, no one could have been. After four and a half months they were shipped back to South Africa and replaced with fresh intakes just as they were beginning to display the promise of the potential fighting force they could be.

The Rhodesian Army too has made mistakes but after years of bitter, bloody, terrorist fighting it has learnt the lessons well and has emerged as a highly competent and efficient fighting machine.

Consequently the SAP simply couldn't begin to compare. Certainly not after such a short stint at the sharp end. And they knew it. So they snarled, boasted and displayed extreme contempt for us. The South African Press, depending on the editorial posturing of each individual newspaper, hailed the SAP either as the saviours of Rhodesia, or the spoilers of Zimbabwe, which did little to increase their popularity-rating with the Rhodesian forces.

But the SAP did fill a gap, for which we were grateful.

Powers went into a huddle with the SAP warrant officer, and I went into a huddle with my foot. I eased off my boot and blood-soaked sock as gently as possible. My foot was throbbing and hurt like hell. The gash in my heel was black and yellow round the edges and a thin red line had worked its way up along the vein past my ankle. I called the RLI medic over.

'Blood poisoning, sir.' He didn't look particularly worried about it. Why should he? It wasn't his foot. He gave me a couple of shots in the backside which grabbed hold of the muscles and twisted them like molten-steel fingers. I grinned at him to prove that I hadn't felt a thing.

'Better stay off that foot for a couple of days, sir.'

Fat chance.

He walked away looking disappointed that there were no bullet holes for him to practise on. A lousy blood poisoning was no challenge at all. Not to him.

It challenged me. I was sweating freely by the time I managed to lace up my boot. My foot had swollen and with the added bulk of the dressing I had to force it into the blood-wet leather. Next time I drink champagne in bed I'll use a straw.

Powers came back and squatted down just as I finished lacing my boot. He picked up the empty penicillin phial the medic had dropped and cocked an enquiring eyebrow at me.

'I cut my foot. The medic gave me a shot, just in case.' The explanation seemed to satisfy him.

‘I don’t understand it.’ Powers shook his head. ‘The ters appear to have vanished. The SAS are covering both flanks and the stop-line has been in position since early yesterday afternoon. Nothing! No sightings, no contacts, not a bloody thing. They had no way out. Unless they sprouted wings.’ He shook his head angrily again. ‘The SAS think we missed them in the escarpment. They’re doing another sweep through the area we’ve just covered. If they find anything, I’ll crawl from here to Bulawayo eating crow all the way.’ His expression was one of rage and frustration.

Where the hell were they? I opened the map and spread it out. We had them boxed in. They were sealed, stamped and delivered. Only the box was empty. There was just no way for them to get out, but they had found a way, and somehow we had to figure it, and fast. There was very little time left. We were only twenty-five miles from the border, and we had to work out where they were and stop them. After the way they’d been running, twenty-five miles was an easy day’s stroll for them. They were bastards, but very fit bastards. Christ, we couldn’t let the Ronson children down. Not again!

I measured off the northwest bearing on the map between Nyamahamba Farm and the Zambezi River. It passed through the SAP stop-line about two-thousand yards east of the dam. I called Mitcher over.

‘Take Hill, Rawson, Henderson and Sergeant Moses.’ I traced out the course of the Hell’s Gate/Mana Pools Road on the map. It ran parallel with the dam and half a mile to the north of it, behind the stop-line. ‘If the ters managed to get through the SAP they’d have to cross this road to reach the Zambezi. After the rain last night the road should be fairly muddy and they may have left tracks. Follow the road east for about five miles. If you don’t find anything by then, we’ve lost them.’

The flat, final statement had its effect on Mitcher. ‘We’ll find the bastards, sir.’ His eyes were hard and glittering with hate.

He appeared surprised that I wasn’t going with them, and a little contemptuous. Whether they found tracks or not, Mitcher and his men had to come back to the dam, and my foot needed all the rest

I could give it. In any event, I wasn't obliged to explain my actions to Mitcher, and I didn't.

The patrol moved out, the three blue and grey figures visible long after Rawson and Sergeant Moses' camouflage had blended into the bush. I reminded myself to do something about those uniforms as soon as the opportunity presented itself.

Powers looked at me with faint respect. 'So you're more than just a pretty face, after all.' He yelled for Jamieson again, repeated what I'd just told Mitcher, and sent a patrol westward along the road toward the Makuti/Chirundu Road junction. If the terrorists had crossed the road we should find some indication of it along the nine-mile stretch that the two patrols would cover between them. I hoped.

I agreed with Powers. I thought it was highly unlikely that the terrorists were still in the escarpment area, and if they weren't they must have crossed the stop-line. There was just no other way they could have gone.

The SAP warrant officer didn't enjoy us taking charge in what he considered to be his area, but I flopped down next to the big man and subjected him to my particularly vile brand of schoolboy Afrikaans. It broke the ice and the scowl disappeared from his broad, open features. In five minutes we were swopping war stories and lies about women as if we'd been friends for years. He showed me photographs of his wife and little boy standing in front of a modest house with a neat garden in the little desert town of Kuruman in the northwest Cape Province. I learnt that he had been raised in the Kalahari Desert and that he missed the vast, treeless spaces which to him were home. He had spent a year in Johannesburg with Dog Section and he had hated it.

He had three more months to do in the Zambezi Valley and the time could not pass quickly enough. The brooding violence, the heat and the dense bush of the valley were as alien to him as the moon, and he wanted out. If he had to fight a war he would rather do it on his own ground and in an environment he knew and understood. If I were posted to the Kalahari Desert, I would be a raving lunatic in a week. Each to his own. I sympathised with him.

When he pulled out a couple of bottles of Oude Meester brandy, our friendship was sealed for life. There wasn't enough for more than a couple of sips each in the group, but a sudden feeling of comradeship developed as the bottles were passed round. The troopies relaxed and began sharing rat packs and cigarettes with the South Africans. The suspicions and hostility evaporated and it was a good thing to see.

An hour later Mitcher brought his patrol back into camp. He was carrying a Chinese water bottle and an AK.

'We hadn't gone a thousand yards along the road when Henderson found the spot where they had crossed.' He nodded to Henderson and indicated he should make his report.

'Well, sir,' Henderson said, faintly embarrassed by our attention, 'they tried to cover the spoor by dragging branches across the road behind them, but the drag marks showed plainly in the mud. It was dark when they crossed and they probably couldn't see too well.'

'How do you know it was dark?' Rawson asked him with obvious dislike. Henderson glared back. Mitcher moved into position to stop them if they started swinging at each other again, but he wasn't needed this time.

'Will you two kindly knock off the dramatics,' I said sarcastically. 'How do you know they crossed in the dark?' I asked Henderson.

'There are hyena tracks over the brush marks. Hyenas are nocturnal animals—they don't move around much in the daytime, unless they have to, and then they move quickly. This one was in no hurry. He was moving slowly, probably back to his lair after drinking at the dam.'

I was impressed. Powers was impressed. The SAP warrant officer was impressed. In fact everyone was impressed, everyone but Rawson. He sneered and his expression clearly implied that any ten-year-old child could have reached the same conclusion in less than half the time. He was ignored.

'You mean those sons-of-bitches got through our line?' the warrant officer asked savagely.

'That's right.' Mitcher's tone dripped with contempt. 'We back-tracked for a couple of hundred yards and found the place they came through. We also found one dead ter and two dead SAP. They had been strangled.' He turned to me and pointed towards the dam with an angry gesture. 'It's just beyond the end of the dam, sir.'

The bodies were lying in a thick patch of scrub. One of the dead South Africans was on his stomach and the toes of his boots had gouged little pits into the soft ground. He hadn't even seen the terrorist who had killed him.

The other South African was a few yards away. He was in a half-sitting position with his hands locked round a terrorist's throat. Their eyes were huge and staring, ruptured blood vessels giving them the impression of burning coals in the dead flesh of their faces. They had died together, bitter enemies locked in a final, terrible embrace.

'I don't believe it. I just don't believe they got through our stop-line,' the warrant officer said, shaking his head to clear the nightmare image.

'You don't really have any bloody option,' Mitcher fired at him.

The second dead South African policeman must have been abnormally powerful. A length of insulated wire was buried deeply in the flesh of his neck, the ends twisted tightly at the back. He must have known he had no chance of living, and he hadn't wasted time trying to loosen the wire. He had reached out and grabbed a terrorist, any terrorist. He had been unable to make a sound, but not unable to kill. His camouflaged shirt had split under the strain of his bunched back muscles. His fingers had sunk deeply into the terrorist's neck and his thumbs had penetrated the skin and tissue to disappear into the man's throat on either side of his oesophagus.

If I hadn't seen it, I would never have believed it possible for a human being to exert such tremendous pressure with his thumbs. The knowledge that he was going to die must have imparted the strength of steel claws to his hands. We were all a little awed by the sight.

The policemen carried the bodies to the track that ended on the dam wall. They couldn't release that awful grip, and no one was prepared to break the fingers, so they carried the two bodies together and they lay clasped obscenely to each other on the track until someone covered them with a combat jacket.

Powers got busy with the radio and I let him do it alone. A base camp had been established at Makuti and as this was a combined police/army operation, there was no point in transmitting two reports containing the same information to the same call sign.

I could thank Mr Hamilton for the base camp. I would have a few things to say to the person responsible for turning down my request for protection at Nyamahamba Farm. But not over the radio. It would be a very private conversation.

The SAP warrant officer, who had introduced himself as Hendrik Reitz, and after the second bottle of brandy had asked us to call him Hennie, walked over and asked Powers if he and his men could accompany us on the follow-up.

Powers nodded his permission and turned to me. 'I've requested transport from Makuti base.' He wouldn't meet my eyes. 'It should arrive in about half-an-hour, so you won't have too long to wait. Unfortunately I can't spare anyone to hold your hand. I hope you won't be too lonely.'

He expected resistance, and he got it. I took a step closer and shoved my face within inches of his.

'Not so close, lover,' he grimaced, stepping back. 'You need a shave and, besides, you haven't been using your underarm deodorant lately.'

I was in no mood for a crummy amateur Bob Hope Show. 'What the hell are you talking about?'

'You're a great actor, Rich.' He tossed the empty penicillin phial up and down in his palm. 'Just a little cut, the man says. A couple of shots just in case! I'm not that stupid. I checked with my medic, and if you lose your leg, it'll be your own damn fault, but you're not going to slow down my patrol. You can have your blood poisoning in your own time, not mine.'

He'd caught me by surprise. After the few hours' rest my foot was feeling so much better I had almost forgotten about it. Now I had been forcibly reminded.

'Your medic's exaggerating about my bloody foot,' I said. 'And anyway it's fine now.' I stamped my heel hard on the ground to prove it, and immediately wished I hadn't. The pain shot up my leg and exploded in my brain like a rain rocket. For a couple of seconds red mist obscured my vision and I inhaled sharply between clenched teeth.

'Yeah, very much better,' Powers said. There was no sarcasm in his voice, only sympathy.

I didn't need his sympathy. I needed a foot I could put weight on, and I didn't have it. I limped over to a fallen tree trunk and sat down.

I wished them luck as they filed past me.

Powers stopped to shake hands. 'You can sit in Makuti drinking beer with the rest of the girls round the radio and listen to how we men do the work,' he said, grinning.

'If you don't bugger off now,' I muttered, 'the ters will be in Lusaka before you cross the Mana Road.'

They moved out. The RLI, the SAP and the five BSAP. There was no friction now. They were just men. Men with only one purpose in mind. To seek out and destroy the terrorists. To destroy with bullets, bayonets, grenades and with their bare hands if necessary. I would not have enjoyed them being on my trail. They were very angry men indeed.

I lit a dried-out cigarette and sat watching a small leguaan under a rock about fifteen feet from the edge of the dam. He badly wanted to reach that water, but each time he ventured out from under his rocky protection, the fish eagle, flying in tight circles just above, descended in a screaming power dive, and the leguaan was forced into frantic, scrambling retreat. I wondered why he didn't just stay under the rock. Eventually the eagle would get tired and go away. I suppose he had his reasons.

I was on my third cigarette when the Land-Rover arrived. The noise of the engine and the ground vibrations from the tyres frightened the leguaan and he streaked for the water, a yellow and brown projectile moving very fast, but not quite fast enough. There was a flurry of wings and a small splash at the water's edge, then the big eagle was hopping clumsily away in a jogging half-run, half-flight, its powerful talons firmly clutching the wildly thrashing reptile. The eagle built up enough speed for take-off then it was airborne, spiralling higher and higher, no longer clumsy but the magnificent master of its environment.

Scratch one leguaan. It's a tough life.

I helped load the three bodies onto the open-backed Land-Rover and we took off for Makuti.

4

WE pulled into Makuti Base Camp at 1300 hours. It was just that—a camp. There were two aluminium all-tents, four canvas tents and a small caravan with the legend 'Rhodesia Railways' officially stencilled on the side. I wondered who had acquired it and when the railways would find out about it. There isn't a railway line within a hundred miles of Makuti. Three helicopters rested like giant, squat dragonflies on the landing zone behind the caravan.

For years the officer commanding police, Lomagundi District, had petitioned for a police station to be established at Makuti. The proposal had been vetoed on the grounds that it was too expensive and unnecessary. I didn't think it would be vetoed now.

The caravan turned out to be the Ops Room and a post office engineer was busy stringing wires to it from the VHF tower.

I found Mr Hamilton and Colonel Halman inside the caravan. I knew Halman well. We were old shooting rivals and he had taken the interservices cup away from me in the last competition.

I cleared the Sterling, dumped it into the corner with my pack, shook hands and gave my report. The radio operator sat riveted to his set and paid no attention to me, sweat standing out on his forehead in the confined heat. They listened without comment or interruption—they knew most of it already and I finished quickly.

'Two Commando have been airlifted to Chirundu,' Mr Hamilton told me. 'They have orders to extend as far as possible and sweep southeast toward Captain Powers. If the terrorists are in that area, they will be caught.'

'They're there,' I replied firmly. I didn't tell him that they wouldn't be captured. Not if Mike Powers found them first. They'd be dead.

'A room has been booked for you at the motel,' Mr Hamilton continued. 'The SAP doctor is up there waiting to take a look at your foot.'

'I'd prefer to remain here, sir.'

'Don't argue with me, Kelly. You wouldn't be any use to me with only one leg. I'll keep you posted on any developments. Now get out of here.'

'One thing, sir,' I said, my voice tight with anger. 'What happened to the protection I requested for the Ronson place? Why were those people left alone when the danger was so damn obvious?'

'A PATU stick from Karoi was sent to the farm. Twenty miles out the Land-Rover left the road and plunged down a thirty-foot cliff. Two of the stick were injured and the other three killed. They were found at 0900 hours this morning. Both the injured are in a critical condition.'

Christ! We were having all the luck. It didn't help the Ronson children, but at least we had tried. For all the bloody good it had done. 'Shit!' I said viciously.

'I know how you feel, Mr Kelly, but standing there cursing is rather futile. Now get the hell out of here and let the doctor have a look at your foot.'

'Yes, sir.' I picked up my gear and left.

I used the Land-Rover to reach the motel a mile away on the opposite hill and booked in. The receptionist was an Austrian girl with big trusting eyes that could and did flash fire when she was annoyed. She was very easy to look at. Not beautiful in a glossy way. Her loveliness came from within, like the glow of a far distant bush fire in a night sky. You didn't know what it was, at first, but you knew it was there, and that it would last. She was the only single girl in eight-thousand square, womanless miles and she was engaged to a cop stationed in Chirundu. I hoped he appreciated just how much woman he had inside that nicely stacked five-foot frame. I had known her on and off for a couple of years and I liked her. So did everyone else.

'Hello, Karen.' I leant across the reception desk. 'You look fabulous, as usual.'

'Hi, Rich. Nice to see you again. Mr Hamilton booked you in.' I was crazy about her accent. She sounded more Irish than Austrian.

She reached up to unhook a key hanging from the board. Her blouse stretched tautly across her breasts and I could see she wasn't wearing a bra. She realised how much I could see, and she blushed. It was nice to know there were still women around who could blush. I smiled at her as she handed me the key.

'Number five, Rich.' Her voice was small and embarrassed. 'The porter will take your luggage down for you.'

'I don't have any luggage and you really don't need one.'

'I don't really need one what?' she asked, puzzled. She pronounced it 'vun'.

'A bra,' I told her.

She fled.

I drove down to number five and left the Land-Rover in the adjoining carport. I was just climbing into the bath when someone knocked on the door. 'Come in,' I yelled. I'm over twenty-one and not shy.

An African porter stood in the bedroom and told me the madam said that if I had the time she would have my uniform washed and ironed and returned in about forty minutes. I told him to take it.

When I climbed out of the bath I found a tiny lady's razor and a new blade on the bed where the porter had left them. As I've said, a very nice person, Karen.

I had just finished shaving when the SAP doctor arrived. He wore camouflage, with a nine-millimetre Walther pistol in a leather holster on his belt and lieutenant's pips on his shoulders. He told me his name was Dirk Erasmus, gave me another couple of injections, changed the dressing on my foot, and told me to rest it as much as possible and no drinking.

'I'll meet you in the pub in half-an-hour,' I informed him.

'I'll buy the first round,' he grinned in reply. He packed his bag and went out.

I lit a cigarette, lay back on the bed and wondered what was happening in the valley. The only thing I was positive of was that this time the ters really were boxed. I hoped Powers reached them first. Two Commando hadn't seen the carnage in the Ronson bedroom. I tried to erase the picture of those tormented little bodies from my mind, but without success. Finally I ground my butt out in the ashtray on the bedside table and rang for a beer.

The beer and my clothes arrived at the same time. The beer was ice-cold and my boots had been polished by a master of the trade. My clothes were still slightly damp from the rush ironing job, but they smelt clean and felt good when I put them on. The cut in my foot was no worse and I had less trouble getting my boot on. Dirk's dressing was far smaller and more professional than the medic's had been. It was still uncomfortable, but not seriously so. I ran a comb through my hair and walked up to the pub.

The Lion & Tusk at Makuti Motel is the only pub in the country with a rifle rack against the wall and the atmosphere is totally Rhodesian. Behind the gleaming bar were displayed the finest selection of service plaques I have ever seen outside a regimental mess. There is one stipulation: only plaques of units which have seen service in the Zambezi Valley are displayed. Someone had once tried to put up a Zambian Police plaque and there had damn nearly been a riot. I noticed that a round RPD magazine and a '36' Mills grenade had been added to the collection behind the bar since my last visit. Highly illegal but I didn't imagine anyone would be obnoxiously bureaucratic enough to confiscate them.

I climbed onto a bar stool next to Dirk and he bought me a beer. He was drinking cane spirit and gingerbeer. My constitution isn't up to that sort of thing before the sun has gone down. He had changed into civilian clothes and was wearing a dark blazer with a medical school badge on the breast pocket.

There were three Support Group troopies in the bar who had been stood down and were making the most of it.

One of the troopies leaned across and tapped Dirk on the shoulder. 'Excuse me, sir.' He pointed to the badge on the blazer. 'We were just trying to work out what the Latin inscription on your badge means.'

'It epitomises the high ideals, the self-sacrifice and selfless devotion to duty of the medical profession,' Dirk told him.

'Yes, but what does it say in English?'

'Translated,' Dirk said seriously, running his finger under the words, 'it reads: "Thank Christ for the sick, they keep us alive." '

I grinned and the soldiers burst into laughter. Another round appeared on the bar and the inquisitive soldier said, 'Seriously, sir. Please tell us what it means.'

'All right,' Dirk answered. 'Let me illustrate the point. One afternoon I was walking down the passage in Groote Schuur Hospital in Cape Town when another doctor stopped me and asked me what I was operating on Mrs Smit for. "For two hundred rand," I said. "Oh, what's she got?" he asked. "Two hundred rand," I told him.'

Everyone burst out laughing and it looked like turning into a very pleasant afternoon when trouble walked through the door. Trouble in the shape of four young men who thought they were very tough.

They swaggered up to the bar and the biggest of the four leaned across the counter and shouted at Tom, the African barman, 'Four brandy-and-cokes, and make it fast . . . kaffir.'

Tom hesitated but he served them.

Roughly translated from the original Arabic, 'kaffir' means 'unbeliever', but with the passage of time and prostitution of use it can be more closely related to 'black bastard' today.

The silence in the bar was thick enough to slice with the blunt end of a four-inch plank. Then the trooper who had been enquiring about the badge, turned and asked pleasantly, 'Where you guys from?'

'From Zambia,' the big one said with a sneer. 'Where we make more bread than you'll ever see in your life.'

'Where the hell is Zambia? Never heard of the place.'

'You must have,' another trooper answered. 'That's where the European expatriates act like mice—until they cross the border into Rhodesia. Then they act like the stupid little tits they are.'

'That's right. Now I remember,' the first trooper said. 'Zambia's just north of the Zambezi. That's where the whites pay taxes to finance the ters.'

'You guys looking for trouble?' the big one snarled.

'But of course,' the troopie said smiling, and hit him in the stomach.

The expatriates weren't afraid, and they outnumbered the soldiers four to three, but they had no chance. Although the troopies were only about eighteen years old, they were hard little characters. Hard, fast and fit. It was all over in less than two minutes. They carried the four down the steps and threw them into their car.

'Before you bugger off,' the smiling one told them, 'just remember, there are no kaffirs in this country. Only Rhodesians.'

The car took off, scattering gravel from the rear tyres. They had just come from Zambia and they headed back that way. Possibly they didn't take to our way of life. Tough luck. We didn't need them.

'You're a cop,' Dirk chuckled. 'Why didn't you stop that disgusting assault?'

'What assault?' I asked him innocently.

Tom came round from behind the bar and we helped him pick up the bar stools. There were a few broken bottles and glasses on the floor and more than a little blood. A grinning bar hand with a mop cleared up the mess as the soldiers resumed their seats.

'Tom, stop smiling at me like a bloody imbecile and give us another round,' the troopie said.

'Yes, sir. Thank you very much, sir,' Tom replied.

'What the hell for?' the troopie asked and fished out a note to pay for the round.

The session continued until Mr Hamilton walked through the door. The troopies didn't know him, but they recognised his obvious authority. They shut up. He gestured to me and I followed him outside. We sat down at a table on the verandah as far away from everyone else as possible.

He ordered two beers and waited until the waiter had come and gone before he hit me with it. 'Koster's patrol has been chopped to bits. They ran into an ambush. The terrorists doubled back on their tracks and set up four RPDs alongside the trail. The patrol had no chance.'

I sat in stunned silence. That patrol had consisted of five highly-trained men. It was inconceivable that they would walk into an ambush. Not the entire damn patrol. I didn't believe it.

Mr Hamilton saw that I was about to object and held up his hand. 'I haven't finished. Koster was the only one not hit. One other trooper is wounded, but alive. The rest are dead. The patrol had been chasing no more than ten terrorists. Koster estimates they were hit by at least twenty. If he is correct, and at this stage we have no reason to doubt that he is, it means the original gang has joined forces with another gang, of whose existence we were completely unaware.'

'How the hell . . . ?'

'Let me finish, Mr Kelly,' he said icily. When he used that tone, you listened.

'Sorry, sir.'

'Koster ran the five miles, from the ambush point, to the Chirundu Road and was lucky enough to flag down a passing truck which took him to Chirundu. He made his report from the police station there.'

'But Koster was out of it.' I had to interrupt. 'He was supposed to escort a bunch of old people and kids to the Karoi Road. How did he become involved again? And what was he doing near Chirundu, fifty miles from where he was supposed to be?'

'After the abductees had been transported to Karoi, Koster got hold of an army Land-Rover and was patrolling the main road with his section between Makuti and Chirundu. They picked up tracks on the side of the road sixteen miles from Chirundu, left the vehicle and followed the tracks.'

I waited for him to go on. When he didn't, I asked, 'Why didn't he use the radio to make his report before following the tracks?'

'The radio had packed up,' he said heavily.

'I'm sorry about the patrol,' I told him, 'but it doesn't alter the fact that the ters are boxed in and if Powers doesn't get them, Two Commando will.'

Mr Hamilton didn't look at me. He gazed with unseeing eyes across the hills which stretched away towards Kariba. 'There is one small point I neglected to mention, Mr Kelly.' He suddenly swung round and slammed his glass on the table in front of him. 'Koster's five-mile run was eastwards towards the Chirundu Road.'

The information took a few seconds to penetrate. My mind picked up his words and chased them round my brain until they fell into place like a one-armed bandit paying jackpot. Only we hadn't won. The ters had broken the bank.

'Christ!' I was rigid with heart-gripping, sudden shock. I had been wrong. We had all been wrong. The terrorists had not maintained a northwesterly route. They had swung westwards as they neared the Zambezi. They had outmanoeuvred us. Only just, but it had been enough. They must have slipped out of the trap just before the flanks closed in.

Mr Hamilton had been watching my reactions and I knew my feelings were plainly visible. 'That's right, Mr Kelly,' he said bitterly. 'They were on the western side of the Chirundu Road. Two Commando are moving up the river in pursuit but will certainly be far too late. Koster was ambushed seven miles from the river and we only received the report two hours after it happened. If the terrorists head straight for the river the nearest interception point is fifteen miles from Two Commando's present position.'

He stopped speaking as three Alouette helicopters screamed low overhead, filled with the remainder of Support Group who had been on stand-by at the camp.

The troopies who had been drinking in the bar came out onto the verandah.

'Where the hell are they going at such a rate of knots?' one of the three asked. They weren't left to speculate. An open camouflaged Land-Rover roared up to the steps and stopped in a cloud of dust and a young second lieutenant jumped out.

'Move it, you guys. You're on stand-by as of now,' he bawled.

They ran back into the bar, left their drinks unfinished on the counter, grabbed their rifles from the rack and were gone in fifteen seconds. We watched the Land-Rover drive up the opposite hill and turn into the road leading to the camp.

'Well, Rich, all we can do now is wait,' Mr Hamilton said with resignation.

'Yes, sir.' He never called me anything but Kelly or Mr Kelly unless he was under enormous strain. It was an indication of how we both felt.

Dirk walked over and saluted Mr Hamilton. 'Is the conference over or should I be a good little doctor and go away?'

I used my good foot to push out a plastic-backed chair. He took the cue and sat down.

Mr Hamilton obviously had a lot on his mind. He finished his beer and stood up. 'Excuse me, gentlemen,' he nodded to us.

'I'd like to come back to the camp, sir,' I said to him, half rising.

'There are enough of us fouling the atmosphere in that silly little caravan, Mr Kelly. The engineers are stringing a field telephone line between here and the camp this afternoon. There are no recreational facilities at the camp and we need instant contact with any troops who may be stood down. As soon as it's installed, give me a call at the camp. It'll be reassuring to know something works properly around here.'

'Yes, sir,' I said as he walked down the steps to the carpark.

Dirk made small talk but I was bad company. I was mentally working out Support Group's chances of stopping the terrorists. It didn't look good at all. The patrol had been hit at least three hours ago. The choppers would be at the suspected crossing point now. But only suspected. The Zambezi is a very long river, and the chances of spotting the terrorists from the air was remote. They had had three hours to cover seven miles and get across the river. More than enough time. I didn't think we had a snowball's chance of stopping them.

I watched two army engineers walk up the drive stringing wires behind them, and install a field telephone in the motel office. Highly irregular, but at least there would be communication between the camp and the motel, where most of the off-duty troopers would be spending their time.

I cranked the handle and asked for Mr Hamilton. 'It's working well, sir,' I said into the mouthpiece. 'You're coming through fives.'

'I've some fair news for you, Mr Kelly.' No one could tap this phone and for once he wasn't being circumspect. 'The choppers arrived when the ters were in canoes in the middle of the river. They had no time to drop the troopers and it would have been pointless anyway. There were eight canoes trying to cross. Two made it. We have one casualty. A pilot got a bullet in his hand, nothing serious. Support Group have been dropped and are searching the river bank for any survivors who may have crawled ashore.'

I glanced out of the window. The sun was going down quickly. They'd have a hell of a job in the dark.

'I want you to stand by in case they find anyone alive and capable of talking.' His voice sounded tinny through the instrument. 'You may not be a good soldier, but you're a reasonably competent interrogator.'

A pat on the back and a slap in the face at the same time. Only Mr Hamilton could have put it quite like that. I didn't mind. We hadn't won, but we hadn't lost either. The results were far better than I had expected.

'Yes, sir,' I said, but I was talking to a dead phone. Mr Hamilton had hung up.

The sun slipped off the rim of the world. I walked into the bar and bought myself a whisky. Dirk came in and I bought him another cane spirit.

'What's come over you?' He regarded me speculatively. 'Fifteen minutes ago you were ready to jump off a cliff, now you look as if you've just nailed the bishop's daughter behind the altar on Sunday afternoon.' He poured gingerbeer into his drink.

'Maybe I have, you blasphemous lecher,' I laughed at him.

Karen walked in behind the bar wearing a very becoming long black skirt and a frilly white blouse that buttoned right up to her chin. She had a black choker round her throat over the top of the blouse. The effect was good and it struck me again just how attractive she was. I offered her a drink. She looked down at her bosom, one hand fluttering to the top of her blouse. She blushed very slightly and gave a disdainful toss of her head, her auburn hair glinting in the soft overhead lights.

A fat, balding character in the cocktail bar also offered her a drink.

She smiled graciously at him and accepted. Tom brought her a stool, and she was soon in laughing conversation with the balding romeo. He was flushed and hopeful. I had news for him. Only one man owned her heart and shared her bed, and he was in Chirundu hunting terrorists.

'Looks like you lost out,' Dirk chuckled.

'What are you talking about?'

'Her.' He nodded towards Karen.

'Yeah,' I grunted, remembering the warm, moonlit night I had made my play for her and been gently rebuked. Gently, sympathetically but very firmly rebuked. She had brushed her lips softly and quickly across my cheek and disappeared into her room. I accepted her terms and we had become friends—even if I did embarrass and annoy her now and then. Behind the bar she was the target for every lonely male passing through Makuti. She was charming, sexy and sometimes very naughty, but only behind the bar. Without the protection of that three-foot bar counter she was cool, distant and could be very cutting if the hint wasn't taken. The army would have lynched anyone who said a bad word about her, but it didn't stop them hoping. The fact that she was engaged made no difference at all. In the womanless world of the Zambezi Valley it was every man for himself. But she was strictly a one-man woman, which only served to make her more desirable than she already was.

Some inkling of it must have reached the fat romeo. He suddenly realised that this was not going to be his night, and he started sounding off about everything in general and the security forces in particular. Maybe Karen had said something to annoy him. In any event he wasn't happy.

'Anyone with any intelligence knows the Government is exaggerating the terrorist menace,' he said. 'All they are trying to do is unite the electorate into a solid block behind the Rhodesian Front Party. They're trying to frighten us into going along with their policies.'

He bought himself another double whisky and drank it neat, glaring at Karen. She was the cause of his annoyance. Of that there was no doubt.

She moved away from him and Tom placed her stool opposite me. She sat down. 'You may buy me that drink now, Rich.'

'Not a chance,' I said. 'If I have to sit here and talk to you, you can pay for the booze.'

'You can't talk to a lady like that!' Dirk looked astounded. 'I'll buy the drinks.'

'Don't be stupid. No lady has ever bought me a drink yet, but I'll take one from Karen.'

'Are you implying that she's not a lady?' He was outraged and ready to make an issue of it. Karen and I burst into laughter at the expression of comic indignation on his face. 'Okay, okay. You two know each other better than I thought. But I'm paying for the round,' he insisted, looking sheepish.

'It's a right-wing plot, that's what it is,' the fat man said loudly to no one in particular as he came through the door from the cocktail bar. 'Scare us all into believing we'll be murdered in our beds. It's just a story to keep us voting RF. It's a lot of balls.'

Dirk was one of the old-style gentlemen. No one swore in front of women where he came from. Not if that woman was a lady. He stood up and was about to say something when I grabbed his arm just above the elbow. He seemed surprised at the strength of my grip, and he sat. Karen had heard, and on occasion used, far worse language than that, and a fat, balding drunk was just not worth the trouble. Not as far as I was concerned.

Unfortunately, in his drunken way he had voiced the opinion of a lot of people who refused to believe the evidence which surrounded them and had done for years. They knew about Kaitano Kambadza, an African police reservist who had been cycling home after a tour of duty at his local police station. A gang of thugs in a car had stopped him, stripped him and after pouring petrol over him, had set him alight. His crime—he believed in law and order. He died nine agonizing hours later. They knew about David Dodo, who, after giving evidence against political murderers, had been chopped to pieces with axes as he crossed a football field on his way home from the high court. They knew about Ann Chavouna, who had been dragged from her cycle as she left a church. She had been doused with petrol and set alight. They knew about Ernest Vili, who had been peaceably passing a house where a nationalist leader had been staying. The bodyguard had asked him what political party he belonged to and when he didn't reply, he had been stabbed in the chest and his body transported away from the scene on a bicycle.

The list is endless and the isolated acts of violence against black as well as white had finally culminated into a full-scale terrorist war and the disbelievers were too stupid to realise it.

I would have loved to shove the fat idiot's face in the blood on the bedroom floor in the Ronson farmhouse. That started me thinking about those two mutilated little bodies, and I was suddenly mad enough to smack his teeth down his fat, stupid throat.

'Get out of here, you drunken slob,' I snarled at him.

He spun round, rage turning his whisky face an even deeper shade of red. 'You . . . ' He looked into my eyes and took a step back, anger and bluster draining out of him as his voice trailed off.

His shoulders slumped and he turned into just another pathetic drunk with too much to say and not enough intelligence to think about it. I wondered what his reaction would have been if he had known about Richard Jenge, who had been shot at the eleven-mile peg on the Chirundu Road simply because he had refused to give his 'brothers' a lift. We had caught that gang not ten miles from Makuti.

I was suddenly ashamed of myself. I turned back to the bar and ordered another round. The drunk staggered out, mumbling under his breath. The booze was beginning to catch up with me so I took Dirk and Karen in to dinner. The food was good and so was the company, but after the second bottle of wine I was fighting to keep awake and I felt my eyelids drooping with fatigue. I left Dirk gazing rapturously into Karen's grey-flecked green eyes. He didn't even hear me go. She had captivated him completely. Poor bugger!

I went to bed and fell into a shallow, tortured sleep where arms and legs and dogs and tiny children with terrified faces chased each other round a dead Christmas tree with a hammer and sickle on the top, where the star should have been.

5

I HAD ordered coffee for 0430 hours, and that's when it came. It was still dark outside, with the heavy, impenetrable blackness which comes just before the dawn. The bed was a rumpled mess. The heat of the new day had not yet begun to flex its muscles, but I was sticky with sweat. There was no shower in the bathroom. Baths are for washing clothes and babies, but I used it gratefully, then drank the coffee, black and strong, as I finished dressing. My face was raw and stinging—the blade in Karen's razor had lost its edge and almost peeled my skin off. I threw my pack and the Sterling onto the front seat of the Land-Rover and drove up to the camp.

As early as I was, Mr Hamilton had beaten me. He looked as if he'd been up all night, and he probably had. There were dark rings under his eyes and he needed a shave.

'Morning, sir.'

'Good morning, Mr Kelly.' He shot me a quick glance. 'I was on the point of sending for you. As soon as it's light enough I want you to fly to the contact location by helicopter to conduct interrogations. Although no report of any capture has come through yet, there's every possibility of one shortly as I've had confirmation that some of the terrorists were not in the canoes when they were shot up last evening and are now trapped on the south bank. I shouldn't imagine any of them would have been stupid enough to swim to the Zambian side. With all the blood in the water, that stretch of the river will be swarming with crocs.'

He nodded to a camouflaged figure with air force tabs on his shoulders. 'That's Flight Lieutenant Bristow. He'll be taking you down.'

I walked over and introduced myself to Bristow, stowed my pack on the back seat of the chopper and climbed in. While Bristow warmed up the engine, his technician completed his visual check from his front seat next to the pilot.

The sun rose and we clawed our shrieking way up into the sky. We left the camp behind and the valley opened up in front of us, dark and foreboding, waiting for the sun to clear the edge of the escarpment to give it life and colour.

The trapped ters had to be taken alive. I had to hear them scream, to see them writhing and twisting in an agony far worse than they had inflicted on the Ronson children. I wanted them to die. I wanted them to die slowly. I wanted them to know why. Any information I extracted from them would be incidental. Whether they talked or not, the children would be avenged.

Ten minutes later Bristow flew over the contact point and we could see a couple of overturned, bullet-ridden canoes jammed up against a sandbank in the middle of the river. That's all we could see, apart from the crocodiles. There were dozens of them. As the helicopter passed overhead they shot off the sandbank and out of the shallows, hunting deep water to escape the noisy, stinking monster above. Bristow said something into his throat mike and tapped his technician on the shoulder, pointing to a clearing about three hundred yards from the river.

We landed, and the first person I saw was Mitcher. He looked like an actor straight out of *Combat*, only this was no television spectacular. This was for real. His shirt was torn and ripped in a dozen places, the beginnings of a heavy beard covered his cheeks, his eyes were red-rimmed and sunken with fatigue, he was filthy and he stank. The only clean thing about him was his rifle. It gleamed as if it had just been presented for an armourer's inspection. It might have been an outdated old relic, but it was the only one he had. Somewhere he had acquired an eighteen-inch bayonet and it heightened the World War impression. But there was nothing funny about it. He looked wild, mean and hungry for a killing.

'Morning, sir,' he said.

'Mitcher. How the hell did you get here?'

'The hard way,' he answered, nodding at the helicopter. 'Mike Powers asked me to meet you and give you the full sit. rep.'

'Give.'

'We've thrown a five-hundred yard cordon round the contact point and are gradually closing in. We arrived here about half-an-hour after Support Group set up the initial cordon and reinforced them. Powers decided it was pointless getting anyone killed in the dark so we held the position until this morning. Nothing could have got through. We could practically touch each other, and the police launch from Chirundu patrolled the riverside all night. It was fired at a couple of times so we know the bastards are inside the cordon somewhere.'

'What happened to the launch?' I asked. 'It's not there now.'

'Ran out of fuel, sir. It should be back any moment now,' he shouted as Bristow took off and positioned the chopper two hundred feet above the river, an airborne watchdog.

I followed Mitcher into the thick, lush riverine growth. The sun was up and climbing but even at noon it wouldn't make much impression inside this tangled mess. When Mitcher dropped flat and began snaking his way through the undergrowth, so did I. I saw what he meant when he said it had been a tight cordon. As the troopers closed in they began getting in each other's way, and some had to drop back to form a second line.

The terrorists' camouflage was superb. The trooper in front of me was two feet from the bush when it moved and the RPD blew his head off. The grey-red sticky mush exploded out of the back of his skull and hit me in the face like wet tissue paper. I didn't have time to feel any revulsion. Not right then.

I shoved the Sterling's short, black barrel past the dead trooper's shoulder and fired it one-handed. I pressed the trigger down and held it there. When it stopped firing I thought it had jammed and I jerked it back angrily. The empty magazine surprised me. It didn't seem possible to have fired off thirty-two rounds in such a short space of time. Christ, it had only been seconds. I had slammed a fresh magazine in when I suddenly realised the RPD had stopped firing. The silence had a crushing, oppressive force of its own. Even the scream of the hovering turbo-jet helicopter engine sounded mute and distant.

Slowly, cautiously and reluctantly, the line began moving again. I crawled over the dead soldier, not looking at the pulpy mess that had been his head. I didn't want to go on. Jesus God! I didn't want to die. And I was afraid. Afraid with a gut-churning, nauseous fear that turned my legs to quivering jelly. I swore each move would be my last. I couldn't take anymore. Then I felt those accusing little eyes burning into me. How could I let them down again? I moved forward.

I crawled past the dead terrorist, noting in a peculiar, detached way that I had only hit him once. At two feet with thirty-two rounds I had hit him once. He had caught the nine-millimetre parabellum bullet in the right eye. It had been enough. I lost interest in him. He didn't scare me anymore.

Mitcher moved up beside me as a glint in the grass caught my eye. I kicked his boot and he looked around quickly. I pointed to the taut, speckled fishing line staked out a couple of inches above the ground in front of us. It was almost invisible.

'Stick grenade.' My whisper seemed to shatter the heavy silence. The trooper on my left heard me and the line came to a halt as the message was passed along.

I brushed the sweat out of my eyes with the back of my hand and gently parted the grass along the fishing line, exposing a grenade in a tin. An ordinary, low-explosive grenade, not a stick grenade, thank God. A crude but very effective booby trap. The tin was just large enough to hold the grenade with the lever compressed. The pin had been removed and the tin wedged tightly under the gnarled roots of a tree. The fishing line was tied to the grenade and I knew the other end of the line would be anchored securely about ten feet away, the idea being that you walk into the line, jerk the grenade out of the tin and blow yourself to bits. Works too.

I pulled out my knife and cut the line close to the tin. We left the grenade where it was and crawled on, even more slowly, everyone parting the grass in front, eyes straining for the tell-tale glint of fishing line.

Another RPD opened up in front of us, traversing the centre of the cordon. I snapped my head down so fast I tasted earth. On the left a terrorist was firing short, automatic bursts from an AK. I could see leaves being cut from the bushes and heard the solid smack as the bullets ploughed into wood, but I couldn't see where they were coming from. Two troopers tried to advance and were both hit in seconds. They were pulled back into cover by their heels, one moaning softly and clutching his shoulder. The other didn't make a sound.

Mitcher wormed his way backward and returned in a few moments with the Chinese grenade held tightly in his right hand. Then he was up on his knees and he threw the grenade into the bushes in front of us. As it exploded he charged the bushes, firing as he ran. Somehow, suddenly and without conscious effort, we were all on our feet, running through the bushes screaming obscenities and firing. Not picking targets, just firing, reloading and firing again.

I burst out of the bush and saw Mitcher at the water's edge frantically trying to work the bolt on his rifle. There was a terrorist in the water, striking out strongly about ten feet from the bank. With a high, piercing scream of rage, Mitcher grabbed the rifle just in front of the magazine and threw it like a spear. The bayonet thudded into the terrorist's back as the MAG mounted on the chopper slammed a burst into the swimming figure, and the only trace left of the body was a pinkish stain that rapidly disappeared as the blood mixed with the water.

There was nothing left to shoot at. We stood around in silent groups. There was no banter and no one smiled. If any felt the relief of still being alive, they didn't show it. We had exacted our retribution, but it turned out to be an empty, hollow victory. The elation I had expected to swamp my torment hadn't materialised and I felt strangely let down, a sense of futile anticlimax leaving me depressed and drained.

The bush creatures were still cowering from the pandemonium of man's madness and it was very quiet as Powers came up to me.

'Hello, Rich. Glad you got here for the finish,' he said sombrely. 'How's the foot?'

'Fine. But it's just as well you left me behind at Chimutsi Dam. I doubt if I could have kept up with your patrol. You must have been running to get this far last night.'

'We were, and we made it just in time. Sorry there aren't any ters left alive for you to interrogate,' he added grimly as we moved through the subdued men to the small clearing where the dead terrorists had been laid out. There were only three of them. 'They died too easily. But at least they won't be butchering any more defenceless children.' He paused, staring down at the bodies. 'Bastards!' he spat out and viciously kicked one of the dead terrorists. 'Goddam stinking bloody bastards!' His boot thudded into the body again.

I understood and shared his frustration, but abusing lifeless corpses was pointless. Their pain could only be felt in hell.

'Leave it, Mike,' I said gently. 'You did all you could, and no one could have done better. It's now up to me. Even though I can't interrogate them, I'll find something on them that'll help us track down where they come from and how they are supplied and financed.'

'Okay, Rich,' he said, resigned, 'you take over.' He walked off.

The dead terrorists had been fully kitted out and their packs were piled in a jumbled heap next to them. I was about to search one of the bodies when Henderson came up.

'Morning, sir,' he said. He was wrapping a field dressing round his arm.

'Morning, Henderson,' I nodded. 'What happened to your arm?'

'Bullet crease.' He shrugged it off. 'Excuse me mentioning this, sir, but I think you should wash your face.'

I stepped back in surprise. 'Who the hell do you think you're talking to? Besides you aren't any bed of roses yourself.'

'You've got bits of flesh splattered all over it, sir,' he said and looked away, embarrassed.

The memory of that exploding skull flashed up vividly behind my eyes. God! I ripped off my shirt and ran down to the water. I pushed my head under and held it there. Stuff the crocs. I used my shirt to scrub my face and I scrubbed until my skin felt raw. I could still feel those soggy bits of bloody gore slapping wetly into my face, and I scrubbed some more.

I walked back up the bank. 'Sorry, Henderson. No offence intended. Have a smoke.'

'Thanks, sir. None taken.'

My hand shook as I extended the cigarette pack. Henderson pretended not to notice.

I started going through the terrorists' packs. It was obvious that the troopies had been there before me. I didn't blame them. In their place I would have looted the packs as well, but I wasn't in their place.

Powers finished with the radio and I called him over. I pointed to the packs. 'I don't mind them taking inconsequential items of equipment, and once I've examined all the stuff they can have anything I don't need, but if your little darlings don't return every single item right now, heroes or not, I'll arrest the whole goddam lot of them.'

'Okay, okay. Relax. I'll get the stuff back,' he said and turned away. 'Sergeant Jamieson!'

'Sir?'

'Fall the men in. All of them, right here. On the double.'

They were a ridiculous sight. Filthy, bearded, tattered and stinking to high heaven, they formed up in threes and came to rigid attention when Jamieson gave the order. With their torn uniforms flapping in the gentle breeze they stood like statues as Powers walked slowly and silently along the ranks. I loved every ugly mother's son of them.

Powers finished his inspection and turned to face them. I noticed the SAP and the five Rhodesian cops standing on the edge of the clearing grinning at the troopies' discomfort. I'd get round to them later.

'Gentlemen.' Powers didn't raise his voice. It wasn't necessary. 'Certain items of communist equipment have disappeared. If any of these items have, in some mysterious manner, found their way into your possession, I suggest that now is the time to hand them in. Right here and right now.' He pointed to the ground in front of him.

No one moved. They stood in rigid rows staring fixedly straight ahead. 'I must add that if necessary I will personally strip each and every one of you. If I find anything you'll do your explaining at the court martial.'

Hill moved out from the shade of the tree he had been leaning against. Through the dirt his face was bright scarlet with embarrassment. He didn't say a word. He put a Tokarev pistol in the dust at Powers' feet and walked away, keeping his eyes firmly on the ground in front of him. A trooper stepped forward and dropped a terrorist cap over the pistol. Slowly the pile in front of Powers grew. A couple of SAP added their loot to the pile. With the looks that were thrown at me I should have dropped dead eleven times a minute. My popularity rating was lower than a sewerage pit and it worried me not one damn little bit. I smiled. Finally Powers turned to me and I nodded, satisfied.

The police launch from Chirundu, the *Sir Hubert Stanley*, had arrived during the parade and I told Hill to load all the commie equipment aboard. He wouldn't meet my eyes and his ears burnt brightly enough to light cigarettes every time I spoke to him. I let him suffer.

The bodies of the troopers and the terrorists were loaded onto the boat, the wounded trooper found room for himself in the stern and the launch took off downstream heading for Chirundu, the 75 hp Johnson Sea Horse pushing it effortlessly through the water.

I was damned if I would ride back. I was as tough as the rest of them and could prove it. Besides, my foot felt fine and it was only nine miles to Chirundu.

It turned out to be another stupid mistake. If they were giving prizes for stupidity, I was surely near the head of the queue. I walked the last five miles on my toes. No benevolent numbness took over this time and I felt every yard-long inch of the way. I was dripping wet with perspiration and cursing with pain when I finally lurched into the Chirundu police station yard. Dirk had driven down from Makuti and was dressing Henderson's arm as I staggered past.

'Stupid idiot,' he murmured, without looking up.

I didn't say anything. What was there to say? Hell, I agreed with him. I sat down on the charge office step and took off my boot.

6

0830 HOURS, November 27th, 1972. A dark, wet, morose Salisbury morning in keeping with my mood. Even the train whistles from the shunting yards in the railway goods depot across the street from the Central Police Station sounded thin and mournful. It was hot and humid in my office. The rain streaming down the window brought no relief and the Government issue fan, one—for the use of, standing in the corner was next to useless, not cooling down a thing, only causing the heavy, sticky air to circulate sluggishly round the room.

For the thousandth time in three days I examined the items scattered over the scarred surface of my desk—the personal belongings of the terrorists we had killed on the banks of the Zambezi River nearly three weeks ago.

For two weeks I had occupied a bed in Ward 1a of the Salisbury General Hospital and my foot had slowly healed. The nurses had treated me like a combination of Horatio Nelson and Alexander the Great; the conquering hero returned from battle never had it so good. The trooper who had been wounded in the shoulder during the skirmish had been in the bed next to me and he told the most outrageous lies about our bravery to the open-mouthed and believing nurses.

I wondered how they would react if I told them the truth about my 'wound'. I only wondered. I like my creature comforts, so I kept my mouth shut.

Cathy came every night. On her first visit I told her, 'I haven't got a gun under my arm now.'

'We're not in bed, either,' she replied.

So we talked about every subject under the sun, except love, when all I wanted to do was drag her into bed and love her until eternity ran out of time.

Apart from that I lay there bored, frustrated and chafing at my helplessness. I read *Illustrated Life Rhodesia*, *Playboy* and *Woman's Own* with equal disinterest. I was curt with the nurses and rude to the doctors. My hero's image began to tarnish a little. I couldn't help it. The enforced idleness nearly drove me nuts.

One afternoon Dirk walked into the ward carrying four bottles of whisky in a paper bag and dragging a redheaded floozy behind him. They only let him in because he was a doctor and he insisted that I was his patient. I was very pleased to see him. He opened all four bottles of whisky and threw the caps out of the window. He assured me Johnnie Walker had been a doctor and gave me a healthy slug of Dr Walker's medicine.

He introduced his floozy as Daisy May, which was a little harder to swallow than the whisky. She looked as if she had found oil in the backwoods and had bought a cosmetic shop. She had all the stock plastered over her face at the same time in layers of various depths. She went round the ward dishing out booze and she was at least better looking than the ceiling. The ward began to show some signs of life.

In an hour we had finished the whisky and Daisy May had done an impromptu strip on the table in the middle of the ward.

'For all the brave soldiers fighting for us, don't you see,' she said sweetly as she dropped her dress on the floor.

We saw. We all saw. And we all saw everything. For all the muck on her face she had a very cute figure, and by the time she had tossed her panties over her shoulder there wasn't a sick man in the room. It was a better tonic than any ever prescribed by any doctor. The ward was in a happy, alcoholic uproar when the B-car pulled up outside.

Dirk and Daisy May left through an open window, and the sight of Daisy May with her bra and panties in her hand and her skirt up around her waist as she bent to follow Dirk out of the window, was too much for the bedridden males to bear in silence. The cheering and the clapping echoed through those hushed and dignified passages for a good five minutes. For the first time in two weeks I hadn't been bored. They kicked me out the next morning. Early!

I pulled out a sheet of paper and listed the items on my desk. Two red plastic-covered *Thoughts of Mao*; three primary school exercise books containing detailed instructions on landmines, explosives and booby traps; a cheap Marilyn transistor radio made in Rhodesia; a green plastic thermos flask also made in Rhodesia; two pairs of cheap sunglasses made in Hong Kong; a Parker ballpoint pen and seventeen twists of dagga wrapped in paper torn from the sports section of the *Rhodesia Herald.* Everything else had been standard Chinese equipment, thoroughly examined before being discarded.

I paged through the exercise books again. That's all they were: textbooks of terror, simple to understand but very detailed and similar to many others we had captured. The copies of the *Thoughts of Mao* were the normal Chinese edition distributed by the thousands to the poor and ignorant of the world. Some of the thoughts were naive, a few were brilliant, none of them workable in any society where man has the ability to think and the opportunity to turn his thoughts into actions. It is a great handbook for running a nation of automatons totally devoid of ambition. I dropped them back into my drawer.

I had stripped the radio down to the case. I even took the battery apart. Nothing. But I knew it was there. Something on the desk was vital. There was dynamite within reach of my hands and I couldn't see it. The pile just lay there and mocked me. This was no run of the mill hunch. I knew. More than knew, I was absolutely positive.

I was still staring at the mocking heap when Mr Hamilton walked through the door. I stood up.

'Good morning, sir.'

'Morning, Mr Kelly. Still pandering to your subconscious mind I see.' He glanced at the heap on my desk.

'It's not just a hunch, sir. It's . . . '

'I didn't say it was,' he interrupted. 'And it's a far better pastime for a police officer to indulge in than aiding and abetting in the total disruption of a hospital.'

Dirk and Daisy May had written themselves into the permanent annals of the RLI. One artistic bedridden trooper had drawn a superb pencil sketch of Daisy May's retreat and it now occupied pride of place behind the bar in the regimental mess. I kept my mouth shut.

'I want you to get out to the airport this morning. As you know DPO McLaren has just finished his probationary training. Spend a couple of hours with him and sort out any problems he may have.'

I thought Mr Hamilton was trying to get my mind off whatever those items on my desk were hiding from me. I thought he was being kind in an obscure way. I thought wrong.

'Scarletti is being deported on the 1530 plane to London this afternoon. You might care to hang around and keep an eye on things. There's bound to be a demonstration of some kind.'

And I might not care to. If there's anything I can do without, it's hanging around airports keeping an eye on demonstrations which may or may not amount to anything. That's what uniformed police are for. Mr Hamilton was perfectly aware of my feelings. Standing around in the rain in a trench coat writing names in a grubby little black book with an indelible pencil, like some bad characterization of the Nazi Gestapo, is not a fun way to spend an afternoon. I never took names at demonstrations, and Mr Hamilton knew it. It's one of the points we agreed to differ on. What people say in the heat of the moment is their business. What they do in the heat of the moment could become my business. But only very occasionally. The ravers and the fanatical protesters are ninety percent wind and ten percent horse manure. It's the shadowy, silent ones you have to watch. And they don't wave placards at demonstrations. They do their scheming in the dark and secret places.

'Yes, sir.' My resigned tone reached him but he ignored it.

'By the way, Mr Kelly, your recommendations regarding camouflage uniforms have been studied and you will be pleased to know that full camouflage kit is being issued to all members on border stations.'

'Thank you, sir.' I broke into a grin.

'I had nothing to do with it. It was the commissioner's decision.' He walked toward the door and said over his shoulder, 'He has also authorized the issue of FN rifles to border stations.' He closed the door quietly behind him.

At least the three hours I had spent typing the recommendations had not been wasted. Mitcher would be pleased, anyway. He needed a new rifle and the FN is infinitely superior to the Lee-Enfield and probably better than the SLR the army was issued with.

I cleared my desk and shoved everything into the Chubb safe set into the wall. Whatever it was that was eluding me couldn't get out of there.

I went out to my official Austin Cambridge parked in the station yard. It was grey and unmarked. Unmarked that is, apart from the tyre pressures stencilled in black on the mudguards above each wheel. Very secret outfit, Special Branch.

I drove slowly out to the airport along the Hatfield Road, not wanting to get there at all and hoping something would blow up that would necessitate my return to the station. I had the VHF radio volume turned up as far as it would go, but it remained stubbornly silent.

As I turned into the airport, the rain came belting down hard enough to bounce two feet back into the air, so I parked right in front of the main terminal entrance under the no parking sign. The African constable on traffic duty ignored me. He could see the black stencilling on the mudguards, too.

I walked over to him and flashed my ID card. 'When it stops raining move my car over to the carpark, please.'

'Yes, sir,' he smiled conspiratorially as I handed him the key.

I spent the rest of the morning with McLaren checking flight lists, immigration lists, entry lists, exit lists and air-freight manifestos. There was not much to it and McLaren did what there was very well. The police Alsatian in the basement, sniffing luggage for drugs as the cases moved slowly past on the electric conveyor, snarled at me and I snarled back. Damn Mr Hamilton. I was bored beyond belief.

The Air Rhodesia flight from Bulawayo landed and Jane came through the door from the apron. She was a heaven-sent sight, even in the unimaginative uniform the airways inflict on their hostesses.

I'd never tried anything with Jane, and as a result we had a rather special relationship. Occasionally we went out together. I told her my troubles, she cried on my shoulder. It was a good friendship.

She didn't have another flight that day, so I grabbed her arm and we headed upstairs for the bar.

McLaren looked shocked by my dereliction of duty. The hell with him. Jane was much better company and it was lunchtime anyway. Well, almost. We found ourselves a couple of bar stools. I bought a vodka, lime and water for Jane and a Lion lager for myself.

'You want to watch that stuff,' she nodded at the beer. 'I'll be able to call you tubby, pretty soon.'

'You look as if you could stand a little dieting yourself.' I glanced at her bust. It was an old joke between us. As an air hostess she was continually going on diet and that was the first place she ever lost weight. She pulled a face.

'What's the crowd for?' she asked, gesturing towards the balcony.

'Well-wishers,' I answered. 'Scarletti is being deported this afternoon.' The pack had started to gather early.

'I remember reading about him in the paper. Says he has no idea why he's being deported.' She leaned forward and pulled a thread off my jacket. 'What's he done, Rich?'

'How the hell should I know?'

'Liar,' she smiled, and changed the subject.

We had another drink then went into the restaurant for lunch. We made small talk and kidded around. I hadn't seen Jane for a while and we had a lot to talk about. She raved about the latest development in her love life. I enthused about Cathy. It was an enjoyable hour, and over too soon.

After lunch I walked her out to the airways coach and then stood around in the concourse waiting for Scarletti to arrive. McLaren joined me looking worried. It was his first deportation. I smiled at him. Jane had left me in a very pleasant state of mind and I could even put up with the crummy demonstration.

Scarletti came through the main entrance at 1400 hours. Father Scarletti, late of Gunston Mission, twenty-seven miles from Salisbury. His wet cassock wrapped itself around each leg in turn with every step he took. His spikey red beard stuck out like a rash from his tired, lined face and the rimless glasses on the end of his nose imparted a bewildered look to his features. He had the air of a lost little boy searching for his mother.

He was surrounded by a sea of faces, some white, most black, their expressions a mixture of sadness and indignation that this kindly old priest should be subjected to such tyrannical treatment by the Government of Rhodesia.

A reporter and a television camera crew approached and the crowd made way to let them through to the priest.

'No, I have no idea why I have been singled out for deportation,' he told the microphone in front of him. 'I have searched to the depths of my soul but can find no reason.' There were tears in his eyes and angry mutterings from the crowd. 'I have prayed that the authorities would realise their mistake and find the courage and compassion to rescind this shockingly unjust order, but alas, I fear it is not to be.' His voice was choking with emotion. 'Oh dear God, what will become of my faithful flock?' He wiped the back of his hand across his watery eyes and bowed his head, a bent and beaten old man.

I felt the anger rise up in me. The lying, hypocritical, blasphemous, old son-of-a-bitch.

It had been a little different the night we raided the mission and found two AKs, seven grenades, four thousand rounds of 7,62 mm ammunition and an RPG rocket launcher, all stashed away very neatly under three feet of earth in the cellar of his house. Then he had stood at the top of the cellar steps and cursed us with language a Pioneer Street whore would have willingly given six months earnings to learn. His finger-prints had been found on the two rifles, six of the grenades, the ammunition case and the RPG. I should have shot the old bastard on the steps. I probably would have if I had known the hardest thing he would have to face would be deportation.

I thought of Father Antonio, his head crushed in and his body torn to shreds by hyenas when the search party found what was left of him. He had lived for and died because of his faith, and his God would find little fault with his service. Scarletti served his God with equal fervour, only this one did not live in the temple in the sky. Scarletti's God operated out of a big domed building in Moscow called the Kremlin.

Scarletti was sobbing bitterly into a handkerchief when I laughed. Laughed loudly.

Every head in the crowd snapped round in my direction, all eyes riveted on me, shocked and incredulous expressions replacing anger.

Scarletti stopped his stage grief long enough to look up. His eyes widened as he recognised me. 'May the Lord have mercy on you, my son, for you know not what you do,' he said. It was corny, but he was a good enough actor to carry the lines.

'Screw you,' I said, smiling at him as my hand moved towards my left armpit. He knew what I carried under my coat. He let out a squeal like a frightened warthog and charged through the crowd and into the departure lounge. He bumped the cameraman in passing and the camera smashed itself to bits on the mosaic floor.

'God almighty,' McLaren moaned and ran after him.

No one seemed to know what to do or what had happened. I walked through the crowd and they parted in front of me as if I had the plague. Those with placards waved them round uncertainly above their heads and a few started a chant, but it wasn't taken up.

I began to regret my outburst. Although it made me feel a lot better, threatening Scarletti had been a stupid, childish impulse. I didn't think Mr Hamilton would approve. I was in the slop tank, up to my ears, without water wings.

I bought myself a rare daytime whisky on the terrace and watched McLaren walk Scarletti out to the aircraft. From the balcony it appeared that he was helping the grief-stricken old man. Every few steps Scarletti turned and waved to the crowd. They all waved back with sympathy. I wondered if I was the only one to notice that McLaren had the old bastard's arm twisted up behind his back and was forcing him in the direction of the plane. They stumbled up the steps and my young colleague stayed on board until just before take-off. He most probably had to sit on Scarletti to keep him in his seat.

The demonstration died a slow and confused death. Most of the crowd left the airport before the plane even took off. I walked down to meet McLaren. There were still a few tearful faces around and the television cameraman came rushing in with a new camera looking for the action which wasn't there.

McLaren came up to me and shook my hand with sorrowful condolence. 'Thank you, sir. Oh, thank you so much for not making the dear old man's tragic farewell any worse than it was.'

I stepped back and regarded him with amazement. He'd flipped. I was sure of it.

'When you wished him well,' he continued, 'he was so overcome that his oldest and dearest friend had the courage to defy the Government, to see him off to distant pastures, that he could not bear the strain.' McLaren threw his arm across my shoulders and hissed, 'Smile, dammit. They've got a new camera in operation.' Then he went on loudly, 'To see you standing there smiling bravely was too much for him. He feared his spirit would break if he stayed to say goodbye to you.'

It wouldn't have been his spirit, it would have been his neck.

'I had to sit with the dear old man to console him,' McLaren went on. 'He was far past tears.'

I could buy that.

'Come, sir. Don't make a public exhibition of your grief,' he concluded solicitously.

I let him lead me away from the remnants of the crowd.

McLaren unlocked the Special Branch office and I collapsed into a chair, laughing until the tears rolled down my face. 'McLaren, you conniving twit. Do you know what you've just done?' I controlled my breathing with difficulty.

'Yes, sir. Got you out of a difficult position. That reporter was just about to interview you.'

'Interview, hell.' I laughed at him. 'Mr Hamilton would have had no choice but to fire me after the way I behaved. You've just saved my neck, I hope.'

McLaren grinned sheepishly.

'Don't go coy on me, McLaren. If I can do you a favour, name it.'

He stopped grinning and looked up quickly. 'There *is* something you can do for me, sir. Well actually two things.'

'Go on,' I said, regretting my generosity. Now he was going to tear the guts out of it.

'I need a new pair of handcuffs. I gave mine to Scarletti as a parting gift.'

'Are you out of your mind, McLaren?' I bawled at him. 'What do you mean, a parting gift?'

'I left Scarletti handcuffed to the seat and the key with the hostess. I told her to unlock them at thirty-thousand feet and if he still wanted to get off then, that would be fine.'

'Okay,' I calmed down. 'What's the second favour?'

'I want a posting out of this lousy airport. It's driving me crazy.'

'If I'm still on the force tomorrow, you've got it. Where to?'

'Your office.'

'You *are* crazy. Favours or not, I'll work your backside off.'

'Make a change from sitting on it, sir.'

I stuck out my hand. 'You've got yourself a deal.'

7

'YOU idiot! You complete and utter bloody idiot! For Christ's sake, Kelly, what the devil were you trying to do yesterday? Start a riot? If McLaren hadn't forced Scarletti onto the plane, that's exactly what would have happened.'

I was right. Mr Hamilton did not approve and I had never seen him so angry. He was very close to losing his temper, which was unheard of.

'You're suspended for two weeks without pay and you've lost two years' seniority. You can thank your guardian angel that there was no riot. If there had been you'd be in prison right now.' The fury in his eyes was a hard thing to see. I had taken his verbal onslaught for a solid five minutes. I had to. I admired and respected him and, besides, he was right. But enough is enough.

'May I say something, sir?' I took his silence for consent. 'Will I be returning to duty here?' I fully expected a posting to Sticksville.

He glowered at me for a long, calculating minute. 'Yes, unfortunately.'

'In that case, sir, may I request that DPO McLaren be transferred to my office?'

'You've got a bloody nerve, Kelly,' he exploded. 'I would never subject a promising young police officer to your immature influence. Not if there was a gun pointed at my head. Now get out of my office and off the station.'

I left.

I went home wondering just what I was going to do with myself for the next two weeks. I tossed my jacket and revolver onto the couch, opened a beer and flicked the switch on the tape deck. The low, husky voice of Julie London filled the room with *Cry Me A River*. The song matched my mood. I sat down and looked at the view.

From the eighth floor flat the northern suburbs of Salisbury rolled away from the centre of the city. Salisbury is a sprawling, haphazard city where man defers to nature most of the time. They don't destroy trees to build a road. They build the roads around the trees whenever possible. It's a beautiful city, and my view was one of the best, but I was damned if I was going to sit and contemplate it for the next fourteen days. I got up and telephoned Cathy. She answered on the third ring.

'Hello, kitten,' I said. 'How are things at the dress shop?'

'It's not a dress shop, you ignorant peasant,' she laughed, 'it's a fashion salon.' And it was. Very classy and very pricey, in First Street. 'Exclusive' was the word Cathy used.

I told her what had happened.

'Oh, Rich. I'm so sorry. But isn't it marvellous?'

'What do you mean "marvellous", you dumb broad? Didn't you hear what I said? I've lost two weeks' pay, two years' seniority, I have a black mark on my service record and I probably won't get a promotion for the next hundred-and-ten years. Worst of all I've got nothing to do for the next two weeks. Marvellous!' I snorted. 'Have you been drinking?'

'But, darling, that's just what I mean. Two whole weeks. You and I and fourteen long, glorious days together.'

'Would you mind slowing down and telling me exactly what you're talking about?'

'The season has finished, Rich, and Mrs Simpson can easily manage here. Besides, I've been wanting to get out to the farm to see Dad. Let's go out there for a couple of days.'

'I take it all back. You aren't a dumb broad after all. How soon can you be ready to leave?'

'Give me two hours to clear things here and pack and I'll pick you up at your place.'

'Oh no, you won't. I'm not risking my neck in that jazzed-up German hotrod of yours. I'll pick you up.'

'I'll be ready. Two hours, darling,' she said and hung up.

* * *

We turned into the dirt road leading to the farm just after four o'clock that afternoon. We had left the rain in Salisbury and the few cotton wool clouds in the sky were high and friendly. I stopped the car in the drive in front of the house.

Cathy's father walked down the steps to meet us. His hair was steely-grey and contrasted vividly with the dark tan of his face. His eyes were the same smokey blue as Cathy's and the resemblance was easy to see. They both had the same proud walk and the same direct way of looking straight at you when they spoke. If there was anything of Cathy's dead mother in her, I couldn't see it.

'Catherine, my love, you look fagged out.' He glanced over her shoulder at me and the humour lines crinkled the corners of his eyes. 'What have you been doing to my daughter? Taking advantage of her, no doubt,' he answered himself.

'Oh, Daddy. He has not. Stop embarrassing him.'

'If he hasn't, he's a bigger fool than I ever was.' He winked at me. 'And that would take some doing.'

I grinned at him and handed him the bottle of Ballantyne's Twelve-Year-Old that I had brought out from Salisbury.

'Good God. He must be a fool. No one gives Ballantyne's away.' He lowered his eyebrows. 'Have you been taking advantage of my daughter, young man?'

'Morning, noon, night and all points in between,' I said.

'If that's the best you can manage, you need a tonic.' He held the whisky up to the light. 'Let's go inside and see if they've changed the formula.'

There were forty years of life in the lounge. And it wasn't overcrowded. The furniture was massive, old-fashioned and comfortable. There were skins, spears, drums and an old Spitfire propellor on the wall. A photograph of Cathy's father in the uniform of a Royal Air

Force wing commander hung next to it. The carpets were jackal skins, and a huge polar bear skin was spread in front of the fireplace. It was a room to live in. A room to come home to. A room built on hardship, sweat, tears and love. A lot of love. I felt a real and deep inner peace.

'How is that dress shop of yours doing? Still charging silly old ladies the earth for last year's fashions, I suppose?' They had their arms around one another and the love between them was a tangible thing. They were proud of, and to belong to, each other.

'You and Rich! It's not a dress shop. It's a fashion salon.'

'Sell dresses don't you?'

'Yes, but . . . '

'What do you think, Richard? Is it a dress shop or isn't it?'

'I think if you don't open that bottle I'll die of thirst. I didn't bring it all the way from Salisbury just for you to swing it round like an Indian club.'

'Hell's bells! Just goes to show what a pretty woman can do to a man. Makes him forget life's necessities.' He walked briskly to the sideboard. 'Jephta!' he roared over his shoulder. 'Bring some ice and water.'

The ice and water came. Jephta's smile was ear-to-ear when he greeted Cathy. My welcome was more reserved. I was the intruder, the unknown, and he wasn't sure he approved of his 'picannin madam' being involved with me. For the moment he would put up with me as he had on my one previous visit.

The level in the Ballantyne's bottle sank swiftly and by the time dinner was over, it had disappeared.

We were sitting in the lounge listening to Grieg's *Peer Gynt* and rounding off a superb meal of warthog haunch done in wine. The KWV brandy Cathy's father had unearthed from somewhere went down like liquid velvet and my suspension from the force didn't bother me anymore. The mood was mellow and relaxed. Cathy's father broke it.

'Tell me, Richard. Do you love my daughter?' His tone was conversational but his eyes were intent.

The seconds stretched out between us as I stared back.

'Yes,' I said finally. 'Yes, I do.'

'Are you going to marry her?'

'I'll answer that after I've asked her.'

'Make it soon. Women weren't made to live alone. Dries them up.'

'Please, Dad.' Cathy's voice was small.

'Sorry, Catherine. You're right. I'm just an interfering old man.' He finished his drink, kissed her goodnight and went to bed.

Cathy got up and turned the record over. For a moment there was silence, then as the haunting strains of *Ingrid's Lament* drifted from the speakers, I reached for her. We sank down onto the polar bear skin and I kissed her. Her tongue tracked fire across my lips and it was like tasting honey for the first time. Everything was new, everything was beautiful. Our bodies were vibrating like taut violin strings. I propped myself up on one elbow and looked down at her. Her hair was spread out like a glorious, golden fan and her eyes were alight with happiness.

'You do like Daddy, don't you, Rich?'

'Like him? I love him. Almost as much as I love his daughter.'

'You mustn't mind the things he says. He and Mummy were married when they were eighteen and he thinks I'm almost over the hill. He's worried about me.'

'He loves you, kitten. He wants to see you happy.'

'I know.' Her fingers played with the buttons on my shirt, undoing them one by one. Her hand slid inside my shirt and her fingertips danced fleetingly over my chest. 'And, Rich . . . I'm glad I waited.'

'So am I, Cathy.' I leaned down and kissed her hard. My hand came up and suddenly the buttons on her blouse were undone. She arched her back slightly for me to get at the fastening of her brassiere and then her breasts were free. Gloriously free, proud and demanding. I felt them, each with its hard point of desire, her heart pounding beneath my hand as the passion mounted in her. I kissed her softly, our tongues meeting, parting and twining round each other and I could feel desire rising in me. Her hips lifted off the rug and her skirt and underwear were a tangled heap beside us.

'You're overdressed, Mr Kelly.'

My clothes joined hers as she stretched out on the rug. She opened her body and held her arms out to me. I could feel the blood racing through my head as she guided me into the paradise that was her. Then I loved her. Loved her deeply and with all my heart. We moved to an unwritten and unknown song that climbed higher and higher until we couldn't hear it anymore. There was nothing left but the two of us. We overwhelmed each other with our love, each trying to give more and more, until a searing flash of white-hot flame touched our souls, and the universe exploded.

'Cathy, my darling, will you marry me?'

'Yes, please. Oh yes, please.'

* * *

We roamed hand in hand over the farm. We rode horses. We shot pheasant and guinea fowl. We lay naked on the banks of the Hunyani River. We watched the tobacco being reaped. We inspected the curing barns. And we loved. Always we loved. With our eyes, mouths, hands, minds and bodies. We loved completely. Nothing existed but the two of us, each for the other, and the world of realities was very far away. We were content that it should be so.

We talked endlessly about everything and nothing at all. We planned and dreamed and drank cold wine on hot summer days, and the rains came again and we barely noticed.

'Rich?'

'Umm . . . '

The day was warm and the fresh summer grass was a comfortable mattress. The bottle of Alto Rouge had left a pleasant, contented afterglow. I lay on my back and watched the puffy white clouds chase each other lazily across the arc of the sky.

'Rich, are you listening?'

'Umm.'

Cathy ran her fingernail along the curve of my jaw and down the side of my throat.

'You love this place, don't you?'

I turned onto my side, studying her. Her tone was light but she had something on her mind. I nodded, not speaking, waiting for her to go on.

'I was talking to Daddy last night. He's not getting any younger and we, that is he . . . '

I knew what was coming and I reached for her, not wanting to hear it.

'Please, Rich. Let me finish.'

I dropped my arms and rolled onto my back.

'He was wondering if, after we are married, we would be coming to live on the farm.' She paused, choosing her words with care. 'You and Daddy get on so well together and he really does need some help to run it.'

This time when I reached for her, she came.

'Cathy, my sweet, your father and I like each other at the moment. What would it be like in a year, or even six months? It could possibly be fine. It probably would not be. And if it wasn't, life would be hell for all of us. Me on the one side, your father on the other and you caught in the crossfire. It would tear us all apart and reduce our love to a farce. I respect him and I love you far too much to gamble irresponsibly with our future. Besides, I know more about selling eggbeaters to Eskimos than farming.' I brushed her cheek lightly with my lips, trying to soften the words. 'A man makes his own way, kitten, or he goes nowhere. Irrespective of who he is or what he's got. I'm a cop, not a farmer, and that's the way it's going to stay, Cathy.'

'Does that mean it's no, Rich?'

'That's what it means.'

I expected tears, or at the very least, disappointment, but she surprised me. She laughed with genuine happiness. 'I told him you'd say something like that.'

I laughed with her, pleased that there was no disagreement between us.

'I told him that if you consented to his ridiculous suggestion I'd have to think twice about marrying you.'

'You mean if I had opted for the easy life you would have turned me down?'

'Oh no, I'd have just thought twice about it,' Cathy said, and she pressed herself against me. 'Take me now, please, darling.'

'Again? Woman, you're insatiable!'

'I know. Isn't it fabulous?'

And it was.

* * *

She stretched her arms above her head with the contented feline grace of the cat that has had the cream—and the canary.

'It was heaven, Cathy, my love,' I said, studying the woman I had chosen. She was poised, sophisticated and confident, and there was nothing shallow about her. When she gave, it was completely. And she would accept nothing less in return. The feeling between us was in its infancy. It would grow and would fuse us one to the other in an incorruptible bond of love. I didn't want it any other way. I loved her.

'Would you like a cup of coffee before we go back, darling?'

I nodded, lit a cigarette and put it between her lips.

She took the thermos out of a saddle bag. 'Oh, damn. It's leaking.' She held up the empty thermos in disgust. 'That's strange. The top seems tight enough.' She tugged at it and the glass insert suddenly came out of the metal casing. 'Sorry, darling. The service in this place is lousy. No coffee.'

'You've ruined my day.' I took the cigarette out of her mouth and kissed her.

I saddled the horses and we rode slowly back to the farmhouse, silence stretching out between us yet drawing us very close. We were attuned to our surroundings and in total accord with each other. Life was very, very good.

* * *

It hit me at four-thirty the next morning. I sat up in bed, instantly awake and knowing I had the answer at last. It was so blatantly obvious and simple. And it had taken me weeks to see it. I knew I was right. I had to be.

'Cathy, my love, wake up.' I gripped her shoulder and shook her softly. Her eyes flickered dreamily and she nuzzled into my chest. I shook her again, a little harder. 'Come on, Cathy, wake up.'

'Um ummm . . . ' She snuggled closer.

'Wake up, dammit.' I shook her really hard. 'I have to get back to Salisbury.'

That finally penetrated the misty layers of sleep and she sat up. 'What did you say?' Her eyes were wide with disbelief.

'I said, my sweet, that I have to get back to Salisbury now.'

'Right now?'

'Right now.'

'Oh why, Rich?' There were sudden tears in her eyes. 'You can't go back to work for another six days. Why the sudden urgency? I don't want you to go. What could be more important than the two of us being together like this?' she cried, digging her nails into my arm. The dimly remembered world of realities was back.

'We have the rest of our lives to be together, kitten.' I disengaged myself gently and slipped out of bed. 'Our time is only just beginning. But I still have a job to do and I have to go. Now.'

'I don't understand.' She looked at the luminous dial of the clock on the bedside table. 'It's only twenty-five to five. What could possibly be so important that you have to leave so ridiculously early? It's hardly even light outside.' She had stopped crying and was beginning to show the first traces of anger. 'And what's more, why wait until now to spring it on me? You could have told me last night.'

'I didn't know last night. It's something I've only just thought of. If I wasn't such an idiot I would have seen it long ago. It really is important, Cathy, and I must get back to Salisbury.' I climbed into my pants as she slid her arms round my waist.

'Sorry, darling. I was being a bitch. I'll have to get used to sleeping with a policeman. I'll be ready in fifteen minutes.'

'You don't have to come. Just because I go rushing round in the middle of the night doesn't mean you have to.' I grinned at her.

'That's right,' she said. 'I don't have to, but I'm coming anyway.'

Twenty minutes later we found her father in the grading shed.

Life begins with the sun on a Rhodesian farm. If he was surprised by our sudden departure, he didn't show it. Just told us to hurry up and set the date. Not that he thought a piece of paper would make an honest woman out of Catherine. He hadn't thrown a party for years and we were having the reception on the farm, weren't we? I told him definitely we were, thanked him for his hospitality and we left.

My old Zephyr hadn't been driven so hard for years. The tyres squealed, the engine protested and the exhaust was about ready to fall off, but it kept going.

At 0745 hours I dropped Cathy off next to her car with a quick kiss and a promise to call her. Her new white Mercedes made my Zephyr look even more of a wreck than it was.

The clock on the wall read 0758 when I walked past a surprised duty sergeant into the Central Police Station in Railway Avenue. He should have stopped me, but he didn't try. As I turned the corner I saw his hand reaching for the telephone.

I walked into my office, closed the door and took the green plastic thermos flask out of my safe. I sat down at my desk and used the point of a paper knife to ease the plastic lip off the rim running round the top of the flask. Just as I finished the door of my office was hurled open and it smashed into the wall with almost enough force to rip the hinges out.

'Kelly! You insubordinate bastard!' Mr Hamilton bellowed. He had finally lost his temper. It was quite a sight.

'Morning, sir.' I glanced up briefly.

'Morning, sir?' Rage sent his voice booming along the passage. 'Morning, sir? Is that all you have to say? You're under arrest. This time you've gone . . . '

His voice trailed off as the flask came apart in my hands. The sheets of rice paper slipped off the glass insert and curled up on my desk. He shut the door quietly, then pulled up a chair and began examining the sheets. He looked up at me. I stood at rigid attention.

'What are you up to now, Mr Kelly?' The storm of his temper had passed and may never have been.

'Waiting to be marched off to the cells, sir.'

'The arrest is revoked. Temporarily.' He didn't smile, but it was close. 'Let's see if these scraps of paper have saved your neck.'

They had. They were dynamite.

There were seven sheets of very thin rice paper, covered with single-spaced typing. Every police station, army camp and SAP camp within seventy-five miles of the Zambian border was listed. The names of the officers and the numbers of men they commanded appeared on the third page, together with patrol areas and normal frequencies of radio communications, and the various call signs. It also listed the total strength of the Rhodesian Air Force. The information was very detailed and almost one hundred percent accurate. The last page contained a list of four names and addresses. The information given below these stated that the four could be trusted as true friends of Zimbabwe and could be called upon for aid at any time. They were all Europeans and the addresses listed were in the upper-income bracket area of Salisbury. The names meant nothing to me, but they sure as hell would. The page ended with the slogan 'ZIMBABWE SHALL BE FREE' typed in red and underlined.

That the seven pages had been destined for either the ZAPU or ZANU terrorist headquarters in Lusaka was obvious. But there was no indication where they had originated.

'What action do you propose taking on this, Mr Kelly?'

I didn't answer him. I walked over to the Xerox copier and fed the first sheet into it. It was an expensive piece of equipment and the copy was perfect. I cut it vertically into three sections so that no section on its own provided any meaningful information. The seven original sheets went into a large envelope. The forensic boys could examine them and if we were very lucky, they just might be able to lift an identifiable print. I picked up the phone and told Rawson to come into my office.

'Good morning, Mr Hamilton. Morning, sir.' His expression reflected puzzlement as he glanced from Mr Hamilton to me. Which was understandable. The entire station must have heard Mr Hamilton place me under arrest.

'Who have you got on duty at the moment?' I asked him.

'Giles and McLaren, sir.'

'McLaren? From the airport?' I raised my eyebrows.

'Yes, sir.'

I looked at Mr Hamilton in surprise. He pretended not to hear and was staring intently out of the window at nothing at all. Possibly he hadn't been very fond of Scarletti either.

I handed the three cut sections to Rawson. 'I want the machine these were typed on found. Use Giles and McLaren. Start with the agents. Someone will be able to put a name to it. If possible get a list of names and addresses of all the people who have purchased this model. Check the agents' repair and maintenance records. Go down to Customs House and check through the import manifestos. I want to know where every single typewriter of this model in the country is located, and I want to know yesterday. Got it?'

'Got it, sir.' He smiled and appeared to be genuinely pleased that I was back in business.

'Okay, move it,' I shot back.

As the door closed behind Rawson, I picked up the pad on which I had written the four names and addresses. 'I'll need sixteen men,' I told Mr Hamilton, 'to provide continuous surveillance on these four peopie. Starting immediately.'

'Sixteen men seems a little excessive to me, Mr Kelly. Why so many?'

'I'd like four details assigned to each of the subjects, sir. They would work in two-man teams. Even then they'll be working in twelve-hour shifts. It would be unfortunate to blow this because someone was sleepy or bored and missed something vital.' Unfortunate hell! It'd be criminally irresponsible. I lit a cigarette. 'I don't think the surveillance can be maintained properly with any less.'

'Very well, Mr Kelly. I'll have to obtain the commissioner's permission to use uniformed personnel in plain clothes. As you are aware SB simply don't have the establishment to mount an operation of this scale.' He took a cigarette out of my box. 'I expect vou'd like to conduct the briefing yourself?'

I nodded, shrugging into my jacket.

'Please be available at 1200 hours. I'll have the sixteen men ready for you.'

'Thank you, sir. I'm taking these sheets up to Doc Stanlake at the lab. He may be able to lift a couple of useful prints.'

Mr Hamilton looked doubtful, but he nodded, then said, 'I see you're still carrying a non-issue revolver, Mr Kelly.'

'Yes, sir.' He was well aware of my sentiments regarding the standard issue .38 Webley and Scott. It is clumsy and very seldom accurate. As one fellow police officer put it, 'If you aim at a barn door you'll be lucky to hit the barn.' I agreed with him. My Smith & Wesson hit what I aimed at and was a simple, uncomplicated piece of machinery. It had cost ninety dollars at Harrison's in Baker Avenue, and I considered it money well spent. It had saved my life on two occasions. The Old Boy Club at the top in the BSAP refused to consider any police equipment which wasn't British. The Smith & Wesson, while vastly superior to the Webley, is American and therefore infra dig. To hell with them. I'd stick with it. Besides, I knew Mr Hamilton carried a nine-millimetre short Beretta. He had no time for the standard issue revolver either.

I took the envelope containing the sheets of rice paper, put it into my pocket and was heading for the door of my office when Mr Hamilton said, 'The arrest is revoked permanently.' He grinned suddenly. 'Good luck, Rich. We can't afford to foul this one up. Let's see if we can get enough solid evidence to take it to court, for a change.'

I knew what he meant. The Government has a decided penchant for deporting terrorist supporters. No Government can deport murderers. And I was going to prove that the author of those pages was as guilty as the terrorists we had killed on the banks of the Zambezi. In fact he was doubly guilty. He hadn't faced the risks. He hadn't died with bullets churning through his guts. He'd been sitting somewhere in his fancy lounge drinking whisky and watching the news on his remote-control television set. He hadn't chopped the arms and legs off the Ronson children. No, he hadn't done that, but he had given the power to do it to a primitive and gullible group of people. And he would die for it. I walked out.

8

CORPORAL Lance Koster was enjoying himself. The thundering group on the bandstand of the Moonraker Club brought back memories of the old rock sessions in Hillbrow and if the tunes the band was belting out had hardly altered in two years, it didn't matter a damn. He knew his style of dancing was very much better than most of the other couples who crowded the minute dance floor and Lindy was at her radiant best. He smiled at her as the music ended and slipped his arm round her waist protectively as he guided her back to their table. He ordered two drinks from the bikini-clad waitress without noticing the smouldering, provocative look she gave him and stretched forward to place his hand on Lindy's stomach.

'Are you sure you feel all right? Why isn't he moving? Surely the little bugger should be kicking and jumping around a lot more now?'

'Lance, honey,' Lindy said as she took his hand and squeezed it tenderly, 'I feel fine. You know I'd tell you if I didn't and it's only six months. I'm a woman, not a pressure cooker, and the baby can't be kicking all the time. And what makes you so certain it will be a boy anyway?' She smiled impishly.

'It will be. No doubt about it. I'd look pretty silly trying to teach a girl to fish and shoot and ride a motorbike.' Christ, she's lovely, he thought to himself. And she looks so happy. His life had taken on added meaning, and he knew he loved her as no other woman could ever be loved.

Gone was the swaggering Hillbrow hood. When Lance had joined the army just over two years previously, his only desire had been for a place to hide. Somewhere he could wait in anonymous obscurity letting time and the unsuccessful investigation dampen the fervour of the hunt for him. He considered three years would be long enough and that's what he had signed up for. And he hated it.

The short hair, the shouting and bawling of orders, the endless parades and inspections and the bulldust bored him. He did everything the others did, sometimes even better, but always in a lazy and disinterested manner. He was cynical and contemptuous of everything military and he despised the recruits training with him. Anyone who joined the army because he really wanted to become a soldier had to be a sub-human moron. His attitude showed and gradually the others learned to leave him alone.

At the first pay-parade one of the troopers said, 'Money. At last. I'm going into town tonight to get laid and smashed, in that order.'

'Money!' Lance sneered. 'In the old days I wouldn't have bent down to pick up that piddling amount if it had been lying in the street. You don't know what real money is, you ignorant sod.'

'Why don't you just bugger off back where you came from, Koster? We don't need your kind round here,' Cormack said. He was the biggest man in the squad and reputed to be very tough. He had dominated the rest of the squad since the first day and was considered the unofficial leader.

'Screw you, Cormack.' Lance turned to face him. 'No one asked for your oar. Keep it out of my business or I'll ram it up your backside and snap it off short. Understand, mama's boy?'

'You can't talk to me like that, you bastard.' Cormack stood up, rage and anger written clearly across his blazing features.

'When you're big enough to stop me you'll be too bloody old,' Lance taunted him, savouring the coming fight which he was now determined to provoke.

'Christ, I'll kill you, you Jo'burg tit!'

'You terrify me, Cormack. I want my mummy!'

'Apologise or I'll smash you up good.'

'Screw you,' Lance repeated, and spat accurately onto the toe-cap of Cormack's highly polished boot.

'You son-of-a-bitch!' Cormack snarled and leaped forward swinging his great ham of a fist.

It never connected. It took an officer and two MPs to stop Lance. Cormack was destined to spend six weeks in the barracks' hospital with a broken jaw, suspected skull fracture, three broken ribs and two broken fingers.

Lance was unmarked. He was sentenced to fourteen days in the guard house.

When he came out he was left totally alone. He was watched like some dangerous wild animal that could go berserk at the slightest hint of provocation. The ease and savagery with which he had demolished Cormack set him apart from the rest of them and he preferred it that way.

If the men left him alone, the officers and NCOs did not. He was wholeheartedly disliked by the majority of them and they set out to break him. Lance was not a fool. He knew exactly what they were trying to do, and he was equally determined that he would not break. It developed into a grim contest of wills. He drew every crappy detail, he was posted on guard duty almost every night, he received no passes, he was confined to barracks every weekend for misdemeanours as trivial as a fly on his pillow during weekly inspection, but he did not break.

In a strangely perverse way he began to enjoy it. His turnout improved with every inspection, he read every manual he could lay his hands on until his knowledge of arms, drill, tactics and regulations was far in excess of his fellow recruits and sometimes matched that of his instructors.

Four months after attesting he received his first weekend pass. An officer and two NCOs on Saturday morning inspection could find nothing wrong. And they really tried. His turnout was perfect and no other recruit in the depot came anywhere close to matching it. He hadn't broken. He had won. And with the realisation of his victory he discovered a strange new pride in himself, in his uniform and the army. He didn't know what it was at first, and when he finally understood it, he didn't believe it. Gradually his acceptance grew until he could no longer deny it. He was happier than he had ever been in his life. With each passing day his contentment increased. He was turning into a soldier, and a good one. The pressure on him eased slowly as respect for him rose, but his standards did not drop. He worked harder than ever until at last he knew that this was the life he had been born for, and he wanted no other. At the end of six months he passed-out of the depot at the top of his squad and one of the most promising recruits that had ever been through it. Lance Koster had come home.

* * *

Lance met her in the Pink Orchid the night of the pass-out party. A group of them had decided to go looking for girls and excitement in the city and had picked the Pink Orchid because it was the cheapest joint in town and there was always a supply of illicit booze available if you had the right connections. And if you picked your girl carefully you could generally avoid a dose. Lance was included in the group and even welcomed. Trouble between the army and the civilians who crowded the Pink Orchid was a very real possibility and if it came to that, they wanted Lance on their side.

Lance grinned cynically to himself as he paid the entrance fee and the doorman stamped the back of his hand with a rubber stamp. The management had stopped issuing tickets when it was discovered that patrons inside the hall were passing their tickets through the gents' toilet window to friends outside to use to gain free admission. Couples moving in and out of the building were no novelty. The large, empty, overgrown lot next door was ideal for five-minute quickies and traffic was generally heavy. If you were unlucky enough to obliterate the stamp on your hand in the frenzied clenching outside you paid again or you didn't get in. A few of the regulars managed to avoid the necessity of washing too frequently and obtained free entrance for three or four successive nights on the same stamp.

She was leaning against the wall near the band when Lance walked through the door and she was the first person he noticed. Her long blonde hair was worn in a swirling pony-tail which caught and held the flashing lights from the bandstand. She wore a tight black dress with a miniskirt. Her figure was superb and her eyes were a sort of cloudy sea-grey. Lance stopped in his tracks. For an impossible moment he thought it was Carol, then the cigarette smoke cleared partially as the door behind him opened, and he realised his mistake. But the resemblance was almost uncanny. The band started up as he crossed the floor towards her.

'Hello,' Lance said as he stopped in front of her.

Her eyes flicked quickly over his face and she apparently liked what she saw. She smiled. 'Hello, yourself.'

'Would you . . . would you like to dance?' Lance stammered over the words. He didn't understand it. He wasn't shy with women. He liked them and generally they fell for his line. He'd advanced way beyond the stammering stage years ago. But the back of his throat was dry.

'Why not?' She pushed herself away from the wall. 'That's what people come here to do, isn't it?' She raised her eyebrows in a teasing question.

She gyrated backwards across the floor to the pop tune, her legs flashing and her pelvis undulating in time with the beat. Lance could feel his tongue sticking to the roof of his mouth as he watched her. God, she was Carol. But she wasn't Carol. The resemblance was great, but so were the differences.

A big, husky character with long, slicked-down hair and wearing a black leather-jacket, stepped onto the floor between them and put his arms around her, squeezing her buttocks. Lance saw her hands against the big man's chest and her savage expression as she tried vainly to push him away. Then he was beside them, his fist smashed into the man's kidney, and he crumpled. Lance stood over him as he came slowly off the floor, animal hatred glowing deep in his eyes.

'I'll get you for this, you bastard.'

'Any time, any place,' Lance said, his arms hanging at his sides, relaxed but ready.

'My time, my place, but you'll know it when it comes,' he snarled, and backed off into the crowd.

Lance steered the girl over to a vacant table and pulled out a chair for her. She put a warm hand on his arm. 'Thanks, but you shouldn't have done that. That was Luke Mason and he can be a dangerous animal.' She took her hand away and reached into her purse for a cigarette. 'My name is Lindy, by the way.'

He grinned down at her and lit her cigarette. 'Would you like a drink, Lindy?'

'God,' she smiled, 'a gentleman. In this place yet. Yes, please. A coke.' Then she added warningly, 'Just a coke. Without a booster charge, okay?'

'Just a coke,' he nodded and flicked the burnt-out match under the table. He walked over to the dispenser smiling to himself.

He came back with two cokes and sat down next to her. Luke Mason and two of his friends were three tables away, glaring at them. Lance shrugged it off. If they wanted it, they could have it, with interest.

'You haven't told me your name,' Lindy said.

He smiled at her and covered her hand on the table with his. She made no effort to remove it. 'Lance. Lance Koster,' he said . . . and the cold, sticky coke hit him in the face.

She was on her feet, white and trembling with anger as she backed away from him. Lance was astounded as he watched her park herself on Luke Mason's lap. Mason's arm came round her waist and his thumb stroked the front of her dress just below her breast. She swivelled on his lap and said something Lance couldn't hear, and the four of them burst into raucous laughter. Mason's hand came up with his fingers spread in the old V sign, directed at Lance.

Lance was too confused to even notice it. He sat immobile in stunned disbelief. What the hell had happened? What had he said or done to produce this violent and unexpected reaction? One of Lance's squad mates sat down next to him, tears of uncontrolled laughter streaming down his cheeks.

'Man, oh man,' he gasped. 'You sure as hell know how to pick them, don't you?'

'What's going on around here? What are you talking about, for Christ's sake?' Lance was still confused.

'You mean you don't know? You really don't know? Man, that's rich. That's really rich.' His laughing fits redoubled.

'What do you mean, pig face?' Lance reached out and twisted his hand in the other's shirt. 'What's really rich?'

'Christ, Lance. I thought you knew. That was Lindy Cormack Big Cormack's sister.'

Lance released him and slumped back in his chair. He lit a cigarette and attempted to wipe away the moist traces of coke from his face with the back of his hand. No wonder she had come on strong, like that. Cormack would carry the marks of Lance's fists on his face for the rest of his life. He hadn't the slightest regret for what he had done to Cormack, but he did regret that Lindy turned out to be his sister. He had known her for only a few short minutes but no other woman had ever affected him like this or left him with the crazy feeling of walking on air. Just like in the sob magazines. And there was nothing he could do about it. Christ, what a lousy deal.

Lindy, Mason and his two cronies stood up and Lindy held onto Mason's arm possessively. She sent Lance a withering glance of contempt as Mason's hand clamped on her backside and the four of them walked out.

The trooper took Lance's coke, sploshed half of it onto the floor and refilled the paper cup from a half-jack of Mellowood brandy which he took from his jacket pocket. He held the cup out to Lance. 'Here, have a slug of this. For Christ's sake, Lance, this is a celebration, not a funeral. So you lost out—so what? There's a dozen more easy lays in here.'

Lance sipped the brandy slowly and ran his eyes round the room. It was true. There were girls all over the place and he would have no trouble picking one up, but suddenly he didn't want to. He wanted the unattainable. He wanted Lindy and he couldn't have her. His mood had changed and he felt depressed. What was there to celebrate? Who the hell celebrates a loss? He knocked back the remainder of his drink and stood up quickly. 'Thanks for the drink, Len. See you around.'

'But we only just got here. Where the hell you going?'

'Who knows?' Lance shrugged disinterestedly. 'Cheers.' He walked out into the darkened carpark and lit another cigarette. He didn't know what to do with himself. He didn't want a woman unless it was Lindy; he didn't want to get drunk; the thought of returning to the empty barracks in Cranborne depressed him. He stood next to the big Vincent wondering what to do with the rest of the evening. What a cockup. He flicked the half-smoked butt away into the darkness, swung a leg over the saddle, and heard it. It came from the direction of the overgrown lot next to the Pink Orchid. Could he have been mistaken? He cocked his head and listened intently, concentrating on the night sounds under the noise of the band inside the hall. For a second there was silence, then it came again.

'No, no. Please, no.' It was too muffled to be a scream but it was desperate. And it was Lindy's voice.

Lance was off the motorcycle and running through the undergrowth before he realised it, and he burst through into a small clearing without any rational thought at all.

Lindy was completely naked and stretched out on her back. Her clothes were a torn and rumpled heap on the grass and Mason stood over her, monstrous in the dim light, his trousers down around his knees. One of his companions held Lindy's legs pinned wide to the ground and the other stretched her arms viciously above her head.

'Christ, hurry up, Luke,' the one holding her legs panted. 'I can't wait all night.'

It was the last thing he said for a very long time. The toe of Lance's heavy-soled shoe slammed into his back with insane, sickening force and he screamed once, very loudly, as his spine shattered. Lance pivoted and Mason's face was a mixture of lust and fear as Lance's instep swung up in a terrible, berserk arc between Mason's open legs with all the power of his rage-filled body behind it. The kick lifted Mason two feet off the ground and he was unable to scream as an incredible agony burst behind his eyes and then a merciful blackness claimed him. The one who had been holding Lindy's arms suddenly realised he was alone and tried frantically to scramble away, a terrified whine coming from his throat. Lance leapt high into the air, flipped his legs back and landed with crushing force on his knees on the man's chest. He felt ribs snap but it didn't stop him. There was nothing scientific about his punching. He swung his fists with blurring speed and awesome power, trying to drive the face under him into the ground. He felt a hand on his shoulder, swung round savagely and almost smashed his fist into Lindy's face. She clung desperately to him, sobbing hysterically, her body shuddering uncontrollably as she gulped air into her starved lungs.

Lance's killing rage died slowly as he stroked her hair. 'It's all right now, Lindy. It's all right, girl. They can't hurt you anymore.' A strange tenderness, almost longing, came over him as he dressed her gently in the tattered remnants of her clothing and buttoned his jacket over the torn bodice of her dress. He couldn't find her underwear and he didn't waste time looking for it. Her shuddering gradually subsided and she clung gratefully to his arm as he steered her in the direction of the Pink Orchid, in search of a telephone.

Johnny Collins, the one Lance had kicked in the back would never walk again. His back broken, his world was now confined to the squeaking rubber of wheelchair tyres. Luke Mason would walk with difficulty for months and would never feel the stirrings of passion again. His manhood had been mashed to pulp and he was permanently emasculated.

They both drew a sentence of twelve months suspended for three years. The magistrate considered that they had been punished enough. Jerry Pistorious would never do anything again. He was dead, a jagged, broken rib had pierced his heart.

At the inquest Lance was praised by the coroner for his prompt, if somewhat over-violent, action. Lance's only regret was that it had been Pistorious who had died and not Mason.

Three months later Lance Koster married Lindy Cormack in a simple ceremony at the RLI chapel. Big Cormack was on operational duty at Hoya River and could not attend. He sent a telegram which read, 'Welcome to the family and thanks.'

* * *

The Moonraker was filling up and Lance recognised Kelly as the policeman threaded his way through the closely-packed tables and sat down with a crowd near the bandstand. He had been in the contact on the Zambezi where the four ters had been killed and had been responsible for the recovery of the communist equipment looted by the troopers from the packs of the dead ters. Typical bloody fuzz, Lance thought with a sneer, confiscating souvenirs from soldiers who had risked their lives in action when those souvenirs were completely useless to the cops and would only lie in some forgotten storeroom until they rotted away. But the cops were not all that switched on. He grinned at the thought that Kelly would have a pump attack if he knew of the Tokarev pistol and the three ter bayonets he had managed to bring home after previous contacts. Two of the other men at Kelly's table had also been on the banks of the Zambezi that day but Lance ignored them all. Cops were for avoiding when possible and outsmarting when you couldn't.

Suddenly Lance had had enough of the Moonraker. The sight of Kelly had reminded him of the screams, the blood, the fear and the death that was part of his job and the way he made his living. Tonight he didn't want to be reminded of it. Tonight he wanted to lie next to Lindy, to make love to her and to know the kind of peace and security that was impossible in the bush, where to relax for the slightest instant was to invite death. He wanted to hold her tightly in his arms and to sleep without the constant fear of a sudden bullet or the vicious crump of an unexpected grenade. He had been reminded of that part of his world which Lindy could not share, for he told her very little of what went on in the bush. And he hated Kelly for it. He pushed his chair back angrily and stood up.

'Come on, Lindy,' he said loudly. 'When the fuzz start snooping round, they screw the whole scene up. They can't even leave us alone in a joint like this, for Christ's sake. Let's get out of here.'

Lindy was bewildered but she stood up obediently and followed Lance.

9

TWO weeks and nothing. Absolutely nothing.

I finished typing my report and scanned quickly through it before passing it on to Mr Hamilton for his perusal and comments. The typewriter had been identified as a Hermes. A fairly new one. The agents, Underwood Business Machines with offices in Pax House, Union Avenue, had imported a batch of two hundred and fifty similar machines six months previously. All had been sold. Twelve had been re-exported by people leaving the country, two hundred and thirty-one were in the original purchasers' possession, mostly businesses, and seven had been resold privately. We had traced five of the seven.

Rawson, McLaren and Giles, posing as service mechanics, had checked them all. Comparison tests had been carried out by the forensic branch. Some were close, very close, and had been rechecked. With the same result—only close. We hadn't found the typewriter.

The immigrants' import manifestos had been examined for the last twelve months. It was pointless going back any further. The machines had only been in production for a year. Same result. Nothing.

I took the report through to Mr Hamilton. He read it slowly and looked up.

'I presume Underwood Business Machines are the sole agents for Hermes.'

'Yes, sir.'

'And they have only imported the one batch?'

'That's right. They've used up their allocation of foreign currency and no typewriters will be imported until about July.'

He dropped the report on the desk and leaned back. 'In that case, Mr Kelly,' he mused, 'unless a Hermes of this model has been smuggled into the country, and for the present we will give our excellent customs personnel the benefit of the doubt, it has to be one of the two machines which you have been unable to locate.'

I nodded. I didn't share his regard for the Department of Customs. Ever since Britain had persuaded big daddy at the UN to impose sanctions against us, the amount of contraband smuggled into the country had increased considerably. But that was beside the point.

'How do you propose finding those two machines, Mr Kelly?'

'I don't know, sir,' I shrugged. 'I can't take the chance of advertising for them, even obscurely. It could alert whoever we are after, and a typewriter is an easy thing to dump. It would be impossible to check every machine in every private home and office in the country. Firstly, because we don't have the men; secondly, because no magistrate in the country would grant a search warrant with such wide scope and, thirdly, because the press would be bound to get hold of it and play it up and the person responsible for those sheets could conceivably connect the search with his own machine and get rid of it.' I drew deeply on my butt. 'I'm completely out of ideas, sir. I'm stuck.'

'It's unthinkable that we should allow this to peter out on us. It will be a long time before we get another lead as conclusive as this. Go away and have one of those famous flashes of inspiration you are so fond of.' He smiled slightly.

I stood up and walked towards the door.

'Mr Kelly.'

'Sir?' I turned round.

'Has it occurred to you that one of the four parties listed on the rice papers may be the author of that document?'

'It did occur to me, sir,' I told him. 'There are no Hermes typewriters in any of their offices. Three of the parties have typewriters in their homes for private use. One Remington, one Imperial portable and one Olivetti.'

'Are you satisfied your information is correct? There's no possibility of a mistake?'

'Quite satisfied.' I had hoped to avoid this. I was becoming uncomfortable and he could see it.

'Who supplied you with the information?'

'I obtained it myself, sir.'

'I presume you didn't walk up to the front door, produce your ID card, inform them you were from Special Branch and enquire if they had a typewriter on which a subversive document was thought to have been typed.'

'No, sir.' Sarcastic bastard. My face was wooden.

'Then how did you find out? I haven't cleared a search warrant for you.'

'I didn't apply for one.' Here we go, I thought. 'I used a master key to obtain access to the homes when the occupants were out.'

'Mr Kelly.' He looked resigned. 'As a police officer you break more laws than most of the inmates of Salisbury Central Prison. And one of these days, that's exactly where you'll land.' Then more lightly. 'Now shove off and think of something.'

'Yes, sir.'

I walked along the passage to my office and fiddled around with some paper work that should have been attended to days ago. But it was a waste of time. I could not concentrate. There must be a way to trace those two machines. But how? I pushed the papers aside and looked at my watch. The day had crept around to 1315 hours.

I walked out of my office and went up the stairs to the NCOs mess for a beer. There are three pubs in the Central Police Station building—the patrol officers' mess, the NCOs mess and the officers' mess. All very regimental. In fact the BSAP does enjoy regimental status which was earned in bitter, bloody fighting far from Rhodesia and conferred by a grateful British Government not so very long ago. Short memories some people have.

The pub was crowded. I had a couple of beers, got a dart in my leg when it hit the wire and glanced off the board at a tangent, bought a pack of thirty Gold Flake and went back to my office.

The paperwork hadn't been done by any helpful little elves during my absence, so I sat down at my desk and started on it after shedding my jacket.

I was still busy at 1700 hours when Rawson knocked and stuck his head through my doorway. 'You haven't forgotten about my stag party this evening have you, sir?'

'Hell, no. Of course not.' I had completely forgotten about it. I had even forgotten that Rawson was getting married on Saturday. 'At the Moonraker, right?'

'Right, sir,' he grinned. 'Starts when the first person gets there.'

'Fine. I have a little work to catch up on here, then I'll be right over. Okay?'

'Yes, sir.' He withdrew his head and closed the door.

Rawson and I were rapidly approaching what could in a loose way be termed a friendly relationship. He even grinned at my sarcasm now. But then I wasn't sarcastic in my dealings with him very much these days. He had proved himself in the hot hell of the Zambezi Valley and it had been enough. Besides, he had worked doggedly for over two weeks on the typewriter investigation. As soon as he passed his promotion exam for section officer I was recommending him for his own station. He deserved it.

I reached for the telephone, dialled and caught Cathy just as she was locking up her fashion salon for the night.

'I'm sorry, kitten. I won't be able to make the play tonight,' I told her. It was the Reps production of *The Diary of Anne Frank* and reputed to be very good.

'But, Rich, it's the final night. This is our last opportunity to see it. Can't whatever you have to do wait until tomorrow?' she asked with mild disappointment.

'No, Cathy. I'm going to a stag party. One of my detectives is getting married on Saturday.'

'A stag party! You mean to tell me you're willing to pass up the chance to see this play just to go boozing?'

'There are thousands of plays, kitten. A guy only has one stag party in his life, if he's lucky.'

'All right, but don't be surprised if I'm not here when you come looking for me.'

'I'll go to the ends of the earth to find you. No stone shall be left unturned until you are mine once more.'

'To the ends of the earth?'

'Yes, my fairest one. Well at least as far as Enkeldoorn.'

'Oh, you big, mean swine,' she chuckled. 'I'll have the aspirin and coffee waiting.'

'I love you, Cathy.'

'I know,' she said softly and put the receiver down.

I cleared my desk, locked the safe and left. The rush-hour traffic had thinned to a trickle as I swung my old Zephyr right at the lights and headed up Kingsway.

The street looked a little sad as the blank and empty offices in the buildings on either side stared out at it. Night was falling and life had ended for another day. One kind of life, that is, where no one kicked you in the crotch or slipped a knife between your ribs, but instead cut your throat with a writ of execution or castrated you with mortgage bonds and hire purchase agreements. Soon a new form of life would emerge on the streets, nowhere near as deadly: the night people. The scum who knew they were scum and pretended to be nothing else, and in a perverse way they may have been more honest than the relentless sharks that inhabited the sunshine hours. Hell, philosophy wasn't my forte. I shook my head and swung into the curb.

It was 1730 hours when I walked into the Moonraker through a battered wooden swing-door and the noise almost blasted me back onto the street. The place was packed. Most of the racket issued from the stage where a long-haired band screeched into long-suffering microphones and tortured amplifiers threw the result out of half-a-dozen speakers within an ohm of blowing a fuse.

Most of the customers were off-duty security force personnel and they emulated the band, clapping, stamping and banging on the tables. The resultant din was enough to make me wish I had brought ear plugs. The ceiling lights tried to illuminate the place, but they fought a losing battle with the three-foot deep cloudbank of smoke which hung above the tables.

I had never been in the Moonraker before, but I had heard about it. Nothing good from my point of view, but it did serve a purpose. It catered almost exclusively for off-duty security force personnel. It was the one place in Salisbury where they could cause havoc and the police were never called. If anyone passed out cold, the management poured them into a taxi, paid the fare and sent them home. Harvey Williams of the Licence Inspector's Squad had told me about it. The floor show was often obscene, usually featuring some stripper the other nightclubs wouldn't look at. The serving was done by girls in skimpy bikinis and fishnet stockings. There were five rooms belonging to the Moonraker in the building next door. What the girls charged didn't interest the management; they weren't running a brothel. But most of the waitresses made the trip three or four times a night. Their take-home pay was probably higher than mine.

The police left the place alone apart from the odd visit by Drug Section. There was a need for the Moonraker. After six weeks of loneliness, blood and death, the troopies returned to hit Salisbury for a week before being sent back to the sharp end, and they had a lot of living to catch up on during that week. If the Moonraker could handle it without too much fuss, it saved the other places of entertainment and prevented clashes between the army and civilians and saved the police a hell of a lot of work. It was crude and it was cheap. If you puked on the floor, they didn't throw you out; they simply cleaned it up. Which was probably one of the reasons Rawson had chosen it for his stag party.

I fought my way through the noise, smoke and crowd until I reached the eight-seater table where Rawson was holding court. He had seen me coming and as I sat down a young waitress put a whisky on the table in front of me. If she had bent any lower her breast would have popped out and contaminated my drink. There was perspiration running down her sides from her armpits and a few straggly hairs drooped limply over the dirty top of her bikini pants. She turned me on like a glow-worm competing with Kariba. She smiled at me and I wondered when she had last brushed her teeth. I shuddered.

Everyone at the table was Special Branch, with one exception:

Henderson. My surprise showed. The last time I had seen him he had not been very well disposed towards Rawson. And vice versa.

'What the hell are you doing here?' I asked, glancing at Rawson who looked away, embarrassed.

'I'm the best man on Saturday, sir,' Henderson said. He looked as embarrassed as Rawson.

Everything changes and everything is relative. Wonders never cease and miracles still happen. I sipped my whisky and found it surprisingly good. At the low prices the Moonraker charged I wondered how they made a profit. I buy my whisky wholesale and I know what it costs.

A young man across the dance floor suddenly rammed his chair back and stood up. He was tanned and from the length of his hair was obviously a soldier. In one of those freak silences which sometimes happen in the most crowded of places I heard his angry words clearly, 'Come on, Lindy. When the fuzz start snooping around they screw the whole scene up. They can't even leave us alone in a joint like this, for Christ's sake. Let's get out of here.'

The attractive blonde girl with him got up hesitantly. I could see she was pregnant, she was also bewildered.

He was staring straight at me when he spoke and I recognised him. He was the young corporal who had been sitting next to me in the chopper during the flight from Salisbury to Malopa Mission and had subsequently lost his patrol in an ambush in the valley the day the Ronson children had died. His name was Koster and he didn't seem to like me a whole hell of a lot. But then that's an attitude towards the police shared by plenty of soldiers, and sometimes it's justified. Ever since the RLI had been formed they had caused so much trouble in Salisbury that it had become automatic to blame them for any disturbance, whether they were guilty or not. The mere presence of troopies near the scene of trouble was generally enough to ensure that they were picked up and questioned. Eight times out of ten they were the cause of such trouble, but it was the couple of times when they had nothing to do with it that led to the bad feeling between the police and the army. There was justification on both sides but my own personal opinion was that no one should be picked up without solid evidence to back up the arrest. If Koster didn't like cops, I could sympathise with him but it didn't bother me overmuch.

He had to pass the table where we were sitting to reach the exit, and with the instinct for trouble that all good police officers and barmen develop I could sense that he was itching to start something. He was level with us when Rawson laughed uproariously at something Henderson said and, unaware of the soldier's presence behind him, pushed his chair back. It slammed into Koster with enough force to be painful. His reaction was swift and savage. He grabbed the chair and jerked it out from under Rawson. The policeman hit the floor with jarring force and looked up with astonishment, the expression on his face slowly turning to anger.

'That was clever, my friend, very clever. Let's see how you like this.' He came off the floor like a coiled spring and swung a round-house punch at Koster's jaw. Koster didn't even bother to move his feet. He shifted his head a fraction and as Rawson's fist whistled past his face he sank a hard, vicious punch into Rawson's solar plexus. The policeman gagged, turned white and tilted slowly toward the floor.

'Any more of you bastards want to take over where he left off?' Koster taunted the table of stunned policemen.

'Please, Lance.' The girl's voice was small and frightened in the tense atmosphere. 'Please leave it. Let's go home.'

'Like hell, lady,' Henderson roared. 'He isn't going anywhere.' He kicked his chair back and advanced threateningly towards Koster.

I stood up. It was time I helped myself to a little of the action. Koster's fist was drawn back to swing again when I caught his arm and gave him an elbow in the kidneys which was hard enough to discourage any further violent action on his part. It did nothing to discourage Henderson and I had to shove him back, hard.

'Sit down, Henderson,' I said.

'Get out of my bloody way,' he snarled as he tried to get round me. 'I'll kill the bastard.'

'Who the hell do you think you're talking to?' I said harshly and the anger suddenly drained out of him. He wasn't about to get away with that sort of behaviour with me and he knew it. 'Sit down and shut up,' I told him. He did.

'What was all that about?' I asked Koster quietly.

'Up yours,' he grunted through compressed lips as he struggled to catch his breath. 'You bastard fuzz are all the same, big shots in a crowd. If you don't like the way I act, be a big shot—go ahead, arrest me.'

From the corner of my eye I saw Henderson stand up, his face contorted with anger.

'Sit down, Henderson,' I snapped. 'And that's an order.'

'But, sir, I'm going to call a B-car and have this garbage,' he gestured towards Koster, 'thrown into stocks.'

'Sit down, God dammit!' I spat it out. 'This garbage, as you call him, was responsible for locating the ter tracks in the valley after you had lost them.' That was a little unfair. Henderson had done his best and under the circumstances no one could have done any better. He winced at my words, which was what I meant him to do. 'This garbage,' I continued, 'lost his entire patrol in an ambush and damn nearly had his head blown off while you were pussyfooting around Chimutsi Dam. If anyone is tossed into the can tonight, it'll be you for disobeying a direct order. Is that clear?'

'Yes, sir,' Henderson said in a subdued voice. 'I'm sorry. I just got a little carried away.'

'Please don't arrest him,' the girl said tearfully. 'He's just come back from the bush and is very tense. He doesn't normally behave like this. Honestly, he doesn't.'

'Are you his wife?' I asked her gently and smiled.

'Yes,' she returned the smile hesitantly.

'Then I suggest you take him home and get him to cool off. If he pulls another stunt like this he will wind up in a cell.'

'Thank you, oh thank you so much.' She turned to Koster and tugged at his arm. 'Let's do as he says and go home, Lance, please.'

'Thanks for nothing,' Koster hissed at me, and tried a sneer that didn't quite come off. His kidneys were still painful.

'Cut out the heroics, son,' I told him. 'You don't have to impress anyone around here. Just listen to your wife and go home.'

'Stuff you,' he answered and walked out with the girl clinging to his arm pleading tearfully with him, her concern and love clearly showing through her distress.

Maybe I should have arrested him. He was guilty of an unprovoked attack on a police officer. But then he was also a member of the security forces, and in his own small way something of a hero. It's not easy to live for weeks on end with your nerves stretched to breaking point and beyond, as the boys in the bush had to if they wanted to stay alive. I considered Koster's behaviour to be a direct result of just that kind of tension and I wasn't about to arrest anyone for it. I knew the conditions they lived under. Possibly I was getting soft, but what the hell. I shrugged and turned back to the party. I had difficulty calming my cops down but managed it finally and when Rawson joked that it was lucky he hadn't been kicked in the crotch just before his marriage, the conviviality returned.

We talked about this and that, bounced the ball of politics around the world settling all the problems en route and drank quite a lot. I found out that Henderson had saved Rawson's life in the final engagement near the Zambezi and that he now jokingly considered it to have been a waste of time.

'Saved him from one kind of terrorist only to hand him over to another. Should have let him die on the Zambezi. At least he would have been at rest,' he shouted across the table. 'No rest after Saturday, Rawson. Still have time to change your mind.'

They were getting canned and I was stone cold sober. By 1900 hours I was ready to leave when the band changed and the sweating waitress brought a menu to the table. She had either tucked the hairs back where they belonged or someone had pulled them out. The crowd had thinned considerably, running out of staying power or money or both. The new band was good, not world class, but after the last one, superb. It must have been a performer's dream of heaven to follow an act like the previous one. A young blonde sang sticky sentiment in a low voice, the air-conditioning plant sucked most of the smoke out of the room and my headache didn't get any worse. I ordered steak tartare from the waitress, hoping the chef was cleaner than she was. She took all the orders and dropped the menu onto the table.

The lights dimmed, the band struck an opening chord and a woman of about thirty-five, dressed as a schoolgirl ran out into the spotlight. She took off her clothes with as much finesse as a rhino in a mud wallow, made love graphically to the floor a couple of times and flopped down on my lap. I grinned at her and flicked my hip. She hit the floor on her backside with enough force to rattle her brain, bounced a few feet, stood up, snarled at me and went away.

My steak arrived and like the whisky, it was surprisingly good. I took a chance and ordered coffee. I lost. The coffee was out of an instant tin. A very cheap instant tin. I pushed it aside and was about to leave when I remembered to ask Rawson what he wanted for a wedding present.

'Hell, sir, I don't know. My fiancée is handling that end.'

'You must have some idea.' I had been to weddings where the happy couple had received fifteen electric toasters and no bread knife.

'I have a vague idea, sir,' said Henderson taking a pen out of his pocket. He flipped over the menu and listed about six items on the back of it.

I slipped it into my pocket, then stood up. 'If you will excuse me, gentlemen.'

I got the usual bull about the night being young, let's go somewhere else, you can't leave a stag party sober and all the rest of it.

'Try to stay out of jail, gentlemen,' I said. 'I may need some of you in the morning.' That shut them up and I walked out.

I jumped into my car, broke the speed limit getting to Cathy's flat, picked her up and we just made the curtain at Reps Theatre.

For the next two hours I watched Anne Frank and her family being hounded by the cruel and relentless Gestapo. Not once did they do anything to help themselves. They hid until they could hide no more, then they went passively into captivity. Not my kind of people. Not my kind of play. Cathy loved it. She cried almost right through it and said afterwards, 'Oh, Rich, that was beautiful. To think of the horror and tragedy those poor people went through.'

Only a woman could call horror and tragedy beautiful. I should have stayed at the Moonraker. If Anne Frank's father had had any guts he would have grabbed a machine-gun and taken some of those Nazi bastards with him. I couldn't see the new style Israelis marching off to the gas chambers like a flock of docile sheep.

'Beautiful,' I answered Cathy and dragged her off to Le Matelot for a nightcap.

Like the Moonraker, Le Matelot is also a nightclub. But there's a world of difference between the two. At Le Matelot the tone is hushed, the floorshow sophisticated and the band very, very good. We watched a naked girl with a thirty-eight inch bust limbo her way under a flaming rod ten inches from the floor, we drank Irish coffee, we danced slowly and dreamily to the muted tones of an alto-sax and I took her home at 0230 hours.

* * *

The sun chased the night away much faster than I did. I dragged myself out of bed, tipped my blend of Inyanga coffee into the percolator and forced myself under the shower, regulating the temperature from hot to icy cold. I stood under it for ten minutes and then used a rough towel, hard. After the second cup of coffee I felt halfway human and took a couple of slices of toast and two cups of coffee into the bedroom.

Cathy had kicked the sheet off and was lying with her arms stretched out above her head, slowly coming awake with the unwritten poetry that belongs only to the truly beautiful. The breeze from the open window swayed the net curtains gently and the rising sun dappled her body with illuminating light and mysterious patches of shadow. I put the tray down and kissed her. Her arms wrapped around me and she drew me down next to her. She didn't have to use much force.

I was half-an-hour late for work. No one noticed.

The SB duty office looked like the aftermath of an Irish wake. It seemed Rawson's stag party had finished up at the station. I didn't care. I was still remembering a halo of fair hair, smokey blue eyes, long sensuous legs and arms with a life of their own. Rawson hadn't shown up and I mentally granted him an unofficial day off. I was in a very good mood.

I walked into my office, shut the door, shed my jacket and pretended to work. It wasn't until ten o'clock when I dug into my jacket pocket for another pack of cigarettes that I found the list of possible presents Henderson had written on the back of the Moonraker menu. It was a toss up between a warming tray and an electric kettle. I put my jacket on and went shopping.

I bought an electric kettle that wasn't more than thirty percent overpriced, and while the sales assistant was gift-wrapping it for me, I began to get the faintest glimmerings of an idea. As I stood watching her finish off the parcel with a fancy satin bow, the fragments began slipping into place and slotting into each other like a line drawing in a TV advertisement. It only needed the typewriter—the final conclusive fact—to cement the whole picture together permanently . . . and maybe, just maybe, I had found it.

'That will be fourteen dollars thirty-five cents, please,' she smiled as she handed over the parcel. 'Wrapping's free.'

Not at that price it wasn't, but I didn't say anything. I paid her, picked up the parcel and walked back to the station. I climbed into my official Austin Cambridge, put the kettle on the seat next to me and drove up to the Forensic Science Laboratory in the grounds of the Police Training Depot. I asked the pert brunette receptionist for Doctor Stanlake.

'One moment, sir,' she said and got busy with the telephone. 'He'll be out in about five minutes. Would you care to take a seat?' She nodded toward a chair.

I sat down and paged through an outdated copy of *Outpost* until it bored me. I lit a cigarette, drank the cup of coffee the brunette brought me, and waited. It is generally the same at the Forensic Lab. The scientific boys get carried away with some experiment and forget everything else.

Once on a previous occasion I had become annoyed with the long wait and had gone looking for someone to complain to. I had opened the wrong door and ruined an experiment it had taken weeks to set up. I had learned my lesson, so now I swallowed my rising impatience and waited. I was lucky—it wasn't more than half-an-hour later that Stanlake came through the door into the reception area.

'Morning, Kelly.'

He was a tall, imposing character with a full head of greying hair, a hawk nose and a stubborn, jutting chin. He looked more like a tough, unscrupulous lawyer out of a Dickens novel than a scientist, and he was brilliant. He had been the first forensic scientist in the world to separate ballpoint pen ink into thirteen different and identifiable components and one certain gentleman with mayhem on his mind had been sentenced to six years' hard labour because of it.

His voice was gruff and curt when he greeted me. It had been his experiment I had ruined and he would be a long time forgetting it.

'Morning, sir.' I didn't smile, it would have been a waste of effort. I took the Moonraker menu out of my pocket and handed it to him. 'Would you run a comparison test on the typing on this with the sample of the Hermes typeface I brought in a couple of weeks ago, please.'

He took the menu card. 'Wait here,' he grunted and stamped out.

This was his castle and he was the king. I waited.

The phone rang on the receptionist's desk. She answered it, looked up at me and said, 'Doctor Stanlake would like you to go through to the lab. Second door on the left along the corridor.'

'Thank you.'

'He said only that door,' she added, the corners of her mouth twitching. I grinned at her and nodded.

I walked into the laboratory and Stanlake indicated an electronic comparison microscope on the bench. 'Take a look.'

I looked. Jackpot! The two specimens matched perfectly. I stepped back. 'The same machine?' I asked, although I knew the answer.

'Yes. I'll let you have a full report on points of similarity by 0900 tomorrow.' He sounded almost happy. 'In the meantime I assure you that there is not the slightest possibility of these two specimens having been typed on different machines.'

'Thank you very much, sir.' I left him with the menu to use in the composition of his report and almost ran out of the laboratory.

'Good luck, inspector,' he called after me. He sounded as if he meant it. Maybe he wouldn't keep me waiting so long next time.

I drove quickly back to the station and walked into Mr Hamilton's office. I gave him a full report on my findings, ending off with the information that Doctor Stanlake would be sending me a written analysis of the comparison in the morning.

'How did you initially connect the Moonraker with this, Mr Kelly?' he asked when I had finished.

'It was so obvious that at first I couldn't see it,' I said. 'Why is the Moonraker the only place in town that never calls the police, never reports drunken behaviour or fights? They put up with all the nonsense the troopies can give them, and that's plenty. In fact they seem to beg for more. It's a perfect system for gathering information. Feed them good booze but at supermarket prices until it's coming out of their ears, send them to bed with a stupid little slut who doesn't know any better, tell her to ease his burdens by being sympathetic and ask her for everything he said about the army afterwards.' I paused as the full impact of my words sank in. 'Hell, what better way of getting information is there? The troopies come back from the bush so gash happy that they are the easiest game there is for any woman with a pair of hot panties.'

'You're assuming that the girls are actively and knowingly involved in this information gathering?'

'Actively involved, certainly. Maybe knowingly as well, but I wouldn't like to say at this stage, sir.'

'But you intend to find out?'

'Yes. I need an ID card from the Municipal Fire Department identifying me as a fire inspector. A complaint from a member of the public alleging the Moonraker is a fire hazard can easily be arranged. That will give me unquestionable entrance to every room in the place.'

Mr Hamilton held out his hand for a cigarette and I gave him one. Ever since he had stopped smoking I was getting through twice as many butts as normal.

'The club opens at 1700 hours, sir, and I would like the card before then, if possible. I would also like a complete report on everyone even remotely connected with the Moonraker, from the floor sweeper to the managing director and any hidden or sleeping partners there may be.'

'Very well, Mr Kelly. I'll have the card for you by this afternoon. The personal dossiers will probably take a little longer, but you'll have them as soon as it can be arranged.' He dismissed me with a wave of my cigarette and was reaching for the telephone as I walked out.

At 1635 hours the municipal fire inspector's card with my photograph on it was delivered to my office by a young policewoman from CID studios. At 1700 hours I was standing in the foyer of the Moonraker talking to the hard-faced chemical blonde behind the cash desk. Her hair had been dyed so often she probably couldn't remember what colour it really was.

'Fire inspection,' I said, flashing the card. 'I'd like to speak to the manager, please.'

She looked me up and down slowly, ran the tip of her tongue across her lips and seemed to be mentally debating if I would taste better with or without salt.

'Today, if you don't mind.' I glared at her. Tough lot, fire inspectors.

She threw me what she thought was a withering look and disappeared through a door behind the desk which was padded with cheap, cracked imitation leather. She came back a couple of minutes later with a tall, willowy character in a dress suit that would have set me back two months' pay. He came towards me with dainty, mincing steps and fluttered his hands effeminately when I told him I wanted to inspect the premises for possible fire hazards. The girls would be safe round this one. They probably borrowed his make-up, too.

'I'm afraid it is absolutely impossible, my dear man,' he said, as waves of very feminine perfume drifted over and nearly choked me. 'We are on the very verge of opening and simply cannot spare the time. You do understand, don't you, dearie?'

From his condescending manner he could have been the maitre d' at Maxims. Perhaps he thought he was. He signalled to someone I couldn't see, and a bouncer came towards us from the direction of the bar. He was big, topping me by at least five inches, with shoulders as wide as a Mack truck, a nose that had been spread all over his face giving him a featureless look and brown eyes that were dull and empty. Apart from his present occupation the only other job he would have been any good at would be between the shafts of a milk cart.

'This gentleman is just leaving,' Pretty Boy said. 'Be a sweetie and show him out, Christopher.'

Christopher! I didn't believe it.

'Look, Mac,' I said to the flouncing manager, 'I don't do this job because I love it. We received a complaint and it's got to be checked out. But suit yourself. I go ahead with the inspection or you don't open tonight. Either way it's no skin off my nose.'

Christopher grabbed me by the shoulder and spun me round. I let him do it, although he left himself wide open and I could have dropped him on the spot. I was playing fire inspector not kung-fu instructor.

'Unless you want the cops swarming all over this joint,' I told Pretty Boy, 'you'd better get this ape off my back.'

Pretty Boy looked annoyed but he waved the bouncer away. Christopher left us looking neither pleased nor disappointed. Just empty.

'Well?' I straightened my jacket.

'This is most inconvenient.' He stamped his dainty, well-shod foot angrily. 'Surely you have to make an appointment before you come barging in like this?'

I didn't answer him but walked over to the pay phone on the wall.

'What are you doing now?' he shrilled.

'Phoning the cops. I've got the authority to close this place down until an inspection has been carried out and, besides, I've taken enough crap from you.'

'No, wait.' His hands drew agitated, girlish circles in the air. 'Oh dear, what would Mr Stanislau do if he were here?'

'I wouldn't know,' I said disinterestedly. 'I don't even know who Stanislau is.'

'He owns these premises and the club. He's away at Victoria Falls at the moment.'

'That's your problem.' I had to shout to make myself heard. The band had started up. 'Do we get started on the inspection or not?'

'Oh, very well.' He tossed his head disdainfully. 'Where would you like to begin?'

'Offices first, then the kitchen and the toilets.' Anything to get away from the racket. The band were tuning their instruments, very loudly and very badly.

I followed him up a steep flight of stairs which led up from the main dining area and along a corridor which ended at a closed, locked door. I knew it was locked because I tried the handle. 'What's through here?'

'That is Mr Stanislau's private entrance. It leads to the building next door. Mr Stanislau owns that as well.'

'You don't say.' I tried to sound impressed. 'He must be pretty rich, hey?'

'Stinking, my dear, absolutely stinking rich,' he said, letting me know I was playing around with the big time.

'Do you have a key?'

'Oh, yes. Mr Stanislau trusts me implicitly.'

'Open it, please.'

He pulled out a bunch of keys and opened the door. I noticed he was wearing a solid gold Patek Philippe on his left wrist. Maybe I was playing around with the big league. You don't get that sort of watch out of a cornflake box.

A passage led away from the door to the head of another staircase going down to street level. There were doors on either side of the passage. This must be where the girls brought their clients. Very convenient. I had no excuse to go through so I stood on the club side while he relocked the door, then I followed him into the office. There were actually two offices, one leading from the other. They appeared worked-in but tidy.

The Hermes was in the second office.

It sat on the desk—blue, modern, efficient and harmless. It just might help to hang someone. I paid no attention to it, but I could feel triumph surge through my body. I looked at Pretty Boy and smiled.

I pulled a few wires, checked the light fittings, grunted and walked down the stairs to the kitchen. I heard the lock snap in the office door as he locked it. No problem. It was an ordinary Union two-lever and I had a master key in my pocket.

The kitchen was long, narrow and had been designed for maximum efficiency. The fittings were old but spotless. The white uniforms worn by the African staff could have been used in an after-shot for a Persil advert. I was impressed.

'Nice kitchen,' I said.

'Yes, it is, rather. I designed it myself, you know.'

'Congratulations,' I said and meant it.

'Thank you.' He lowered his eyes with what he imagined passed for coy modesty.

I poked around looking at gas-pipe connections, played with the light switches and generally tried to give the impression that I knew what I was doing. A few meal orders came in and were executed with speed and economy. If this was Pretty Boy's organisation, he was extremely good at it. I walked over to him and stuck out my hand. 'My name is Richards.' At least that was what it said on the municipal ID card. 'I didn't catch your name.'

He was surprised but let his fingers dangle in my fist for a few seconds. 'George Gretson. My friends call me Georgie. Like in the song, you know,' he simpered.

I could believe it. I wondered why I had suddenly been elevated to the ranks of his friends. Maybe he liked compliments.

'Well, Mr Gretson,' I wasn't hankering to be one of his friends, 'I can see you are a very busy man. I won't take up any more of your valuable time. Just one thing,' I flashed him a conspiratorial wink, 'there's a loose light switch in the office. I won't mention it in my report, but you'd better get it fixed as soon as possible.' There was no loose switch but it amused my childish sense of humour to have Georgie going frantic trying to find one.

'I'll have it attended to first thing in the morning.'

'You run a fine club here, Mr Gretson. Cleanest restaurant kitchen I've seen in years.' Which was true. It was also the only one.

He positively glowed. He put a slim, white hand on my arm and I had to stop myself swatting it off. 'Would you like to stay for a drink and a meal?' He did thrive on compliments. 'On the house, of course,' he added.

I was about to refuse, but changed my mind. It would be a lot easier to open one door than come back when the club was closed and possibly have to open three or four. 'That's very nice of you, Mr Gretson,' I said as he led me to a table next to the sample-sized dance floor.

'We have a new strip act tonight.' He tried to give me a man-to-man look that didn't quite come off. 'I'm sure you'll be enchanted.'

'I'm sure I will,' I said. He ordered me a drink and excused himself.

The crowd and the band were no worse than they had been on the previous night and the steak was, if anything, better. Or maybe it was because I now knew that the cleanliness of the waitresses and the kitchen staff bore no relation to each other. I had VIP service. Georgie had certainly put the word out. The bands changed just in time to save my hearing and the new stripper came on. She shed her clothes with as much interest as a starving whore at a kitchen tea and chewed gum the whole time. She was less sexy than Roy Rogers riding off into the sunset, and from the back she looked like it. The horse I mean.

I drank a lot and slowly began slurring my words. Georgie came over once and I looked glassy-eyed at him.

'S'great. Ever'thin's jus' great,' I leered. He clucked disappointedly and walked away. He didn't come back. Maybe he was shocked.

At about 1945 hours I decided I had played the drunk scene long enough. I clutched awkwardly at a passing waitress. 'Shay, baby. There shomewhere I can get a li'l rest? Can't go home like this. Wife's a bitch. She'll kill me.' I missed the edge of the table with my elbow and spilt half the whisky on the cloth.

'Of course there is, you poor darling.' She put her tray down on an empty table. 'It'll cost you ten dollars, though!'

This was one thing Georgie was not going to pay for, but what the hell, I was on expenses. I dug out a note and gave it to her. She walked over to the bar and came back with a key.

'Up you get, my sweet. Let little Laury help you to a nice soft bed and a little bit of paradise.'

I staggered to my feet and lurched into her, almost knocking her over. 'Who's li'l Laury?' I mumbled.

'I am.' The hard veneer of her smile cracked a little. It must be a hell of a way to make a living.

I let her guide me up the stairs past the offices. She used a key to unlock the door leading to the adjoining building and I followed her into a room leading off the passage. She switched on the light, closed the door, shed her bikini and spread herself on the bed. She didn't even bother to get out of her fishnet stockings or her shoes. She was as inviting as last week's left overs and twice as cold.

'Come on, love,' she said. 'Do hurry up. I have to get back to work.'

'Don' wanna.' I stood swaying at the foot of the bed holding on to the old-fashioned brass rail. 'Wanna sleep. Few minutes, s'all.'

'Don't be silly, darling,' she said, gyrating her pelvis.

She was a pretty little thing. She was someone's daughter and may even have been their pride and joy. But that had been a while ago. I felt like belting her. It was her body and she could treat it in any way she chose, but I didn't have to stand and watch the performance. I staggered over to the side of the bed, shoved her leg out of the way and flopped down on my face.

'Jus wanna sleep, s'all,' I mumbled into the pillow.

She shook my shoulder a couple of times and I snored back at her. She gave up. 'Takes all sorts,' she muttered to herself as she dressed and walked out. At least she was honest. She hadn't tried to lift my wallet, which for her sake was just as well.

I gave her five minutes and sat up quietly. I slipped into the passage and tiptoed to the private entrance. I didn't have to use my master key—little Laury had left the door open. I moved through, closing it gently behind me. I had to use my key on the office door. I went in and locked it from the inside. The lights were off but a flashing Air France sign on top of the opposite building gave me all the light I needed. I took the cover off the Hermes, fed a sheet of paper into the roller and typed a couple of rows of the alphabet in small letters and capitals. I ran through the figures and all the punctuation marks, pulled the paper out of the machine, replaced the cover and left the office, locking the door.

I moved back to the whore's room and was only just in time. I heard the private entrance door open and close softly and the sound of someone moving cautiously in the passage. I eased down onto the bed and lay facing the door. Through my lashes I watched the handle depress slowly and Georgie was suddenly in the room. A very different Georgie. His face was flat and cold like a woman scorned and he had a small automatic pistol in his hand. It looked like a .22-calibre, which figured. Another woman's toy. He came into the room.

'Do sit up, Mr Richards, if that is your name. The time for pretence has passed.'

I snored loudly.

'Oh dear,' he sighed, 'I see we shall have to do this the hard way.'

The shot sounded like a damp cracker going off on a rainy night. I felt the wind of the slug as it tore into the pillow half an inch from my eye. With shooting like that it was no longer a toy. I sat up.

'What the hell do you think you're doing, you bloody lunatic?' I yelled. 'You could have killed me.' I was shaking and very little of it was sham.

'It may come to that yet, Mr Richards,' he said conversationally. 'And there is no need to shout. My hearing is perfectly normal.'

'You're crazy. I'm getting out of here.' I moved towards the door and the pistol cracked again. I looked down in surprise as a thin red trail of blood opened across the back of my left hand. He might have been as queer as a three-humped camel, but he had put in a lot of hours with that pistol and they hadn't been wasted. 'What's the matter with you?' I yelled even more loudly. 'You can't get away with this. I want the police.'

'Do shut up, dearie.' He was beginning to get bored with me.

I opened my mouth to object some more when he pointed a delicate finger up at the ceiling. A light fitting similar to the kind used in art galleries to illuminate paintings nestled in the corner of the ceiling opposite the bed. Only it wasn't a light fitting.

'Closed circuit television, Mr Richards—with video tape recording. It begins operating when the light is switched on.'

There was no point in protesting any further. 'Efficient,' I said. 'Sneaky but efficient.'

'That's not all, sweetie.' He moved to the foot of the bed and unscrewed the ornamental brass knob from the rail. I could see wires trailing from it. It was a well-concealed microphone.

'We like to see and hear what goes on,' he said and fluttered his eyelashes at me.

'Kinky. Must do your education a power of good.'

'Oh yes. You have no idea how inventive some of the girls can be,' he giggled.

'Give you plenty to try out on your boy friend. Or does he try it out on you?' I asked. Georgie didn't like that much, but my fear was fading and I was beginning to get just a little bit annoyed with him.

'Turn round and face the wall,' he snapped.

'Turn my back on you? You've got to be kidding,' I grinned nastily at him.

'Turn round, damn you.' He stamped his tiny foot and his finger tightened on the trigger.

I turned.

'Back off two steps from the wall and lean against it with your fingertips.'

I did as I was told. The classic frisk position. There are three ways to get out of it. All of them dangerous. I stayed where I was. He ran his hand expertly over me, lifted my Smith & Wesson and stepped back.

'My, my. Fire inspectors are the most curious people. Are you normally in the habit of walking around with great big guns, Mr Richards?'

'Self protection,' I said and changed the subject. 'You must pay the girls a hell of a lot to go through all this.'

'Don't be stupid, dearie. They don't know anything about the recordings or the films we make from the video tapes. They'd pee green if they knew how much those films are worth. We have a very select group of clients who pay almost the earth for them. You'd be surprised at the very top names we have on our list.' He giggled again. 'Oh no. The girls don't know anything about it. We simply tell them to leave the light on in case they have any trouble. Don't know what good it would do, but they seem to believe it. They are nothing but stupid sluts,' he said with a trace of hatred. His hormones were more confused than a Chinese jigsaw puzzle.

'You really are a warped, little tit. Aren't you, Georgie Girl?'

He didn't like that very much either and smashed the butt of my revolver down on the back of my outspread left hand. It hurt like hell. I lost leverage on the wall and collapsed. I curled up on the floor with one leg stretched out and the other tucked up in a foetal position, and moaned softly.

'You're far more attractive in that position, Richards. Now, shall we have a little talk?' he enquired girlishly.

I moaned again.

'Come, come, lovey. Nothing's so bad it can't get any worse.' He kicked me in the kidney to demonstrate the point. Not very hard, but it half winded me. With his gun handling and his knowledge of body points, it was obvious someone had taken a lot of trouble over Georgie's training. I wondered just who that someone had been.

'No more,' I croaked. 'Don't hurt me. I'll tell you anything.'

'Just a little one, dearie, to make up for all the nasty things you said about me.' He drew back his foot, his eyes glittering with anticipation as he stared at my exposed groin. His training hadn't been so good after all. From that moment I had him.

As his foot left the ground I jammed my left instep behind his ankle and launched my right heel at his kneecap. I wasn't fond of Georgie Girl, and my heel slammed into him with all the power I had. His knee shot out backwards as the cap broke and the joint dislocated. I felt a savage joy as I saw it happen. He felt quite a lot too. He screamed once, high and loud like an injured horse and passed out.

I stood up, favouring my injured hand. The bullet crease didn't bother me, but my hand was swelling fast and I couldn't move my fingers. I hoped nothing was broken but I wasn't left to worry about it as the door crashed open and Christopher came into the room like a berserk bull buffalo. He must have been monitoring the closed circuit television and I had forgotten all about it.

His shoulder hit me in the stomach and hurled me across the bed onto the floor on the other side and my injured hand lashed against the brass rail in passing. I was winded, pain obscured my vision and I scrambled desperately across the floor to escape Christopher's follow up. I knew I couldn't do it, but I had to try. Nothing happened. I dragged myself to my feet, using the wash basin in the corner for support, and saw why.

Christopher sat on the floor cradling Georgie's head on his lap, and he was crying. Tears of pure grief ran down his cheeks and his shoulders were shaking as he crooned, 'Georgie, Georgie. Speak to me, my love. It will be all right now, Georgie. Chrissie's here now. He'll look after you.'

The poor slob was in love. His voice was as gentle as a rockfall and I suppose I should have felt sorry for him, but I didn't. I took a deep breath, crossed the floor and slammed the edge of my hand into the back of his neck. He went out like a match in water.

I had only one pair of handcuffs and I used them to secure Christopher to the outlet pipe from the basin. I took a sheet off the bed and ripped it into six-foot lengths, then I tied Georgie's spread-eagled body to the four corners of the bed. It was awkward work with only one hand and I was sweating freely by the time I was satisfied he wouldn't work himself loose in a hurry. I picked up my Smith & Wesson and walked out.

There had to be a master control panel for the closed circuit television somewhere close and the logical place for it was in the office. It took me twenty minutes to find it. A solid-looking safe moved slightly when I leaned against it. I pulled at it and it swung easily away from the wall on a pivot. There was a neat locking device attached to the back of it, but Christopher must have forgotten to operate it when he went charging to his lover's rescue. I crawled through the gap it left in the wall and into a darkened cubby-hole of a room. There were five screens set into the wall about head height and three were throwing out a picture. From one of them I could see that Georgie and Christopher hadn't moved. The performances on the other two screens were positively acrobatic. Those young ladies could have taught *Penthouse* magazine a couple of things. The pictures were remarkably clear. Beneath each screen was a tape recorder. It was all highly sophisticated. There must have been a pretty large and slick organization behind the set-up to have installed the equipment let alone brought it into the country. Certainly no legitimate importer or dealer could have been involved.

The recorders beneath the three live screens were revolving slowly. A thin spiral of smoke climbed to the ceiling from a cigarette in the ashtray where Christopher had left it. No wonder they used queers for this operation. Any normal, red-blooded male would have been out of his mind after ten minutes in front of those screens.

I rewound the tape on the machine under the picture of the room I had just left, depressed the erase control and ran it right through. I left it switched off. I crawled out, swung the safe back into position without locking it and went back to the lovers. They hadn't moved, but one of them soon would.

I ripped the two-strand electric cable out of the bedside lamp, split it and bared the ends. I took off one of Georgie's shoes, removed his sock, wrapped one of the bare wire strands round his foot and forced his shoe back on. I switched on the current, holding the other strand in my good hand.

'Come on, my sweet little fairy.' I shook Georgie's shoulder. 'It's time we had that cute little chat you appeared so keen on.'

He didn't respond. He felt boneless. I pushed back an eyelid and saw white, lightly veined. I held the polished, stainless steel back of my watch under his nostrils for a few moments. It didn't cloud over. Georgie wasn't breathing. Which was not surprising. Georgie was dead.

I moved a chair under the closed circuit camera, flipped it open, and then closed it after a few seconds. No one was going to read anything from that exposed video tape. I sat down, lit a cigarette and regarded the late, unlamented Georgie with distaste. He wasn't much of a man but I hadn't expected him to die of shock from a lousy broken kneecap. Alive he had been a possible source of information. Dead he was useless. I had no idea what to do with him. If he had been the boss of the outfit, I wouldn't have minded, but I didn't think he was. And any publicity about his death during a police investigation would screw our chances of nailing whoever was the boss.

Christopher was breathing noisily at my feet, but I didn't think I'd get anything useful out of him. He had nothing between his ears but solid bone.

Finally I decided Georgie would have a tragic accident. Christopher would hole up with his grief somewhere and no one would miss him. The fact that he would be in a room with a steel door and bars on the window would not be publicised.

I stubbed my butt out in the basin and flushed it down the plug hole. I searched around until I found the two expended .22 cartridge cases. I untied Georgie and went through his pockets, finishing up with a gold Dupont lighter and thirty Westbury. Nothing else. I stuffed them back into his pocket, replaced the little .22 in his chamois-leather shoulder-holster, draped him over my shoulder and dumped him in the doorway.

Christopher was out cold and would stay that way for at least another twenty minutes. I removed the handcuffs and dropped them into my pocket. When I moved it would be fast and I didn't want trivial details holding me up. I climbed onto the chair after switching off the light and closed the camera.

By the time I got Georgie Girl to the head of the stairs I was dizzy with pain. I had banged my injured hand against the wall twice and from the agony that shot up my arm I knew something was broken. I got him onto my shoulder, bent my legs and heaved. Georgie hit the stairs about halfway down and every head in the place swivelled towards him as he lazily somersaulted the rest of the way. I shouted in anguish as the body hit the floor. Which was no lie. My hand was giving me hell. It wasn't my fault that fairy club managers tripped over their own dainty little feet going down steps.

I didn't expect the corpse to smash into an African waiter who was preparing a crêpe suzette in traditional style, but that's what it did. The flaming pan flew out of the astonished waiter's hand and into the curtains. The flames were as hungry as the customers. Everyone started screaming at the same time and there was a panic rush for the door. I turned and ran back to Christopher.

I used my arms under his armpits to drag him down the private staircase, and out to my car. No one took any notice of me. The crowd was going frantic trying to get away from the burning club. I cursed my hand as I struggled to get Christopher onto the back seat and finally managed to close the door. I eased the lever into first gear with the heel of my palm and drove away. I had almost reached the main station when I suddenly remembered the Hermes.

I did a screeching one-handed turn and raced back to the Moonraker. But I was too late. The flames were forty-foot high and rising. Two fire engines jerked to a stop in front of me and a uniformed cop came running over.

'Get out of here, mister. You blood seekers make me puke.' He didn't see the man on the back seat.

'Sorry, officer.' I drove away, chastised.

Well what do you know. The Moonraker had been a fire hazard after all. Which didn't help me one little bit. Of all the stupid things I had ever done, leaving that typewriter was in all probability the worst. I would gladly have traded Christopher for it. I mentally kicked my backside all the way to the station.

I called a couple of Charge Office constábles to help me get Christopher out of the car and into the cells where I booked him on a charge of manufacturing obscene material for sale. It was enough to hold him for a couple of days, and by then I would, I hoped, have something far more substantial to throw at him. He regained consciousness as we completed the details and complained of a headache. I told the Cells Detail to give him a couple of aspirin and if that wasn't enough, another belt in the neck. Christopher stopped complaining, and I left.

10

I COULD have received far faster treatment at the General Hospital where they have a doctor on duty all the time, but I wanted to avoid questions about the bullet crease on my hand and, besides, I wasn't very popular at the General. I swung into the drive of the BSAP Camp Hospital in Morris Depot and pulled up behind a camouflaged SAP Land-Rover. I walked through the door and bumped into Dirk in the casualty section.

'What the hell are you doing here?' I asked in surprise as we shook hands.

'Hello, Rich.' He looked sheepish. 'Remember Daisy May?'

'Who could ever forget her?' I said, grinning.

'She gave me the finest dose I've ever seen in my life.' He paused wistfully. 'But it was worth it.'

'Physician heal thyself,' I laughed.

'Easy to say and damn near impossible to do. Have you ever tried to ram a syringe full of penicillin into your own backside?' He looked hurt.

'No, not lately. Anyway, I don't need to. I'm riddled with health.'

'What are you doing here then? And at this time of night?'

'Playing Florence Nightingale. What else?'

'Don't bulldust me. If you want to see Dr Divide you'll have a long wait. He went to Gatooma for a wedding and won't be back until tomorrow afternoon. What's the problem? Maybe I can help.'

I didn't have any spare hours to play with. I held out my hand silently. It was very swollen and the bullet crease stood out like a wet, red river bed in the desert. Dirk examined it briefly and looked up.

'That's a bullet wound.'

'So?'

'So you must move in charming circles.' He squeezed my hand gently and I felt the sweat spring out on my forehead. 'That hurt?' he asked.

'Only when you laugh,' I said through my teeth.

'Move your fingers.'

'Yeah. And for my next party trick I'll ride a porcupine bare-back.'

'Something's broken,' he said as he stood up. 'Let's see what it is.'

I followed him through to the office. A male state registered nurse was busy writing a report. I didn't get up to the hospital very often and I didn't know him. Dirk introduced us. 'Rich, Mike.' We shook hands.

'I need an X-ray on this hand,' Dirk said. 'Can do?'

Mike nodded and we trooped through into the X-ray room. He took five or six shots and told us to wait in casualty while he developed them. Dirk walked out to his Land-Rover and came back carrying a bottle of Johnnie Walker Black Label.

'Special stuff,' he grinned. 'Reserved for special occasions.' He knew I wouldn't tell him what had happened to my hand and he didn't bother asking. He found a couple of glasses in the small ward which led off the casualty section and the bottle of whisky was a long way from full when Mike brought the developed plates out to him.

'Fractured metacarpal,' Dirk said after examining the negatives. 'Nothing serious.'

'Not to you,' I replied.

He put a thick gauze dressing over the bullet crease. 'I don't want you getting blood poisoning again. You're running out of hospitals.' He dropped a couple of plaster of Paris bandages into a bowl of hot water.

'Make it a heavy cast.'

'Why? You want to hit someone with it?'

'I just might.'

He went out to the Land-Rover again and came back with two thin strips of lead. 'Old battery plates. I use them for making fishing sinkers.'

He set and bandaged my hand, placing the lead strips along the outer edge of my palm away from the broken bone. 'Try not to hit anyone for a couple of hours. I don't want to have to reset your hand.' He took a sip of his drink. 'And I didn't put that lead in there. I'm supposed to save life, not help take it.'

We walked out to the carpark after I had thanked Mike, and as Dirk climbed into the Land-Rover I told him to give Daisy May my love.

'I'll give her my own.' He held up a phial of penicillin. 'In a couple of weeks. After I've rammed this into her.' He laughed and pulled away.

I drove back to the station, bummed a cup of coffee in the Information Room and took it up to my office. I telephoned Mr Hamilton and gave him a full report on the evening's events.

'You're a menace, Kelly! You leave a trail of destruction behind you like Kitchener marching through the Transvaal.' He did not sound pleased. 'The only possible lead you have left is Stanislau. Charter a plane from Skywork and fly up to the Falls. I'll arrange for the member-in-charge there to meet you and book you into the same hotel as Stanislau. Stick with him and try to leave some of the Falls Township standing.' He took a deep breath. 'Have you read the report on Stanislau yet?'

I picked up the red folder with the black cross that was lying on my desk. 'STANISLAU, PJ' was typed neatly in the top left hand corner.

'No, sir.' It had arrived after I had left my office. 'I'll read it on the plane.'

'Do that. Keep me informed and good luck, Mr Kelly.' The phone went dead.

I used my battery-shaver while I contacted the twenty-four hour Skywork Charter Service at Mount Hampden Airport, about ten miles from the city. I finished shaving, took six hundred dollars from my safe and got a B-car to drive me to my flat, where I picked up a suitcase, and then out to Mount Hampden Airport.

At 0025 hours we took off in a twin-engined Cessna. I spread the Stanislau file across my lap and fell asleep.

The pilot reached back and wakened me just before he began his descent towards Victoria Falls Airport. I looked at my watch. It was 0300 hours.

I thanked the pilot as he handed my bag down from the Cessna and walked across the dark apron into the dimly-lit airport terminal. There were no immigration or customs officials on duty and the baggage counters looked lonely and neglected as I passed them. Perhaps they only came to life to greet the hordes of tourists from all over the world who jammed the airport buildings every time a scheduled flight landed. Then it would be colour and life and excitement as people flocked to see one of the seven wonders of the world. A fall of water that dwarfed Niagara and conjured up visions of great romance and glory. But now the buildings were dark and deserted, looking ominous in the black night setting and I felt the fairy fingers of apprehension playing up and down my spine. I suppressed my ridiculous emotions and walked to meet a young uniformed patrol officer who stood waiting for me near the main entrance.

'Detective Inspector Kelly?'

I nodded. Stupid twit, who else was he expecting at 0300 in the morning? I was tired, dirty and in no mood to be civil to a young cop who thought he was playing a role in a James Bond movie. This one had a definite 007 gleam in his eyes.

'I have transport waiting outside, sir,' he said excitedly. He was prancing around like an anxious young puppy and I expected him to jump up at me any minute. I let him take my bag and followed him out to the grey police Land-Rover in the carpark. A constable with a shotgun greeted me courteously from the back as I settled myself uncomfortably on the hard slab of a seat. I grunted a reply.

I lit a cigarette I didn't want and sat morosely watching the headlights consume the black tar of the road as we drove towards Victoria

Falls Township. The patrol officer tried to talk to me for the first couple of miles, but gave up and concentrated on his driving when he received no response from me. He looked hurt.

It wasn't a premonition or fear or anything I could put a name to. It was just a feeling of vague apprehension that would not leave me alone, and I didn't like it. I forced it down but could not get rid of it entirely. I flicked my butt out of the window and closed my eyes.

Finally, we pulled up outside the police station, or Pete Station as it was known locally. There were seven European police officers stationed in Vic Falls and six of them were Peters. The PO led the way to Pete Fuller's office and opened the door for me.

'Mr Kelly is here, sir.' He didn't sound as impressed as he had been at the airport.

I walked through the door and dumped my bag on the floor. Pete Fuller was forty-five years old, balding, fat and sloppy. He had been an inspector for the last ten years and it was as far as he would ever get. He knew it and he didn't care. He was despised by his superior officers with an intensity that was matched and probably exceeded by the loyalty and reverence of his subordinates. If you worked under him and did a good job, he told you so. If you fouled up he kicked your backside and forgot about it. If you were in trouble he helped you out. If you were an officer he told you to get knotted. Not that he disliked every officer. There were exceptions in his book, but as far as he was concerned it was the principle that counted. One had to be consistent. And Pete Fuller was nothing if not consistent. He also happened to be a pretty good cop.

He was dressed in a pair of rumpled, khaki police shorts and a loud floral shirt that would have had a Yank tourist reaching for his wallet. He had a pair of rubber Bata slops on his feet which were propped up on the desk.

'Rich, you old rascal. How the hell have you been, boy?' He waved in the direction of a small fridge in the corner. 'Beer's over there. Get me one while you're at it, mine's about finished.' He beamed at me over the rim of the can.

'At this time of the morning? I'll settle for a cup of coffee.' I grinned back at him. It was good to see him again.

'Coffee!' he bellowed like a gut-shot buffalo. 'There isn't any coffee on the station. Keeps you awake, you know. What would happen to our reputation if someone walked into the Charge Office and found everyone awake. Hell, the public would lose all faith in us.'

He tossed the empty can over his shoulder without looking and it landed in the waste basket in the corner. I wondered how long it had taken him to perfect that throw. I gave up and opened two beers.

Fuller tossed a green Sudden Death Docket cover across the desk to me.

'What do I want with an SDD, you drunken bum?' I asked.

'Security, Rich. Security,' he growled like a 1930s Hollywood gangster. 'No one reads SDDs. Too boring. Best place to hide classified information. You never know who has a key to the safe. Besides, it was handy when I finished the report on Stanislau. What the hell have you done to your hand?'

'I broke a bone.'

'No! I thought you were wearing a cast just for fun. How did you do it?' He drained the beer and the can followed the first one into the basket.

'I fell down some steps.'

'Ha,' he grunted disbelievingly, but didn't push it. 'How about another beer?'

'Get it yourself,' I grinned. 'You look as if you could use the exercise.'

I flipped open the docket cover and read:

STANISLAU PJ

Arrived Vic Falls flight RH 828 Monday 18/12/72 1100 hrs.
Accompanied by efa STELLA RANDALL and ema GERALD (JOHNNY) HART—both subjects of Special Gazette 13/7/70 re IDB. Salisbury CR 233/5/70 refers.
STELLA RANDALL using name SHEILA STANISLAU.
GERALD HART using name PETER BRADSHAW.
Subjects booked into Victoria Falls Hotel; one double room for

STANISLAU and RANDALL (No 127); one single room for HART (No 129).
Since arrival subjects have followed same daily routine: Coffee in rooms at 0815 hrs. Breakfast at 0915 hrs. All three then proceed to hotel swimming pool until 1200 hrs.
Lunch.
STANISLAU and HART take launch trip to Kandahar Island every afternoon. RANDALL remains at hotel.
Dinner 2100 hrs at Casino Hotel, then all three proceed to casino.
STANISLAU plays roulette.
RANDALL and HART play blackjack.
All gambling appears to be financed by STANISLAU.
All three return to Vic Falls Hotel at 0200 hrs approx.
STANISLAU has hired a BMW registration 60-874R, but uses it at night only between the two hotels. Uses tourist transport during the day.

P FULLER INSP. 4772
0200 hrs 21/12/72
VICTORIA FALLS.

A copy of the gazette, with photographs of Randall and Hart clipped to it, was attached to the report. The gazette told me that they were thirty-four and forty years old respectively.

I looked up as Fuller put a beer down next to my elbow. 'Thanks, Pete. This is all I need for the moment.' I pushed the beer away. 'That, I don't need.' I didn't ask him how he had obtained the information at such short notice. He could not have had more than a couple of hours to do it, and it would have offended his pride if I had asked. Vic Falls was his town and he knew virtually everything that went on in it.

'No stamina,' he said and hooked the beer across to his side of the desk. 'The first qualification of an officer. I don't hold out much hope for your future.'

'If I make superintendent, you haven't got a future,' I retorted. 'What transport have you arranged for me?'

'Avis BMW. A white one. It's outside.' He tossed the keys

across the desk to me. 'Try not to wreck it. I had to wake the Avis manager to get hold of it. Lucky he's a friend of mine.'

'Who isn't? Did you get a room for me at the hotel?'

'Yeah. Number one-thirty-five. It's the closest I could swing to Stanislau.'

'Thanks, Pete.' I picked up the docket and my bag and headed for the door. 'I'll check with you later today.'

'Rich.'

'Yes?' I turned to face him.

'All I know of what's going on is the little Hamilton told me over the phone when he woke me up, and at the moment I don't want to know any more.' His chubby face was suddenly hard and there was no mirth in his eyes. He no longer looked like a fat joke. 'But if anything happens that could even remotely affect the safety of anyone, and I mean anyone, in my area, I want to know before it happens, not afterwards. Clear?'

'Sure, Pete. You know damn well I'll fill you in on any details which could affect you, so don't pull your hard-eyed act on me.'

'Just to get the record straight, boy. That's all.'

'Bull. You know me better than that.'

I walked out.

Damn the rivalry that exists between the uniformed and plain-clothed cops. Sure there were things I knew that I would not share with Fuller, and they wouldn't affect him in the slightest way. Things he didn't have to know. Information that would be completely useless to him. Hell, I didn't go snooping in his Crime Register. The need to know. Curiosity killed the cat and all that manure. For God's sake, we're all on the same police force, and we spend more time fighting each other than crime. Screw it.

The car was a BMW 2800 and a beauty, but I was too tired to enjoy it. I booked into the hotel via a sleepy night clerk, and ordered coffee. The crisp, cool sheets felt good against my body and I fell asleep before the coffee came.

* * *

The telephone rang shrilly. I cursed it before remembering that I had requested a call at 0800. The four hours' sleep I had seemed like four minutes.

I answered the telephone and asked for a large pot of coffee, then stood under the cold shower for five minutes and tried not to get the cast on my hand wet. My hand throbbed painfully. I snapped on the radio and listened to some idiot tell me what a beautiful day this was going to be. He should have been able to see it from where I stood. His false cheerfulness irritated me and I switched him off in mid-sentence. I dressed in casual slacks and shirt, not unpacking anything else in case Stanislau took off for Salisbury when he heard about the fire, if he hadn't already.

It was 0825 and according to Fuller's report I had fifty minutes before Stanislau was due in the dining-room. I poured out a cup of coffee, fired up my first cigarette of the day and settled down with the file I should have read on the plane.

Stanislau had been born in Pest in Hungary in July, 1934, which made him thirty-eight years old. He had gone through both junior and high schools as an average scholar and had been attending the University of Budapest when the Hungarian Revolution had erupted to sear the consciences of the Western world. He had apparently been one of the leaders of a student revolutionary movement and had been forced to run, getting out of Hungary just ahead of the KGB. He had begged his improverished way around Europe for a while, mainly in Austria, before settling in South Africa, where he opened and managed a very successful restaurant specialising in Hungarian dishes. He emigrated to Rhodesia early in October of 1970 and before the year had ended he had opened the Moonraker. Six months later he purchased the premises in which the club was situated and the adjoining building. The combined purchase price of the two properties had been $390 000. He had paid an initial sum of $180 000 and had obtained a Central Africa Building Society bond to cover the outstanding balance. Apart from this bond and monthly trade creditors he had no outstanding debts, paid his accounts promptly and was considered to be a rising star in the business world. He had no criminal record, associated with no undesirables, was a member of the Salisbury Police Field Reserve and lived in his own house in the suburb of Highlands.

I tossed the file onto the bed and stared out of the window toward the Zambian border, considering Stanislau. His rise from penniless Hungarian refugee to respected Rhodesian businessman had been meteoric. According to the file he had brought seven thousand rand into Rhodesia in October, 1970, and by June, 1971, had been able to put up $180 000. Calculated on a monthly basis, that averaged out at $30 000 net per month. I didn't believe it. The Moonraker sure as hell was not showing that kind of return, and if his pornographic films were pulling in that kind of loot I was in the wrong business. He had to be receiving his backing from somewhere. I was becoming very interested in Mr Stanislau. Very interested indeed.

I picked up my old 35mm Pentax and walked down to the dining-room. The Vic Falls Hotel had undergone a remarkable facelift since my last visit. The building had been repainted inside and out, the corridors were carpeted in soft shades of green and paintings by Thomas Baines and other recorders of early Rhodesiana hung in profusion. The general effect was restful and pleasing. Pretty young girls wearing yellow uniforms and happy Southern Sun smiles flitted around pampering tourists and seemed genuinely pleased if they could render any service or assistance. The whole atmosphere made me wish regretfully that I was on holiday and not at Victoria Falls to kill someone. Because if I found that Stanislau was involved in this suppurating mess, he would die and to hell with the consequences, Mr Hamilton and the courts. I had had the grotesque dream about the Ronson children again during the night and my mood was slightly sour.

I wasn't particularly hungry, but I went into the dining-room anyway. The headwaiter asked my room number and showed me to a table near the entrance to the kitchen. Possibly my clothes and my old Pentax didn't impress him as belonging to the kind of person who would be lavish with his tips. Or it might have been my face or my accent. In any event he could not have done better if I had paid him for it. I had an almost grandstand view of the dining-room and the noise from the kitchen didn't bother me in the least.

As I sat down an overfed, red-faced Hollander a couple of tables away began giving a waiter hell at the top of his guttural voice because the milk for his cereal was hot when he had ordered it warm.

'Vot de matter mit you ploody peoples? Not understood English, isn't it?' he shouted and pushed the silver milk jug away from him. 'Take avay dis and brong varm, understanding? Varm not hot.'

The waiter shrugged his shoulders with a contempt he didn't bother to conceal, picked up the jug and walked past me into the kitchen. The joys of the tourist industry. I grinned at him as he passed and he shot me a look of humorous despair.

The dining-room was about half-full of happy, noisy holiday-makers dressed in everything from almost nothing at all to the latest trends. They looked out of place in the rich, elegant surroundings. So did I if it came to that.

I jammed the fork between the plaster cast and the palm of my hand and was attempting to control an elusive chipolata long enough to cut it, when I looked up and saw them.

Stella Randall compared to her gazette photograph the same way a mother of five preparing breakfast in her curlers compared to her twenty-year-old daughter going out in the evening on a heavy date. The resemblance was there, but they were different people.

Police photographs are generally even worse than cheap passport shots. Subjects are usually lined up in front of harsh, glaring floodlights after a night in the cells and before they have been permitted to shave, comb their hair, put on their make-up or whatever else they would normally do before exposing themselves in public, the shutters snap and a picture which seldom portrays the subject accurately is officially stamped and placed in the file.

In her photograph Stella Randall looked like a raddled whore who had been on her back for ten days and lived on gin. The woman that walked past my table was a sloe-eyed, redheaded beauty with a skin ivory-smooth and just beginning to show a gentle touch of the sun. She was wearing a white towelling wrap that just reached down to cover her buttocks, setting off long, lovely legs. She flowed past me and every man over sixteen watched her hungrily as a waiter pulled out a chair for her. She had the most startling green eyes I had ever seen. They caught the light like fresh-cut, flawless emeralds and added another dimension to her sensuousness. Stella Randall was a doll. She was every man's dream of a woman and every woman's dream of herself.

After a while I got around to studying the two men with her. Johnny Hart looked what he was. A cheap crook with dead, black hair, pock-marked face and a broken nose—and just enough brain to maintain his position in the lower middle ranks of the criminal sewer. He was wearing a green tracksuit top over red swimming trunks. When he reached across the table for the butter I could see the bulge of a pistol butt outlined against the material. In his forty years, he had been arrested eleven times and convicted on four occasions. He had served a total of six years in prison.

The only way I could place him in the group was as a bodyguard. He didn't belong with them any other way, although he had taken a fall with Stella for illicit diamond buying a few years previously. Stella had been using him as a runner and it was pure chance that she had been on the scene when the police trap had been sprung. They both drew two years and both served sixteen months, but Stella had been running the show.

I wondered briefly if she still was, but then I knew that she couldn't be when I switched my study to Stanislau, and found a wolf. In capitals. The short hairs on the back of my neck began to prickle and I could almost smell the gunsmoke and sudden death above the savoury breakfast aroma.

He was around six foot in height with the narrow waist and heavy shoulders of a man who kept himself in shape. His high cheekbones and finely-chiselled nose held traces of his Slavic origin. The whole suave assurance of the man was completed by prematurely-greying brown hair set off by an expensive-looking suntan. He wore a tight-fitting cream, silk shirt and, like the other two, a swim suit. He wasn't armed as far as I could see—not unless he carried a toy similar to the late and fast-decomposing Georgie Girl. Not unless he carried it stuck down the front of his trunks, and he didn't look that stupid. In fact he looked anything but stupid.

There was nothing to set Stanislau apart from any other successful businessman on holiday. Nothing but my jangling nerve ends. He carried the invisible aura of violence and evil around his shoulders like a mantle. This one had been over the hill and back again more than once. Tough guy Johnny Hart faded into the woodwork. Stanislau was the he-wolf in this pack and he would be in just about any other. Yet nothing showed. He smiled pleasantly at the occupants of the nearby tables, was polite to the waiters and gave the impression of a man at peace with the world and satisfied with his position in it. Maybe he was. But he wouldn't be for long, not if I was right about him. I pushed the rest of my breakfast away and walked out of the dining-room.

After changing into a pair of trunks I spread my towel out on a foam rubber mattress at the edge of the swimming pool. The days on the farm with Cathy had left me with a dark even tan and the sun wouldn't bother me. The view was magnificent. The Zambezi gorge stretched away toward the Falls like the monstrous sabre cut of an enraged giant and the railway bridge in the distance was a futile suture spanning the gorge in a lonely and vain attempt to bind the continent together, the black north to the right and the white south to the left. The heavy mist-cloud of spray hung in the sky behind the bridge like a shroud of doom, and my apprehension was back with me, unbidden and fullborn.

A young couple found a spot for themselves under a tree, laid out towels and switched on a transistor radio. You don't get away from it all, these days. You take it all with you. The ten o'clock newscast had just begun when Stanislau, with Stella hanging onto his arm and laughing, strolled past. The duty announcer gave a full report of the Moonraker fire: the manager of the club had tripped on the stairs and crashed into a waiter who had been preparing crêpe suzettes in a flaming frying pan and the flames had ignited the curtains. The overhead sprinkler system had failed to function and the manager, Mr George Gretson, had died in the fire which had completely gutted the club and the adjoining building. Damage had not yet been estimated but was believed to run into hundreds of thousands of dollars. Several people had been treated for shock, but as far as was known at this stage Mr Gretson was the only fatality.

I was one hell of a fire inspector. I hadn't even noticed the overhead sprinkler system.

Stanislau heard it all but gave the report as much attention as a fly in someone else's soup. It was obvious that he already knew about it. One of his employees in Salisbury must have been on the phone to him as soon as it happened. So why the hell was he lounging around a swimming pool in Victoria Falls instead of hurrying back to the city to sort out all the problems which surely demanded his urgent attention? Either he didn't give a damn, which was impossible, or he had far more urgent reasons for remaining where he was. Just what those reasons were I could not figure. Hell, he should have been going frantic trying to book a reservation on the next plane out. But he wasn't.

He stripped off his shirt and did thirty quick press-ups on the lawn. He looked in good shape—not the bodybuilding class, but his muscles rippled easily under his skin. He dived into the pool and swam a fast, professional twenty lengths and wasn't panting when he flipped himself out of the pool and dried off with a towel Stella handed him.

The young couple with the radio were arguing in harsh and bitter undertones. The young man could not take his eyes off Stella and the girl with him knew it. Eventually she grabbed her towel and stormed off in the direction of the hotel building, every line of her body and each movement radiating anger. The young man stayed where he was. I didn't envy him the task of consoling his girl when he finally got round to it.

I splashed around in the shallow end of the pool and did a little one-armed paddling, but it was no fun having to keep the cast out of the water, and no matter how I tried it got wet. Eventually I gave up and used the steps to climb out of the water.

She was brunette, about twenty-five or -six, wearing a bikini small enough to get her a six-month sentence on Clifton Beach and she was lying on my towel. She was reading, or pretending to read, my copy of James Joyce's *The Thin Red Line* and smoking one of my cigarettes. She was also very easy to look at. She didn't turn her head as I sat down on the grass next to her.

'Have you ever heard of the treatment claim jumpers in the old Yukon could expect?' I asked her casually.

'Possession is nine tenths of the law.' Her low, husky voice reminded me of Julie London. She turned a page without looking up.

'Might is right,' I quoted back.

'But you only have one hand.' She dropped the book and turned to face me, pointing at the cast. 'Half your might is out of action.'

'The other half isn't.'

'I would hate people to think I took advantage of a one-handed man.' She would have had a nice laugh if it hadn't sounded a little false and forced.

'One hand is all I'll need.'

I reached out and jerked the mattress from under her. She slid off onto the grass and sat there with surprise and indignation chasing each other across her face in successive waves. She gave the impression of wanting her own way most of the time and was attractive enough to get it. It had been a long time since any man had controlled her scene and it showed in her blazing eyes.

I straightened out the mattress, settled down comfortably and lit a cigarette. The brunette stood up, dusted off her injured pride, and as she walked away I caught her ankle. She stopped and glared at me.

'Hi there,' I smiled. 'What's a delightful young lady like you doing walking around by herself in a setting like this?'

'You . . . you . . . ' She had lost her laugh. 'Let me go. You . . . '

She seemed to be having trouble with her vocabulary and was straining her foot against my hand. I let her go. The release of pressure caught her by surprise and she bounced down on her cute little rump again.

'You . . . you utter . . . ' There were real tears in her eyes when I interrupted her.

'Please stop referring to me as "you . . . you . . . " It's undignified and people will start to talk. They may even think we're married.'

'You utter bastard!' She finally got it out with enough vehemence to prove that she meant it.

'Denied. With a certificate to back me up.' I held out my hand. 'Kelly. Richard Kelly.'

Somewhere in her past there reposed a good education and a well brought up young lady. Reluctantly she shook my hand. 'Madeline Hayward.' She realised I was still holding her hand and jerked it away. 'But I don't want to know you.'

'Why not? I'm lonely and need a friend. Aren't you the friendly type?'

'What the hell do you think I was trying to be when you threw me off that mattress?'

'Sit down and let's try to figure it out.'

She gave me a long look then the beginnings of a smile played across her mouth. She dragged a spare mattress over and settled down next to me.

I grinned at her. 'Hi, Madeline.'

'Don't call me Madeline.'

'Okay, Hayward.'

'Don't call me Hayward either.'

The whole of Vic Falls to choose from and I end up with a nut. 'I just love mysterious women,' I sighed.

'Call me Anne. It's my middle name and I simply can't stand the other two.'

'Hi, Anne.'

'Hi, Richard. Or do your friends call you Dick?'

'No.'

'No what? Your friends don't call you Dick or you don't have any friends?'

'My friends call me Rich.'

'Are you?'

'Am I what?'

'Rich.'

'You mean money-in-the-bank rich?'

'Yes.'

'No.'

'Good. Hi, Rich.'

Enough of this and I would be as crazy as she was, but she turned out to be a very nice young lady and she was pleasant company once the name business had been sorted out.

She was also necessary company, and our meeting was a stroke of luck. Anyone alone in a place like Victoria Falls could attract attention, and that I didn't need. I needed every bit of cover possible, and if Anne provided it, I wasn't about to start complaining. The fact that she was easy to look at was an added bonus.

I got her to pose for some photographs beside the pool. I took a couple, then manoeuvered her in front of Stanislau and Stella. She was about fifteen feet in front of them and completely out of focus. I even caught Hart in the background still wearing his track-suit top. The day was glorious but he couldn't take advantage of it. You can't go swimming at Victoria Falls wearing a shoulder holster. It tends to upset the other patrons.

At 1130 hours an African band that made more noise than music began performing on the terrace. The din they produced would not have been out of place in a foundry. The tourists loved it. It was as close to the real Africa as Pluto and twice as loud. It stank.

Stanislau and Stella walked up to the main building while Hart picked up the towels and followed about twenty yards behind.

I changed, met Madeline Anne Hayward in the foyer and took her in to lunch.

The head waiter seemed impressed with my rise in status and tried to give us a table away from the kitchen door. He looked disgusted when I insisted on my old table. Oscar Peterson's rendition of *My Fair Lady* fought a hopeless rearguard action from the overhead speakers against the screeching wails of the African band on the terrace. I wondered why the management didn't shut one or other up, preferably the band.

'Are you married, Rich?' Anne asked pensively. Her bantering mood had gradually undergone a change during the meal and she sat softly clinking the spoon against the side of her coffee cup. She looked sad, lonely and a little lost.

'No. But not far off,' I said. 'What happened to the sunshine girl I brought in to lunch?'

'She's just remembered she's married. And she feels like a bitch.'

She dropped the spoon into the saucer and looked up at me. 'Is she a bitch?'

'I wouldn't know, girl. I look across the table and see a charming young lady with a nice smile and beautiful eyes who was friendly enough to join me for lunch. It doesn't necessarily follow that she's a bitch.'

'But I am. I deliberately picked you up. You must know that.'

'Wrong, Anne. You tried. Remember? You were ready to call a cop or kick my teeth in when I picked you up.' I grinned at her. 'I'm better at it than you are. More practice.'

She held up her left hand with the back towards me and her fingers spread. 'Tell me, what do you see?'

'A hand.'

'Is that all?'

'And fingers without rings.'

'How did you know?'

'You told me you were married, girl. It's usual for married women to wear them.'

'That's right. It is, isn't it? And do you know where mine are? Upstairs in my room in the dressing table drawer right at the back. And do you know why I'm not wearing them?'

'Because you're putting on weight and they hurt,' I said with a smile, trying to jockey her out of the despondent mood she was building up for herself. It didn't work.

'I've been married for five years. And the magic has gone. Poof. Just like that. You wake up one morning and there's suddenly nothing left. Only the routine, nothing but the bloody routine. I don't even have to cook the breakfast anymore. We have enough servants to staff a medium-sized hotel. So it's tennis and bridge and riding all day and every damn day. And a passionate peck on the cheek when Owen comes home from the office. And he doesn't even notice the new hairdo or the low neckline and it's all such a ridiculous waste of time. The hours you spend making-up in an effort to ignite just one tiny spark of the fire. You stand there wishing he'd take you, right then and right there. On the lounge floor or the kitchen table, anywhere, and you wouldn't care if the whole damn world was watching. Your mind screams and your body aches with wanting him, and he goes outside to feed his stupid pigeons.'

She wasn't hysterical. The words followed each other in flat, toneless succession. It had been a long time since she had confided in anyone. The dam of her pent-up emotions had burst and she couldn't stop the flood. She needed to talk and I didn't interrupt.

'That's when I realised the only time he wanted me was after a few drinks or when the TV packed up and he had nothing to read. A kind of fill-in entertainment. And do you know what I did?'

I shook my head silently. She didn't notice. Her eyes were blank and distant.

'I stood naked in front of the mirror and I thought I looked pretty good and if I was a man I would want to take me to bed. But I couldn't be certain. So I told Owen I needed a break. I packed my bags and came to Vic Falls. To get laid.' Her shoulders slumped and she was dejected but relieved. 'So now you know. Madeline Anne Hayward. Bitch. That's all there is in the book.' She finally raised her eyes. They were misty and it wouldn't have taken much for the tears to start. 'Sorry. Did I bore you?'

'Yes, Anne, you did. What the hell do you think a man's made of? Your only thought seems to be to tart yourself up in a vain attempt to excite your husband, when he probably works with a dozen sexy women all day long. He's been surrounded by fancy hairdos and low necklines for at least eight hours before he comes home to you. And you still expect him to notice yours, for God's sake. Of course you should look nice for him, but the world doesn't revolve on sex, girl, no matter what anyone says. You want to capture your husband's interest, wake him up to the fact that you're still alive? Try feeding his stupid pigeons for him before he gets home. He'll notice you. No other woman in the world could do it for him. It makes you unique and is worth all the fancy French underwear ever produced. A man can find a hell of a lot of outlets for his libido, but he doesn't think with it. Sure, by offering your body you could hold his interest for an hour a day for a month. The next month it would be an hour a week and in a couple of years, if your only talent was on your back, you'd be lucky if you could hold his interest for longer than fifteen seconds at a stretch. And those stretches would be very infrequent. Involve yourself with him, make his interests yours. Become part of him. An indispensable part. It isn't easy, but once you've done it he'll be so hungry for you, you'll be taking a break to get away from sex, not to find it.'

'Are you finished, Mr Kelly?' Her tone was cold and impervious.

'No, dammit, I'm not. Look around you. Most of the men in here would give two years' pay to climb between the sheets with you right now. You're an exceptionally attractive woman. But none of them could satisfy or reassure you. All you'd wind up with would be a feeling of cheap filth you could never wash away. And you'd still have your hangup.

'It sometimes happens, though, that a married woman meets a man and the formula is right and they make love. But it has nothing to do with love. It's just a mutual physical attraction that draws two possibly incompatible people together for a short while. And when it's over there are no regrets, no recriminations and no remorse. Yet they've given something special to each other, and on occasion the marriage is better off because of it.

'But don't wholesale it, Anne. There's a big difference between being desirable and being available. You have to wait for the moment to find you.'

'Wow!' She was sitting straight up and the corners of her mouth twitched.

'Yeah, wow.'

'You mean I'm normal and not a bitch? Or am I a normal bitch?'

'Just normal. With fears, frustrations and passions like everyone else.'

'You too?'

'Me too.' I stood up. The amateur counselling had gone on for too long. 'Come on, let's go and gawk at the Falls.'

11

THE zebra-striped United Touring Company bus left the hotel at 1430 hours. Anne and I had a seat near the front exit; Stanislau and Hart were two rows behind us on the opposite side of the centre aisle. The uniformed hostess began her running commentary as soon as the bus left the hotel grounds. I paid no attention to her. I shifted my position slightly and the glass panel behind the driver gave me a perfect reflected view of Stanislau. He appeared to be following the commentary with avid interest.

I couldn't figure it out. I knew he had taken the same trip five times in the last five days and he could probably have recited the entire script backwards. He could afford to see the Falls in private, air-conditioned luxury, but he chose to surround himself with sweating, over-fed, under-clothed, loud-mouthed tourists. He didn't strike me as the package tour type, and definitely not the same tour for five consecutive days.

The bus stopped in the carpark of the Casino Hotel for another batch of tourists, then took us onto the bridge over the gorge which marks the border between Rhodesia and Zambia. We all climbed out and I dutifully snapped the shutter of my Pentax along with the other passengers. Stanislau did the same, and if this was his routine behaviour he would wind up with so many photographs of the Falls he'd have to hire a truck to take them away. Or possibly there was no film in his camera. It was something to think about. Hart did nothing. He just stood in the sun looking bored. He wouldn't know beauty and grandeur from a kick in the head. He was a backstreet city slob and he looked more out of place than a Chinese general at the UN. He had an expensive black leather Leica sling-bag about twelve inches square hanging from his shoulder, but he never bothered to take any photographs. I wondered why he went to the trouble of lugging it around. Maybe it was just for local colour. I forgot about it.

The actual Falls were not visible from the bridge but the roar of millions of gallons of water, smashing onto the rocks hundreds of feet below the lip to come hurtling through the gorge below us with awesome speed, was strangely disquieting. The gorge was deep and wide but seemed almost too small to contain the water's fury and power.

The hostess pointed out the carcass of a dead buffalo which had fallen into the gorge that morning and lay at the water's edge far below us. At this distance it was just an unidentifiable black smudge but we all obediently pointed our cameras at it. Without at least a 1 000 mm telephoto lens it would come out as nothing more than a flyspot on my slide. The fact that the carcass was still there was an indication of the ruggedness and inaccessibility of the gorge. If there had been any way to reach it, that carcass would have been butchered and eaten hours ago. Even the vultures would not venture into the depths of the gorge and it is a rare event in Africa for any dead animal to rot and decompose with nothing but the elements and ants for company. Not even crocodiles could survive that furious torrent.

We climbed back into the bus and the next stop was the reconstructed, authentic Matabele village. We were herded through by an African guide who spoke perfect English and was as bored as Hart. With Anne next to me I kept just behind Stanislau. What was the bastard up to? He was the perfect tourist in every respect. But five times in a row? I didn't believe it.

A buxom Matabele woman was using a wooden pole to crush maize and a middle-aged German tourist was zapping pictures of her fast enough to burn his camera. Every time the four-foot pole struck, her naked breasts quivered like jelly and the German couldn't get enough.

The Rhodesians in the crowd were obvious by their polite boredom. We grew up with naked brown boobs. The early years of my childhood had been spent around villages far more authentic than this one. The proud Matabele warrior guarding the headman's hut was from a page straight out of history. He was dressed in a kilt of leopard-skin tails and feathers. He wore a waxed induna ring on his head and held a black-and-white cowhide shield with a short stabbing assegai. He was authentic down to the last detail, and no one could mistake him for anything but a savage, proud fighter from the past. In a couple of hours' time he would be dressed in a waiter's uniform and serving drinks on the verandah of some hotel in anonymous obscurity. Sometimes I get the impression that the world is one vast confidence trick.

We watched a very good display of tribal dancing and a witch-doctor fleecing the gullible with horoscopes he had probably culled from last week's *Sunday Mail*. And we stayed just behind Stanislau and Hart.

We walked through the rain forest in plastic raincoats provided by the hostess and still got soaked. The cloud of spray above the Falls was thick enough to cut. December is in the rainy season and not the best time of the year to see the Falls. The Zambezi River is in almost full spate and carries more than twice the volume of water it does in October.

But the little we could see was fantastically impressive. The statue of David Livingstone gazed with bronzed eyes over the scene that had lifted him from the ranks of unknown missionaries and made him a household name in the last century. It is a scene of almost unbelievable beauty. And frightening magnitude. The narrow concrete pathways and steps are the only additions made by man. In all other respects it is exactly as it was when Livingstone first discovered it in 1855, and wrote of it, 'Scenes so lovely they must have been gazed upon by angels in their flight.' Possibly he was not the first white man to visit them, but he was the first to record them and his description of this mighty place is still the best.

The foliage is thick and impenetrable, varying from every shade of green to brown and slashes of black like a Goya gone mad.

Even with the brightest sun overhead the light is murky and grey and the noise is deafening. The water foams white over the snarling lip and it is a vicious and violent place which, through some divine metamorphosis, retains the peace and tranquillity of a cathedral. An incredible two million gallons of water smashes itself to far-flung, scintillating spray every second on the black basalt rocks three hundred and fifty-five feet below the rim. I shuddered. Damn my childish apprehension.

At 1600 hours the bus dropped us at the jetty where a double-decked motor launch was waiting to take us three miles up the river to Kandahar Island in the middle of the Zambezi.

As the launch pulled away from the jetty and began fighting its way upstream through the current, Anne turned to me and said conversationally, 'Owen's an accountant. What do you do for a living, Rich?'

'I'm a civil servant,' I told her truthfully.

'Oh.' It didn't seem to matter. 'How did you break your arm?'

'Not my arm, my hand.'

'Well, how did you break it?'

'I had a run in with a berserk adding machine. It was multiplying instead of dividing and there were little adding machines all over the place. It was chasing everyone around the office and I finally cornered it and strangled it with its own electric cable.'

She gave me a humorous, quizzical look and leaned over the stern rail, staring at the white wake churned by the powerful screws as they forced the heavy craft through the murky water.

'You're a strange person. Most of the men I know would have spun me a wonderful tale about fights with burglars or heroic rescue scenes, or something.' She paused and glanced at me speculatively. 'But not you. You deliberately say something which makes you appear foolish. I wonder why? Did you break it doing something you're ashamed of, or is it none of my business?'

'That's right.'

'What's right?'

'It's none of your business.'

'Oh, goodie. I just love mysterious people, like the man said.'

I laughed but didn't reply.

'Are you always so secretive, or just trying to arouse my curiosity?' she asked, chuckling.

'There's nothing to be curious about, Anne. I broke my hand in a silly accident. Look,' I said, pointing toward the river bank, 'that's the old Imperial Airways jetty where flying boats used to tie up before the 1939 war.'

From the expression on her face, it was obvious that Anne knew I was trying to change the subject. But she didn't push it. For which I was thankful. I liked her and didn't want to lie to her any more than was necessary. She seemed to understand, and moved closer to me as she resumed her study of the wake.

The launch throbbed its diesel-fumed way up the river, and I snapped a couple of pictures of two Zambian Africans fishing from a dugout canoe near the north bank. CID studio would blow the prints up and study them in minute detail, but the chances of finding anything were a million to zero. It gave me something to do and helped justify my expense account. Anne didn't say a word until the launch eased in next to the floating jetty on Kandahar Island.

I waited until Stanislau and Hart were on the jetty before helping Anne over the side. I held her hand to steady her and she squeezed hard.

Stanislau and Hart were nearly at the top of the bank and in a few seconds would be out of sight. I squeezed back and almost dragged her onto the island. We topped the rise just in time to see Hart walking away from the crowd toward one of the numerous tracks which had been trampled through the ten-foot high elephant grass by countless tourists over the years.

Stanislau had stopped next to the trestle table provided by the tour company. Two Africans in white kitchen suits were pouring tea from stainless steel urns into thick china cups and waging a constant and losing battle with a couple of dozen small, grey vervet monkeys which raided the plates of biscuits laid out on the table with impunity.

'What's the hurry?' Anne asked breathlessly. 'Afraid the tea will be finished before we get there?'

'Of course. What else?' I quipped as I watched Hart disappear into the rank, overgrown tangle of bush. I took a couple of steps to follow him but decided against it and stopped. I could read Hart like a cheap comic, I thought, but Stanislau was the one I couldn't figure. I decided to stick with him. It was a mistake, and a big one. But I didn't know it then.

We walked over to the trestle table and helped ourselves to a couple of cups of tea. Stanislau was sitting on a log feeding pieces of chocolate biscuit to a small monkey perched on his knee. The monkey was chattering happily to him. About ten feet to his left another monkey was begging from a child about five years old. The child's parents were gushing proudly and taking photographs. The monkey grabbed a biscuit and turned to eat it. Then the little boy pulled the monkey's tail and it spun round, no longer a soft, cuddly toy but transformed into a pint-sized bundle of outraged dignity and flashing teeth which slashed the child's arm just above the wrist.

The little boy yelled in terror and his father threw the camera at the monkey, which was a waste of a good camera. It hit a rock and shattered. The vervet monkey had taken off for the tall timber as soon as the child yelled. In fact they all had. The child saw the blood on his arm and his yells turned to screams. It must have been painful and I didn't blame him. At five years the combination of fear, pain and blood is not taken lightly. Hell, it never is. His mother snatched him up and ran for the launch, shouting for a doctor. The unflappable hostess hurried after her.

'Did you see that little bastard?' The father was red in the face and very angry as he threw out his arms in an appeal to the rest of us. 'How can they let vicious animals like that run around? They should all be shot. Endangering our lives, that's what they're doing.'

Just who should have been shot wasn't clear. It could have been the monkeys or the tour operators. Probably both if the loud-mouthed father had his way. Stupid ass.

They come to Africa expecting production by MGM, direction by Cecil B de Mille and a conducted tour by Stewart Granger. They know it all because they have seen a hundred Hollywood movies where the hero scratches the lion's ear. It's inconceivable that the lion may scratch back. This is Africa, not Disneyland. The animals are wild.

The tourists huddled together on the ground and the monkeys huddled together in the trees. Both groups regarded each other with hostility.

Hart came back from his lone safari and joined Stanislau on the fallen tree. I wondered if he had felt the call of nature or just a longing to be alone for a couple of minutes. I didn't worry about it. I should have.

The hostess walked back up the bank and herded us towards the launch. Most of the group seemed thankful to get away from the menace of the monkeys. They kept glancing anxiously over their shoulders as they climbed gratefully on board.

'Hey, you,' the red-faced father called to the hostess. 'What's your name?'

'June Sackett,' she replied quietly.

'Well, June Sackett, I am going to sue your pants off. That's just what I am going to do. And your company. They'll wish they never dumped me on an island full of savage wild animals. I'll take them to the cleaners. Yes, sir, that's what I'll do.' He looked round in triumph. 'I got witnesses. All these good people are witnesses. They saw that damn wild animal attack my boy. You people haven't got a chance. Jesus, you know what that camera cost me in Broadwater, Nebraska? Four hundred good American dollars, and you people are going to pay, and pay good. You understand me, June Sackett?'

'Yes, sir. You may file your complaints at the district office in Victoria Falls.' She wasn't impressed. She had heard it all before.

'To hell with the district office. This goes straight to the top man. I ain't messing around with no flunkies.' He sat down looking pleased with himself. 'Boy, I sure told her off,' he said loudly to his wife sitting next to him.

'You did that, Henry,' she said admiringly.

'But that's nothing. Wait till we get off this tub. They'll wish they never heard of Henry Clarkson from Broadwater, Nebraska. This trip ain't going to cost us a dime.' He sat back with a satisfied smirk on his fat, sunburned face.

I wondered when he would get round to worrying about his son. Not that he had much to worry about. The child was sitting on Anne's lap drinking a Coke and enquiring if she had ever been bitten by a monkey. He had a strip of plaster across his arm and a five-year-old tough guy look had replaced the tears.

'Why was my Daddy shouting at that nice lady?' he asked with the round-eyed innocence of the young. 'She was nice to me. She put a Band Aid on my arm.' He held it up proudly.

'He's worried about you. He probably got a fright.'

'Mommy says the only thing he worries about is money. But it was a pretty big monkey, wasn't it?'

'The biggest,' Anne said and ruffled his hair.

'I have to go now.' He hopped off her lap and marched bravely back to his parents, holding up his arm for everyone to see the dressing.

'That's a sweet child,' Anne said, watching him with a strange longing in her eyes.

'Pity he has to grow up,' I said.

'Oh, I don't know. He may turn into a person yet. Even if he has to live with Henry Clarkson from Broadwater, Nebraska,' she laughed.

'With that influence, I wouldn't bet on it.'

The launch tied up at the Vic Falls jetty and Henry Clarkson was the first person off, still proclaiming loudly to the world how he was going to sue the pants off everyone in sight. The other passengers were discernibly embarrassed by his behaviour and avoided him as far as possible.

The bus dropped tourists off at the various hotels along the route and finally stopped in front of the Victoria Falls Hotel. Anne and I were the first passengers off, followed by Hart who missed his footing on the step and lurched into her. I reached out to steady her and Hart's camera sling-bag hit me in the face. He muttered something which could have been anywhere between sorry and stuff off, and walked away. I wasn't listening. All I could see was that camera sling-bag, and the gold Yashica emblem embossed on the front did not read Leica. He had switched bags.

Trailed by Anne I walked into the hotel in a bitter mood of mental self-recrimination. Of all the stupid things to do. I had kept tabs on the wrong party. The only place Hart could have switched bags was the island. He hadn't been out of my sight at any other time during the entire trip. It had to be the island. But I had elected to follow Stanislau, and had backed the wrong horse in the only race.

I left Anne at the foot of the stairs and walked into the cocktail bar. I ordered a beer from the smiling African barman and found myself a lonely table in the corner. Damn Stanislau and Hart. Damn them to hell in every shade of purple. Who could Hart have exchanged bags with? I could not recall any other passenger on the tour carrying a camera sling-bag that size. I thought briefly of Henry Clarkson's smashed camera, and discarded it. The only thing I knew for sure was that Hart didn't have a camera in that bag. Which helped a hell of a lot. I finished the beer and went up to my room.

* * *

According to the information Pete Fuller had supplied, Stanislau, Randall and Hart usually had dinner at the Casino Hotel at around 2100 hours. So far they had followed their daily routine almost to the minute, and it didn't seem likely they would deviate from it. And where they went, so would I. I was sorry I had left Anne so abruptly on the steps and hoped she wasn't too put out to accept my dinner invitation. She was the perfect cover.

I picked up the phone and dialled reception. 'Put me through to Mrs Hayward's room, please.'

'One moment, sir.' There was a pause, then the operator said, 'The number is 728. It can be dialled direct.'

I thanked her, broke the connection and dialled 728. Anne answered almost immediately.

'How about dinner tonight, at the Casino Hotel?'

'Oh, Rich, that would be super.' She wasn't put out. 'What time?'

'We'll wander over there around eight. I'll meet you in the cocktail bar. Okay?'

'Good heavens, it's nearly seven now and I haven't even done my hair yet. I'll have to rush. See you in the bar. Bye.' She sounded happy.

I got through to the Casino Hotel and reserved a table for nine o'clock, then left the room and went out onto the terrace. The blood red orb of the sun had sunk below the horizon, leaving a trail of orange-tipped shafts piercing the misty pink of the spray above the Falls. I hoped Livingstone had been right and there were only angels up there. I was going to need all the help I could get.

Stanislau, Randall and Hart were seated at a table overlooking the gardens. Stanislau was talking, jabbing his cigarette into the air every so often to emphasise a point. The other two were following his conversation with rapt attention. I couldn't get close enough to hear what he was saying without becoming conspicuous, so I continued past them and walked back into the hotel. They had full drinks in front of them which gave me at least ten minutes.

The lock on the door of number 127 gave me no trouble. The interior of the room was identical to mine. I crossed quickly to the built-in wardrobe and opened it. I never would have noticed the match if I hadn't been watching for it. A very careful man, Stanislau.

The wardrobe was crammed with very expensive suits and dresses. Stella had excellent taste and I noted sardonically that most of her dresses bore Cathy's exclusive label. The camera sling-bag was hanging from a hook inside the cupboard. That's all it was, a camera sling-bag—and it was empty. It didn't tell me a thing. I left it where it was and closed the door. I replaced the match in the narrow gap between the top of the door and the frame and walked out, locking the door behind me. I would have given an awful lot to have been able to carry out a thorough search of that room, but it wasn't possible in the ten minutes I had allowed myself, especially as I didn't know what other little tricks Stanislau had set up to indicate that a search had been carried out.

I went back to my room, showered, shaved and changed into a lightweight dark suit. The plaster on my hand was too bulky to fit through the jacket sleeve, so I had to drape the jacket over my shoulder and leave it open. Which meant I couldn't wear the shoulder holster. But the rig had been specially made for me by the police saddler in Salisbury and was adaptable. I unclipped the holster from the harness and slipped it onto my belt. The revolver was uncomfortable in the unfamiliar position, but it would do. At least it was not obvious, and from now on I wasn't going anywhere without my .38. I might not need it, but if I did, it'd be just too bad if it was back home in a shoebox at the back of the cupboard.

I stopped at the reception desk, drew two hundred dollars from the six hundred I had left in the safe and went into the cocktail bar to wait for Anne. I was halfway through my second whisky and the clock on the wall behind the bar read 2030 hours when she walked in, a vision in a glimmering green sheath that clung to her figure like bark to a tree. There was a hush in conversation as she crossed the room and climbed onto the stool next to me. The front of her dress was slashed down to her waist. It was the same Madeline Anne Hayward, but with the night had come a sophistication and poise that hadn't been there before. Or maybe I just hadn't noticed it. She looked terrific.

'Hi. Sorry I'm late,' she said. 'Are you mad with me?'

'That's a nice dress you're almost wearing.' I waved the barman over. 'And you aren't late. What would you like to drink?'

'Brandy and soda, please. And I am late. You said eight o'clock. It's after half-past.'

'That's what I said. But I booked the table for nine, just in case.'

'Very sneaky,' she said. 'If I'd known that I would have had time to make up properly.'

'It's not possible to improve on perfection.'

'Thank you, gallant sir,' she purred as the barman placed her drink in front of her. I tipped the soda into it and touched the rim of her glass with mine.

'Cheers, Anne. Here's to a good future.'

'I'll drink to that,' she replied, her mood sparkling and gay. It could have been because she looked good and knew it, or because she was doing something slightly daring. After all, she was married.

Or maybe it was just my fascinating company. It didn't matter. She was very pleasant to be with and I was enjoying myself.

She finished her drink and said, 'I'm starved. Can we go and eat?'

The Casino Hotel is only a few hundred yards from the Victoria Falls Hotel but we used the car. I had no idea what Stanislau would do when he left the casino and I didn't want to be left standing flat-footed in the carpark if he decided to go for a drive.

The change from the old-world charm of the Victoria Falls Hotel to the glittering plate glass and chrome of the Casino Hotel was startling, almost like stepping from one century to the next. The fittings and decor were luxuriously rich with a wide, carpeted staircase leading up to the dining-room and the casino. The place was packed and jumping.

A maitre d' in a well-cut dinner suit showed us to a table near the band, snapped his fingers imperiously for a waiter and went away. The service was good, the meal was excellent and the bottle of Nederberg Late Harvest was properly chilled, not frozen. The band played music that was mellow and low and between courses we danced.

Anne didn't float. She wasn't as light as a feather or any of the other ridiculous expressions used to describe a first class dancer. She just danced, and very well indeed. She didn't plaster herself up against me but she was close enough to let me know she was a woman.

I had located Stanislau ten seconds after the maitre d' had seated us. He was sitting with Stella and Hart at a table across the dance floor. Hart, in an evening suit, looked as at home as a Ridgeback at a cat show. Stanislau was immaculate and his burgundy tuxedo had never been near a peg. The slight bulge under his left arm was hardly discernible. He looked like a successful tycoon with a yacht in the harbour and a Lear jet at the airport. There was an unmistakable air of mystery and power in his manner which would fascinate women, but for me it reinforced an ominous sense of primal and consummate evil. I knew I was right about the bastard and my palms itched every time I looked at him, which was often. I wondered if I could take him and finally decided if it came to that I wanted a gun in my hand. You don't kick a rabid jackal in the teeth if you can shoot it.

Stella, in a severe black dress, was sensational. She wore very little make-up and no jewellery at all. She didn't need it. There wasn't another woman in the room to match her. Only Anne came close.

I felt a sharp kick on my shin and looked at Anne to find her smiling angelically at me.

'Which one of us are you here with, Mr Kelly?'

'What?'

'Not that I blame you. She really is beautiful, isn't she?'

I hadn't realised my interest had been so obvious. 'Nuts,' I smiled and switched my attention back to Anne.

We were on our coffee when Stanislau and Stella, trailed by Hart, stood up and left the dining-room. I pushed the cup away. 'Time to break the bank,' I told Anne and we walked through into the casino.

Legal casinos were still new enough to be novel and Anne was fascinated by the one-armed bandits. I bought her a couple of dollars' worth of ten-cent pieces and nodded towards the door of the gaming room. 'I'll be through there when you run out of cash.' I left her happily pulling handles.

The roulette tables and blackjack schools were doing box office business. The crowd surged and swayed between the tables in a glittering display of jewels, low-cut gowns and hand-tailored suits.

Stanislau was at the second roulette table, a neat tower of twenty-dollar chips in front of him. Stella and Hart were on the fringe of a blackjack school, waiting for a seat. I circulated, not standing in any one position long enough to become conspicuous. Stella and Hart finally managed to grab stools for themselves and started playing with chips that Stanislau passed over.

Their game was slow and cautious. The dealer must draw on sixteen and stick on seventeen. By watching the cards it is possible to win more often than lose. If the dealer's first card is between two and six and the player has over thirteen, the odds are against the dealer.

I drifted over to watch Stanislau. He was playing red. It only pays out evens and you can't win much. But you can't lose very much either. The dealers moved around frequently, changing position with other dealers, a practice followed by most casinos as a security check. Stanislau had a system but it took me almost an hour to spot it. Every time the dealer changed he bought another two hundred dollars' worth of chips which he passed on to Stella and Hart. He did it five times in two hours. One thousand dollars. Stella and Hart worked the system in reverse. With every blackjack dealer change one of them got up and cashed-in about two hundred dollars' worth of chips at the cashier's grille. I didn't get it. Sometimes they won a little, sometimes they lost. I estimated that they broke about even. But what the hell was the point?

The crowd was beginning to thin and I was becoming conspicuous. I bought twenty one-dollar chips wondering how I was going to justify them on my expense account, and took a seat next to Stella Randall. It took me just over fifteen minutes to lose the lot. So much for my foolproof system. I bought another twenty and began playing more cautiously. They lasted a little longer.

Anne climbed onto a vacant stool on my right and I glanced at my watch. 0045 hours. She had been pulling handles for damn near two hours.

'If I'd known who you were sitting next to I'd have been in here long ago,' she said impishly, nodding at Stella.

'No contest. She's not my type. How much have you won?' I asked.

'Lost the lot.' She pulled a rueful face. 'I was about twenty dollars up at one stage. I should have stopped.'

'No one ever does,' I said and watched Stanislau buy another batch of chips . . . with Zambian kwacha.

Suddenly I knew. I should have seen it before but the tables had been busy and there had been a lot of foreign currency floating around. American dollars, South African rand, Rhodesian dollars, even a few English pounds and German marks. The crowd around the roulette wheel had thinned considerably and Stanislau was the only player buying high denomination chips. He wasn't at the casino to gamble. He was converting Zambian kwacha into Rhodesian dollars. And I knew why. Knowing isn't proof but I had seen enough and didn't need to watch him anymore. The clever bastard. You can't walk into any bank and exchange hundreds of kwacha without a few possibly embarrassing questions being asked. The legal limit is twenty kwacha per person, and then only if a passport with a recent Zambian exit stamp is produced. This is not a Rhodesian ruling. There is nothing wrong with Zambian currency, but large-scale smuggling of cash out of Zambia had left that country with an acute shortage of foreign reserves and they refused to repatriate more than a very limited amount and then only from recognised sources. This in effect rendered the kwacha virtually valueless outside Zambia, and very difficult to dispose of. The casino on the other hand had no problems in banking kwacha as it was one of the recognised sources.

It wasn't easy for Zambians to obtain Rhodesian or any other currency. But Stanislau had found a way. A practically foolproof way, and by waiting until the croupiers changed he avoided speculation. Stanislau wasn't losing. He was changing currency without benefit of exchange control approval, and doing it very successfully. You can't hang a man for currency swindles, you can only put him away for a couple of months. Stanislau deserved more than that. Much more, and he would get it. Five nights at a minimum of twelve hundred dollars a night. Six thousand dollars. He could do an awful lot of financing with that sort of money. Financing of the type I was sure he was involved with.

I cashed in my few remaining chips and put up with Anne's good-natured kidding about my gambling skill being no better than hers as we drove back to the Victoria Falls Hotel.

We walked through the foyer and at the passage leading to her room Anne laid her hand gently on my arm and stopped. 'It's such a beautiful night,' she said, 'and I'm not at all tired. Let's sit out by the pool for a while.'

It was a beautiful night. The wind had dropped, the waning moon shed a pale, benevolent light over everything and I had Stanislau by the shorts. For the first time in weeks I was earning my pay and was, for the moment, content. Tomorrow I was going to nail him.

'Do you have any children, Rich?'

We were sitting at a poolside table where a sleepy night porter had left us a tray of coffee and gone back into the hotel.

'No, girl. I told you I'm not married.'

'Owen and I agreed, no pregnancies for the first four years. Not until we could afford it. Now we can, and I can't,' she said with a faint trace of bitterness.

I knew what she meant but didn't know how to answer her. I kept quiet.

'I was lucky, the doctor told me. I could still enjoy a normal sex life without having to worry about falling pregnant.' She laughed derisively. 'Lucky! What does he know about it? Half woman and half wife. I want a child so badly I can't think straight. No wonder Owen has lost interest. He says sex is only a means to an end, and with me it's like trying to blow up a balloon with a hole in it.' She was close to tears.

'He said that?'

'Yes. No,' she stammered. 'Well, not exactly. But I know that's what he thinks every time he makes love to me.'

'The eternal woman,' I sighed, 'with your preconceived ideas and your God-given ability to determine exactly what your mate is thinking about every subject under the sun at any particular time. Have you ever asked him how he feels?'

'Of course I have. He says it doesn't matter, but I know it does.'

'So every time he comes to you, you know it's only because the TV has packed up or whatever else you mentioned. A kind of second-string entertainment, wasn't it?'

'That's just how it is.'

'Good God, girl. With your subconscious mind kicking you in the head every time he makes love to you, how on earth can you expect either of you to enjoy it? If the fact that you can't fall pregnant really doesn't bother him, he must be going out of his mind wondering what the matter is with you. Have you ever considered that he may think you've lost interest in him?'

She was staring at me in surprise. 'No, Rich. I hadn't thought of that at all. It never occurred to me.' There was an excited tremor in her voice. 'But it is a possibility. It really is a possibility, isn't it, Rich?'

'It's a lot more than that, girl. I'd say it's a definite probability.' I looked at my watch. 'It's also three o'clock in the morning and Mrs Kelly's pride and joy has had a long day.'

She came to her feet and her hand slipped easily into mine as we walked back to the hotel in quiet companionship, not speaking until we stopped outside her door. Then she looked up at me and asked, hesitantly, 'Did you mean what you said at lunch?'

'What was that, Anne?'

'You told me not to wholesale it. You said the time would come if I waited. Did you really mean it?'

'I meant it.'

'Rich,' she met my eyes without guile or deception, 'I haven't waited very long, but I think the time has come.'

I understood her need and, as she gave me her key, I knew I shared it. The moment had found us.

She stood in the centre of the room and her eyes didn't leave mine as I shrugged out of my jacket and managed to slip the .38 off my belt and into a pocket without her noticing it. Her hand moved up her back and came down with the zip and she pivoted as the dress slid slowly down her body and formed a glittering emerald pool round her feet. She stepped out of the pool and walked toward me, not with a lover's look, but with a smile of open affection and trust. She helped me out of my clothes and we lay down on the bed. I reached for the light switch with my good hand.

'Leave it on, please, Rich. I want to see just who it is I'm holding.'

'You have that many you get confused?'

'You know very well what I mean,' she answered dreamily.

'Yes,' I said gently, 'I know.'

We talked for a long time as my hand hovered softly over the body she offered to me in friendship and candour. A pulse began beating rhythmically along her neck and she whispered, 'I'm ready now, Rich.'

There was no urgency or tension and she received me serenely, with quiet passion.

Later she snuggled into me and said, 'This is the first time I've ever been to bed without taking my make-up off first.'

I chuckled and switched off the light. We hadn't been mistaken about the moment; there were no regrets.

12

'I WANT a radio, a couple of water bottles and a lift to Kandahar Island,' I told Pete Fuller.

For once he was in full uniform and not liking it. The perspiration was streaming down his face in rivulets. 'Just like that, hey? Without any explanation!' he growled. 'What the hell's going on around here, anyway?'

'Do you really want to know, Pete?' I asked him.

'Of course I bloody well want to know,' he said angrily as he mopped his face. 'This is my area and I just happen to be the member-in-charge, or had you forgotten?'

I wasn't obliged to satisfy his curiosity and was fully authorised to requisition the equipment I needed without his sanction. But I needed his co-operation, and I wouldn't get it unless he was aware of the broad outline of the situation. So I filled him in on the events which had transpired since my arrival at Victoria Falls Airport and told him what I intended to do.

'You can't sit out on that island by yourself,' he objected. 'What happens if you're spotted and they come for you? I'd better keep you company.'

'No deal, Pete. Two are far more obvious than one and I'll need you in the launch. Someone has to drive it.'

'You're taking one hell of a chance.'

'I don't think so. I'm only going to watch, not win the war by myself.'

'Okay, so be a hero. When do you want to start?'

I looked at my watch. 1230 hours. 'Right now is as good a time as any.'

'Damn, I'm supposed to be playing in the darts semi-final at the club this lunchtime. If they win without me,' he snorted, 'I'll never live it down. Let's go.'

We loaded the equipment I had asked for aboard the grey police Land-Rover and drove down to the Government jetty where the police launch was moored. The African boat guard transferred my stuff into the launch and untied the mooring ropes. Pete Fuller backed the launch into the current, shifted the gear-lever to forward and slammed the throttle open. We were up and planing in fifteen yards. It was a very nice boat.

I waited until we were out of sight of the boat guard, then squatted down in the bow. If we were being observed, which was possible, I wanted it to appear that Pete Fuller was alone. The fact that two of us left the jetty and only one returned could be important in some circles.

Fuller took the launch a couple of miles upstream past Kandahar Island, turned and cut the power until we just had steerage-way. He approached the island slowly from the Rhodesian side and beached in a tiny inlet out of sight of the Zambian bank. I tossed my equipment out of the boat and climbed ashore.

'I'll tie up at the old flying boat jetty and wait for your call,' Fuller said.

'What about your darts match?' I grinned at him. 'You could have a long wait.'

'The story of my life. Good luck, Rich, and watch yourself.' He didn't return my grin. He backed the launch off the sand and was gone.

I picked up the belt holding the two water bottles, slung the heavy TR 28 set over my shoulder and walked into the cover of the dense bush. It took me less than a minute to reach the spot where Hart had disappeared into the elephant grass. The vegetation on both sides of the path was very thick and I could find no indication of a passage having been forced through it. I followed the path for its full length of about three hundred yards and found that it looped back on itself and rejoined near the beginning. There were no other entrances or exits. Yet somewhere along its length Hart had switched camera sling-bags. I walked the path a dozen times, each time more slowly than the last, and wound up with zero. It was there. With a conviction more certain than death, I knew it was there. A Leica bag full of Zambian currency, but I could not find it.

I forced my way into the heavy elephant grass at the apex of the path. It wasn't a perfect position, but it gave me maximum view of the path, which was the best I could hope for under the circumstances. I extended the whip antenna and called Pete Fuller. 'Mike Charlie, Mike Charlie, Sierra Bravo.'

'Sierra Bravo, Mike Charlie. Reading you fives. You got action? Over'

'Negative,' I answered. 'Just testing. Over.'

'Roger. Standing by.'

It was 1500 hours and hotter than the pits of hell. I squirmed around until I found a position which, if not exactly comfortable, was at least bearable. I drained the contents of one water bottle and found myself thinking about Madeline Anne Hayward.

The receptionist at the Victoria Falls Hotel had been mildly surprised when Anne had checked out five days early, but not unduly concerned.

'Rich,' Anne had said as the first rays of the early morning sun crawled redly over the edge of the window-sill, 'please don't be annoyed with me or think I am being silly, or anything, but I want to go home to Owen. Today.'

I didn't think she was being silly. I was pleased for her. The girl was growing up. I helped her pack, took her in to breakfast and drove her to the airport. I parked behind the Air Rhodesia bus and as we walked up the short flight of steps to the terminal she put her hand on my arm.

'Thanks, Rich,' she said. Her eyes were clear and shining and she looked happy.

'No thanks necessary or required. Move it, girl,' I smiled down at her, 'you only have a few minutes before the plane takes off.'

We hurried into the building and I dumped her case on the scale next to the check-in counter. She exchanged her ticket for a boarding pass and a seat number and we moved slowly towards the departure gate. We stopped near the exit as the tannoy boomed its echoing last-minute boarding instructions through the building. She smiled as she stretched up on her toes to kiss me for the last time.

'I'll always be glad I knew you, Rich. Goodbye, my wise man,' she whispered, and hurried out to the Viscount on the apron. She turned halfway up the gantry and waved.

I watched until the aircraft was a minute silver speck suddenly consumed by the wavering heat haze, then drove back to Victoria Falls township, whistling. Dr Kildare may not have approved, but I felt pretty good.

* * *

The long-necked darter perched ten feet from me heard the launch long before I did, and it dropped from the dead stump and slid away on silent wings. A few minutes later the heavy diesel throb was clearly audible as the tour launch tied up at the jetty. I eased the Smith & Wesson out of the holster and held it in my hand, parting the grass slightly as I watched Hart come into view, the camera sling-bag swinging innocently. A young couple, holding hands and laughing were just behind him. He bent down and pretended to tie his shoelace. They ignored him and followed the path out of sight. He turned round slowly, peering intently into the long grass and casting quick, furtive glances along the path. For a second he stared straight at me and I lined my sights on his ugly, broken nose, but he hadn't seen me.

Hart reached into a thick stand of grass on the opposite side of the path and switched bags so fast I would never have realised what he had done if I hadn't been expecting it. He looked round and, satisfied that he was unobserved, walked quickly down the path, the new camera sling-bag bumping on his hip. I let him go and stayed where I was.

A youngster of about eighteen from the boat party came stealthily along the path from the opposite direction and I wondered briefly if he was going to make the pick-up. He wasn't. He unzipped his fly and heaved a thankful sigh.

At 1700 hours the blast from the launch siren summoned the trippers and five minutes later the powerful diesel engines throbbed into life. I waited until I heard the launch move out into the river and then left my cover. Hart's switch had been incredibly fast, which meant the bag had to be easily accessible. It was, but it still took me over ten minutes to find it.

A wooden box, slightly larger than the camera bag, had been sunk into the ground, the lid covered with some type of glue on which sand had been spread. The hinged lid blended perfectly with and was indistinguishable from the ground around it. The Yashica bag was inside. I yanked it out and opened it.

Rhodesian currency. Six bundles of two hundred dollars and one bundle of a hundred dollars. Thirteen hundred dollars total. Stanislau had been to the casino on five consecutive nights. If this was his usual daily stake, he had converted currency worth six thousand five hundred dollars. And it was a safe bet that the bag Hart had picked up contained another batch of Zambian cash.

Terrorists cannot cross the border carrying kwacha. They have to be issued with Rhodesian currency for expenses, and they are, normally around two hundred and eighty dollars each. Stanislau had already changed enough money to finance three of the normal groups of seven terrorists. More than enough. The stinking son-of-a-commie-bitch bastard.

They were fast and they came long before I expected them. Their bush craft was very good indeed. I had just finished replacing the money in the camera bag when I felt it: the creeping chill up my spine and my flesh crawling between my shoulder blades. The alarm went off in my brain with urgent insistence and I knew I was no longer alone. I stood up slowly and moved towards my shelter. I had left the Smith & Wesson on top of the radio set and I wanted it more badly than a hophead wanted a shot of H. My heart was pounding and I could feel the sudden perspiration soaking my shirt.

'Stand still!' The command was harsh and guttural.

I stopped moving towards the revolver and turned slowly. There were two of them. Just two normal, everyday-looking rural Africans. They were barefooted and dressed in tattered shirts and shorts. Even the sunglasses one wore were a sign of normality. Only the AKs weren't normal. They weren't normal at all, and they were both pointed straight at me. The serrated bayonet on one of them was extended and clipped into the business position. If it was meant to impress me, it succeeded beyond the terrorist's wildest expectations.

I took half a slow step to the left with the muzzles following me. The two terrorists looked tense but nowhere near as frightened as I was. I yelled suddenly and dived to the right into the grass, rolled to my feet and took off running. The grass would not stop a bullet but at least they couldn't see me and no shots came my way as I dodged through the bush.

Kandahar Island is very small, and in thirty seconds I had run out of it. I jerked to a skidding halt at the edge of the water, the camera sling-bag hanging uselessly from my hand. I wasted a few seconds debating the possibility of swimming for it, but the idea lost its appeal when I saw the nose and eyes of a very large crocodile just breaking the surface of the water about ten yards out. I turned and moved back into the cover of the bush, crouching down next to a wide-girthed baobab tree which gave me protection on one side. Then I listened, straining my ears to catch any sounds over the pounding of my heart. Apart from the chattering monkeys on the other side of the island, I couldn't hear a thing. I sat there for fifteen minutes, not moving a muscle, breathing quietly through my mouth and waiting.

Finally I decided the two terrorists had been more surprised than I was and had gone back to Zambia. They must have used a canoe to reach the island and could, just as quietly, have decided the sport was not worth the risk and paddled away into the late afternoon. They couldn't know that I was alone.

Yeah. When fishes flew and forests walked.

I eased myself into a standing position to give my cramped back muscles a break and the bayonet, followed by the AK muzzle slid into view round the side of the tree. Fifteen seconds later and I would have walked right into it. I hadn't heard a sound. I reached for the barrel and pulled, swinging the heavy plaster on my left hand in a hard, vicious arc just above the weapon. The terrorist never had a chance. The lead-loaded plaster smashed into his face with a bone-crunching thud and he reeled away, his jaw hanging sloppily and a gaping, toothless hole where his mouth had been.

I spun round still holding the AK by the barrel. The second terrorist had emerged from the other side of the tree and was lining his sights on me. I flicked the rifle, bayonet first, towards his chest. There was no time to do anything else, and it didn't work. My throw was far too low. The bayonet sliced through his calf muscle, but it didn't stop him. It didn't even slow him down. I was completely off balance when he swung the butt of his rifle at my head. I saw it coming and couldn't do a thing about it. I tried to snap my face out of the way, but the butt caught me just above my ear and I collapsed onto my hands and knees, sick and dizzy, with my head hanging down. I could not have moved if a grenade had been tossed under me. I waited for the killing shot but nothing happened. After a couple of weeks I raised my head and found the terrorist standing with his rifle pointed at me, blood seeping thickly from his calf. It didn't make me feel any better.

'You are under arrest,' I said in Shona. My voice boomed round in my skull and sounded like it belonged to someone else. Right then I'd have had difficulty arresting a drunken tortoise on a speeding charge. Carruthers to the last. Go out in a blaze of glory and honour and all that crap. I stopped thinking about it. My head hurt.

'Who are you?' He sounded surprised by my command of Shona.

'Police. You are under arrest,' I told him again in case he hadn't heard the first time. He had heard but he still wasn't impressed.

'Get up. I am taking you back to Zambia for questioning.' He waved the rifle. 'Help my comrade and walk in front of me.'

'I refuse. This is Rhodesian territory. I am a Rhodesian police officer and you are under arrest.'

'This is Zimbabwe. Rhodesia is dead. The country belongs to the masses, not the white pig bastards.' A thin trickle of saliva ran down his chin, his voice was a low hiss and his features took on a fanatical twist. 'Now do what I say or you will die in this place.'

I believed him. I draped his 'comrade' over my shoulder and followed his instructions. He prodded me across the island and onto the shore on the other side. A dugout canoe lay beached in a shallow inlet. I laid the toothless one in the bottom, not gently. He never felt a thing, he was out cold and breathing raggedly. The other terrorist threw the camera bag into the canoe without opening it. He didn't have to—he knew what the contents were.

An eddy caught the bow of the canoe and swung it away from the bank. He waded knee deep into the water and held the bow steady with one hand, keeping the rifle pointed at my chest with the other. 'Get in!' he snarled.

This was it. I didn't want to die. It seemed just a little pointless to have it all ended on the muddy shores of an insignificant island in the middle of the Zambezi River. And by a peasant whose mind had been corrupted by visions of power and riches. A peasant who didn't have the intelligence to appreciate that he was merely a tiny pawn being manipulated by subtle minds in their ruthless quest for world domination.

I stared silently back at him. I couldn't reach him and I wouldn't run. He could point his weapon at me and threaten until the poles melted and hell froze. I was not getting into that boat. Rather a bloodstained corpse and an entry in the death column than a brain-washed zombie when the Chi-coms or the Russians got through with me.

I shook my head. 'No.'

'Get in now!' he spat, his body trembling with hate and anger.

It would have been nice to go out with some world-shattering declaration of deep and profound substance, but I couldn't think of any.

'Get stuffed,' I said in English.

'Then you die where you stand,' he dribbled savagely and his finger tightened on the trigger.

* * *

The old crocodile hung still and motionless in the heavy, darkening water, his only movement was a gentle sweep of his great tail to keep him from drifting with the current and to maintain his chosen position twenty feet above the river bed. He was over nineteen feet long and one hundred and twenty years old.

His tiny brain was receiving minute but insistent impulses which were automatically correlated, without any conscious effort, and transmitted in the form of movement. The periods of his life were measured in terms of stomach content and he hadn't eaten for more than six weeks. The lack of digestible nutrient in his system caused an increase in the frequency of the impulses and his brain forced him down to the river bed in the eternal search for food. He propelled himself slowly downstream about a foot above the mud, his tiny feet folded flat along the ventral surface of his massively armoured, prehistoric body. He disturbed a small vundu which he swallowed in one snapping motion. It did nothing to satisfy his hunger. A flashing orange-and-silver tiger fish shot past within eighteen inches of his snout. He ignored it. He had no chance of matching its speed.

He followed the dark river bed up the sloping contour that led to the island. He drifted into the shallow water under the overhanging branches where he knew monkeys occasionally fell into the water, especially when the small cats began hunting in the high branches at sunset. He was not lucky that evening.

He drifted slowly round the eastern tip of the island where he caught a small crocodile less than a year old and a foot long, and he swallowed it. He was swimming upstream now and had to use his tail more powerfully—a long, black shadow of ancient evil that was unaware of the terror he and his kind had inspired for centuries, and always would, in the heart of man. The fear and disgust with which he was universally regarded meant nothing to him. He survived and it was enough.

For a fleeting fraction of a second, he paused. He lived either by stealth or speed and his reaction to the fresh and familiar pungency in the water was instantaneous. He didn't know men called it blood. To him it just meant food. He swerved and the violent swing of his great tail stirred countless whirlpools of water-borne mud on the river bed. The surface of the water remained calm and undisturbed as the huge reptile moved at fantastic speed beneath it, his highly-developed olfactory senses flashing minute course changes to his brain. He was travelling at over thirty-five miles an hour when he slammed into the man, his incontestable jaw muscles contracting viciously as his teeth ripped through tissue and cartilage, locking into the bones of the man's pelvis. He registered a flash and a loud report as he struck, then he backed quickly into deep water, rolling over and over to kill the feebly-struggling thing he had caught.

* * *

'God almighty!' Pete Fuller exclaimed as we pulled into the station yard. 'You've got to be the luckiest man this side of paradise.'

I concurred, wholeheartedly. I had just finished telling him about the island, and I found it difficult to believe myself. That bloody monstrous croc had erupted out of the water like a missile and had taken the terrorist a split second before he pulled the trigger. The bullet, meant to kill, had only nicked the flesh of my upper arm. I hadn't even felt it at the time. The water had been churned into a foam-lashed white maelstrom stained with red as the croc had twisted away from the bank. But in five seconds no trace of the reptile or the man remained. The ripples dispersed rapidly and then there had been only the gently-rocking canoe, the unconscious terrorist lying in it, and me.

Slowly the evening sounds which had ceased abruptly when the croc struck, began again. Sudden and violent death is no stranger to the bush creatures and as soon as the danger had passed they resumed the desperately serious and all-encompassing search for food. In the wilds even the demanding and instinctive reproduction cycle plays a poor second to rumbling bellies. The falling of the night cast a deepening shadow and a tranquil mantle over the scene, and the killing, like the night, would pass. Both would come again but leave no scar to mark the time or place of their passing.

I turned and walked towards the centre of the island, looking for the radio, revolver and my cigarettes. The sun had fled before the cold, harsh menace of the stars and the darkness was almost absolute, which helped neither my concentration nor my confusion. I could still hear the crunch and grind of the decay-infested teeth as they had torn through gristle and flesh, and it took a little while before I found my equipment. I smoked two shaking cigarettes in silence, a thankful silence, and noted with supreme detachment that the burning sensation on my upper arm was a bullet crease. Then I used the radio to call Pete Fuller and he picked me up ten minutes later.

'What do you intend to do now?' he asked as we climbed the steps leading into the police station and walked through to his office at the end of the regulation cream-coloured passage. 'Apart that is, from inaugurating a benevolent fund for ageing crocodiles.'

'Lock this away for me.' I pushed the camera sling-bag across his desk. 'And get a doctor for the ter we brought back from the island.'

He nodded and took the camera bag into the strong room. He made use of the phone and finally located the doctor at the club. He replaced the receiver, popped a beer can and looked at me. 'Now what?' he asked.

'I know that Stanislau is the top jackal in this pack,' I told him. 'But so far, what have we got on the bastard? We can prove that Hart is guilty of evading currency control regs. Big deal. He would probably pull eighteen months at the very most, and then only if the magistrate was in a bad mood. And where does that leave Stanislau? Free as a bird and laughing up his bloody sleeve,' I said angrily. 'As for the terrorist connection, even if we get anything from the one we caught, a slick lawyer like Puceni would slaughter us in court and have our case against Stanislau tossed out in minutes. Pete, we just don't have enough solid evidence to force a conviction. Not at the moment. But there might be a way.' I looked across the desk at him. 'It's not strictly legal. In fact, it's not legal at all.'

'How?' he asked, alert and interested.

'You must understand that it's not just bending the rules. It's distorting them beyond all recognition. You may even wind up on the other side of the law.'

'Rich, this is me you're talking to. Me, Pete Fuller. Not some defective officer with more weight on his shoulders than between his ears. If you've got any ideas in that head of yours, give them out, boy.'

'There are times, Pete, when the legislated law is not adequate to deal with certain situations, and I think this is one of them.'

'So the law is for the guidance of the wise and the slavish obedience of the foolish. So what else is new?' The beer can followed the path of numerous predecessors into the waste basket in the corner. 'Stop screwing me around, Rich. Give.'

'We push him,' I said slowly as the idea formed in my mind. 'We get him so jumpy and confused he'll have to phone the met. office to find out if it's raining. We turn on the pressure and we watch. Sooner or later he'll foul up. He has to.'

'I doubt it.' Pete Fuller was sceptical. 'From the little you've told me he doesn't sound the type to go running to his mummy with a cut finger. He's more than likely to cut you back, twice as deep.'

'I hope to God he tries,' I said fervently. 'But short of praying that he may fall down the steps and break his neck or throwing him in front of a train and to hell with the consequences, there's no other way of nailing him.'

'Just what do you have in mind?'

'Nothing concrete, Pete. The only thing I *am* certain of is that I can't do it alone. Are you in?'

'I'm in.'

'Thanks, Pete. Let's have a beer while we kick a few ideas around.'

13

I WALKED into the casino at midnight. I had shaved, showered, changed into my lightweight suit and washed the blood off my cast. I had three cups of insipid instant coffee and two double whiskies inside me. I had my Smith & Wesson on my hip and a consuming rage in my soul. What I had told Pete Fuller had been the truth. I needed neither God nor the law on my side that night. I had things to do and the devil could turn puce before I would hesitate. As a kid I had broken the law for fun and kicks and, more by good fortune than skill, I had got away with it. Times, things, people, everything changes, and I had become a cop. The law I once flouted became a guideline in my life. I applied it with vigour and belief, occasionally with compassion, always with impartiality. Now one man had chosen to set himself above the law, and where he climbed I would follow.

Stanislau was at the roulette wheel. Suave, sophisticated and smiling. I no longer hated or loathed him. I was going to kill him and, as I considered him already dead, I had no feeling for him. I could curse and damn him for things he had done, and I would do so as long as I drew breath, but for the man himself there was nothing. I had decided that he should die and from that moment he did not exist. The only problem he presented was the manner in which he would join his compatriots in hell.

The crowds round the tables were more tightly packed and noisier than they had been on the previous evening, and I suddenly remembered it was Friday. I collected a handful of chips and bought into a roulette game. I played on the corners for a while and broke about even, not concentrating on the spinning wheel but devoting my attention to Stella at one of the blackjack tables. Her flaming hair stood out like a beacon and the dealer almost lost his flow every time she bent forward to examine her cards. He dealt her an ace and a king, paid her out three to two and his eyes followed the contour of her plunging neckline as she smiled at him and slid off her stool. I moved away from the roulette table to follow her, and the croupier called, 'You win, sir.'

'Let it ride,' I said. 'I'll be back in a minute.'

I watched Stella leave the gaming room, cross the floor of the main hall and disappear through the padded door of the ladies toilet. The hall was jammed with excited handle-jerkers jostling for position in front of favourite machines and ramming coins into slots with compulsive disregard of final costs. The continual clanging of the one-armed bandits as they paid out started my head throbbing again. The spot above my ear where the terrorist had caught me with his rifle butt was tender and felt as big as an egg.

Stella came back into the hall with regal dignity and granted me a smile that should have had me turning handsprings around the room as I stepped in front of her. She tried to move round to my left and I blocked her off. Her eyebrows moved towards each other in a delightful, quizzical frown at what she obviously thought was a new slant on the pick-up routine.

'Excuse me, please,' she said as I smiled at her and blocked her off again. The frown faded and was replaced by a cold, contemptuous flash of emerald green. 'If you don't get out of my way, I shall call for help,' she said with just the right touch of anger.

'That would be fun,' I grinned. 'Be my guest.'

'Get out of my damn way!' This time there was no controlled anger and she looked ready to call for help when I showed her my ID card.

'Stella Randall, you're under arrest,' I told her. 'Let's go.'

'My name is Mrs Stanislau. Mrs Sheila Stanislau. I've never heard of Stella Randall. Please stop wasting my time and let me pass.'

'It wouldn't make any difference if you were Mary, Queen of Scots. You're still under arrest.'

'Look, I don't know what this is all about,' she said, playing it to perfection, 'but my husband is in the gaming room, and if you would care to talk to him, I'm sure he can straighten everything out.'

'I'll be talking to him, all right. A long, private talk. But not right now.' I dropped my bantering tone and turned on my cop voice. 'Let's go. Hard and fast, or slow and easy. Suit yourself.'

'What's the charge?' she asked and for the first time her eyes showed a small trace of fear.

'Anything between soliciting and subversion. Take your pick.'

'You can't arrest me without informing me why. I know my rights. It's illegal and you can't do it.'

'Don't bet on it, Stella. Let's go.'

'You bastard. You bloody cop bastard,' she spat, but she came.

Pete Fuller was waiting for us in the carpark in my hired car. 'Any trouble?' he asked as I opened the back door and forced Stella onto the seat.

'No,' I said and handcuffed her to the back door armrest. 'But watch this one. A lady she isn't.' She had tried to knee me in the groin on the way down the steps and wound up with a sore leg for her efforts. 'How did things go at the hotel?' I asked Fuller.

'No sweat. The manager's a friend of mine and he owes me a couple of favours. We cleaned all her things out of the room and she booked herself out.' He laughed at Stella. 'She looks the type who could wind up with a split personality.'

'You're sure you removed everything of hers?'

'Positive. Right down to her toothbrush and birth control pills. Everything's in the boot.'

'Better give her the pills back. We don't want an increase in the prison population.' I stepped back as Fuller laughed and drove out of the carpark. Stella glared at me like Circe with a toothache, but turning me into a pig would have fallen far short of her ambitions.

She had been absolutely correct about one thing. Her arrest was completely illegal and if I miscalculated to the slightest degree I would never see another payday as a cop. Neither would Pete Fuller and I doubted if he would appreciate learning to sew mailbags as part of the Salisbury Prison's occupational therapy programme. It didn't appeal to me a whole lot either. I shrugged and climbed the stairs back to the casino. Events within the next twenty-four hours would dictate whether or not I swapped my ID card and gun for a suit of arrowed Government grey.

'Hey, mister,' the croupier called excitedly as I resumed my seat at the roulette table. 'Your bet built up to over four hundred dollars. But you lost it on the last spin,' he shrugged apologetically.

'That's the way the baby bounces,' I said. 'Always knew I couldn't trust my bladder.'

He laughed and I got a few sympathetic chuckles as I moved away and bought myself a whisky. Stella's arrest had taken less than five minutes and it took Hart another ten to realise that she hadn't come back. He played a few more hands, looking around and searching the crowd with a puzzled expression on his unornamental face, then he cashed in his chips and walked over to Stanislau. They held a hurried, whispered conference that lasted no longer than thirty seconds and Hart abruptly left the gaming room, walking fast. Stanislau continued to play, looking cool and nonchalant. He didn't appear to have a care in the world, but he soon would have.

Half-an-hour later Hart came back and I moved up behind Stanislau, stretching round him to place a bet.

'. . . booked out and all her things are gone,' I heard Hart say. He looked white and shaken.

'Don't panic,' Stanislau replied so quietly I had to strain to hear him. 'If she has left the hotel I'm sure she did so for very sound reasons, although it does appear rather peculiar that she should have done so without any explanation.'

He beckoned to the croupier and said pleasantly, 'Please cash these in for me.' He pushed a pile of chips across the green baize, then turned to Hart. 'In any case,' he continued in the same low tone, 'there are only two more days left and we cannot allow anything to deviate us from our plan.'

I left the casino and covered the few hundred yards to the Victoria

Falls Hotel quickly. I moved into the bushes to the left of the main entrance where I would be shielded from approaching headlights but still have a good view of the reception area inside. I pressed back against the wall as Stanislau and Hart drove up, left the BMW in the drive and entered the hotel, passing not three feet from me. I watched Stanislau as he stopped at the desk, in complete control of himself and the situation, or so it seemed. He smiled at the African night clerk, offered him a cigarette and from appearances could have been holding an amicable conversation about the weather. Hart prowled the fringes of the conversation like a bewildered bull buffalo.

I couldn't hear any of the conversation, but I had a very reasonable idea of how it was going. Soon, if he hadn't already done so, Stanislau would learn that there is no public transport out of Victoria Falls at night and as Stella did not have a car, she must have been picked up by someone. I hoped that worrying about the identity of the person would keep him awake. The less sleep he got, the more nervy he would become and consequently more prone to make a mistake.

I left the shelter of the bushes and moved over to Stanislau's car at a crouching run. I climbed into the back and flattened myself on the floor, arching my stomach over the transmission tunnel. I had the Smith & Wesson in my hand. Patience is learned early in police work. It can, and often does, mean the difference between success and failure on a case. But after sixty-five minutes of breathing carpet fluff and dust, I was ready to admit that I had miscalculated. I was on my knees and reaching for the door handle when I heard heavy, measured footsteps crunching on the gravel. I dropped flat as the driver's door opened and someone settled behind the wheel. Stanislau or Hart? The door slammed and the starter kicked the engine into throbbing, powerful life.

I straightened slowly and jammed the .38 barrel behind the driver's ear, not bothering to be particularly gentle about it. It was Hart, thank God. He cursed with shock and the car leapt forward, coming to a shuddering, stalling halt within a few yards.

'Who the hell are you?' he growled, swivelling his head.

'Eyes front, Johnny,' I said and tapped him gently on the jaw with the front sight. 'Start up nice and slowly and I'll tell you where to go.'

'Like hell!' He was recovering from his intial shock and getting his nerve back. 'I'll tell *you* where you can go. You can go to . . . '

'Johnny, Johnny,' I said reasonably and ground the muzzle into the back of his neck. 'It's been a long, hard night and I'm just a little tired. I don't want to have to hurt you. Well, not much anyway. Just be a good little gorilla and do as you're told.'

'You think you can heist me, you stupid bastard?' he snarled, snaking his hand towards his left shoulder.

'Of course,' I told him and smashed the plaster cast down hard on the back of his right hand. A bone snapped audibly and I hoped it hurt him as much as Georgie Girl had hurt me. More, in fact.

He hissed in pain and drove his head back towards my face. His skull met the butt of the Smith & Wesson travelling forwards, and Johnny Hart suddenly lost all interest in playing the tough hood. He hung limply over the steering-wheel and I waited patiently for him to recover. If he wanted any more rough stuff I was more than willing to oblige. But he didn't.

'You can't get away with this,' he finally moaned.

'You and Stella must have gone to different schools together,' I said. 'You both believe in fairies and there aren't any round here to stop me.'

'Just who the hell are you, anyway?' He tried to sit up and I ground the .38 barrel into the back of his neck.

'Questions, always questions,' I said. 'All that's required of you is to do as you're told. Then maybe, with more luck than you deserve, you'll live to see the sun shining through the bars in the morning.'

I didn't think he would give me any more trouble, but to be on the safe side, I belted him across the side of his head with the cast. He sprawled sideways and puked on the seat with hollow, retching sounds and I was glad it was Stanislau's car. I twisted my fist in the back of his jacket collar and slammed his face into the steering-wheel. 'Drive,' I snapped at him.

'Okay, okay,' he groaned and fumbled with the ignition key.

He drove slowly and clumsily but appeared to have recovered most of his limited faculties by the time I had managed to direct him into the police station yard, where Pete Fuller was waiting for us.

'Out!' I told Hart.

'Say, what is this?' He looked from me to Fuller. 'Are you a cop?'

'Observant, isn't he?' Fuller said.

'Jesus, am I pleased to hear that.' The relief on Hart's face would have been comic if it hadn't been so pathetic. 'I thought I was being robbed.'

'You are,' I said, 'of twenty years of your life at least.'

He swung round to face me and I hit him with a short, hard, four-fingered jab. He was in fair shape but my fingers sank into his solar plexus easily. He slumped over the bonnet of the car heaving for air and I put my foot against his hip and shoved. He sprawled face down on the sharp granite chippings. The stones gouged deep tracks through the skin of his face as I jerked him to his feet, and the blood quickly covered the front of his shirt.

He had been arrested eleven times, so being hauled into a police station was nothing new to him. But the treatment was. He was used to policemen calling him 'sir', even as they locked him up. He was used to calling them every vile name he could twist his tongue round and still being accorded all the courtesies, because that is how the men of the British South Africa Police are taught to react. He was used to demanding instant access to a phone to contact his lawyer. And he had always got it. But not this time.

Just to make sure Johnny (Gerald) Hart, alias Peter Bradshaw, got the message, I curled my fingers into a fist and drove it into his mouth, hard. The Old Boy Club would not have approved. It simply wasn't cricket. But then I wasn't playing a game. I was dealing in human lives and in my business there are no dirty tricks. There are only the dead and the living. And the Ronson children were dead. I swung my fist again, almost hard enough to break Hart's jaw, and the contact sent a savage pain along my arm.

'Christ, Rich! What are you trying to do? Kill him?'

Pete Fuller didn't know how close to the truth he was. I swore an oath when I joined the BSAP. I swore to protect my Queen, my God and my country. So Elizabeth the Second, or at least her Government, had kicked us in the teeth. It did not invalidate the oath, and the time may not be too distant when she will be in need of all the assistance she can get. And being the misguided idiots we are, we'll give it to her willingly. My God needed no assistance. But my country was a story of a different colour. And that colour would not be red. Not as long as I could pull a trigger.

I turned away and lit a cigarette as Pete Fuller lifted Hart's .45 Colt and forced him up the stairs into the police station. Legally we could hold him for forty-eight hours prior to appearing in court on a charge of possessing a firearm, which as a person with previous convictions involving violence he was not permitted to do. Forty-eight hours may be a long time in the life of a High Court judge, but during a police investigation it was seldom long enough.

In this case it didn't matter. Neither Stella Randall nor Hart had been officially booked and there were no records to show they had ever been detained at Victoria Falls Police Station. The lack of interest shown by the officer on night duty had been commendable. His only action had been to offer me a strip of Elastoplast for the split skin over my knuckles. I used it.

We spent ninety frustrating minutes interrogating Hart and got absolutely nothing out of him. Short of using thumbscrews, which I would have if I'd had any, there was no way of forcing him to talk. Eventually Pete Fuller sent him, under escort, to the local clinic to have his hand set and his abrasions patched, then he dug out a bottle of White Horse and two glasses.

'I don't like this,' Fuller said as he poured out the drinks. 'I've never beaten up a suspect in my life, and I've never allowed it on my station. It's wrong, and all your damn cockeyed moralising doesn't alter the fact.'

'I warned you, Pete. I told you that you could wind up on the wrong side of the law. You came into this of your own free will. No one twisted your arm.'

'I know. I know that. But it doesn't make it any better. I sure as hell didn't expect you to pull any third degree stuff on helpless prisoners just to satisfy your hot-shot ego.'

'Ego? Don't talk crap. Ego has nothing to do with it. Hart's in possession of possibly vital information. Information that could save lives, innocent lives, and I want it.'

'You're supposed to use your brains. That's what you've been trained for. Where do you carry your brains? In your fists? Anyway, you never got a thing out of Hart. Not one single peep.'

'Which bloody side are you on, Pete? Do you want to see that murdering commie bastard walk away from this just because you had an attack of conscience and turned squeamish at the sight of a little blood? Is that what you want? Then go ahead and turn Hart and Randall loose. Let them go running back to Stanislau with their little tales of woe. Screw the investigation and set me up to take a fall for illegal arrest and assault. Send your conscience to bed with the overworked bitch of complacency and sit back in the proud glow of your smug duty. But just remember every time a farmer is murdered, a kraal head has his genitals shot off, a woman is raped, a child is butchered or a landmine blows a truck to hell, that maybe—just maybe—it's your fault. And make no error, it will be. When you wake up sweating in the middle of the night you can always let your sense of righteous duty coax your conscience back to sleep. Stuff the people who'll be killed and maimed because your tender-hearted soul cringed at the sight of a murdering son-of-a-bitch's blood. Go ahead and do it. Turn them loose and damn you deeper than hell.'

I stopped, knowing I had been shouting but unable to control it. I picked up my drink and walked over to the window, staring out at black nothing, fighting the urge to toss the rest of the whisky into Pete Fuller's face. Sure I had enjoyed hitting Hart. Revenge is Mine, said the Lord, but when He didn't appear to extract it, I would gladly lend Him a hand.

A couple of minutes passed before Pete Fuller said, 'You fit to talk to yet?'

'Yeah.' I turned from the window. 'Sorry about that. I guess I got a little carried away.'

'A little. And you aren't sorry at all. You meant every word of it, and I must admit there's a small seed of logic mixed up in your crazy reasoning.'

'What's that supposed to mean?'

'That Randall and Hart stay locked up and we go ahead. Okay?'

'Okay.' I walked over to the desk. 'I want to phone Mr Hamilton.'

'Private call?' He looked up quickly.

'Hell, no. You know as much about the set-up as anyone.' I pulled the phone over to my side of the desk and dialled. It rang for a long time and I let it carry on. I took a sip of my drink and looked at my watch. 0300 hours. My own personal bewitching hour. I was sick of the sight of it. I had half a bucket of coarse sand under each eyelid and some crazy musician was using the base of my skull for a drum. I didn't only want my bed, I needed it. But I had to talk to Mr Hamilton first.

'Hamilton,' he answered, sounding fresh and crisp, as if he lived in a world of far away sanity.

'Morning, sir. Kelly here.'

'Ah, Mr Kelly. How are you enjoying yourself? Not too many late nights, I hope. You sound a little jaded.'

Jaded, hell. I was almost finished. I brought him up to date and then made my requests. 'I want a full report of the Kandahar Island business to be included in the hourly radio news bulletins starting at 0600 hours this morning.'

'The Tourist Board and the Vic Falls Publicity Association will pull every string they can to have that report stopped, Mr Kelly. It could scare people away for months and have a disastrous effect on the tourist industry in the area.'

'There are millions of tourists, sir, but only one Stanislau. Anyway, if it's handled properly they won't know anything about it until it's too late to stop it. In my opinion it's vitally necessary. We've no chance of forcing Stanislau's hand unless he is utterly convinced that the net is about to close in on him.'

'I'll see what can be done. Anything else?'

'Yes, sir. I think it would be advantageous to us if Stanislau were under the impression that one of the terrorists was alive and talking.'

'I don't follow your reasoning. Those two were obviously very low calibre. The one we hold couldn't possibly tell us anything of importance, not as far as Stanislau is concerned, and he would know it.'

'I realise that, sir, but it could be just one further pin prick.' I was so tired I hardly understood what I was saying myself.

'I'll consider it. Keep me informed.'

'Yes, sir.' I broke the connection and finished my drink. I had deliberately avoided any mention of arresting Randall and Hart. Mr Hamilton would have gone through the roof. What he didn't know could hurt him very badly, but there was no point in worrying him prematurely. And if he didn't know they had been arrested he couldn't order their release.

'If that broadcast comes over I'll be running the quietest police station in the country.' Fuller said.

'Does that bother you?'

'Hell, no. Give me a chance to catch up on my darts practice. I've been missing out just lately.'

'I'm bushed. See you, Pete.' I moved towards the door as the telephone rang. I ignored it and went out to Stanislau's car. The stink of Hart's vomit caught in my nostrils and I opened the window quickly. Fuller came out into the yard as I started the engine.

'That was the clinic on the phone. Seems you hit that ter a bit too hard. He just died.'

'So what do you want me to do? Send flowers to the funeral?'

'I thought you should know about it, that's all,' he said sharply. My bad temper had got to him.

'Sorry, Pete. I am so buggered I can hardly see.'

'That's okay.' He sounded mollified. 'What about your car?' He nodded towards my hired BMW standing in the corner of the yard where he had left it after bringing Stella Randall in.

'Get someone to drive it over to the Victoria Falls Hotel carpark first thing in the morning and leave it with the keys in the ignition.'

'Sure. Sleep tight.'

I drove out of the station yard and along the Bulawayo Road for five, fast miles. If Stanislau kept a check on the odometer, and he seemed the type who would, I didn't want him to have any idea where the car had been. By the time I got back to the hotel, the grass and bushes on the side of the road had come alive and shadows were jumping out at me. Fatigue soaked through my body and my throat was harshly dry from too many cigarettes. I left the car in the carpark with the keys in it, wondering what Stanislau would make of the vomit on the front seat. I hoped it would help to make him sweat. I walked through the foyer, leaving instructions for a call and coffee at 0530 hours with the night porter. I crawled into bed and was asleep almost before my eyes closed.

14

LANCE Koster was worried. Worried sick and scared—with a total, unrelenting fear that built up and up until it controlled every thought, every facet of his brain. It took hold of his mind and ruled him with a ruthless domination more compelling than anything he had ever experienced. It left his mind a seething, whirling vacuum which sucked all rational thought down into the vortex of his despair.

Ever since the contact on the Zambezi a few weeks before when he had first seen Warrant Officer Reitz, the fear had been building up in him and now was ready to swamp him. The sight of Reitz brought back the vivid memory of a rainy night, an alley, a dog, a gun and a cop. It had been dark in the alley, but the darkness had been relative to the street. There had been enough reflected light for Lance to see the cop's face. And that face had been Reitz's.

He was sure Reitz recognised him. The news that Three Commando was to conduct a seek and destroy patrol down river to Mana Pools did nothing to allay his fear. The SAP were going with them. Dear Jesus God, it can't happen now. Not after all this time. It's not true. It can't be. But it was.

For the tenth time in as many minutes Lance shot a quick, furtive glance in Reitz's direction. Was the bastard watching him? Did he know? Was he playing some kind of crazy cat and mouse game? Jesus Christ! Lance's tormented mind screamed. If he knows, why doesn't he say something? Just sits there staring at me with those little pig eyes. What's he trying to do to me, the stinking son-of-a-bitch?

Warrant Officer Reitz was puzzled. He couldn't understand why the RLI corporal watched him so intently. Ever since the patrol had pulled out of Chirundu he had felt those eyes on him. Darting, calculating eyes, evaluating his every move. He could find no reason for the scrutiny and he was becoming uncomfortable. It was also beginning to annoy him. If the bugger had something on his mind, why didn't he just come out with it?

He did not for a moment connect Lance with the wet night in the Hillbrow alley when his dog had been killed. He couldn't. He recalled very little of that night . . . a confused whirlpool of light and darkness, of people shouting and the dog whimpering. And the pain. Mostly he remembered the gut-searing, agonising pain. But he'd been lucky, the doctor told him later. No permanent damage had resulted from the kick he had received in the groin. Reitz thought he would have been even luckier if someone else had been kicked. It had been a pain-filled, unpleasant stay in hospital but he had recovered and seldom thought of it now.

The patrol was moving slowly and cautiously through the thick, tangled undergrowth near D Camp, when he sensed those eyes on him again. Hell, even in a situation like this he's watching me instead of the bush. Stupid idiot. But maybe he knows me from somewhere, or maybe I look like someone he knows. He glanced back over his shoulder. Lance was twenty feet behind him and to the left. Their eyes met and locked briefly, then Lance looked quickly away.

Finally Reitz could stand it no longer. When the patrol bivvied for the night he walked over to where Lance was heating water for coffee. Lance saw him coming and his heart started hammering against his ribcage hard enough to be heard. Reitz squatted on his heels next to him and held out a packet of thirty Lexington.

'Smoke?'

Lance's throat was dry and he had difficulty forming the words. He could feel sweat running down his back and on his face. 'No.' His voice was a hoarse croak. He swallowed desperately. 'No. No thanks.' What was the bastard trying to do to him? He poured the boiling water into an aluminium mug containing a couple of coffee bags. His hand was shaking so badly he sloshed half of it onto the ground.

'You all right?' Reitz asked in a puzzled tone.

'Of course I'm all right,' Lance spat, fear adding a harshness to his reply that he couldn't control. 'Why the hell shouldn't I be?'

The vehemence of the reply startled Reitz. 'Calm down. Sorry I asked.' He looked at Lance speculatively. 'Are you a South African?'

'No, I'm not.' Maybe he doesn't recognise me, Lance thought. Jesus God, please don't let him remember my face. 'What difference would it make if I was?'

'You sound like one. And from the way you've been watching me I thought possibly you recognised me from somewhere.'

He knows. Christ help me, he knows. He recognises me. The message screaming through Lance's brain. The sweat was pouring off him. The bastard's playing with me. He's playing with me. He fumbled in his shirt for a cigarette and his hands trembled violently as he lit it.

'Thought you didn't smoke,' Reitz said.

'What the hell's it to you?' Lance's face was a twisted mask. 'Why don't you bugger off and leave me alone?'

'I outrank you, corporal.'

'In which army, copper?' His hand was on the bayonet at his belt and he looked wild and mean. If the bastard says another word, I'll kill him.

Reitz had been a policeman for far too long not to recognise the danger signals. He was in the valley to help finish a war, not start a personal one. He looked into Lance's face and saw death. He had seen that same look many times on other faces and had challenged it. But always for a reason. Here there was no reason he could understand. He stood up and walked away. Koster was mad. A raving, bloody lunatic.

'For Christ's sake, Lance, what was all that about?'

He spun round to face the trooper who had spoken. 'Shut your bloody mouth, Marsh!' he snarled and stood lowering over the seated trooper.

Marsh took a sip of hot coffee. 'But, corporal . . . '

It was as far as he got. Lance kicked the mug savagely out of his hand and the hot coffee hit Marsh in the face. He backed away quickly and Lance looked round the circle of seated soldiers. 'Anyone else want to join in the conversation?'

Most of them knew him. Those who didn't, knew of his reputation. None of them said a word. Lance picked up his pack and moved deeper into the bush by himself.

He knows. He knows. He knows.

The words spun round in his head and took on the regular, insistent beat of a compelling drum. He lay down and tried to sleep but it was impossible. He couldn't even close his eyes. Why now? Sweet Jesus, why let me go through all this and spring it on me now? He cursed the gods and damned the fates that had sent Reitz into the valley. But it didn't help.

He knows. He knows. He knows.

It was 2100 hours before Lance suddenly made up his mind. He was not going to hang. Not for killing a bastard like Roy. Zambia was only three hundred yards away. Three hundred yards across the Zambezi River. He was going to swim the river and ask for political asylum.

To hell with the RLI. To hell with Rhodesia and stuff the South Africans. He was only twenty-one years old and that was too young to die. He would be welcomed on the other side of the Zambezi. That he knew without a doubt. Especially if he said the right things. He would tell of police and army brutality, of inhuman treatment of Rhodesian Africans and of how it sickened him. He would be lying in his teeth but that didn't matter. He would be alive and that did. He would be fêted by the anti-white block throughout the world. Hell, he might even make some money out of it. Above all, he would be safe, secure and alive. Even if the South African Government announced that he was a wanted criminal, who would believe them? It would be considered a smoke-screen to cover themselves. The more he thought about it, the better it seemed. He couldn't miss. To hell with them all.

He picked up his rifle and worked his way soundlessly downstream. It was a bright, moonlit night and he had to get well away from the camp before he attempted the crossing. It would be stupid to be shot by his own sentries. Slowly and quietly he moved through the bush, eyes and ears straining for the positions of the perimeter sentries. Once he thought he had been seen, but he was lucky. The sentry turned away.

He was seventeen hundred yards from the camp when he decided it was safe to cross the river. He took off his boots, strung them round his neck and was waist deep in water when he saw the canoes.

There were five of them. Dugouts. They cut across the silvery surface of the water leaving black ripples behind them. They made no sound and he could see the moonlight glinting from the rifle barrels as the canoes beached fifty feet from him. He sank slowly and gratefully into the water until only his eyes and nose cleared the surface. The sons-of-whorebinding-bitches, he thought, as he watched the nine terrorists unload their equipment onto the sandy bank. Who do they think they're playing around with? It's the RLI they have to face. We'll slaughter them.

Hold it, Lance, an inner voice whispered, you're crossing the river, remember? You're on their side.

I don't need you to tell me which side I'm on, he cursed back vehemently. I'm on my side and as soon as those canoes bugger off I am crossing the river. I'm crossing, understand!

Then a vision of Lindy's face hit him. Lindy, her face alight with the soft angel-glow of the life inside her. Aglow with a glorious peace and a wondrous contentment with the life she carried. His Lindy, swollen with his child and he knew he couldn't do it. Sometimes the easiest things turned out to be the most impossible. He could not cross that three-hundred-yard stretch of water and walk out of her life. He loved her.

The lightened canoes returned to the Zambian bank as quietly as they had come. The terrorists picked up their packs and moved into the cover of the Rhodesian bush. Lance was suddenly alone. Desperately and chillingly alone. He waded out of the water, laced up his boots, picked up his rifle and ran back to the camp.

'Halt! Who goes there?'

'Corporal Koster, you stupid tit. Get out of my way.' He shoved the startled sentry aside, ran into the camp and grabbed Captain Powers by the shoulder. 'Captain Powers. Wake up, sir.'

Powers rolled out of his sleeping bag, instantly alert. 'What's the trouble, corporal?'

'Nine ters, sir. Just crossed the river about a mile downstream.' Lance was sweating and panting from the run.

Powers didn't waste time trying to find out what Lance had been doing a mile from the camp, or why he was soaking wet. He called for Sergeant Jamieson and in three minutes they moved out with Corporal Koster as lead scout. He was the only one who knew where they were going.

It was 0900 hours when they walked into the ambush. Lance Koster's second and his last. When dawn had broken the tracker had taken over the lead position from Lance, but Lance had stayed close behind him. Reitz, not wanting to be left out of any action and itching to make up for the mistakes at Chimutsi Dam, had moved up with him, on his left. Lance ignored him. He was no longer frightened and his concentration on the surrounding bush dominated all other feelings. Time enough to worry about Reitz later. Now he was doing precisely what he had been trained for, and that training over-rode everything else. He was totally unaware of the mopani bees trapped in the sweat on his face and the tsetses that had found them as soon as they moved away from the river.

The tracker was ten feet ahead of Lance and had walked right past the AK barrel when Lance saw it poking out of the bush, directly at Reitz. His reflex action was instant—he dived to his left, into Reitz, knocking him from his feet as the AK fired. The bullet smashed into Lance's chest and he staggered back and tripped over a rock. Reitz opened up with his Walther. The policeman's aim was good. There was a rasping cry from behind the bush and the terrorist toppled slowly forward and died tangled in the branches.

Reitz ignored the furious action which was taking place all round him. 'Medic!' he yelled over his shoulder. 'Come here. Quickly!' He sat down in the dust and cradled Lance's head on his lap. 'You saved my life, man. You saved my life.' There was wonder in his voice as he looked down at the wounded man.

'Makes up for the last time, doesn't it?' Lance gasped raggedly.

'What last time?'

'You mean you don't remember?' Lance coughed up blood. He wiped his mouth and stared for a moment at the thin red smear across the back of his hand, then looked up at Reitz. 'You really don't remember?'

'No, corporal, I don't remember,' Reitz said. The man was delirious already. 'What should I remember?'

Lance gagged and a bright glob of brilliant blood shot out of his mouth. It splattered against Reitz's leg and Lance suddenly realised he was dying.

Jesus Christ, dying! All because of a bloody cop. All cops were bastards and he was dying because of one. They were all bastards. Dying! It just wasn't fair.

'Don't worry about anything now.' Reitz's voice seemed to come from a great distance. 'We'll have you fixed up quicker than you can say Jan van Riebeeck.' He tried to smile but couldn't hold it.

Lance's heart was pounding and the sky had taken on a strange, yellow tinge. He wondered why he felt no pain. 'You can't con me. You know I'm finished.' Lance coughed weakly. 'And you don't remember?'

'No, soldier, I don't.' Reitz shook his head, puzzled, and bent low to catch the words.

'All for nothing.' Blood was bubbling up through the hole in his chest. 'Jesus, it was all for nothing. Tell Lindy . . . tell Lindy . . . Lin . . . ' His voice trailed away and a great gout of rushing blood spewed out of his mouth.

A medic ran over and knelt down next to Lance. He felt for a pulse, rolled back an eyelid then pulled the camouflaged cap down over Lance's face.

'Dead?' Reitz asked quietly.

The medic nodded, stood up and walked away. And no great bloody loss, he thought to himself. His name was Luke Mason.

15

'NO!' The harshly-spoken word cut through the discussion as the speaker's clenched fist hit the table with enough force to rattle the cutlery. 'It is completely out of the question. Have you gone mad? Have you forgotten your positions and the oppressed people who consider you the leaders in our struggle? To even consider such a proposal is to be a traitor.' He glared round the table at the four men seated opposite him and only one of them returned his look without flinching.

The five men were immaculately dressed in well-cut, dark business suits. The room was large and well furnished, the table round which they sat was covered with an expensive woven cloth made in Rhodesia. The cigarettes they smoked were Rhodesian, the wine which had accompanied the meal and the brandy which followed it were products of the Republic of South Africa. The location was the main dining-room of Liberation House, Lusaka, Zambia. The two-storey building had been placed at the disposal of black Rhodesian nationalists by the Zambian President, Dr Kenneth Kaunda, and it was the nerve centre in the war against Rhodesia.

Gara Paratema had been the speaker. He had come a long way since his days at Malopa Mission. He had been one of the six survivors to reach the safety of Zambian soil after the burning of the mission. He had arrived in Lusaka penniless and in rags, but his superior education and sharp mind had been noticed immediately and within a week he was on the organizing staff of the proscribed Rhodesian nationalist movement, the Zimbabwe African National

Union. He was fast-moving and ambitious, climbing rapidly through the lower ranks of his less-educated and slower-witted co-workers. Six weeks after his arrival in the Zambian capital he had been appointed personal assistant to the organizing secretary.

A week later the secretary, a vigorous man in his early forties, had died suddenly and mysteriously. The official cause of death had been listed as heart failure, but the capital seethed with rumours and speculation and the name of Gara Paratema was mentioned often—softly as a suspect and loudly as the obvious successor to the secretary. Gara denied the former strongly and supported the latter with ruthless determination, spending large sums from the party treasury to ensure his nomination. If he was appointed to the post of organizing secretary he could cover the losses. If he was not, he could always ensure that the caprice and extravagance of the late secretary had been responsible for the shortfall. The accounting procedure was chaotic and it would not be difficult.

'It has never been traitorous to save the lives of our people. To say such things is stupid, or even worse to be seeking personal glory.' The speaker was Titus Magaba, director of operations, Zimbabwe African Peoples' Union, also based in Liberation House, also outlawed in Rhodesia, and bitter rivals of ZANU. He alone had not flinched under Gara's tirade.

'Personal glory!' Gara retorted. 'What do you know of it? You who have never faced the white guns. I have fought the white racists and killed them. I have been hunted by them like a dog. I swam across the Zambezi River with a bullet in my leg to reach Zambia so that I could continue the fight. And you talk to me of glory. You who know only the beer halls and the whores of Lusaka.' Gara smashed his fist into the table again, the black skin of his hand contrasting vividly with the snow white of the cloth. His gold cufflink shone richly in the glow of the wall lights.

'You killed an old man who had been your friend. You killed him because you had a gun in your hand and no brains in your head. If you were hunted like a dog it is because you ran like one. You swam the river because to stop swimming was to drown and become food for the crocodiles. You are nothing but Korekore rubbish and yet you seek to tell the Matabele how to fight a war. You are less than the urine of a jackal on the ground.' Titus Magaba had not raised his voice, but the automatic pistol in his hand stopped Gara as he reached across the table with a steak knife pointed at Magaba's throat.

This had been the way of things ever since M'Zilikazi's impis had swept north across the Limpopo River to escape Chaka's wrath and laid waste to the country white men were soon to call Rhodesia. The Matabele nation had been born, the roots of their heritage deep in Zulu tradition, their only pride in the arts of war, their only way of life to command, and they had rolled the pitiful warriors of the Shona people before them and eaten their kraals like the lion eats the impala. The black bull elephant had put his foot upon the land and the people trembled.

The Shona nation had fled to the northern part of the country and only the coming of the white man, with his strange ideas of fair play and completely incomprehensible laws had saved them from total annihilation. If you were a Shona and you killed a Matabele, the white man hanged you. But they did the same to the mighty Matabele. Even the powerful Lobengula, successor to the immortal M'Zilikazi, bowed his headring in the presence of the whites. He went to his death somewhere in the high granite hills of the Matopos Range, cursing the fates which had brought these strange people into his country—beardless boys whose noses shed skin and whose legs grew ugly, red blisters in the light of the sun. Beardless boys who fought like lions and defeated his impis with terrifying ease. The Matabele had scored only one significant victory. They had slaughtered a patrol under the command of Major Allan Wilson on the banks of the Shangani River. The induna in command of the impis had looked down on the hairless faces of the BSA Company patrol and restrained his men from the usual superstitious mutilation, declaring, 'They were men of men, and their fathers were men before them.' In the Matabele vocabulary there is no higher compliment.

The whites took on a new perspective in the eyes of the Matabele and the rule of law was gradually imposed throughout the fledgling

Rhodesia. The animosities of tribal differences and hatred still flourished and now nearly eighty years later, despite their avowed and common aim to overthrow the white Government and rename the country Zimbabwe, had resulted in the Matabele formation of ZAPU, trained by the Russians, and ZANU, consisting mainly of Shonas and backed by the Chinese communists.

'Gentlemen, you are behaving like children in the cattle kraal,' Sibanda said from the head of the table. He was the oldest of the group and although his sentiments leant towards ZAPU, as liaison officer it was his job to promote harmony between the two groups, and he was determined to do it. 'We will never defeat the white racists and rid Zimbabwe of Smith's illegal regime if we continue to quarrel between ourselves like women around the cooking pot.

'We are here tonight for one reason only, and it is not to abuse each other. Smith, through the South African Prime Minister, Vorster, has contacted Dr Kaunda with proposals to hold a conference to discuss our constitutional demands and to stop the war of liberation. We are here tonight to decide if we want to speak to Smith or not.' He looked calmly round the table. 'Comrade Paratema obviously does not support any contact with the illegal racist regime. Perhaps you will tell us why?' Sibanda asked, pointing at the ZANU man.

'Of course I don't support any talks with Smith. He is a white racist liar and would give us nothing but words. Every speech he makes confirms his belief that there will be no black majority rule in Zimbabwe during his lifetime. Holding talks with a man like that is a waste of time. We would gain nothing and lose the respect of our followers. And why does Smith want to talk?' Gara kicked his chair back viciously and leaned, flat-palmed over the table, staring intently at each man in turn. 'I will tell you why. Because he is afraid. All the racists in Zimbabwe are afraid. The white will is crumbling before the victorious advance of our gallant liberators and they know they cannot stand against us. They are white sheep bleating at the scent of leopard smell on the wind.

'So they wish to talk, to promise us a lot, perhaps give us a little and keep the rest for themselves. The whites have stolen our country and we cannot rest until we have got it back. All of it. We are not children or beggars to go with our hands out pleading for that which is already ours. We will kill them and take it, like men. No, I say! No! There can be no talks with Smith.' He sat down, perspiration standing out on his forehead and trembling with the passion of his conviction.

Titus Magaba waited a few moments, sitting quietly twirling the stem of the Waterford goblet in his fingers, aware that Gara's words had had a profound effect on the others. Magaba was a realist. He knew that the Shona had taken the land from the little yellow Bushmen, killing them or forcing them to flee into the arid, inhospitable desert of the Kalahari. The Matabele had done exactly the same thing to the Shona and only the arrival of the whites in 1890 had prevented their annihilation. The whites had taken land from both groups and so become the common enemy, to be dealt with first. Once that had been accomplished the Matabele could again walk tall in the land and drive the Shona dogs back into the kennels from which they had sprung.

If Magaba was a realist, he was also an opportunist and a conference with Smith would be the ideal method of gauging the feelings and morale of the whites in Zimbabwe. It was a foregone conclusion that nothing else could result from such a conference. Magaba did not want a settlement with the whites any more than Gara did. Any settlement would extinguish his dreams of a Matabele-dominated society with the Shona subjugated to the role of second-class citizens and servants.

Even in the unlikely event of Smith agreeing right now to all the demands of both nationalist groups, Magaba would ensure that ZAPU's subsequent demands became absolutely unreasonable and would force the Rhodesian Prime Minister to withdraw from any talks with the African nationalists. He neither loved nor hated the whites. They existed merely as a stumbling block to his dreams of a Matabele empire, and they therefore had to be eliminated.

'If the white men are no more than bleating sheep in the wind, why did you run before them? Why did you not attack Salisbury and slaughter them all? For an armed man with the blood of warriors in his veins it should have been an easy thing to do. Or can it be that the Shona warriors are less than the sheep they despise?'

For a moment Magaba thought he had gone too far. The threat of the gun in his hand seemed almost insignificant in the face of Gara's rage. He was on his feet, his face contorted with hatred as his lips twisted in savage effort to reply through his violent anger. The shocked silence round the table filled Magaba with the knowledge that he had overstepped the bounds of acceptable conduct, and he could very easily find himself in an unenviable position of condemned isolation.

'I apologise, Comrade Paratema,' he said quickly, forcing sincerity into his tone with conscious effort. 'Your personal bravery is beyond question and I withdraw my remarks. It is just that I feel we should agree to talks with Smith. We should listen to him to discover exactly how desperate he has become,' he ended lamely, knowing he had lost the attention of his audience and damning his loose tongue and inability to conceal his contempt for the Shona, and for ZANU.

He would have to be very careful in the future. Gara had killed a white man, inoffensive and old he may have been, but still a white man. He had been involved in a series of clashes with Rhodesian soldiers and had been wounded, if only slightly. He was the hero of the hour and could do no wrong. Very few of the staff at Liberation Headquarters could claim to have even seen a Rhodesian soldier, let alone been in action.

Sibanda went round the table pouring out KWV brandy and making small talk to relieve the tension. Gara sat back in his chair, not mollified but no longer dominated by killing rage. Magaba had apologised and publicly attested to Gara's bravery. That the words were insincere he did not doubt, but they had been spoken in front of the most influential nationalist leaders in Lusaka, and he knew the story of Magaba backing down to him would circulate like wildfire through the ranks of ZAPU and ZANU and enhance his own prestige considerably. With his stupid, loose mouth Magaba had virtually ensured Gara's nomination to the post of organizing secretary. He was satisfied to let the matter rest, for the moment.

'Very well, gentlemen,' Sibanda said as he resumed his seat at the head of the table. 'We will put the motion to the vote. All those in favour of a constitutional conference with the rebel Smith, say aye.'

'Aye.' Magaba's voice was thin and lonely in the silence.

'All those against such a meeting say no.'

Four voices answered 'No!' simultaneously and four pairs of eyes subjected Magaba's reaction to close scrutiny. He shrugged without any display of emotion and lit a cigarette.

'The request from the rebel regime in Salisbury is denied,' Sibanda said into the void. 'Copies of this meeting's minutes will be prepared and delivered to all interested parties in the morning. I will personally inform Dr Kaunda of our decision this evening. The meeting is closed. Goodnight, gentlemen.' He shuffled his papers together, put his pen into his pocket and walked out of the room.

Gara was the next to leave and Magaba watched him go with hooded eyes. That one was too ambitious for his own good and one day he would have to die. Magaba's devious mind was already planning the details of the death and although it might be postponed for months, or even years, when the time came for Gara to die, the plan would be ready and perfect. He sat back in the padded chair, sipping brandy and considering the details. For the first time since the meeting had begun, a small smile played across his lips.

Gara climbed into the back of the white Mercedes-Benz parked in the dark street and shook the sleeping African chauffeur roughly by the shoulder. 'Wake up,' he snapped. 'If you were paid for sleeping I would buy you a bed. If this happens again you will be fired and I'll make sure you never get another job in Lusaka. Do you understand?'

'Yes, sir,' the shaking driver replied. 'It won't happen again.'

'It had better not. Now take me home.'

'Yes, sir,' he said and reached with a trembling hand for the ignition key.

When he had been promoted to assistant to the organizing secretary a whole new, undreamed of world had opened up for Gara, a world of big, gleaming motorcars, luxurious hotel suites, hand-made clothes, servants, expensive liquor, after-shave lotions, deodorants, women. White women.

Her name was Jacquetta Duval and she came from a small town

near Paris, the name of which Gara found it impossible to pronounce. She was a qualified nurse and had been attached to the Flying Doctor Service before he had taken her over. She cost him in excess of a hundred kwacha a week and finding the money was a constant problem, but she was worth every bit of it and more. Just thinking about her tightened the muscles of his stomach and his body tingled with anticipation. He leaned forward and prodded the chauffeur in the back. 'Drive faster, you fool.'

Gara walked into his three-roomed flat twenty minutes later. When he had first seen the flat and been told that it was one of the perks which went with the position of assistant to the secretary he had been like a child with a much desired and unexpected present. He had run round switching on all the lights, burnt his hand on the electric stove and flooded the bathroom by forgetting to turn off the bath taps. But now that he almost had the appointment of organizing secretary in his pocket, the solid comfort of the flat faded into depressing ordinariness when compared with the opulent luxury of the modern, split-level house on three acres that went with the organizing secretary's job.

He walked into the lounge and threw his jacket over the back of a chair. Jacquetta was lying on the couch with her feet tucked under her. She was wearing a housecoat and had a French magazine spread out on the cushions beside her.

'You look tired, cherie,' she said as she stood up quickly. 'Come and sit down.'

He flopped down into a chair and ran his eyes appreciatively over the lines of her body. 'Get me a drink.'

She moved over to the liquor cabinet, opened it and poured an inch of brandy into a glass. She handed it to him, then walked round behind him and began massaging his neck with strong, kneading fingers. He reached for her and pulled her down onto the arm of the chair.

It amused him that he, Gara Paratema, who a few short months ago was welcome in the white man's home only as a servant and condemned to live in a pigsty of a kia at the bottom of the garden, now had one of their women to serve his drinks, rub his neck and gratify his whims. He had never been a white man's house servant, but he identified with those who had because it helped to increase his sensation of dominance over Jacquetta.

Suddenly he pushed her away and walked to the window with the drink in his hand and stood morosely watching the traffic in the street below.

'What is it, cherie? Have I done something to upset you?' She slid her arms round his waist.

'No, it has nothing to do with you.'

'What is it then? Tell your little Jacquetta what troubles you. I may be able to help.'

'There is a man I have to kill,' he said softly.

'You aren't going back to Rhodesia, are you?' she asked with quick alarm. She didn't give a damn about Gara but the one hundred kwacha he paid her every Friday was a different matter altogether. That, she cared about. If he went back to Rhodesia he could be killed and she would have to go back to work. The idea did not appeal to her.

'Zimbabwe, not Rhodesia,' he said angrily. 'How many times do I have to say it? Rhodesia is dead. It is now Zimbabwe! Do you understand?'

'I'm sorry. Zimbabwe.' She found it difficult to predict his mercurial changes of mood with any accuracy. 'But you aren't going back, are you?'

'No. The man I have to kill is here.'

'Here? In Lusaka?'

'Yes. Right here in Lusaka. A mad dog of a Matabele hyena spawn.'

'Who is it?'

'That is not your concern.'

She shrugged her shoulders and returned to the couch and her magazine.

16

I HAD left instructions for a call at 0530 hours the next morning and told the night porter to hammer on the door until he was sure I was awake. I couldn't take the chance of oversleeping. And hammer he did. He damn near broke the door down before I stumbled over to open it. But at least I was up. He put the coffee tray down on the bedside table and I told him to bring another pot, a big one, in fifteen minutes.

I stood under the shower for five minutes, then used some eyedrops I found in the bathroom cabinet. The drops turned the sand under my lids to mud. I used some more and after a couple of minutes I could blink without cringing. The fresh coffee came just as I finished dressing. I poured out a cup, strong and black, lit a Gold Flake and turned on the radio. I sat through five minutes of soft-sell religion and the six o'clock time check. The report was the first item read out by the newscaster.

> '*Security Force Headquarters have issued the following communiqué: Late yesterday afternoon, a terrorist was killed and another captured during an engagement with security forces on Kandahar Island near Victoria Falls. The terrorists were members of a banned organization with offices in Lusaka and were armed with Communist weapons. The captured terrorist was found to be carrying a large sum of money in Rhodesian banknotes. He appears to be a senior member of the banned organization. The reasons for the terrorist presence on the island are not yet known, but investigations are continuing. There were no security force casualties.*'

I was about to switch the radio off when the announcer continued:

'*Security Force Headquarters regret to announce, in a different incident in the operational area, the death of Corporal Lance Koster. Corporal Koster was aged twenty-one and married. Four terrorists were killed in the engagement and a number of others captured.*'

I snapped the set off savagely as a vision of Koster's wife flashed into my mind. The poor little kid . . . pregnant and left to face the world without her man. She was so obviously in love with him. I could only begin to imagine how she felt. Damn it. It was a dirty war, and Stanislau was part, a large part, of it. He had to die and the false communiqué Mr Hamilton had somehow managed to have broadcast would help. If it didn't get Stanislau climbing the wall, nothing would.

I cleaned the Smith & Wesson, using no oil and leaving the barrel dry. If my predictions were correct, I would soon be using it and I didn't want unnecessary burnt oil deposits in the grooves between the lands of the barrel. I flicked out the cylinder and slid the six bullets snugly home, then nestled the revolver into the holster on my hip and left the room, checking my appearance in the mirror on the way out to ensure the gun was fully concealed by my shirt hanging outside my slacks.

It was 0610 hours and the hotel passages were deserted. I walked through to reception and asked for a couple of pints of fresh orange juice to be sent out to the terrace for me. It was a beautiful morning, still cool enough to be crisp and not a cloud in sight.

The orange juice was cold and tangy, and I was no longer tired. I felt invigorated and expectant as I sat back and waited for Stanislau to react. If he had been a normal tourist he would have been frantically trying to trace Stella and Hart through the other hotels and he certainly would have contacted the police. But being Stanislau the last thing he would want would be any type of police involvement. There was just no way he could discover what had happened to them. He would consider all the possibilities. An accident? That was a possibility with Hart, but not Stella—not after booking out of the hotel. A double cross? Turning State's evidence? I grinned to myself. By now he should be going round the twist. But by 0730 hours, when he still hadn't appeared, I began to wonder if he had checked out before breakfast, and I went back to the reception desk to find out.

The foyer resembled the deck of the *Titanic* just before she sank. It was packed with over a hundred agitated tourists, all demanding instant attention and their bills.

That report had really started something. The hotel manager and four flushed assistants were doing their utmost to cope with the rush, but it was impossible. As soon as they tried to deal with one person, another would grab them and insist on being first. Finally, the harassed manager jumped onto the counter and cupped his hands round his lips. 'Ladies and gentlemen, please!' he bawled. No one paid any attention to him.

One thing was certain. I wasn't going to be able to check if Stanislau had beaten the rush.

'Will you bloody idiots shut up and listen!' the manager yelled at the top of his lungs. '*Shut up!*' This time he got about eighty percent attention. He was about to continue when a louder voice cut him off.

'Who you telling to shut up? If I ain't got my bill in five seconds I'm walking out and stuff you.'

The crowd burst into violent sound again with, 'You tell him, buddy,' and 'Me too,' and 'I'm not hanging around this dump to get slaughtered.'

I couldn't see who the first objector had been but I didn't need to. I would have recognised that voice in my sleep. Henry Clarkson from Broadwater, Nebraska. There is no public transport in Victoria Falls apart from the buses operated by the tourist companies and Air Rhodesia and they would sure as hell not transport him away from an unpaid hotel bill. If Henry wanted to leave that badly, he would have to steal a car and I'd be delighted to arrest him.

The crowd was beginning to turn ugly. A couple of women had fainted and no one seemed to give a damn. A fist fight had broken out between two men, each trying to reach the desk first. When I requested the broadcast, I had anticipated a little local reaction but had not expected the situation to develop into a panic-fed riot. I moved into one of the phone booths lining the wall and dialled the police station. I asked for Pete Fuller and got him. 'Pete, you'd better get down here fast. There's a large crowd in the foyer on the point of turning into a mob.'

'Christ! Thanks a lot. Ever since that damn news bulletin of yours came over, my bloody telephone hasn't stopped ringing. Every mother's son from the mayor to the camp labourer wants to know what's happening.' He sounded a little flustered.

'So you have to earn your pay for a change,' I said. 'If you don't get down here now you'll have more than telephone calls, you'll have bodies.'

'Oh, for God's sake. Okay, I'm on my way,' he groaned, and slammed the receiver down.

I went back into the foyer just in time to catch a woman who had been hurled out of his way by none other than my old friend, Henry Clarkson, in his frantic scramble to reach the desk. If I hadn't been there she would have fallen. I helped her to a chair and asked, 'Are you all right?'

'Yes, thanks,' she panted, brushing hair out of her eyes. 'I believe in Women's Lib, but this is ridiculous.'

I grinned at her and walked into the crowd, just behind Henry. He was using his elbows as rams and making progress. I pressed up behind him and as he tried to ram me, I brought the plaster cast down sharply on the point of his elbow, not with crushing force, but hard enough to hurt. He yelled loudly and suddenly lost all interest in reaching the desk. He lurched out of the crowd, moaning and holding his elbow. I smiled at him as he passed me but he didn't return the smile. It didn't hurt my feelings in the least and was not something I'd lose any sleep over.

Pete Fuller sailed into the foyer like a four-masted galleon under full canvas and bulled his way through to the reception desk. The sight of his uniform had an immediate calming effect on the crowd and they quietened down considerably. For a long moment he remained silent, tapping his swagger stick on the counter and surveying them with kindly sympathy. There was a little isolated muttering, but the majority were unexpectedly ashamed of their conduct, and self-conscious grins began to appear.

'Ladies and gentlemen. I fully understand the position in which you think you find yourselves and I sympathize completely. But I must stress that there is no danger to any . . . '

'Why aren't you armed?' a voice called from the back of the crowd.

Fuller extended his arms in front of his body and looked at them with surprise. 'These are legs?' he asked loudly.

The laughter was spontaneous and when it had faded he said, 'As I was saying, there is absolutely no danger to any of you. None at all. And there's no reason for anyone to terminate their holiday prematurely—if any of you had contemplated such action.' He smiled at the crowd like a benign grandfather at an Italian wedding. 'Should any of you still wish to leave today, I'm sure the hotel management will be delighted . . . ' He paused. 'Well, maybe not delighted, but they will make up your accounts. They can't do it all at once, though. So let's give them a chance, shall we?'

He had them eating out of the palm of his hand and he hadn't once mentioned the bulletin or terrorists. His technique was masterly and his control of the situation complete.

A babble of chatter broke out and the majority of the crowd drifted out of the foyer, most of them wondering what the hell they were doing there in the first place. Only eight or so remained clustered round the reception desk. One of the eight was Stanislau.

I watched him settle his account and followed him through to the dining-room for breakfast. For a man who should have been on the knife-edge of panic he appeared remarkably calm. He ignored the two empty chairs at his table and gave the waiter his order. He was his normal, urbane, smiling self.

God damn him. Didn't he have any nerves?

His reactions were totally beyond comprehension. His nightclub and building burn right down to the ground; his whore vanishes with all her belongings; his tame ape disappears without his; his money-changing racket is blown wide open and as far as he is aware, a captured terrorist is being interrogated by the police and could possibly incriminate him. And he sat there, apparently quite unperturbed. The son-of-a-bitch. He had to crack.

After breakfast he returned his hired car to Avis and then spent the rest of the morning in the residents' lounge, paging through magazines. At 1030 hours he went up to his room to supervise his luggage and half-an-hour later his cases were stacked in the foyer waiting to be loaded onto the airport bus.

I was desperate. He hadn't put a foot out of line—and I was in trouble, deep trouble. I knew he was guilty, but that wouldn't help explain to Mr Hamilton how I had just let him walk away. Not after all the rigmarole we had gone through to get him. But that wasn't the main consideration. I would have to live with myself. Myself and a dream of mutilated children, blood, bullets and screaming death. The face I'd have to shave every morning would be mine and the man behind it would be a fraud. A fraud without the guts to back up his convictions because the laws of our society dictate that guilt is innocence until proved beyond a reasonable doubt. I had the certainty, but not the proof.

I watched the porter load his luggage aboard the bus which had pulled up outside the hotel. Stanislau tipped him lavishly, then took his place in the queue, waiting patiently for those ahead of him to take their seats.

The bastard was walking away from me. Not only from me, from everything he had done. And legally there wasn't a thing I could do about it, not one tiny, damn thing. Sure I could arrest him. On the evidence in my possession we could hold him for at least fifteen seconds, and that was an optimistic estimate. You can't fight evil with a copy of the constitution in one hand and a good housekeeping manual in the other. I decided to take my chance and walked over to the bus.

I tapped him on the shoulder. 'Mr Stanislau?'

'That is correct. Who might you be?' His voice was low and controlled, without a trace of accent, and his lips formed a polite, enquiring smile. I had to force my hands down at my sides as the memory of the Ronson children flooded my brain and the bitter, yellow bile of seething hatred welled up in the back of my throat, suffocating me. At that moment I could easily have killed him—without compassion or remorse. I should have.

'Police, Detective Inspector Kelly.' I flashed my ID card and had difficulty forming the words around my hate. 'I would like you to accompany me to the police station to assist in an enquiry which is under investigation.'

'I'm afraid that is not possible,' he answered. 'I have a plane to catch and the bus leaves for the airport in a few moments' time.' His eyes were laughing at me and the mockery they contained almost tipped me over the edge of self-control.

'It is possible. And I insist,' I said, knowing my lips had stretched across my teeth in a savage grin.

'Are you intimating that I am being placed under arrest?' His eyebrows arched in supercilious surprise.

'It could be arranged, if you prefer it that way.' My voice was cold and hard, betraying none of the anxiety or doubt that was hitting the high notes in my brain. If this didn't work out I was in more than trouble. I was finished. I wondered briefly if Cathy's father's farm option would still be open when I was released from jail.

'Spare me the dramatics,' he said. 'It would appear that I have no choice in the matter. I have several important business meetings scheduled for this afternoon in Salisbury, and I'll exact full compensation from the relevant authorities for any losses I may incur as a result of this delay. Is that clear?' he added heavily. 'If you are hurt in the process it will be entirely your own fault.' He gave the impression that the more hurt I was the more pleased he would be.

I told the porter to unload Stanislau's luggage and put it in the boot of the hired BMW which Pete Fuller had returned to the car-park.

'I am only accompanying you under the most rigorous protest. I hope you understand that.' His condescending manner reached all my raw spots at the same time.

'Get in,' I said, holding the passenger door open for him. He didn't appear to be carrying a gun, possibly because of the stringent anti-highjacking security precautions in force at the airport. He settled comfortably in the seat as if he was going for a pleasant

Sunday afternoon spin in the country. I climbed into the car and turned the key in the ignition switch. 'I wonder which side of Parliament Square you were on in Budapest that October?' I said, watching his reaction with hawk eyes. Only he didn't react.

'I beg your pardon?' he asked conversationally.

'Did you enjoy the sight of the Danube running red with the blood of your countrymen when the Mongolians took over the city? Or did you prefer the entertainment in the cellars of AVO Headquarters at sixty Stalin Ut?' I grated harshly at him. 'As a spectator, of course. Or did you participate in the fun, from the dark side of the interrogation lamps?'

'You are obviously aware that I am Hungarian by birth and was involved in the October Revolution. Possibly you are not aware that I was one of the junior leaders of the Revolution and was forced to leave my country by the Russian pigs. I am now a naturalized Rhodesian citizen,' he said and smiled easily.

'You're a naturalized bastard, recruited either by the Soviet MVS or the KGB.'

'If you would care to repeat that in front of independent witnesses I would sue you for so much that the amount would make your head spin. But, of course, not being able to prove it, you won't.' He was still smiling, but it was no longer easy. It was fixed and mechanical. 'I was under the impression I had left this sort of police persecution behind the iron curtain. It was most unpleasant then and I find it no more enjoyable now.'

His tone hadn't altered, but the artery in his neck had begun to pulse noticeably and I realised I was getting to him at last. He was a long way from blowing, but the fuse was alight and burning. I turned the screw a little tighter.

'For whom was the persecution in Hungary unpleasant?' I asked, biting the words. 'Those who died for freedom from the Russian bootheel or the ones like you, who brought the survivors back into the fold and re-educated them with Mongolian savages, tanks, firing squads and torture?'

'This has gone on long enough,' he said and the smile was a shadow of its former self. 'When we get to the police station I insist upon seeing a senior officer and laying the severest charge possible against you.'

'If it's severe charges you want you'll find them in plenty when we get there. But I'll tell you a little story before we do. A story of a misguided idiot of a terrorist who died on the bank of the Zambezi River and was found to be carrying a thermos flask which contained much more than tea—seven sheets of rice paper covered with interesting facts. A story of a blue Hermes typewriter which was removed from the Moonraker before the fire and of cute little Georgie Gretson who sang such a sweet, interesting song and signed a statement before he died. A story of a whore named Stella and a henchman named Hart who suddenly found themselves overcome by fits of patriotic fervour and revealed all.'

I paused to let the lies sink in. Then angrily gave the screw a final twist. 'I know exactly what you are. A murderous commie bastard,' I spat. 'Have you ever seen children hacked to bits and lying in their own blood, Stanislau? You and your sodding Marxist friends. You financed that to perpetuate the stinking schemes of your Russian masters. You burnt down a hospital and the patients in it, you killed a harmless old priest and Christ knows what else you'll have to answer for in hell. But first you'll answer to me, and I think you'll find the devil an easier inquisitor.' I felt the urgent need to lash out, to destroy, and controlled myself with difficulty. 'The MVS don't have the resources to mount your kind of subversion. So you've got to be with the KGB. That's right isn't it?'

I slid my hand imperceptibly towards the .38 hidden under my shirt. Do something, I screamed silently at him, give me the excuse I need to finish this now.

He didn't. The look of contempt he flicked over me froze my hand, sending me mentally reeling. 'You are marvellous, Kelly,' he sneered. 'You really are. Does your stupidity know no bounds? What has a thermos flask filled with typed sheets and carried by an obscure revolutionary got to do with me? Even if the typing was done by a machine in my office, how can I be implicated? I spend a lot of time away from Salisbury and several people had access to that typewriter. George Gretson is dead, Kelly. As a police officer, you of all people should know that only deathbed statements are acceptable by the Rhodesian courts as admissible evidence in criminal cases. If Gretson signed any statement, which I doubt, he is no longer with us and cannot be cross-examined. So such a statement has no legal standing. Or did he sign it as he was consumed by the flames? That would have been a remarkable achievement.

'As for Randall and Hart, what are they?' he snorted. 'Two inconsequential criminals bred in the gutters of your decadent society. They both have police records and any testimony they offered would be suspect. And what could they tell a judge, even if he was inclined to listen? That the despicable Mr Stanislau had broken foreign exchange regulations and was engaged in the heinous crime of illegal currency deals? This sort of thing goes on all the time and, as you know, occasionally with official sanction. An offence which carries a paltry fine.' He regarded me with malicious amusement. 'Do you take me for a fool, Kelly?'

'Yes, Stanislau. And like all fools you talk too much. How did you know,' I asked quietly, 'that the information on the rice paper was typed on your machine, or even that it was typed at all?'

I felt a surge of triumph at the sudden doubt that flashed in his eyes. But he was good, a professional, and he recovered instantly.

'Clever. Very clever,' he said slowly and with deliberation. 'But is it clever enough? Where are your witnesses? The weak and ineffectual system of justice in this country will not convict a man on the unsubstantiated word of a policeman. It is *your* word against *mine*, Kelly.' He paused confident of his immunity. 'You need solid evidence, but you don't have it. Do you?'

'No, I don't.' My fingers touched the cold butt of the Smith & Wesson.

Stanislau didn't hear me. He didn't see the movement. He sat staring through the windscreen, his face alight with victory and burning fanaticism.

'You are close, Kelly. Closer than anyone has ever come. No, it is neither KGB nor the MVS. I am a regional director of the Africa Department attached to the Soviet Ministry of Foreign Affairs,' he boasted, now that he knew I couldn't touch him, 'and my command encompasses Rhodesia and the entire province of the Transvaal in South Africa.'

I sat rooted to the seat as the realization dawned on me. This was no ordinary communist agent. This was the brain that controlled every Russian-backed group of terrorists in the country, and there was nothing I could do about it. Or so he thought.

'We have been operating under your capitalist noses since 1960,' he continued expansively, 'and Phase One is almost complete. That is the infiltration of armed revolutionaries who are at this very moment gaining control of your rural areas. The chiefs, the school teachers and the headmen who are stupid enough to oppose them must die and in such a manner that discourages any further opposition. The deaths, the murders you squeal about mean nothing, less than nothing, compared with the Soviet conquest of Africa and you with your pathetic laws and senile system of Western democracy cannot stop it.' His breathing was fast and shallow. A film of perspiration covered his face and I realized then that Stanislau was a raving megalomaniac. He had commanded total power for so long that he thought nothing could stop him . . . and he was right. He would deny every word and I couldn't even enter his name on a charge sheet let alone try for a conviction on the grounds of what he had just told me—not without witnesses.

'How does it feel, Detective Inspector Kelly,' he taunted, 'to be so close to the glory of arresting me? Think of the promotion and prospects that would have stretched out so pleasurably in your future. Then think about reality. Think of what you know and cannot use, and of the fact that I will be free and untouchable. I think there will be more joy in my future than in yours,' he said and the contempt was back in full force.

'You don't have a future,' I told him flatly. I'd had enough.

The revolver slid into my hand. Stanislau regarded it with disdain. 'You have lost, Kelly. Your childish theatrics do not impress me.'

I didn't reply. There was nothing left to talk about. I felt empty and emotionless. I was about to commit cold-blooded murder. I was about to reject every principle I had ever believed in, and I didn't care. Stanislau had to die and what happened after that was of no consequence to anyone but myself. My decision was final and irrevocable.

Stanislau's sneer of amused contempt froze on his face. For a moment he looked at me intently. Then surprise and sudden fear clouded his eyes and I knew he realized I was going to kill him. Involuntarily he steeled himself as I tilted the gun barrel up toward his heart.

And then the child screamed.

The split-second distraction was enough for Stanislau. If I hadn't caught the flicker of movement out of the corner of my eye I would have been dead. His hand, board-stiff with thumb extended at right angle to the palm, came out of nowhere and whipped with vicious power toward the lethal spot just below my nose. I jerked my head aside and the edge of his palm smashed into my temple, then he was out of the car and running. I hung over the steering-wheel dizzy and blind with pain. The child was still screaming and I heard a concerned voice trying to calm it: 'There, there, poppet. It was only a little bee. Mummy will rub some onion on it and kiss it better.'

Damn the bee. Damn the child. Damn them both to hell.

By the time I stumbled out of the car, Stanislau had disappeared round the corner of the hotel and there was no chance of a shot. Not that I could have done anything about it even if there was. I was swaying like a drunk and had difficulty focusing.

Nothing had worked out. By now Stanislau should have been dead, with a couple of bullets helping him along the road to hell. I had turned a rabid dog loose on the unsuspecting population of Victoria Falls, and I had to find him before he killed somebody. I eased back into the car and drove fast to the police station, my eyes screwed up and squinting through the pain.

17

'THE road block is set up twenty miles out on the Bulawayo Road. Not too far for it to be out of touch but not close enough for Stanislau to walk round it either,' Pete Fuller said confidently and tossed the pencil he had been using as a map pointer onto the desk. 'The road to Kazungula is practically impassable at this time of the year but I've put a block on it anyway. The customs post at the bridge has been alerted and armed patrols are searching the river bank and guarding the boats at the same time. Section Officer Mills is out at the airport so all the exits from the township are sewn up tight. Unless Stanislau wants to commit suicide by trying to walk out through a couple of hundred miles of bush, we've got him.'

I wished I could share Fuller's confidence. The idea of a constable with a Greener shotgun confronting Stanislau left a picture of a dead constable in my mind and there had been far too many innocent deaths already. Only Stanislau's death was necessary now, and I had screwed it up. Any further loss of life caused by him would lie heavily on my conscience. I cursed myself bitterly. I'd had the chance and blown it. Letting him get the edge on me like that, especially when I had been expecting it, was unforgivable, and I couldn't shake the feeling of dark foreboding.

That sort of thinking wouldn't help to catch the bastard. I shook my head and tried to concentrate on what I would do in his position. I thought about the hot, endless miles of dangerous, desolate bush country to the south, but there was nothing attractive in it as an escape route. The lure of Zambian safety was compellingly close.

If I were in his place it would be the river, which meant the bridge or a stolen boat. Which meant that someone would die, unless we were very, very lucky. I didn't feel lucky. I smashed my fist into the side of the desk and cursed.

'Relax, Rich. There's nothing to get uptight about. He's running, he has no way out and he's stuffed. He has to show himself soon and when he does we'll have him.'

Oh sure, I thought, he'll show and how many people will die when he does? But I didn't say anything. Sharing the load with Pete Fuller wouldn't make it any lighter. I reached for the can of Lion lager he put down in front of me and took a long swallow. I desperately wanted to be out hunting Stanislau but I had to stay in the police station. It was the central point and the only one in contact with all units.

We played cut-throat stud poker with a dog-eared pack of cards bearing the casino motif, and Fuller took twenty dollars off me. I was nervous and jumpy and my concentration was lower than nil. By the time the clock on the wall had crept round to 1530 hours I was very near breaking point. Then the telephone rang.

'Inspector Fuller,' Pete barked into the mouthpiece and I watched his features harden as he listened. 'We're on our way,' he growled and slammed the receiver down. 'Stanislau tried for the bridge,' he said as we ran out to the carpark. 'He crashed a car into the barrier and shot a customs officer.'

'Did he get away?' I shouted over the racket as Fuller gunned the Land-Rover out of the station yard.

'Don't know,' he yelled back and swung onto the road leading to the bridge. My hired BMW would have been faster but it wasn't fitted with a radio. Fuller brought the vehicle to a tyre-shredding halt outside the border post a couple of minutes later. The senior customs officer, wearing gold-braided epaulettes, was waiting for us. He clutched a cumbersome old Webley .455 in his right hand and looked furious enough to use it.

'What happened, Jim?' Fuller asked, ignoring the gaggle of open-mouthed tourists who stood around gawking increduously and talking in hushed, shocked whispers.

'The crazy bastard!' the senior customs officer exploded. 'He came down the approach road and must have been doing close to seventy when he hit the boom. Look at that!' He flung his arm out angrily towards the bridge.

The boom had been ripped from its supports and lay like a twisted, metal python amid the debris and shattered glass that littered the road. The car—a white, two-door Cortina—was crumpled against a concrete support beam, the roof almost torn off. Part of the engine had been forced back onto the front passenger seat and although the car might not have been doing seventy miles an hour when it hit the boom it couldn't have been much less.

'Andrews tried to stop him but the swine shot him in the chest.' The tremor in the customs officer's voice was distinct.

'What happened to the driver?' I asked him quietly. 'Did he make it across the bridge?'

'No. I fired a couple of shots at him.' He held up the antique Webley. 'He climbed the embankment over there next to the security fence and disappeared into the bush.'

'Did you hit him?' Pete Fuller asked hopefully.

'No,' he said, shaking his head. 'No, I don't think so. I wish I had. The bloody bastard.'

Andrews was young, about twenty, and lay on a wooden bench in the customs building. Someone had opened his bloodstained shirt and used a field dressing to stop the bleeding from the hole in the left side of his chest. His breathing was slow and irregular, and his face was grey. He would be a hero if he lived. It didn't seem likely. I had been wrong: Stanislau was armed—a small-calibre pistol judging by the size of the hole in Andrews' shirt.

'Have you called the clinic?' Fuller asked.

'Yes,' the customs officer nodded. 'The doctor's on his way here now.'

There was nothing we could do for Andrews.

'Let's go, Pete,' I said and walked out to the Land-Rover.

'Where to?' he asked as he heaved himself in behind the steering-wheel.

'The river. It's his only chance now and time's running out. He knows it. He has to get across before we saturate the entire area with troops and flush him out. He's desperate and running scared. He's going to steal a boat.'

'You mean try, don't you? All the boats are guarded.'

I sat silently for a moment, mentally debating possibilities. 'Pete, how many men do you have on the boat-guarding detail?'

'Four ACs with Greeners and a PO with a .303. Why?'

'I want them pulled off. Immediately.'

'Are you out of your tiny mind?' Fuller asked incredulously. 'What the hell do you want to do? Help him escape?'

'Do you really think a constable with a shotgun can stop him? He's going to steal a boat and I'd rather he didn't leave a trail of bodies behind him doing it.'

'If any of my men get hurt . . . '

'You can prevent them getting hurt. He's armed, highly trained and extremely dangerous. Dammit, Pete, they haven't got a chance against him. Use the radio. Call those men off. Do it now, before it's too late.'

He stared at me for a few seconds, then reached for the VHF radio microphone and gave the necessary orders. 'I hope you're sure of what you're doing,' he said to me. 'If we don't stop him we'd better start making plans to cross the border ourselves.'

'So move this heap down to the police jetty, unless you want to sit here gabbing while he gets away.'

He revved the engine savagely and we took off for the river.

* * *

Fuller slowed the launch and turned to me. 'We're opposite the Southern Cross Safari launch site. The only other two sites are on either side of it. No boats are moored any further downstream, the current is too strong. They would be washed over the Falls. If Stanislau is going to steal a boat it has to be in this area.'

'How far are we from the Falls?' I asked.

'Two and a half, maybe three miles by river.'

It was hard to believe. It seemed we were a lot closer to them, the water was moving so fast. A clump of floating weed swept past the boat and disappeared in seconds.

There were two islands between us and the Zambian shore. A small one named Kalunda and a very much bigger one called Long Island. Both are Zambian territory.

All the boat launching sites on the Rhodesian shore were directly opposite Kalunda Island and the total river frontage they occupied was less than a mile, with the United Touring site nearest the Falls and the Victoria Falls Boat Club furthest upstream.

We had been cruising the narrow channel between Kalunda Island and the Rhodesian shore for about twenty minutes. Fuller swung the launch round opposite the United Touring jetty and in the middle of the turn we saw him.

He had chosen well. It was a sleek, blue, open fibreglass deep-V, about sixteen feet long and, judging by the speed he was travelling, it must have been equipped with at least an eighty horsepower motor. It came out of the Victoria Falls Boat Club inlet like a missile and was up and planing before it shot round the top end of Kalunda Island. Stanislau was seated in the stern, gripping the tiller. He raised his hand in a derisive salute just before we lost sight of him.

Fuller slammed the throttle forward and the six-cylinder Austin Healey engine screamed in protest as the Hamilton Jet hurled us through the water in pursuit.

We rounded the tip of the island in a shuddering turn as we cut into his wake.

He was heading downstream in the channel between Kalunda and Long Island. Possibly he was unaware that both the islands were Zambian territory because he didn't attempt to beach on either of them. If he had I would have risked international repercussions and followed him, something I wouldn't have done on the Zambian mainland.

The deep-V was travelling very fast but it was outclassed by the police launch and we were gaining on him, the distance between us closing rapidly.

He cleared the end of Long Island, swung left and headed straight for the Zambian bank, three hundred yards in front of him.

'Move, you bitch! Move!' Fuller snarled, smashing his palm against the throttle control in frustrated rage.

Stanislau was fifty yards from the Zambian bank and we were thirty yards behind him. We weren't going to make it, it just wasn't possible. Then he twisted the throttle grip and the bow of the deep-V dug into the water as it slowed down.

The bank was sheer and twenty feet high, cut off clean by flood waters with no low spots or beaches where he could have run the boat ashore. To hit the bank at speed could only result in an accident in which Stanislau would be hurt, and he realised it. So he slowed down.

Pete Fuller had no such inhibitions. He tipped the launch onto its side in a tight, spray-spewing turn and shot into the opening between Stanislau and the bank, crashing violently into the deep-V, ten feet from Zambia. The force of the impact jarred the Smith & Wesson out of my hand and it spun lazily into the water. The crash also sent Stanislau sprawling on the bottom of the stolen boat.

Fuller leant on the wheel and forced both craft away from the bank in an erratic, grinding manoeuvre.

It had been very close. Zambian foliage brushed across my face as we turned, but there was no time to think about it. It wasn't over yet.

I lurched to the side of the police launch and dropped into the other boat, grabbed the tiller and swung away from Pete Fuller. I twisted the throttle as the bows came round and headed back for the Rhodesian bank, hoping the boat hadn't been holed in the crash.

Stanislau was bleeding from a deep gash in his forehead and he appeared to be unconscious. I hoped to God he was, and would stay that way until I got him ashore. In any event there was nothing I could do about it. It was impossible to handcuff him and control the boat at the same time. Doubly impossible with only one hand operational.

Pete Fuller kept the police launch upstream and parallel with me, grinning all over his fat face like a cherub. I knew how he felt.

We were a hundred yards from the Rhodesian shore when Stanislau erupted. He came off the floorboards like a cat, a small nickel-plated automatic pistol in his hand. I felt the boat swing in the current as I dived off the stern seat. My shoulder hit him hard in the stomach and for an instant he paused, fighting for breath. I grabbed his wrist and smashed it down on the gunwale with enough force to make him drop the pistol and it fell into the water. I had caught him by surprise. He had expected the pistol to scare me, but my reaction had been instinctive.

I released his wrist and whipped my left hand up from my knees with all the power I had. This was one fight I wanted to end quickly. I felt the cast graze his cheek and it left a few scratches under his eye which immediately filled with blood. But only scratches.

He was lightning fast. I realised with sudden horror that I couldn't match him. I was still trying desperately to regain my balance in the wildly-rocking boat when his toecap came out of nowhere and my solar plexus exploded into a million white-hot fragments of agonising pain.

I collapsed on the bottom of the boat, fighting back nausea. He landed on top of me, one knee pinning the cast down and I didn't have the strength to free it. His hands wrapped round my neck and his thumbs sank deep into my throat. The kick had forced the air out of my lungs and his thumbs cut the supply completely and I could feel blood vessels bursting behind my eyes. His face was a vague, undefinable blur floating in a sea of red mist, blood roaring through my head.

My right hand fluttered weakly over his face and he laughed. The bastard was killing me and laughing. I forced every atom of my dwindling strength into my index finger, rammed it up his nostril and ripped.

I didn't feel the fine spray of blood that covered my face as his flesh tore and he staggered back holding his hands over his nose, making a strange mewing sound.

Cold, sweet air rushed into my starved lungs in fantastic relief as I sat up slowly, shaking my head to get rid of the roaring in my brain. But it didn't subside. The roaring wasn't in my brain.

The boat was about fifty yards from the Rhodesian bank and the shoreline was flashing past at tremendous speed. The mist wasn't in my head either, it was real and wet.

Christ! The Falls!

With a gutroot fear that was close to panic I reached for the tiller, twisted the throttle wide open and pulled the rudder over, trying to steer for the bank.

The deep-V twisted and slewed in the furious white water and almost capsized. It bucked and surged in the frenzied waves and was more than a quarter full of water by the time I brought it round to run with the current. There wasn't the slightest chance of reaching the shore across that churning hell.

Stanislau was kneeling in the bows, clutching the sides of the boat. His mouth hung open and his eyes were wide with terror. The torn flap of his nostril was plastered across his cheek and his face was a mess of blood. He didn't try to reach me. There was no point. In a few seconds we would both die.

The thunder of a hundred million gallons of rampaging water smashing every minute with violent, uncontrollable fury into the tormented rocks three hundred and fifty feet below the snarling lip of the Falls hammered into my brain with a crushing depair that banished coherent thought, and I cringed against the stern seat in fear. I had no control over the boat and the tiller twisted and turned in my hand with a demonic life of its own. For a crazy instant it seemed to me that the boat understood what was happening and was going through its death throes.

A thin, black slice of land suddenly loomed out of the mist and raced toward us, ten feet to the right.

I leant my weight on the tiller and held it over, without reason or thought, and felt the boat begin to tip as the full force of the current thrust greedily at the beam. I was frozen in terrified position and couldn't move, my mind a separate entity which hovered just above my head, watching with casual interest as we hurtled towards the rocky projection.

The tilting bow ground against a partly submerged rock, swinging the boat violently round and driving its side into the land with irresistible, splintering force. The impact picked me up and I felt myself turning slowly through the air as I was tossed helplessly onto the rock. I was stunned and long moments fled to oblivion before I realised, with slow-dawning incredulity, that I was still alive. Alive and safe. No lover has ever been hugged with the passion and intensity with which I embraced that cold, black rock.

I stood up gingerly, my rubber legs threatening to collapse under the weight as I put one foot in front of the other and my vision cleared to the limits of the clinging mist.

Mosi-oa-Tunya the men of the Makalolo tribe had named it. The Smoke-That-Thunders. They had erred on the conservative side. It wasn't just thunder, it was a solid wall of sound which through its very magnitude lost some of its awesomeness. It was too loud, too overpowering to comprehend and in consequence the mind denied a little of its total existence, but it was still crushing.

The mist curbed my field of vision to about twenty yards, which was enough to show that the boat had gone. The only trace of it having existed was the engine cowling which had been thrown up onto the rock with me.

Of Stanislau there was no sign. Possibly he had gone over with the boat. I fervently hoped so. I was in no condition to handle him.

I followed a rising contour and discovered my rock was the peninsula of an island and connected to it by a narrow ridge of high ground. The island itself was covered with dense, tropical growth and criss-crossed with elephant trails. I picked one which appeared to lead west and stumbled along it. I had no idea where I was and only knew that to the east lay Zambian territory, which I had no compelling desire to visit. If elephants could get onto the island, I could get off, or so I thought.

The trail I had chosen led to the brink of the Falls and I realised I had been walking south, not west. My mental compass had taken a beating, but Saint Christopher hadn't let me down. I was on Cataract Island with the Devil's Cataract on my right—Rhodesian territory. The thankful sigh I heaved was cut short as an apparition weaved ghostlike out of the mist and took on solid form as Stanislau came towards me in a menacing crouch, the thick, four-foot branch held in his hand like a club.

I was on the very edge of the Falls. Stanislau blocked my path to the centre of the island and Devil's Cataract cut off my retreat.

I couldn't cross that thirty-five yard wide maelstrom of insanely twisting, tortured water. The only other choice was to go over the Falls or wait for Stanislau. I waited.

He came on slowly, his eyes burning fever bright in the pale, almost translucent flesh of his face. The mist had washed the blood from his features and the cuts under his eye and dreadful tear along the side of his nose stood out in disgusting relief leaving his face a hideous mockery of the sophistication he had once affected. Raw animal hatred blazed from his eyes. His lips distorted into a soundless snarl as he raised the club and charged towards me.

I braced myself to meet him. There was nothing else I could do. I was standing on a bare stretch of rock devoid of vegetation apart from a few small shrubs clinging to life with precarious tenacity in the sparse soil which lined the rim. Beyond them smooth rock reached downwards at an angle of forty-five degrees for about ten feet and then the world ended.

I ducked under his first wild swing and lashed out with the cast. I hit his shoulder hard and he dropped the club and pivoted, arcing his foot toward my groin. But this time I was ready for him. I stepped back, caught his heel in my right palm and put everything I had into the throw. He should have landed on his back and if he had, I could have killed him. But he didn't. He twisted in the air and landed on his hands and launched himself backward like a lance. His heels thudded into my chest and hurled me back another two steps.

It was enough. I was on the sloping rock and fighting desperately to regain my balance. I almost made it. Almost, but not quite. My feet shot out from under me and suddenly I was on my side, sliding over slime-wet, green fungus with nothing between me and death but ten feet of steeply-slanting, glass-smooth black basalt. Aerial roots from the shrubs which lined the rim hung down the rockface, and I grabbed one but it snapped under the sudden strain of my weight. A short, narrow crack climbed swiftly past my face and with desperate convulsions and a frantic, unfamiliar prayer on my lips, I twisted onto my stomach and rammed my left hand into the crack as far as it would go. I slid another six, sickening inches and stopped abruptly with a shoulder-wrenching jerk. My feet were dangling over the edge into space and I could hear my heart pounding above the thunder of the Falls. The cast had jammed in the crack and I clung to life by the thickness of a plaster of Paris dressing.

I looked up and saw Stanislau standing on the rim, the branch poised in his hand like a spear, nothing in his eyes but madness. The vengeful madness of a demented devil in agony. Then he laughed and threw the branch.

I watched helplessly as it came at me. To move was to die. It thudded into my back and I slid another gut-churning foot before the cast jammed again. The edge of the rock, and of time, pressed into my body just below my pelvis and the gods danced on Olympus. Damn them. I couldn't die. Not here, not like this.

Stanislau disappeared from the rim, but not for long. In a few short seconds he was back with another branch in his hand, his wet shirt flapping lethargically in the water-borne wind. I watched his feet carefully, not wanting to die but determined that if I had to, he would die with me.

Just one more step, you bastard. Jesus, God, I prayed frenetically, please make him take one more bloody step.

He raised his arm for the throw and his foot came down in front of a small shrub growing in the shallow soil of the rim. I closed my eyes and jerked the tangle of roots I had wrapped round my right fist. The weak soil surrendered without protest and the plant pulled out easily, snagging Stanislau's foot. I quickly jerked the roots again, not caring if I fell as long as the incarnate son-of-a-bitch came with me. For a mind-stopping moment I thought I had lost.

He stood on the rim eight feet above me swaying like a drunk, spine arched and arms windmilling, fighting with every ounce of his being for balance. The weight of the branch in his hand betrayed him, and he was suddenly on the rock.

For an infinitesimal fraction of eternity he remained on his feet, sliding down the rockface like a trick skater in a grotesque ballet. Then he was on his stomach, slipping slowly past me four feet to the left.

There was no crack to stop him. The roots he reached for in panic snapped in his hands like cheap cotton as he pressed his face hard against the rock in a futile attempt to stop. The mirror surface defied him. The torn skin of his nostril peeled slowly back until it covered a wild, staring eye, leaving a gaping hole where his nose had been. He dug his fingers into the rock, gouging tracks in the slimy green gunge and as he slid past me I watched his fingernails rip out one by one and his hands turn into bloody, mangled claws. His feet went over the edge and he raised his head, the uncovered eye flat and without intelligence, like a fish.

With sudden, irrational feeling I knew I didn't want him to die. Not this way. A quick bullet, a rope, these he deserved. But not like this. This was not just death, it was a hideous torture that no man should suffer. I wanted to help him. To reach out and grab him, but I couldn't move. I hung in motionless suspension, feeling his need but dominated by my own.

His belt buckle snagged on the edge of the rock as he checked himself, and his expression was no longer vacant. His single eye blazed savagely, not at me, but at fate, and he screamed once, long and high. He placed his hands palm-down on the rock and pushed, his scream lingering as his body catapulted away from the rockface and disappeared into the void.

The pain in my shoulder penetrated the layers of misty horror and I stopped feeling sorry for Stanislau. Right then I didn't have any sympathy to spare for anyone—I needed it all for myself. The rim was eight feet above my outstretched, aching arm. Eight lousy, stinking, slippery feet. From where I hung it looked to be at least eighty.

Cautiously I moved my feet, trying for a toe-hold and found empty space. I gathered a dozen hanging roots and twisted them together. Sliding my hand up the tangled length to the limit of my reach, I took a deep, reverend breath and slowly, very slowly, pulled. They held.

The relief as the strain came off my left arm was indescribable. Then the real pain hit me and I knew I would have to move before movement became impossible.

By alternately taking the strain on my left arm and inching my right hand up the roots I finally got my left foot into the crack. The smooth leather sole of my shoe had no adhesion and I had to ease my agonizing way back down the rockface until I managed to bring my feet together and jettison my shoes. I blessed my lifelong preference for slip-on footwear, but my eyes were stinging with perspiration and I could taste salt on my lips by the time I curled my sock-clad toes round the sharp edge of the crack.

After that it was simple. With my foot in the crack the rim was only twelve inches above my head and I wrapped my arms round a projecting rock and slithered painfully over the edge to safety.

I lay back with my chest heaving and my heart pounding. Red mist which had nothing in common with the natural type that surrounded me, swirled behind my eyes and I was closer to complete exhaustion than I had ever been.

I will never know how long I lay there.

After a lifetime I climbed reluctantly to my feet. A brightly-dressed crowd of tourists lined the edge of the gorge in the rain forest across the unbridgeable void which separated them from the face of the Falls. They were waving and jumping around like ants at a picnic. A couple of them had their hands cupped to their mouths in a vain attempt to make themselves heard above the roar of nature. It was a pretty good sight. They were the same tourists but there was not an underdressed, overfed, sweating person among them. They were the most beautiful bunch of humans I had ever seen. I waved to them and sat down on a rock.

The plaster cast on my left hand was ripped and torn, the water had softened it to a mushy pulp. I unwound it and tossed the whole thing, lead and all, into the howling waters of Devil's Cataract. The crease from Georgie Girl's bullet looked clean and healthy but the bone would have to be reset. I hoped Dirk was still around to do it. I owed him more than a couple of bottles of whisky. I owed him my life.

I also owed Randall and Hart a bucketful of grief, particularly Hart. Then I thought of the documentation, and groaned aloud at the amount that had to be completed before they could be brought to trial. Paper work had never been my strong point, and there was going to be even more of it when I got round to dealing with the four characters listed on the rice paper. I didn't think they'd enjoy my devoted attention and I was going to make bloody certain they wouldn't.

For no reason at all I remembered that Rawson had been married three hours ago and his wedding present still reposed, unopened, on the seat of my official Austin Cambridge. I grinned to myself, knowing that electric kettles would be the last thing on his mind. For a while, anyway.

I hoped it wouldn't take Pete Fuller too long to figure out a way to get me off the island. The sun was dropping fast and it would soon be dark.

I lay back watching the fairyland clouds drift across the misty sky and thought about Cathy.

Epilogue

ZAMBIAN DAILY MAIL, May 17th, 1975.

LUSAKA.

A GOVERNMENT spokesman, speaking from State House in Lusaka, today confirmed that Mr Gara Paratema, organizing secretary of the Zimbabwe African National Union, based in Lusaka, was killed late last night when he returned to his home in the Ridgeway suburb of Lusaka.

He had been attending a meeting of top ZANU, ZAPU and ANC officials where he spoke out strongly against the detente moves initiated by the South African Prime Minister.

Unconfirmed reports state that Mr Paratema was killed when the car in which he was travelling detonated a landmine which had been laid in the driveway of his home.

A woman, believed to be an expatriate French nurse, who was travelling in the same car, was also killed.

Sources close to President Kaunda revealed that the President did not believe that suicide squads from Rhodesia had been responsible for the atrocity, despite local rumour.

The spokesman reiterated that Zambia would not be turned into a battleground for warring factions of Rhodesian Nationalists. President Kaunda later stated that no stone would be left unturned until the perpetrators of this heinous crime have been located and punished to the full extent that the law allows.